MW01599692

Sweet Charlotte Series

Sweet Charlotte in the Higgs Field
A Small Goddess
Heart String Theory

S C Schneider Publishing, 621 W. Mallon Ave., Ste. 505, Spokane, WA 99201 ss@stevenschneiderlaw.com

Cover design by Masha Falkov and Ruby Devine
www.mashafalkov.com Art and Glasswork
Spindly Orbiter copyright Masha Falkov
Icon design by Steven C. Schneider from artwork of Br. Claude Lane OSB

In the Still Pond

Still pondering ripples
In whitecaps
Steering by reflections
Of unseen islands
Below the horizon
And galactic north

And in the depths below
Compressed and shining
In the Higgs field
Companions speak in
Silent light
Of the same destination

And do we both,
Each as creature,
Rise and descend
Forsaking familiar physical
Principles to wash ashore
On a strange land?

Or have we simply circled back
To the arms of our forgotten
Fathers; and from this false
Womb to our true Mothers,
To breathe again at last
In the ether and the air?

Editor's Note:

This special edition contains additional material supplied by Charlotte Pritchard, F.S., PhD. This material fills in and extends the story as originally presented. The comparison between the two versions is easily made by scholars and laymen alike and we are certain that concordances will follow. Nonetheless, at Dr. Pritchard's request, the new or revised material is not identified here, honoring her commitment to provide an enhanced and hopefully seamless experience of the material. Dr. Pritchard has the final word on those contributions but does not confirm whether any particular fact, as portrayed by Mr. Schneider or by her, is true.

Note on Ashokan Reckoning Dates:

Ashoka the Great was born in the year 304 B.C.E. on Earth and established a Buddhist Empire in India in 232 B.C.E.. Ashokan Reckoning, the standard dating system on the planet of Charlotte's second lifetime, Mara. A.R begins in the year of Ashoka's birth. A.R dates are equivalent to C.E. (Common Era.) B.A.R (Before Ashokan Reckoning) dates are equivalent to B.C.E. (Before Common Era) dates on Earth offset by 304 years.

Charlotte's *transitus* on Moving Day, 2109 C.E. therefore, corresponds to 2143 A.R. on Mara. 304 B.C.E. is 1 A.R. on Mara. 1 C.E. is 304 A.R. So, take any C.E. or B.C.E. date and add 304 to calculate the Ashokan Reckoning date, e.g.:

Moses 600 B.C.E. equals 296 B.A.R.
Gallic War/Gallic Accords 50 B.C.E. equals 254 A.R.
Crucifixion 30 C.E. equals 334 A.R.

On Earth, colloquially, the time period before the first *transitus* of the historical Charlotte is referred to as B.C., Before Charlotte.
Pre-historic dates are rendered in Years Before Present, Y.B.P. Cosmological dates begin with T = 0.

I saw Beauty, It was my Destiny . . . Therein lies all

- Edith Södergran

To meet the challenge before us, our notions of cosmology and the general nature of reality must have room in them to permit a consistent account of consciousness. Vice versa, our notions of consciousness must have room in them to understand what it means for its content to be 'reality as a whole'. The two sets of notions together should then be such as to allow an understanding of how consciousness and reality are related. - *Wholeness and the Implicate Order*, David Bohm.

HEART STRING THEORY

Sweet Charlotte in the Dark Forever
By Steven C. Schneider

Introduction

You wouldn't have heard of me unless you have read a book called *Sweet Charlotte in the Higgs Field*. Now, when I say you wouldn't have heard of me, I realize that you know about Charlotte Pritchard, Charlotte Pritchard, F.S., and the Bodhisattva Xià lù dì. I am none of those people. I'm a second generation hybrid spook but I have *never* inhabited a spook ball and even though my bodies are gone, the shape of this spook now includes two lifetimes and a post graduate education. We did alright.

That book, *Sweet Charlotte*, was written by Mr. S. C. Schneider, and he told the truth for the most part, the truth of a man trying to stay out of trouble with the arbiters of truth. That's understandable. He had a family, something to protect from his inability to stop writing the truth

I wrote my own version of that story in a place where most of the truths in it were lies, but not dangerous lies. I had at least that advantage.

In that other universe, on Mara, my second home, the title was *Heart String Theory*; and I lend that title here, no charge, for his sequel *Sweet Charlotte in the Dark Forever*.

The title kept with his theme and I have no quarrel with it. But, after contributing to the text, I thought he wouldn't mind. At least, I didn't have to explain my title as much as Mr. Schneider had to explain *Sweet Charlotte*. It was obscure even then; a reference to an old movie that just popped into his head.

It wasn't obvious that the title would be exactly what he needed at first. He had to let it sit for a while. He said that he trusted his intuition and non-cognitive processes in general. He would keep a random phrase like that on the back burner until he had wrung the obvious clichés out of it and its true meaning was revealed. I can't dispute his process and I did appreciate his baseline assessment of me in that title. For all the trouble I caused, given half a chance, I was pretty sweet.

To be clear, I didn't know him personally since his book was written and he was long gone before I came home for good. But, that title *Sweet Charlotte* makes me think maybe he had a crush on me, at least as an imaginary friend. It seemed that he understood me, or was projecting his own true love on me. I'm not being condescending or finding fault. He had access to more information about Daniel Pritchard and me than anyone outside of our family. And he got the source and goal of theological transcendence right, the simple oneness that can be experienced between two entities.

There were, of course, some truths that Mr. Schneider stretched, but we both took differing artistic license for the same reasons. We aimed to preserve the truth in an entertaining lie until it could be freely told and heard.

I did reach out to him in the manner that spooks can, nudging through the mist. He certainly could have sensed me, a small quiet voice inside. Like Dan Pritchard said, something was throwing pebbles at the window. I was however, further away than the universe next door, so perhaps it was only a feeling that came through, some sweet delight, sugar and spice. It was the sort of thing that might just give a guy hot flashes or the shivers. I'll also admit; I've always been a distraction to someone.

That's what the power of love and longing can do. I remember something I wrote, naively, when I left Dan the first time:

> *I do not want to hurt you ever again. There's room in this heart for all, I realize that now, if I do not place restrictions on it. It's time to create new ideas of love, who can love whom and in what ways. I'm getting ready to make my own rules, not live by someone else's. It's gonna happen, I know.*

Well, I was only twenty when I wrote that; what did I know? I knew it would cut him deeply. When I saw those same words in Mr. Schneider's book and how he treated me with kindness in spite of them, it seemed like he had a love of his own in mind. I want to honor that as the great tribute it must have been. As it says in the Golden Wire Sutra:

> Longing is the antenna, the golden wire divining all frequencies leading back to love. Ultimately, it is the same oneness experienced in the birthing field, a mother's eyes, the embrace of lovers, the symbiont bond and the face of the Goddess. Longing is like a solar wind emanating from the source of all light and filling the universes, ever more diffuse but ever present. Longing opens the Library, spins the arrow of time and unerringly bows the strings of the field. Do not therefore, despair from longing, longing is not unskillful. Longing is not attachment; rather, longing is the only key to oneness. Only longing will bring you without fail to the salvation of love.

Both Mr. Schneider and the Bodhisattva Cult, though sometimes at cross purposes, got this right. Wherever in the infinities of the multiverse we come together with this power to guide us, there will be love and oneness. I honor those that will take the risk of that step in spite of fear. *It's gonna happen, I know.*

Thanks S.C.; see you in the Dark Forever.

Charlotte Pritchard F.S., PhD.
2130 C.E./2434 A.R.

PART ONE

Rare Earths

One day a goddess came to earth and,
Holding up my fingers to frame the shot,
My life and longing compressed into
That small moment.

And what could she know of it?
That I had safely desired her from afar?
That I never meant to catch her?
That I had no idea what I had caught?

I mean, a boy must have his goddess,
But what of requited love?
What of the alien other suddenly
Manifesting and saying "I am for you."?

Excerpt-A Small Goddess, Poetry of Dan Pritchard, Devi Sheridan, editor, Centennial Edition, Modern Europa Press, 2199.

Boiling it all down to brass tacks, the Aesthetics War started about one hundred years ago, when Charlotte came back from the dead. In summary, in 2030, quantum gravity devices enabled field sentients, who at that date thought they were human souls, to communicate with the corporeals they left behind.

Humans also, at first believed they were in contact with their departed loved ones. But not every human had a symbiont field sentient, so they could not be what each had hoped. By 2035, contact had however, been made with the home universe of the field sentients. At the same time, direct contact with the Andromedans began; a species that had been observing Earth for millennia.

By the end of the 21st century, these three species had built the Orbital Collider and created the tachyon anomaly we know as The Library, enabling transit through fractal nodes to universes and timelines in the multiverse. The last puzzle piece in this paint by number set was the application of 3MI graviton technology to space elevators.

Before Dan Pritchard built the first space elevator at Spaceport America, they could only be placed at the Equator in geostationary orbits. With graviton retros, the same science that made the Orbital Collider possible, space elevators could be built anywhere in geosynchronous orbits. They quickly proliferated until there were twelve, all connected to major population centers, making off planet travel as easy as taking the hoverway.

From these events, the life of the historical Charlotte Pritchard and her symbiont, Charlotte Pritchard, F.S. and the urge to follow the Way, the yearning of billions constructed the myth and the Cult of the Bodhisattva Xià lǚ dì.

By the first Moving Day, April 1, 2109, the autonomous Transdimensional Personhood Movement, the Cult pilgrims and the Library, started an Exodus that led to fully twenty percent of the population of Earth disembarking to the System, other worlds, universes and timelines as a religious imperative, a haj; The Way

This Exodus also gave birth to reactionary movements among the eighty percent left behind which eventually became known as the New United Futurists, whose stated goals, though deliberately obscure, seemed to include retaking Earth from the Star Orphans, as they named the pilgrims.

We can see therefore, that although the Aesthetics War, more accurately, the Siege of Earth, lasted little more than a year, it had been one hundred years in the making. It is no surprise then, that the pent up passions and wisdom of generations contributed to the future we live in now, including the self-planned 'Fall' of the New United Futurists.

The Rise and Fall of the New United Futurists, S.C. Schneider, Modern Europa Press, 2130.

*

In the Dark-Forever
T = - 0

C: This is not a shaggy god story, one of those stories where everything about religion is explained by some alien who looks like the devil, or where two stranded space pirates happen to be named Adam and Eve.

D: Yeah, who'd believe that?

C: And what's this Dark-Forever bullshit? Is it a noun? Or am I just, in the dark, like forever? Is the dark-forever still a noun if you take out the hyphen?

D: It's not an insult.

C: Forever is an adjective, but dark-forever is a noun. Am I just in a place; the dark-forever?

D: You were the English teacher, Miss Brooks.

C: You liked Miss Landers better. Anyway, I didn't name it, just be quiet.

D: Should it be The Web of Hercules?

C. That wasn't real. Just call it the multiverse field.

D. Many worlds, inflation?

C: We live in it, that's all, and now we have something to tell them.

D: Communication is hard, not like this at all. But we have to try. Something threatens this place.

C: It's their place too.

D: Eventually.

C: We have a job to do. Like Bulgakov said, we are spiritual beings with work to do in the world.

D: He said that about angels, so now we are a shaggy god story.

C: If it saves the multiverse, then I guess I don't care. Let's go make a crack in the sky.

*

Earth
2110 C.E.

Uluru, Northern Territory, Australia

You don't know this story. It's not your story, not yet anyway. But you might need it later on. You might learn something about how to live proper way in the worlds.

Uluru is red in the sunrise and sunset but mostly pink in between. Even up close, Uluru is pink. On the southwest side of Uluru there is a cave close to the ground. Goanna Man, he made this cave when he made the worlds. A long time ago, my ancestors knew about this cave. Now everybody knows about this cave because it is shaped like a vagina, a pink one, and it smiles. You didn't know that, did you? I am not making this up. Men won't go there. Nothing stopping them, but they know better. It's in sacred women's space. Men are at least smart enough to be scared of it. They got their own man cave far around Uluru. No wide screen streamer and Lazy Boys, just a cave.

Tourists not supposed to climb on Uluru, do it anyway but I'm not their mama. Their mamas should tell that mob this story, but their mamas don't know it. Anyway, since Moving Day, a whole lot less tourists coming by. Whitefella tourists now mostly headed to some other Dreaming, their Dreaming, their story, the songline that sings them off planet. They just figured out they have their own story, their own Dreaming. Suddenly they got religion. Good luck with that. Mostly starfella lizards coming by now. Starfellas seem to know how to live proper way.

Anyway, women who want to get pregnant go to the women's cave. Pregnant women go there to have strong babies. Nearby is the birthing cave. Women go there to give birth proper way with no pain. The birthing cave has a vagina too, a small cave off the larger one. There, ancestors and powerful beings gave birth. The knee marks of the long ago ancestral midwife made grooves in the cave floor in front of the small cave. Women have birthed there in the same place for 40,000 years. So far, so good, eh?

*

Kumpaya was there because she was a midwife and doula to the Pitjantjatjara Anangu. Kumpaya was an old blackfella lady, eighty-four years old, with thinning, fuzzy cotton hair and white whiskers around a mouth that couldn't stop smiling. Her white clay and red ochre painted saggy tits and bandy legs were exposed with just her fanny pack and string skirt for practical decoration. Out in the bush, she felt relaxed and at home.

Kumpaya was taking Bindi to the women's cave. Bindi followed behind Kumpaya, each with a long walking stick, as they crossed the scrubland and started up the trail to a low rocky bench in front of the cave. Bindi surveyed the cave mouth and said, "Well, it doesn't look like *my* vagina."

Kumpaya said, "You don't got a vagina."

"Cloaca is the correct term."

"I know, everything goes in and out one hole, bad idea, don't put the sewer in the amusement park, eh?" She laughed.

Bindi said, "We have other erogenous zones."

"Well, anyway, don't see any lizard man chasing you out here to get some, how's that working out for you?"

"You wouldn't understand, I'll have my egg time."

Kumpaya said, "Just kidding. Don't get so serious." She chuckled and started to make a fire in a rock circle for some warmth and to cook a goanna she had caught on the way and slung over her shoulder.

She placed the goanna next to the fire among the hot rocks and put more rocks and burning wood on top of it. Soon it was sputtering and popping. She cut off the tail, which was done first. Grinning, Kumpaya offered lizard tail meat to Bindi, "Want some a you little brotha? . . . just kidding."

"No, that's fine, that's how we got to the top of the food chain." Bindi took the chunk flaking delicately off the bone and gulped it down without chewing, Andromedans not having grinding molars.

Kumpaya said, "Big lizard eats little lizards, just like here, world goes round."

"It's the Circle of Life, Simba."

"Does the Pope shit in the woods? Is a bear Catholic?"

"Does a cow go moo?"

"Exactly."

"Just some old proverb, m'sayn?"

Kumpaya said, "Yep, the Dreaming's outside of time all over, ain't it?" She tilted her head a bit, eyeing her friend, and said, "You know, Bindi, you sit like a kangaroo." Bindi made a dismissive snort out of her nose holes as she rolled her eyes.

"As if . . ."

But Kumpaya was right. Bindi leaned back on her tail, double thumbed hands on her knees, forming a stable tripod. Her chameleon scales were mimicking aboriginal tattoos and body paint. Other than that, she wore no adornment. The males liked parachute pants and aloha shirts, but that was just cosplay. Like all ladies, they indulged their men's nonsense up to a point, as long as they did their chores. In Bindi's work however, there weren't many males of her own species to get in the way. She thought, *Probably all at the intergalactic curling bonspiel, drinking earth beer and eating chicharrones.*

She watched the scrub brush below. Three old black ladies in mu'u mu'us were hunting feral cats with long metal pikes. Kumpaya said. "They're getting dinner, cats ate all the small game so now they eat the cats."

This was a part of weekend camping for the people that lived in towns. They hunted and slept under the stars with a campfire and their worries and frailties disappeared for a time.

Scrub and grass provided some cover for the cats but any movement betrayed their hiding place with a telltale shiver of grasses. The ladies approached a clump of grass from three angles, smacked the sticks down all at once and a cat ran out and tried to find another clump, but the ladies were too fast. Running and shouting in their language, they bashed it in the head until it was dead. One tied it by the tail to another dead cat and slung it over her shoulder.

Kumpaya said, "Cats pretty good, taste like chicken."

Bindi said, "So do you, I hear."

"Oh, ok, you funny girl now, eh? Fair play to you."

The three ladies started to survey the area for goanna burrows, which descended at a low angle under the grass clumps. One poked her pike into a burrow while another poked straight down to where they thought the lizard was, to block it from going further. Then, number three knelt down, stuck her arm in the burrow and pulled out a four foot long goanna by the tail. Holding it up, again they all bashed its head with their pikes. Everybody satisfied with the catch, they chattered happily as they dug a pit next to the fire, threw the carcasses in with hot stones and smoldering branches, covered up the pit with dirt and sat back to have a smoke while the cats and lizards cooked.

Kumpaya said, "You better keep out of sight. Maybe they mistake you for Blue Tongue Lizard Man, come after you next. Bash *your* head." She held her belly and laughed, her smile twitching her white whiskers. Bindi laughed too, not a pleasant noise the first time you heard it, with teeth clacking and snorts out the nose holes, it seemed more like a threat. "Snk shhs shhs snk snk."

Andromedans did not give the impression of easy game. They had the look of bipedal dinosaurs evolving into ostriches, roundish head, face moved under the frontal cortex like humans, shimmering scales that could change color and pattern, nose holes on the forehead. Short arms with clawed fingers and two opposable thumbs, nictating membranes and a good set of sharp teeth in a short muzzle, completed the picture.

Up the trail came a young girl, some old blackfella's third wife, looking for favor by getting with child. She greeted Kumpaya, gave Bindi a nod and sat by the fire. Then she gave the doula a cooked cat as an offering. Kumpaya started to skin and debone the cat and sample the rib meat. She said, "Scrawny but good," and began to tell the girl a story.

"This is your story. This is how you get born in the time of your ancestors, and now. It's not about you now but it will be. Maybe show you how to live proper way in the worlds. Long ago before he was born, a boy was a little fish in his waterhole. Nice shady waterhole, cool water and warm breeze, good things to eat. Nice. He stays there between death and birth. He's happy, no ambition. But, one day his father comes by the waterhole and the little fish asks, 'Who is my mother?' His father shows him where all the people are living near the waterhole. He points to his third wife and says. 'That one, that's your mother.'

"Now, that little fish starts thinking. What's the harm of a little swim, check it out? Now he's excited, not sure why, wants to swim upstream, from his waterhole into her vagina and to her belly. That little fish swam real fast and settled in her belly. The next day the husband says, 'I had a dream, you got a baby boy in you now.' The husband and wife were so happy they had sex right away. Pretty soon she was big fat pregnant and that little fish turned into her boy and was born.

"But *your* husband, he gotta wait; you gotta make him wait. Stay here in the cave tonight, tomorrow go home. Your husband will say. 'I had a dream. You're gonna have a baby now, a boy.' Husband's so happy he wants sex right now. You make your husband wait three days and no sex. Now the fish are jumpin'. After three days, get sex with your husband, that little fish, your boy, he'll swim up there quick. Gonna get big fat pregnant soon." Kumpaya lit some grass and eucalyptus leaves and brushed smoke all around the girl's belly to drive out any spirit or sorcery that might try to stop that little fish.

Meanwhile, Bindi took out a graviton compass and surveyed the cave. The legends of a magnetic anomaly at Uluru were easy to confirm. The quantum gravity measurements were however, harder to explain. There were no quantum devices here, obviously, but the instrument showed a bleed-through of some kind, a natural connection to the holographic universe event horizon, brane gravity, something like the Library but naturally occurring; for more than 40,000 years, before people came here. The readings showed it was more like 400,000 years old. *So far, so good, eh?*

Mara

2316 A. R.

At the Bodhi-Ganapati Week Slumber Party

Since Charlotte had Dan well in hand in September, he wasn't cuckolded by Melanie when Lindsey's parents were out of town during Bodhi-Ganapati break. Instead, Charlotte went to the sleep over with Dan and spent the night with him and other friends who had orchestrated a cherry poppin' slumber party. Melanie was there alright, and she still put out for Kent, the college man, but in this timeline Dan was never in that loop. There was some drama and tears among the other guests but there were no distractions or awkward moments between Charlotte and Dan that night.

When the pizza was gone and the couples began to desert the streamer binge in the living room, Dan led Charlotte to the bed in Lindsey's brother's old room. He had come to know that he was allowed to roam over every inch of her. First base, second base, third base, *Ah yes, the lady garden*, exploring with kisses, inhalation, fingers. It was understood that there was a certainty of more in time. They both had done it before with others, so the end of it was not the only goal. But, this was their night to start something, to take their time, to be drunk with pheromones, anticipation and surrender.

They climbed in under the covers, having already shed their clothes, shivering till the sheets and their skin warmed and they could take a deep breath and look into each other's eyes. He wasn't in a hurry; he held his body above her without touching her and then leaned down only to plant kisses. Continuing, still with nothing touching her but his breath and lips, he kissed the top of her head, her hairline, ear and neck. He said softly *"I'm a spy, in the house of love."* Charlotte stifled a laugh, trying to look entranced, but she knew that he knew that, from here, it could go either way, ecstasy or comedy.

Having successfully preserved the mood, he lingered over her topography until he had revisited every sacred and profane spot on her body. He liked the edges of things, the places where her hair started, contrasting with the smoothness of her skin. He liked the darkness of her hair against the paleness of that skin, the tiny hairs and goose bumps in the skin that his passage made rise up. He liked her toes and fingers, liked putting one at a time into his mouth. He liked the spot under her breasts where their curve started and the spot between them, the taste of the salt and sweat there and the different salt and sweat at the nape of her neck. He loved all her curves and hollows, her sharp angles too, chin, elbows and knees. Every bit of her was endlessly engaging.

"Stop breathing in my ear."

"I'm not; I'm blowing in your ear. Girls like that."

"Don't get your sex tips from Playboy. Just read *me*."

Charlotte gave each present moment to Dan as a gift. She understood how many of those moments are ignored or wasted in a human life. She had been through that kind of life, and then life as a spook in Purgatory and Over There, where present moments could get mashed into one eternity. On either Earth it was an exceedingly rare experience for most people. Some who could experience it in the world called it the Dreaming. With that perspective, she was not impatient with present moments. Mindfulness was not a distraction from the present, but a mode of fully experiencing it.

Dan said, "Now turn over."

"No, no, no, no. Don't get distracted. You're on a mission; Missionary Position."

"Aye Aye, Cap'n"

She did kind of want him to get to it but that just made her anticipation build while something spectacular waited in the wings. This body hadn't had a real live orgasm yet, neither had her first body at the same age, having ignored Dan for about six more months then. She had suppressed those past life memories so that it had been a bright but indefinite lure to her corporeal body, something deep in muscle memory that made her pelvis start to move involuntarily at the brush of a thought across its hiding place. Tonight however, she was going to let her host body know all that it had to do, and feel everything it was meant to feel, so that the rush of hormones and bonding chemicals would once again tie her and Dan together for life.

All of this obsessive hovering under the covers also created static electricity that made all of their body hairs stand on end, reaching for their counterparts, enlivened by the ionized crackling of potentialities. When their bodies finally touched, a short sharp shock arced like lightening, brightening the air under the sheets momentarily. Charlotte laughed and yelled, "Ow! I can't take it, you're tickling me and it's too slow! Put it where it goes!" He did what she told him. After that they didn't waste breath on words, wordlessness carrying all meaning. They took only a few minutes, then let gravity reassert itself as they fell together into the bed and wrapped arms and legs around each other.

Charlotte said, "I'm all sweaty now."

Dan said, "I like it." Her hair was wet near the scalp and sweat ran down her temples in drops like tears. Her whole body had a sheen of moisture over the red glow of dilated capillaries.

He tasted her neck again at her collarbone. "Hmmmm. . . You're salty, dirty neck, almost as good as dirty toes." He was also awash in an elixir of olfactory dreams, the female body odors that had evolved to trap a man, all infused with her *Tea Rose* perfume.

Dan said, "Did I say I love you?"

"You did, more than once. You don't remember?"

He said, "I was distracted. Did you say it?"

"I did. I do."

"Is this a 'next level' thing? Just sex could go either way."

Charlotte said, "You are never going to have 'just sex' with me."

"Sounds like a threat."

"A promise; afraid of commitment, Dan?"

"Not."

"You are so peculiar."

"That's *why* you love me, right?"

"Nonsense, your obsessions . . . amuse me, " she said regally.

"You talk a lot."

Then she put her hand behind his neck, pulled him to her for a kiss and spoke in rhythm with her hips "Enough talk . . . I . . . like . . . this . . . better." She moved against him and said matter-of-factly, ". . . and . . . I . . . want . . . more."

He willingly took her lead and after another few minutes, they finished again. Now, even more exhausted and hungry as well, they got dressed and started for the kitchen to forage. Charlotte backed up to the kitchen counter, put her hands on the edge and eased her butt up onto it. She grabbed some cereal from an open cupboard and started munching out of the box while Dan looked for any available ingredients that might be scrambled into breakfast.

Charlotte thought, *I'm glad Captain Crunch tastes the same in this universe; but those blue monkey bugs in Lucky Charms? Creepy.*

Coming down the hall after slamming the bedroom door on the college man, Melanie lit a cigarette and stomped out onto the patio, another slam. She was lucky the glass slider didn't shatter. Then they saw Susan sitting under the dining room table crying, her boyfriend nowhere to be found. Dan whispered, "Nothing much to eat here. Let's walk down to Starbucks. Don't want to annoy everybody by being happy."

Charlotte locked her arm in the crook of Dan's elbow and squeezed him tight to her side. She thought, *This is working out so much better than my first life.*

This planet of her second timeline was called Mara following Buddhist tradition arising out of the Ashokan Empire. In her private inner narrative that other Earth was 'back home.' In broad strokes, Mara was pretty much a duplicate of Earth. It wasn't confusing, usually. The grass was green and the sky was blue. Some of the bugs *did* have monkey faces, their little jaws chewing like hamsters with cheeks full of peanut butter. She just got used to the differences.

She wasn't sure how any of this worked though she had staked her life on one dive through a fractal anomaly, now eighteen Earth years ago; the first Moving Day. One brand of physicists back home held that each measurement that collapsed a wave function necessarily created a new universe. Infinity being what it was, she supposed that could make sense. But, each new universe so created must also create its own new universes with any observation. It wasn't hard to see that was too much information to deal with.

What was the saying back home about the Higgs Bubble Drive? You don't need *all* of infinity just to make a star drive. It was like *pi.* You don't need *all* of *pi* just to calculate the radius of a bar stool; made sense, after all, *all* scientific theory was an approximate modeling of some corner of reality.

When she had planned her third *transitus* and had identified her target fractal node in the Library, she thought long and hard about where in that timeline she should enter her new human host. There was already gnosis for this as revealed to initiates. It really had to be done in the womb so that the Field Sentient component was just a part of the self, the big Self. Once there, the field sentient, the *effie*, could just take the wheel. Otherwise, at any time after birth, a separate personality was growing. Charlotte certainly did not want to subject the host personality to mental illness, a real split personality.

No, this was the way it had been done back home, back on the old Earth, for millennia and this me is still me, even better. It came instinctually when the symbiosis began. The effie just curled up in the hippocampus of the host until it became fully conscious with the infant. The infant experienced non duality, the unitive experience, oneness, for the first few months, in a state very close to human pre-consciousness. The effie was in the same state, unaware, learning as the infant learned.

What was different was the grafting of an effie that already had lived a lifetime onto an embryo. A certain amount of freedom and sensory input had to be given up. In effect, Charlotte was her own babysitter and then walled off most of the information from her past life, just letting it drift in on dreams and intuition. So here, she waited until that fateful day in her senior year when Dan pulled over and asked her if she needed a ride, and said 'yes' instead of 'no' this time. She was now ahead of things, swamping Dan with unequivocal love.

As they wandered back toward Lindsey's house with their coffee, a phalanx of boys on bikes issued from the alley and rushed past. One yelled, "Susan's mom's on the warpath!" So, Dan walked Charlotte right to his '87 AMC Eagle jalopy and they drove back to their own neighborhood. He dropped her off at her home and they kissed goodbye as Dan went on to work at the vegetarian pizza shop.

Charlotte went into her mother's house. It was still something special for Charlotte to see her mother in the beauty of her youth, even now in her forties. She still remembered watching her mother die, holding her in her arms and rocking her through the fear, feeling the tension subside and the spirit flow out of her body. This was all burned in Charlotte's memory of that other life. She could appreciate her mother so much more now that she knew what she had put her through. Charlotte still gave her mom a little shit but no full blown contrarian tantrums. No "You just don't get me!"

bullshit. Just enough pouting to seem normal; but her perennial Mother's Day gift was to spare her mom the particular horror of hormone driven teenage girls.

She went to her room and started her meditation. Her first stop was to monitor her cell checker. She had developed this mindfulness program back home to automatically scan her cells for precancerous abnormalities, breast cancer hormones, etc. trying to keep her promise of staying alive past her fortieth birthday on this second go round. With that buttoned down she turned her attention and her energy body outward.

The striking thing about Mara was the silence that greeted her in the direction of Purgatory. Here, it became quickly apparent that there was no stressed space time between universes allowing interaction, no Purgatory, no other spooks, nothing. This did not distress her, because the existence of her home universe was assured even if it did not touch this one. She certainly wasn't lonely for non-hybrid spooks, and their absence removed the need to manifest. No non-corporeal interaction was necessary at all. It was sort of a relief to not be challenged by such a complex existence on a daily basis. She could perch, prim and proper, on the hippocampus and just *be.*

But, she kept one eye open in that direction anyway, like SETI, waiting, waiting for that melodic close encounter signaling the other half of her heritage. Her entry point in the sky was burned into her cognitive map for sure. It was catalogued in the Library and so was as accessible as any other. She couldn't know if any pilgrims had come through with her or for a few years after, until her toddler self started to reboot her memories. But, *since then,* no one else had come through in her eighteen years on this planet. Out of infinite multiverses, she supposed, it was too much to expect someone to drop in to say hi, and be stuck forever. Then again, if anyone had come through when she was an infant, they might also just be attaining full awareness.

She also had another focus. She knew that the human 'soul' must still leave the body after its death. Because of effies occupying the place of the self, the inference had confused humans and effies back home. Here, without a Purgatory-like dimensional interface, there were no disturbances to be mistaken for miracles; No ham handed Andromedans chewing the scenery and violating the Prime Directive. Here, the silence let her focus without distraction on what seemed to be the path of that consciousness she knew as *silvers*, Silver Dan and her own companion with which she had shared a skin suit, Silver Charlotte.

On a more pedestrian level, the History Channel, PBS and NPR, as well as twelve plus years of public education had piqued her interest as soon as she could focus her eyes and attend her hearing close enough to catch snippets as her mother puttered and hummed lullabies while making bottles and changing diapers. Through that haze it became clear that this was not an identical timeline. Somehow, an alternate history had unfolded, highly likely in the multiverse. And yet history had still developed in a way that, improbably, put Dan and Charlotte in the same neighborhood and high school in this time and place. Charlotte had made that timeline her business by becoming a history major and then an academic at the University of Colorado.

She had fiddled about in her first life, wasn't expected to go to college, did some flower arranging, took a course in retail sales, word processing, then aimlessly ran Dan's love into the ground before she took off for L.A., got married, got divorced, crashed and burned and Dan took her back.

Well, there's no temporal paradox in not fucking up this time, right? I'm not in my own past, so que sera, sera, what will be, will be, right?

It was amazing how living without a plan through one life gave her the perspective to actually accomplish something in this life. She didn't reveal her full knowledge but kept a little bit ahead of her age level from pre-school on, not enough to be a prodigy or get skipped ahead. She still needed to be in the same grade as Dan so he could make his move when they both were seventeen.

Her mom here had no idea the shit she had put her through as a teenager the first time. But, this time, she made a point of getting the grades necessary to apply for scholarships, took AP classes, got SAT scores in the 700's, joined DECA, volunteered at the homeless shelter and even got on the track team. So, she was accepted at CU Denver and would attend with Dan in the fall. She was going to mark her territory and keep her eye on him this time.

Her smart phone trilled and she swiped the screen. Dan said, "I'm off work, the folks are going to the Moose Club. You want to come over?"

". . . hmm, uh huh, pick me up?"

He said. "Almost there."

*

Earth
2040 C.E.

Sparkle Plenty and the Rodeo Laser Bowl Bar and Grill

Mike Sandifur wasn't surprised to see his new bowling ball sunk down in the middle of the trampoline. His son, Archie, was repeatedly rolling a tennis ball around the curved surface like a croupier at his roulette wheel. The family's fox terrier was popping up and down and yapping frantically at its ball. The high containment net around the trampoline kept the dog out. Archie, sitting on the edge, focused with similar intensity, was oblivious, seeing only trajectories into the gravity well of the Brunswick Strike King Black Pearl.

Led to the scene by an accusing little sister, Emma, Mike recognized the classic attempt to model the time-space continuum and the warping effect of gravity. *As old as Einstein.*

Archie was carefully launching the tennis ball's hapless test pilots to burn up spiraling into the planetary atmosphere or freeze forever on the event horizon of a black hole. Mike had learned a long time before that day; the humble student approach worked best. Put a smartass genius kid in the position of teaching *you*, and he gets serious about that responsibility rather than questioning your authority.

He said, "What are you doing? I need my bowling ball."

"It's the old model of gravity, twentieth century old." In his shorthand speech he telegraphs, "The bowling ball is a planet . . . maybe a black hole, gravity warps space time."

"Ok, but if that's the old model, why are you making it for the science fair?" Archie was usually at the cutting edge.

"It's about gravity *and* the Higgs field."

"Of course, old *and* new, but isn't the trampoline kind of big for a school project?"

Archie shook his head, mostly talking to himself, "Gotta start over, doesn't work, doesn't sink enough, scale it down, a balloon in a frame, a lead sinker in the middle and marbles maybe, to roll into the black hole. . . "

"One of those new spookballs might do the trick."

"That's a person, not a t-t-t-tool!"

"Ok, ok, it can do *something* with gravity."

"They're not *its*, they're p-p-p-people, just *different*."

Emma joined in, "Yeah Dad; not cool, 'A person's a person no matter how small.'"

Shit. Transdimensional Personhood Empathy Training. . . mandated after the riots. Kids just got done with that at school. Now they're recruiting Dr. Seuss. Distraction. . .

"I know, I know, forget that; what part does Sparkle play in all this?" Archie had lugged his sister's goldfish bowl out into the yard as well; no damage done, yet. "Nothing sinister I hope?"

Calmer now, the stutter disappeared. "That was sarcasm." Archie could recognize when something non-literal had occurred, an exaggeration or a joke; he just didn't see the point. *But, people can't seem to stop.* "She's a subatomic particle. Particles get mass from moving through the Higgs field. Like a fish in water. The fat fish has more drag."

"She's not fat!" Emma chimed in.

"Roundish, whatever. One fish, two fish, red fish, blue fish. Fat fish, more drag. Skinny fish, less drag. The skinny fish eats the fat fish."

Mike said, "Theoretically, right?"

"Just an example, point is, how do gravity and the Higgs field interact in one system?'

"You mean like the balloon *and* the fish bowl together?"

Archie said, "In a Grand Unified Theory of Everything. GUT's and TOE's."

Mike said, "How about a water balloon?"

A pause, and to himself again he said, "Exactly!" Dad was now some kind of hero or idiot savant. *From there to here, from here to there, funny things are everywhere.*

Mike said, "But I need my bowling ball, league tournament today, you know, science will have to wait." Archie retrieved the Strike King Black Pearl from the singularity and surrendered it to Mike. *If it* was *a black hole I'd get a strike every time.*

*

Archie wasn't as good at math as people assumed he was but neither was Einstein. Einstein could feel and see the concepts that composed his theories but had to enlist his friends to help make the equations work. This was not unusual; while there is a clarity in equations, what was being described was, after all, the real world. The fact that a watch on a table ticks faster than a watch on the ground was proven easily once clocks could register nano-nano-seconds. If you only told the story of relativity with extreme examples of black holes and traveling at the speed of light, you miss the physics all around you. Gravity or acceleration both mess with time and produce the same result.

But gravity does that on every scale; your head is aging faster than your toes. That's something you should feel, like neutrinos. They are all around us and zipping through us every second. If you pay attention, feeling it is the only sure confirmation. Like Archie said when asked, "What are you doing?" "Just catching photons." It was true; it was only photons that came into his eyes, while his brain used them to weave a whole world in the dark. It composed poetry out the alphabet of the electromagnetic spectrum, spun straw into gold, in the dark.

Archie had this gift; like Einstein and David Bohm, he could feel the spin of an electron as easily as a Harlem Globetrotter could twirl a basketball on his finger. He had a memory from when he was very young, perhaps two years old, of seeing a juggler on the streamer. This juggler, from Cirque de Something, made a ball seem to stand still in the air as he passed his hands, arms, his whole body under, over, around it. The ball was clearly spinning, rolling, moving, but to the juggler, and to the audience, it did not move in three dimensions. It did however, have supersymmetry, any change that occurred did not destroy symmetry as to the observer.

He had told Coach Brodie: That's string theory, a loop in three dimensions, spinning perpendicular to its axis. That's where the extra dimensions are.

Archie could feel particles by feeding them through that memory as he became the juggler, his eyes focused on the particle standing still while the rest of his body, the whole universe, moved relative to it. In effect, he took on spin like the stigmata, so that he could observe without really collapsing the wave function. It wasn't true, but he could imagine it and then actually feel it in his body.

OK, think of it like this Coach; take this pencil, a round pencil. Roll it in your fingers around its long axis. See, it can spin

relative to itself, but be motionless relative to you. Now, take an O-
ring, got one right here. Roll it with your fingers about its axis, it's
still motionless to you. So, that loop is a quantum string and the
spin is through another dimension of space. String theory has ten.

Brodie knew the answer already but was fascinated by how Archie got there, finding the quantum world right at his fingertips. When he learned about gyroscopes and how they gave a glimpse of something outside of normal reality and Newtonian physics, he felt those effects with his entire body, as Einstein felt the equivalence of acceleration and gravity in an elevator.

Intuitively, he was correct. On every scale, the toy gyroscope, the magnetic moment of electrons and the spin of planets were analogous. These, along with the gyroscopes on submarines and the Hubble Space Telescope, all of them connected conservation of angular momentum to Archie like an ice skater spinning on a Planck scale rink.

In his reading (always above his age level) he became fascinated with the life of David Bohm, one of the founders of Quantum Physics. Amazingly, Bohm described this same feeling, being a human gyroscope. But beyond that, Bohm seemed to be able to feel major concepts of the unseen quantum world directly.

Like many of the starry eyed mystics in his future, and not a few of his contemporaries, Bohm wanted to find that the human scale was the manifestation of the invisible realm beneath. Bohm went a few steps further, wanting to find that the human scale certainty of classical physics was an emergent quality coming out of the uncertainty of quantum physics. He called it the Implicate Order.

It was because of this feeling that Bohm began to think in two heretical directions. First, he could not agree with physicists who were sure that effects of quantum physics could not be felt in the macro world. And here, it is important to note just why quantum physics, with all its contradictions, was still a viable theory. Simply put, its ability to predict results in the 'real' world surpassed any other scientific paradigm. The effort and passion behind its support in spite of its surreal nature was therefore, derived from its essential usefulness.

The effect of the theory on the human scale began to be proven with the invention of lasers and superconductors which were only possible because of quantum effects. In the other direction, Bohm did not believe that Heisenberg's Uncertainty Principle and Schrodinger's Cat were true reflections of the nature of the quantum world. These theories, or more accurately thought problems or puzzles, provided that the state of any particle was only established when observed. It was 'proven' therefore, that for particles to have any properties at all there must be a conscious observer, or more conservatively, a 'measurement,' an awkward necessity. Bohm felt that there was some underlying process that had the same effect as an observer, and it wasn't, simply could not be, God.

Here was the real problem; the established scientific paradigm, the Standard Model, the one its aging discoverers jealously guarded, the most successful theory ever for predicting results, had an essential element of pure fantasy, *reducto ad absurdum*: A sentient observer was required for the existence of the entire infinite universe. Some factions got around this by redefining the terms, manipulating equations or generating multiverses; still it was awkward.

Archie understood this problem. In the same way that monotheism had been saddled with the necessity of an omnipotent, omniscient, omnipresent God, so physicists were stuck with necessity of a sentient observer. These ideas led Bohm, and then Archie, to the conclusion that there was something else, like a Quantum Mind, made of the particles of consciousness, something not made of physical states of matter that nonetheless existed between and underneath these observed states.

Archie was sure that an imperfect god and Bohm's implicate order could solve both of these problems. Indeed, the sentient observer, of necessity present since the big bang, sounded a lot like a perfect God. "Who needs 'em?" Archie said out loud. "Feel it directly, stick your head out the window, feel the wind, feel the rumble strips."

This feeling and rant did nothing to make him fit in, but he had his own crowd anyway, kids that would at best listen, and at least wouldn't run away. His teachers were also in two camps. Some just wouldn't put up with his shit, others tried deflect or redirect his passions. More than once a previous teacher would take him by the ear and force him into a program that would challenge him. "It's ok to be an autodidact Archie, but you're not *that* smart."

"I'm not just an autodidact, I'm a high functioning Asperger's spectrum autodidactic polymath."

"My point exactly; that's a diagnosis, not a résumé. Just do what I tell you."

Not naturally athletic, at gym he just wandered on the outskirts of the playing fields, internally pondering or having intellectual discussions with friends. When he had to actually play, he chose a position with the least activity like center back in soccer or deep outfield in baseball, less chance of action. Once he did catch a ball out there. He was so surprised he had to think a little about what to do next, while his teammates yelled and waved their arms.

He was the short guy who stood under the basket, "waiting for the rebound." In football, he would politely step aside to let the linemen on the other team waltz right through. *After you, kind sir, no, no, I insist.* Finally, he just ran laps for the full hour of gym in middle school. One coach gave him a 'D' but Coach Brodie gave him an 'A.' Brodie enjoyed watching any kid stick it to the man, even if he had to impersonate 'the man' once in a while.

And even though Archie didn't do the Rainman bit, visual patterns captivated him and made him feel safe. He wore the same horizontal striped shirts daily, like a caricature of a cabin boy. For an OCD quirk, it was practical. *Necessarily* repetitive, he bulldogged his tics into something that didn't appear symptomatic. It kept his hands free. So long as he actually did wear that shirt, his body became the pattern.

Within this rigid framework, his thoughts were however, spinning fractal geometries. Like an old jungle gym made out of metal bars, that framework allowed within it infinite creative variations.

*

Mara
2316 A.R.

Pillow Talk

> But though Ailell was king, Maev was the ruler
> in truth, and ordered all things as she wished,
> and took what husbands she wished, and
> dismissed them at her pleasure; for she was as
> fierce and strong as a goddess of war, and knew
> no law but her own wild will. *Táin Bó Cúailnge*

Charlotte and Dan lay facing each other, the image of the figures gracing the lid of the most famous Etruscan sarcophagus, the one carved in the form of a marriage bed. Even on Earth, that particular carving had been preserved and wondered over.

What if. . . .?

The Etruscans constructed their tombs to duplicate their family homes. All of the perishable materials, wood, thatch and rope were duplicated in stone. This was the reason archaeologists knew so much about Etruscan physical culture.

A part of this culture involved the sarcophagi of married couples. They were shaped like the marriage bed or like reclining couches. The covers featured the top of the bed or couch with the occupants sculpted as well; just part of the furniture for eternity.

The scenes were very different from the Roman or Greek artifacts she was familiar with back home. In those cultures, art showed women subordinate, smaller in size or absent altogether from gatherings, certainly from Plato's all male symposia. Charlotte had often wondered what kind of world would have been built if men and women honored each other equally. On Mara, the thought problem was reality all around her.

On the banquet couch sarcophagus, an Etruscan man and woman recline, she in front, he behind, essentially spooning; both smiling. Their feet are entwined, his arm around her, his hand pointing to something, her eyes following. Maybe they are gazing at the entertainment, enjoying a private, silent joke, finishing each other's thoughts and sentences, so different from the all-male Greek and Roman scenes.

The top of the marriage bed sarcophagus was even more remarkable; a man and woman in bed lying on their sides facing each other. The stone was carved with impossible craft, delicately forming a sheer sheet, beautifully draped and covering their naked bodies up to the waist.

He has his right arm on her shoulder. She however, has her right arm behind his neck, her hand is there pulling his head to her. *She* is the one initiating the kiss, and so much more. They both smile. It is the loveliest expression of the commitment and joy of marriage. What a world, indeed, a world that might have been.

Well, now she knew. The Etruscans, not the Romans, had dominated in this time line. Etruscan style respect and honoring of spouses created something rock solid, something unlike mediaeval romantic love, which gave lip service to chemistry in order to justify infidelity. No, this was a different channeling of human chemistry, to tend and defend, till death us do part.

That's the normal expectation here; how strange. The thing that everyone back home hopes for and very few achieve in the deception of western psychology.

Here, she saw that what was fleeting back home led to something that could indeed last forever. Of course, there still was deception, betrayal and lust for another. But at least the very basis of the myth, the knight and the lady, was not hopelessly flawed from the beginning. That's the difference; here, the white knight and the goddess know each other as equals from kindergarten on; there is no deception. They know where the chemistry leads, where the alchemy leads; to a transcendental love. But after that, do the dishes. *Do the fucking dishes every day and love it. Then you will achieve true love and true enlightenment.*

*

Dan's folks left for the Moose Club to cut a rug. Dan expected a few rug burns himself and a quick tussle before relaxing for the evening. Instead, as they sat on the floor and Dan put on his best come hither pout, Charlotte said, "Do you think we will stay together forever?"

Dan said, "Ahh, I don't want to talk about that."

"But, what kind of life should we have? Seems like people will break up no matter what they say. What do they all want?"

"I don't know what *they* want. I just want you to love me."

"That can't be all."

Dan said, "Well, we'll get older and we'll get married and have a bunch of money."

"You really haven't thought this through have you?"

"It's simple, I'm going to love you forever and I don't want things to change."

"But things will change, we'll live for like sixty more years."

"We'll figure it out."

Charlotte said. "Let's figure it out now. Let's make our own rules, we decide who gets to love whom and in what ways."

"You get to love me and I get to love you."

"Will you get tired of me?"

"Ok, this is not fun," he said. Charlotte pushed him back flat on the floor and rolled over on top of him, pinning his arms with her hands on his wrists above his head.

He said, "Is this like Strip Twister 'cuz that was. . ."

"No."

"Or, Hijacker and Hostage? The rope's under the . . ."

"No!" She arched her body over him. It felt like she was holding his ankles like his wrists, with opposable toes. For an instant, a vision brushed past his optic nerves: An impossible warm breeze blew her hair to the side, backlit by a glow of static electricity. The ceiling disappeared revealing the sky outside darkening as storm clouds loomed, crackled and boomed.

"Is that thunder. . ."

Her voice registered a bit lower than normal. "I am the Sky God and you are the Earth Goddess."

Then the storm subsided as her flickering menace morphed back to the sweet Charlotte he knew. *That other thing, what was that?* He lost it as if it were a dream.

He said, "But the Earth Goddess is a girl."

"That's the point honey, submit to my will, or we might have to play Operation next."

"Ok, got it, I can work with this. . ."

She sighed, "You are so difficult. Ok, listen to me, I'm going to kiss you after every question and if you are still scared, I will *force* you to have sex with me. Understand?"

"I'm pretty scared right now. I was anyway. . .I think."

"Never mind that." She kissed him. "Will you get tired of me?"

"You're pretty entertaining, all right. Life is full of distractions. But, I don't know how to say this; there is no other right combination, there is no other right 'us' than 'us.' I don't need you to be anything but what you are and what you will become."

She thought, *I'm still thinking like a Roman and he's Etruscan all over. I should believe him.*

"But you'll meet someone else you'll fall in love with. I probably will; just some shallow infatuation. I'll still get mad at you. I know you'll get mad at me. So, what if I had sex with someone else?"

"I would forgive you eventually. And what if I had sex with someone else? And you forgot the kiss."

She kissed him. "I would have to kill you, after I ran you over."

"That doesn't seem fair."

"Too bad for you."

"Now I'm really scared. Can we have sex?"

"Not yet." She kissed him. "What would you do if you wanted to have sex with someone else?"

I'd go to the temple. The Vestal Virgins put out for free."

"Not so free, you have to register and start tithing and learn stuff."

"I'll do that tomorrow, how long until I can poke a virgin?"

"I don't know, and obviously they're not really virgins."

"Even better, I need training, discipline."

"What if I was a monotheist?"

"Then I'd just poke you."

"What if...."

"Do you *want* me to poke a virgin? I'm getting mixed signals here. Why don't you just go into the future and fix everything so we will never have to deal with that?"

"And the past too; I think I'm going to do that right now."

"Can we have sex first?"

"That's the great thing about time travel. I'll go and come right back here in the same blink. You would never know. In fact I just did it."

"Great, can we stop talking now?"

"What if we had a three person relationship?" She kissed him.

"If I can help pick the girl, sure."

"What about a guy?"

"Now it just sounds creepy; igloo brothers is one thing, but I'm not crossing swords. . ."

"Be serious. If this 'us' is certain, not on the table, can that be a basis for a lifetime relationship?"

"Like the Constitution?"

"Or the Ashokan Accords."

"So, you're proposing diplomacy? We can promise to solve problems and agree on how to do that?"

"Why not agree to that at the beginning of a relationship instead of at the end. That's what doesn't change."

"That's a great idea, let's do that. Then we can get married and have kids."

"Whose uterus are you renting out without permission?"

"Or not, but we can get married. "

She said, "I just want to be your unconditional lover, the one that won't leave, so you will never be afraid."

"Sounds good to me "

"So, you will always love me too?"

"Uh huh, I will love you forever. My fantasy is right here, like how you look so beautiful in the morning before you put on makeup or even rub the sleep out of your eyes or brush your hair."

"Gods, you are incorrigible."

"I'm *encouragable*."

"Yes you are, now we can have sex."

"Hmmm." She loosened her grip on his wrists and ankles and descended onto his body like nightfall, like the moon seducing the earth, her lover. She let him roll her over as she changed subtly into something so soft, warm and fragrant that he forgot what they were talking about. His only thought was, *She smells like roses.* She kissed him.

From the beginning, she had given him gifts of her physical and energy bodies that she knew he could find nowhere else. This was the one reality where she still manifested, when she surrounded him with arms and legs, when she took him inside. She wanted him to stare at her with wonder afterword, so that in the future, when she allowed him an indiscretion, he would know, *know in every chakra,* that there was no one and nothing like her, so that when he bragged indiscreetly to his male friends, they simply did not believe him. *Get out of town!* But, at the same time, they really, really wanted it to be true, wanted it to be possible in their world too. She wanted those men to actually ask their wives if it was true and their wives to say 'Not tonight, I have a headache.' to punish them for being so stupid.

Any woman could learn some of things she knew, with pelvic floor muscle exercises and hareem gyrations, but *she* could manifest an extra pair of hands, *she* could have wings, *she* could be a tantric Green Lantern if she wanted to. *No, too flashy.*

And she didn't give him everything all at once or every time either. She wanted him to long for it, to lose consciousness for a moment as his body took him over, to believe that it had as much to do with his prowess as with hers and then lose all certainty. Sometimes, she took it all for herself and didn't even let him finish.

Wham Bam thank you man, aaaand, I'm done, you take care of yourself the rest of the way; I'll make breakfast.

She would slip on her kimono and tug assertively on the ties, locking away the prize, the chalice, and give him a dismissive look down her nose as she walked out the door like a runway model, knowing how much he enjoyed even that.

But, just often enough, when he was inside her, at the moment when he wanted all of his strength to be concentrated in one final motion with no yielding or holding back, when he was sure he could overpower *her*, she grabbed him with her energy body, clamped him so he could not pull out, *and then, inside of her, she grabbed him and did the rest for him.* Her physical arms held him too, one hand on his neck, the other on his hip, so that he wasn't quite sure *how* she was doing it.

As his eyes rolled back, his mouth watered and his pleasure was spent, she released him. *"Deus fucking Pater, Char, I . . . Where did you . . ."*

"A wicked aunt taught me."

"Aunt Ollie Mae?"

"Oh please. . . an aunt you will never meet, don't worry your pretty little head about it."

Then, she enveloped him in arms and legs and feathery wings, turned down the gravity and shushed him to sleep.

Needless to say, they worked things out, went to college, started professions and had a child. All and all it was a happy life, a little excitement, a little sorrow. About fifteen years later, there was a solo law practice, a tenure track professorship and a five year old with a pre-Copernican view of the cosmos. Shanti was definitely the center of their universe.

*

Earth
2040 C.E.

At the Rodeo Laser Bowl Bar and Grill, Mike watched the Strike King not live up to its name, "Should have been named 'Gutter King'" he muttered. Brodie said, "Just aim at the pins Mike," and tried to give him a high five.

"Don't patronize me; that's a fist bump at best."

"Yeah, but we need your handicap."

"I don't want to be a ringer, I want to win!"

"You, know Mike, bowling is like a woman, she hurts you and humiliates you, and then just when you've had enough and are walking out the door, she gives you just one little bit of encouragement, one little strike, maybe just a spare, and you're down on your knees, begging for more."

"You're fulla' shit."

"And . . . they both involve three holes."

"Now, you made it creepy."

"Suck it up, you're on."

Mike was bowling with his teacher's lounge team from Obama Middle School where he taught science to 7th and 8th graders, including Archie. His teammate, Walter Brodie, was a better bowler and would have been a better science teacher too. He certainly had a good enough grasp of trajectories, mass and momentum to lead the league in strikes.

Mike and Brodie had both started on the science track at Revelle College at UCSD, both eventually ending up at San Diego State, but for different reasons. After two years at UCSD, Mike believed he wouldn't make it in the rarified air of the Physics Department, grad school, research assistant, dissertations, publish or die; all of that. Like so many kids who dutifully impressed their parents and teachers in high school, he burned out on the treadmill early and had to escape.

In the third quarter of his second year he just walked away, looking for an idea, a dream, something at least worth trying to make sense of. After a year of industrial arts classes (to support a short-lived imaginary career path in photography) he volunteered at a youth center's after school program. That seemed to be a step in the right direction and he never regretted the decisions that followed. Becoming a teacher led him to his wife Anna, his kids Archie and Emma and a daily dose of human potential in the guise of awkward, emotional and sullenly enthusiastic tweens.

Brodie's academic career was a different matter. He could have done the whole nine yards in physics right up to a Nobel Prize but he found the idea of structure, tenure and research politics too constricting. He too was a polymath and an autodidact, an Ayn Rand devotee and Richard Feynman fan, an angry populist-anarchist; something for everybody.

Since CERN found the Higgs boson in 2012, everything he needed scientifically was on the internet, including a constant stream of data from the Large Hadron Collider. After all, CERN *invented* the World Wide Web *and* used the web and volunteer computers all over the world to continually analyze collider data. It was no problem for Brodie to use the LHC primary data stream with a minimum of hacking and apply his own sweat equity on homemade hardware and software.

He simply didn't want to be constrained by rules. His paradigm was Edison, the Wright brothers and Popular Mechanics. So, he majored in Phys Ed instead of Physics. He liked the idea that it made no sense to anyone except him, and Mike. To Brodie, PE was practical applied geometry and physics, just like spaceflight.

He was 5'5" and had a compact and muscular frame. He liked nothing better than to do squats and lunges and planks, not just keeping up with students but leaving them in the dust. With a blond buzz cut and a square jaw, he stood authoritatively, thumbs hooked on his jock strap waistband, shouting "Take a lap! You! Take a lap!"

He had never been in the military but endeared himself to these hormonal boys by yelling at them like a drill sergeant and teaching them to answer "Yo!" to roll call. None of this however, and this was the point, none of this disturbed the constant flow of ideas that was the actual work of his life.

Mike and Brodie liked to commiserate at sixth period gym, watching the boys go through their track and field module.

"Know why I hate squints, Mike?" "Squints" was Brodie's word for real physicists.

"Do you need more reasons?" Mike played the straight man somewhere between Eeyore and not quite contrary Mary. Brodie was always mad about something but rarely got angry.

"Always. They have the biggest, most expensive machines on the planet to play with, and they have to saddle the whole study of physics with a seventh grade sense of humor. They find the fundamental building blocks of the universe and then name them quarks, squarks, gluons, WINO's and WIMP's."

"Charmed and strange."

"Yeah, sounds like they're describing themselves. But I have some hope now that the spooks are shoving the Planck scale right up their asses. They used to swear they couldn't affect the human scale with their experiments. Now that spooks and gravitons have proved that wrong, they just want to ramp it up to higher power, more dangerous experiments on smaller and smaller scales."

"So what would you prefer?"

"Why don't they start out by saying they want to make a bomb or an engine or a universe and quit pretending they're doing 'pure research' with no responsibility for the consequences?"

"Is that what you're doing in your garage?"

"Damn straight." He points to some goof-offs: "You, you, take a lap! And you two, planks!

"The thing is, now, the squints talk and talk about how nothing bad can happen while at the same time trying to duplicate the creation of the universe by force. The whole point of the Orbital Collider they're talking about now is to create greater and greater speeds, more violent collisions."

"Maybe the more fanciful the vocabulary, the safer they feel."

"It doesn't help the world to keep the squints feeling safe, Mike. It's dangerous not to see the danger. At least I see it.

"Remember when we were kids and had cap guns and rolls of caps? The cap gun is the sophisticated engineered "safe" way to make a bang. What did I do? I hit the caps on the sidewalk with a hammer."

"I remember that! What were we, seven, eight?"

"I never stopped, just made bigger bangs. One cap makes a good bang that way, but eventually, at least once, I just hit a whole roll with a hammer, bigger bang, recoil, temporary hearing loss, count your fingers, pure joy. *Joy because you didn't die or put your eye out.* I think that's the thrill of science. That's what everybody at Alamogordo felt.

"So they've got their Large Hadron Collider, but what we need is a hammer. I can make a *hammer,* a Redneck Hadron Collider. *Now that's funny!"*

Mike said, "For a minute there, you were sounding almost enlightened, Brodie. It's not ok to be reckless just because you're willing to admit it. Unintended consequences are the problem. Even Edison and the Wright Brothers were part of the industrial revolution that led to environmental disasters and global warming."

Brodie said, "But *they* couldn't destroy the world with one experiment."

"And you can? Perfect. Anyway, gotta run, lesson plan, wife, kids, dinner, you wouldn't understand"

"*You* need to take some laps, Mike. You should come over and check out my garage sometime, absolutely."

*

The next Sunday, on the way home from the Rodeo Laser Bowl league tournament, Mike tailed Brodie into his three-car garage driveway at the end of a cul-de-sac. It was an ageing 1980's California neighborhood; Spielberg-esque, circa *E.T*, now suffering from deferred maintenance and bad contractors, disintegrating ranchers alternating with cube shaped houses filling every square inch of a lot.

He didn't open the garage door but led Mike through the house, each grabbing a ritual beer from the fridge on the way. The hollow core door from the kitchen to the garage had been recently replaced by a metal one. Mike noticed the heavy hinges and felt the heft as he pushed it open against self-closing springs. *It's not just for show*, he noted. A motion sensor turned on overhead arrays of painfully bright lights.

"Jesus Brodie, what are you making, moonshine?"

Metal tubing in spiral coils about the diameter of classic slinky toys extended in no recognizable pattern all around the newly cleared space, junk piles having been relegated to corners. On closer inspection, the tubing itself was wrapped with fine copper wire along its entire length, like a metal guitar string. Mike thought, *That's quite a project right there.*

Galvanized metal ducts hung from the ceiling in large diameter curves. In cross section, the ducts were the size of the diameter of the coils. Two separate ducts spiraled like DNA gently sloping down until they both ended on the floor, facing each other but unconnected. Attached to the end caps were pipe connectors, not quite finished.

Brodie said, "It's the Redneck Hadron Collider! See, the coils go in the ducts, the ducts are filled with liquid nitrogen and the wire generates a superconducting magnetic field. All I need is a proton beam generator on one end and detectors on the other.

"The super-conducting magnetic field will keep the proton beam centered in the tube as it accelerates. See, it doesn't have to be a *large* hadron collider, just a long one, the right length."

Mike recognizes the general design. "Fermilab's Mu2e experiment used a smaller bore and tighter curves like that back in 2016."

"Right, the Transport Solenoid, a tight s-curve wrapped in magnets to concentrate the beam. But even with that small diameter, it's like spittin' in the Grand Canyon."

"And eventually the military co-opted that to make a particle beam weapon."

"Not surprising, but irrelevant. This is different Mike, more curves wound tighter with a liquid nitrogen cryostat. Mine has even smaller diameter tubing and the particles still aren't really affected by the curve.

"I think I can get the proton beam up to LHC speeds, 15 Tev's at least. But eventually, have no fear, the music goes round and round and it comes out here!" pointing to the ends. "Little Big Bang!"

"There's so much so wrong here, I don't know where to start, Brodie." Mike says, though not really surprised.

"I'll work it out, it'll be great."

"You're lucky you have a day job. You couldn't get near CERN with this jury rig and the quench protocols would shut it down automatically if you tried."

"Prissy French piece of junk. Swiss watch, my ass. Who needs it?"

After another beer and some teamwork stuffing the coils into the ducts, Mike says, "Archie's modeling the Higgs field in a goldfish bowl for the science fair."

"I like that kid. He's a riot; and he's really intuitive. You should bring him over here."

"Then my whole house would look like this!"

"Don't be a buzz kill on his creativity, man."

"I'm not. He's hard to contain. And I'm just a happily married husband and father who wants to stay that way, *man*."

"Exactly! That's your problem right there; you're addicted to risk avoidance."

*

Mike arrived at his own driveway, entered the house and was giving Anna an almost-sober kiss when a shrill voice killed the mood. "Dad, Archie's got Sparkle in a water balloon!"

"Emma, Archie wouldn't hurt Sparkle."

"He melted Barbie's head playing nuclear holocaust!"

"I know, but . . .just . . .stay out of the way."

Into the inner sanctum he went, into the lair of a serial obsessive. There was the geodesic sphere that was too big to get out of the room, tensegrity polyhedra, the gross of ping pong balls turning into a Buckminster Fuller closest-packing-of-spheres project and various Star Trek, Star Wars and Battlestar Galactica model ships hanging from the ceiling, most having lost all structural integrity, shields down, inertial dampeners offline, hanging askew, burnt and listless from photon torpedoes, phaser blasts and firecrackers. Barbie might have just gotten innocently caught in the crossfire, after all.

"Archie, you are not helping . . ." He had to pause however, and take in this new scene. A net grocery bag hung from the ceiling, a water balloon made from a large surgical glove resting inside, its fingers protruding through the net like they were purpose-made to anchor the balloon. It was filled with water and had expanded to such a size that it was almost transparent. The balloon was backlit by a desk lamp. There, happily swimming in this precarious island universe was Sparkle, no worse for wear.

"How did you get her in there?"

"Cut the end off of a funnel, stuck it in the glove, she slipped right in with the water. The net supports it, it won't pop. She's safe."

Talk about relativity. "Ok, how long are you going to need her?"

"Tomorrow's the science fair."

"Does she have enough air?"

"Duh; see the tubing connected to the pump?"

The aquarium pump bubbled inside the balloon, also compensating for air seepage. *Well then, never mind. . .* Mike turned to his younger child. "Emma, let your brother borrow Sparkle for the day and you can come check on her at the science fair after school. I'll be there too, ok?"

"No, but ok and you owe me." Sort of a proto-squint herself, Emma had learned at age seven that, on average, she would get more things her way if she managed her expectations and *appeared* reasonable when Dad needed to *appear* to be in control.

He said, "Put it on my tab."

*

The next day at 3:00, Mike walked into the multi-purpose room and surveyed the science fair projects. A papier-mache volcano was featured, a potato battery powering a transistor radio kit and Sparkle. Brodie was standing there in his shorts and tank top, but in uncustomary silence, furrowed brows contemplating something . . . different.

The gravity well was nowhere in sight. The real project hung from a hook stuck in the metal frame of the acoustic ceiling panel. As Mike approached, Archie was fiddling with something protruding from the opening of the water balloon. Instead of the plastic tubing and aquarium pump, there was a glass pipette tube sticking out of the glove opening, rubber bands sealed the opening tight around the tube. On the other end of the tube, *in the water,* a small round balloon was similarly attached and sealed. He had fixed a couple of bendable straws to the protruding end and bent them down and then parallel to the equator of the blown up glove.

Mike recalls a science lesson he had recently taught. *Like Hero's revolving steam engine.*

"Hi *Dad*! This is your idea. Watch this!" Archie blew into the straw and the balloon inside the glove began to inflate. Sparkle curiously bumped against it with her mouth. Archie let go and the air escaped through the nozzle with a hiss. The little universe began to spin. "See, outside of her universe is 'nothing' connected now to the 'nothing' inside her universe. I cleared the Higgs field in the center. Now Sparkle can see *outside* of her universe while she's still *inside* her universe. It's like a Klein bottle where the inside and the outside are one continuous surface."

Mike said, "Thanks for the attribution," although he wasn't quite sure what Archie decided he had thought up. "What's with the spinning?"

"Hmm, not sure, it's going somewhere, I like it."

Brodie said under his breath, "I like it too. Jesus, *I get it!*" He spun with a start and stomped out, car keys twirling on his finger like a six shooter. As Emma showed up to check on Sparkle, Brodie's classic 64 1/2 Mustang rumbled to life and its tires squealed.

*

Mara
2326 A.R.
Enuma Elish

"I get my bedtime story, Daddy," Shanti said.

The nursery and the convertible crib-youth bed were about to outgrow their usefulness. The bed was a nice blond oak piece of furniture that Dan and Charlotte had worked together to build from plans. Then, they had sat together on the floor with a quilt board, patterns and rotary cutters, to make a special quilt, not so easy at seven or eight months pregnant. On their hands and knees, they had cut out the sections of a pattern that had been in the Pritchard family for generations, straight from Cave-in-Rock, Shawneetown and Cairo, Illinois. Little Egypt, they called it, and Hell on the Ohio. Dan's river pirate ancestors had tucked in their wee bairn with the same quilt pattern in that Scots-Irish hole in the wall two hundred years before.

The quilt had an eight pointed star on a black background, outlined with triangles intersecting. The lines from the points inward then made eight smaller triangles framing an octagon in the center. Dan thought, *Just like my grandmother Alma Tabitha Pritchard made for my mom and her brothers.*

The beautiful thing about this quilt was that, after piecing the sections together, the outlines of the stars were embroidered with Scottish twilling stitches and then with embroidered flowers and wild roses around the border and filling in the triangular sections. The piecing followed the colors of the rainbow in sequence, running clockwise and the flowers mirrored the same colors. It had green stems and leaves in a Celtic braid pattern that still looked natural, fractal. On the black background, similar embroidered flowers in light grey outline were evenly spaced like a sampler, completing the design.

Dan's first job at sixteen had been at a big craft store where he unpacked yarn and notions and then cut up the boxes for recycling. He had learned embroidery, needlepoint, cross stitch, even knitting. His paternal grandmother had been a seamstress and so his father had no qualms about making a dress for Dan's mother. He could fix the sewing machine and make the clothes.

So, it was natural for Dan and Charlotte to sit on the floor piecing the quilt, hand stitching and embroidering together while watching the streamer, exchanging smiles, threading each other's needles and biting threads off of knots. A peaceful silent oneness settled like a mist around and between them and the baby in her womb.

Five years later, that oneness continued as they stood by the bed they had also built together. They tucked in the quilt around this girl of theirs, wood and cloth and thread grafting their love to her.

Years from now, worse for wear, Shanti will pull the quilt lovingly out of a bag or box, maybe only once every few years as she moves from the family home to dorm room to married student apartments, back home, then on her own again, a new home in the suburbs, until she knew it intimately as the oldest true thing she could remember. Later, with a baby inside of her own womb, she'll sit on the floor, cut her own triangles and piece together her own newest true thing for her child.

Shanti surveyed the bookshelf above her headboard, Winnie the Pooh, Little Bear, Frog and Toad, Anaximander's Fables, Dr. Seuss, and all the myths and stories that she will love throughout her life. Charlotte stocked the bookshelf herself, the selection of creation myths for children being much wider than the Christian dominated American libraries of her first life.

The difference was more than selection however. On Mara, all the stories were treated as valuable myth, not as superstitious products of a forgotten age. No, here the power and truth of myth was the whole point.

"Which story do you want?"

"About how the world began," Shanti said.

He looked at the shelf of books. "Which one? We have the Vedas, Egyptian, Etruscan and Greek, the *Táin Bó Cúailnge,* the *Popul Vuh.*"

She said, "You left out the Syriac one."

Dan said, "I like that one too. How did you know?"

"When I was little, you told me," Shanti said.

Charlotte peeked around the door jamb. "What's 'when I was little' to a four year old?"

"When I was a *baby* Mom! And I'm four and a half."

"*Sorry,* I forgot. Can I listen?" she asked.

Shanti said seriously, "Ok, but don't interrupt. Grown-ups are so annoying."

"Yeah, just watch it Mom," Dan said as he picked a well-worn book from the shelf and sat on the bed.

Charlotte propped up the pillows and tucked-in Shanti between them like bookends. All the warmth and love that anyone could hope for was in that scrum. Three interconnected beings, all one yet all separate. *A Holy Trinity from another planet.* Dan opened the book and began to read the *Enuma Elish.*

"This I have heard with my own ears: In the Beginning, when on high. . ."

Shanti settled down into the pillows, Charlotte's arm cradling her neck and head, but still fidgety with anticipation. Dan continued with the ancient creation myth, alternating passages with showing the pictures in the book.

"When on high the heavens had not been named,
And the ground below had not been named,
And nothing but a formless void and darkness
Covered the face of the Deep
The face was that of Tiamat, the salt waters of Chaos
Upon which the world would float.
Then Apsu, the fresh waters, her husband,
Swept over Tiamat
And their waters flowed together as they slumbered.
And as they slumbered, their waters seeded the womb
of Tiamat with the first gods, Ea and his brothers."

Shanti said, "They didn't mean to make babies, they just wanted to sleep, right Daddy?"

"That's right." He looked at Charlotte. "Sometimes it just happens."

"But, on the seventh day there was no rest for Apsu

Because Ea and the others caused a great uproar
Inside of Tiamat with unceasing movement."

Here he always added, "Jumping! Leaping! Throwing things, constant noise and babbling . . .and because of all the noise and commotion, Apsu wanted to kill them, just so he could rest."

In a stage whisper, Charlotte said, "Now, *I've* never felt like that."

Dan turned the page and ad-libbed, "But, after all, being sleep deprived, his child Ea got the best of him and killed Apsu instead while Tiamat slept. What?!"

Shanti chimed in, "And after that the other gods jumped on the bed until Tiamat woke up and they said please, please, please do this one thing and we will never, ever ask you for anything ever again!"

"She wanted them to stop begging, so she created an army of monsters and Qingu, a new husband to defeat her children.."

Shanti said, "And Ea says to Qingu, you're not my real dad, and not the boss of me."

"Right, but Qingu and the army of monsters defeated Ea and so the children tell Marduk, the grandson, that he can be their king if he defeats Tiamat and Qingu. Marduk defeats the monster army and kills Tiamat. He splits her lengthwise and separates her body into the heavens above and the earth below."

"Yuck!"

"Well that's the story, baby. Then Marduk was the chief god and he created humans from the blood of Qingu to be slaves so that on the seventh day all the gods could rest. But on Monday, back at work, Marduk created Babylon and the humans got to have a civilization and that was that, la la la. The End."

"That's not how it ends!"

"Tonight it does. I'm tiered of the novies. Time for bed."

She tried a serious whine, "Let's not and say we did. Tell me the one about Utnapishtem and the Flood, I really wanted to hear that one."

"No, not tonight, Mommy and I really need to get some rest."

"Please, please, please, I'll never ask for anything ever again!"

Charlotte said, "Were you even listening to the story? It didn't turn out well for the whiners that kept their parents from sleeping."

Dan said, "And we have to get up early to go to grandma Amy's house for Kali-Bahkti."

"And the museum! Okay, you guys go to bed."

Dan said, "Good night baby, gods' blessings on you."

"And on you, Daddy."

Dan put out the light, took the hand of his own sleepy goddess, led her to the marriage chamber and lay her gently on the bed, the two of them ready to comingle the waters of chaos and spoon creation through the evening to the morning of the first day.

They lay close together on their left sides. In this position his belly fit into the small of her back, her butt fit snugly into his lap, the front of his thighs conformed to the back of hers, Dan thought, *Just like plate tectonics. Miss Africa, meet Mr. South America.*

Their calves and feet intertwined, his chin was just over her shoulder, his left arm was under her head and his right hand cupped her right breast. She drew him close, pulling on his arm and gently exploring the tangle of legs and feet. His pelvis moved a bit forward and hers answered back, just a kiss goodnight that he repeated with his lips on her neck. He squeezed her breast and then just held it, needing nothing more. He thought, *Now this is the best feeling, the only thing that matters. If we make it through the day, I can do this again tomorrow night.* Charlotte said, "Remind me to cut those toenails." Dan just said, "Hmmmmm."

Charlotte waited for Dan's deep rhythmic breathing to start and then reached out with her energy body to encircle him and Shanti, to complete the cocoon she wove each night. She started her cell checker practice to monitor their three bodies as one, automatically repairing damaged DNA, fending off microbial attacks and building immunities. Then, she silently chanted a prayer from another space time:

Thank you Kali – Ma
Thank you for all things
Thank you for Creation, Sustenance and Destruction
Thank you for Universes and Arrows of Time
Thank you for the Three Realms
Thank you for the Worlds in the Realms
Thank you for the Love and Longing
Of Sentient Beings
Thank you for Respite in your arms
Thank you Kali – Ma

*

Earth
2040 C.E.

Something about Archie's project clearly clicked, or snapped, with Brodie. The next bowling night, Mike and Brodie had another beer, this time at Mike's house. Their attention was first drawn by some mess and stink that Emma was making at the kitchen table. Brodie always assumed that something scientific was going on. *Most of life involves chemistry, physics and geometry. Cooking is just chemistry.*

Emma sat at the kitchen table hunched over a binocular microscope, staring at something in greenish liquid under the lens, the image fed to the wall mounted flat screen. Archie was just bringing his post-dinner snack of a bowl of

Captain Crunch to the table in one hand and clutching his phone-pad in the other.

Brodie said, "What's that smell?" He wrinkled his nose. Archie paused with his next spoonful in midair, not lifting his eyes from the pad. "*Her* Science Fair project, tardigrades, water bears, moss pigs, you know."

Emma said, "Not pigs, I don't like that name."

Mike said, "I know what they are . . . "

Archie whatever'd a "Hmph."

Brodie said, "These kids are endlessly entertaining, gotta get me some."

"They're not virtual pets, you know."

"Well, there's got to be a mom in the mix somewhere, to do the dirty work, you know, to complain how I just get to be the fun parent and she's the disciplinarian."

"You're counting on the mother not being able to stand you? Do you get *all* your minimal social skills from popular culture?"

Brodie said, "Life imitates art imitating life. That's all you need to know, unsullied reality is long gone. Cork 'em and pork 'em and then you just get alternating weekends, fun, fun, fun."

"Well, there you go." Mike said to Emma, "Put it outside for now."

Emma tossed the green slush out the back door. Archie drank the last of the crunchberry juice, tossed the bowl in the sink without looking and headed for the living room, eyes still glued to his phone-pad. Emma routed the microscope feed to her pad and started making notes for her project.

Mike said, "So what's up with the science fair fallout? You blew out of there like you had seen a ghost."

"Ghostbuster, maybe." Brodie turned to Mike after chugging the bottom half of a bottle of fine domestic pilsner.

"And . . . another archaic pop culture meme and . . ."

"Classic." Brodie dropped the phony redneck bravado and talked fast but clearly. He'd gone over this in his head a million times. Mike kept up, following the gist of it.

"Look, take Archie's project at face value. The goldfish is inside the balloon which is space time and the balloon is filled with water. The water is the Higgs field, just like Archie says. It's the one field that's always there, like water in a water balloon.

"What if there was a bubble of whatever is outside the universe, now inflating inside the universe, like the bubble of air in the center of the water balloon? That was Archie's point; how do you get outside of something that there is no outside of?

"You want to make what's outside of our universe accessible right here on the workbench?"

"Stay with the water balloon, what would make a stable bubble?"

"Just tell me."

"Right. A semi permeable membrane, a cell wall. It's made of molecules that attract water at one end and repel water at the other end, they naturally orient to make a bubble; certain things can pass through from outside to inside but not the other way."

"Ok, that's seventh grade science, and so . . ."

"Now think about the Higgs boson, Squints think one triggered the Big Bang."

"That assumes that a Higgs boson existed before the Big Bang."

"Exactly. All particles arise from potentiality in a field, so a Higgs field existed somewhere, before this universe. And the Higgs must vibrate another field, one that carries the potentiality of universes, a multiverse field. In a multiverse, that field must still exist between universes."

Mike waxed poetic, ". . . and Brodie was on the face of the Deep."

"Amen, brotha'. But where did the Higgs boson come from? Where did it exist when it triggered our Big Bang?"

Now Mike squinted. "From somewhere else where a Higgs field *does* exist."

"Right." Brodie continued, "From a universe at least *that* similar to ours. So, there must be a way out. I think I can find it. Look at these Feynman diagrams." He put the familiar drawings with lines, squiggles and arrows in front of Mike.

"This diagrams how particle collisions can make the Higgs."

"Visualize them oriented in the same way the cell membrane molecules do but relative to the Higgs field, one end of the process is stable and at the other end unloads all the potential of the field. Think of a sphere made of these."

"Feynman diagrams are not molecules."

"*I said visualize.* It's a metaphor, a concept, jeez, this isn't that hard . . ."

Emma laughed as a fuzzy creature in soft focus appeared on the flat screen. It was a pudgy little thing like a sausage with eight fat legs and long claws. No face really, but mouth parts sucking on moss and crinkles that looked like eyes. It swam or slogged through the juice like it was grazing, sometimes twisting its body like a manatee to move off in another direction. For something the size of an amoeba, it actually seemed like it could have a personality.

Brodie, momentarily distracted, said, "That's awesome Emma. Do you have your talk ready?"

Emma said, "Oh yes, water bears. . . "

Eavesdropping from the living room, always on the lookout for topics about which he really *should* be consulted, Archie loudly interrupted, ". . .also called Moss Pigs, tardigrades, means slow walker, discovered by some Dutch guy 200 years ago, can live 100 years without water, lost in space, everybody knows already."

"Stop it! You always spoil everything!"

Mike said, "Archie, let her do it. It doesn't matter if it's not perfect according to you. We've already had this conversation."

Archie, turning on his full Asperger's savant routine, started to rock and moan and raised the volume on the streamer.

Emma yelled, "Just cuz you got Asperger's doesn't mean you have to be an Ass-burger!"

Archie smiled to himself and yelled. "So tell him yourself if you're so smart!"

"Go ahead Emma."

"Well," referring to her phone-pad for notes, but mostly extemporaneous, she said, "Water bears were discovered in 1771 by a German pastor named Goeze. He named them Kliene Wasserbar, little water bear, cute. So they are maybe less than half a millimeter long, have four pairs of legs and claws, later named tardigrades, meaning slow *stepper!* They can live in just about any environment on earth where there is water, but can survive by drying up to only three percent of their body mass, into a little ball called a tun. They have been rehydrated after ten years and came alive just fine. They have even survived exposed to radiation and the cold and vacuum of space, and had normal babies after they came back. Did I say they had eight legs?"

Mike raised his eyebrows at Brodie. Brodie said, "See, she's a genius, Hardy Har Har." Then to Emma, "And do any other animals have eight legs?"

Emma said, "Spiders!"

Archie yelled, "Barsoomian Thoats!"

That's not real!" she yelled.

Mike asked, "What's a thoat?"

"Jeez Dad, you know, John Carter of Mars, Edgar Rice Burroughs. All the Martian life has multiple legs. Thoats have eight. Tharks use them like horses. Don't you read?"

Brodie jumped in, "Yeah Mike, Dejah Thoris, *A Princess of Mars.* When we were Archie's age that graphic novel version, oh man, that's why I have unrealistic expectations of women. She was mostly naked all the time and had the most beautiful and well developed. . ."

"Personality?"

Archie yelled, "No Dad, boobs! It's the lower Martian gravity, I got it right here on the pad . . . ."

Emma put her fingers in her ears, "La la la la la la la! I can't hear you! La la la la!"

Mike said, "Ok, ok, I'm sure she was a really nice person too, but that's not real guys."

Archie said, "Whatever, but if water bears can survive in space, maybe they came from space, on a Martian meteorite, then evolved for a billion years and here we are."

"Ok," Mike said, "but those books are fiction; not trying to be picky, but they *are* fiction."

Undaunted, Archie replied, "The author says he was given the book by his uncle, John Carter, maybe it was real and he just pretended it was fiction to throw everybody off."

"But we have pictures from Mars."

Brodie said, "Not from a billion years ago, and anyway they all look like Texas to me. Can you prove that water bears *didn't* come from Mars?"

"Well, no but that's not even logic.. . ."

"Ha, so there, it could've happened."

Archie said, "So when we melt the Martian ice caps, guess what? Thoats and water bears, wanna bet?"

"No, but if you're right, I'll admit you're right."

"*That's the way, Uh huh, uh huh, I like it, Uh huh, uh huh.*" Archie did some retro disco hustle back to the couch as Emma headed to her bedroom and slammed the door.

Mike said, "Alone at last, continue."

Brodie said "Boy, that made me remember something else from high school, Wonder Woman!"

"No, no, no, you'll get all poetic and misty and. . ."

"Ok, More beer, then."

"As much as it takes."

Brodie cracked his knuckles and put on his sort of professor voice. "In our universe, the Higgs field is coextensive with expanding space time. So, by definition, there is no natural place *inside our particular universe* where the Higgs field does not exist. But, there *is* a place where there is no Higgs field and that place is the field between universes in the multiverse."

"Hypothetically." Mike handed a fresh bottle to Brodie.

"You know, I really liked it when they stopped making the screw tops. The classic crimped on ones you can open like this . . ." He stuck the bottle top into his bicep, tensed the muscle and popped the cap. "Girls love that trick."

"Girls you don't pay for?"

"Any girls; fuck you, you know, if you paid for one you might have a different perspective on the value of sex workers."

"Hooker with a heart of gold?"

"Jusayn; don't knock it till you knock, knock, knock it."

"Still married, Brodie."

"Don't expect sympathy from me. Ok, stop distracting me, call it the multiverse field. The point is to imagine a space inside our universe without the Higgs field which therefore, also contains the multiverse field. There's never just nothing."

Mike said, "That's Archie's balloon in the balloon."

"But how do you build that in the world? That's the problem."

"You want to make a wormhole?"

"No, a wormhole connects different parts of the same universe. We need to get out of this universe altogether. I want the escape hatch, I want *out*."

"*OK* . . . continue"

"First, we have to make the space, the bubble."

Mike said, "Where's the math, white boards, equations?"

"Math is for squints, Mike, I can *feel* it."

"Jusayn. Usually there's math."

"I'm not hiding behind math. I'm not that good at it; better at Feynman diagrams. No, I want to build something with nuts and bolts; listen. Higgs bosons will pass through the bubble like the semi permeable membrane. The particles are going *somewhere* at up to the speed of light, faster maybe since they go outside this universe. The energy generated by this departure has to push the bubble *somewhere else,* in an equal and opposite reaction, and there you go, instant GUT ship drive!"

"That's another one of those cute acronyms you hate so much. GUT's and TOE's."

"This one I like. It's a contraction, Grand Unified Theory Of Everything, GU'TOE."

"Which still hasn't been successfully demonstrated."

"Patent that idea and it's move over Dan Pritchard."

"Jesus Brodie, you can't just cobble together all the unrelated bits of physics that you happen to like and call it a theory. You start with a great theoretical mechanism to create the Big Bang and end up as the billionaire playboy of your dreams."

"But, that's the part I really like. Bruce Wayne and Tony Stark used their fortunes for good, not evil. I could do that."

"Those guys were morally conflicted anti-heroes."

"You're such a buzz kill. Look, if it works, I've automatically proven the multiverse."

"Because. . . "

"Because, if both the bubble and the universe are permeable, the closed system is not our universe, it's the multiverse. Particles can therefore, leave our universe through the bubble without violating physical laws."

"You're saying that you can leave the universe and still conserve mass and energy?"

"*You* can't leave, but, the *bubble* allows for particles to cross over into the multiverse field. If the bubble does not reach equilibrium, if the particles keep flowing, then that proves the system is not closed."

Archie yelled from the living room as he walked toward the kitchen. "Boys, b,b,b,boys, Ask me, ask me."

Brodie said, "You tell it Arch."

Back at the table, Archie continued, "Right. One, a sphere that shoots bosons from all points on its surface to its center,

"T't'two, Feynman diagrams predict the colliders make a smaller sphere in the center,

"Three, that surface duplicates the edge of our universe, n'no d'doubt,

"Four, Higgs bosons can pass through that surface, right right,

"Five, conservation of energy, check, conservation of matter, check,

"Six, *Go Dog Go*, thank you very much, Ha!"

Mike said, "You're talking about reverse-engineering the outer edge of the universe."

"Good b'b'boy."

"You don't have to be a smart ass *all* the time, Archie, take a rest."

"I'll be in my ready room Number One." Archie saluted and mounted the stairs.

Brodie said, "The result is practical. When particles start seeping through, then the bubble begins to move through four dimensions. That's Archie's spinning water balloon. We just need a nozzle, the straws.

"It's like a turbo jet, or a jet-ski nozzle, the same continuum sucks it in and blows it out. So, the bubble moves within the isolate field at the speed the particles leave, up to the speed of light. If you can control the direction the nozzle points, you should be able to 'steer' the bubble. But, we can't really know what will happen until we make it work."

Mike said, "This is what you complain about with the squints, 'trust me, the math says it's ok.'"

"No, this is much less refined, more dangerous. Don't trust me, I don't know what I'm doing but I'm going to do it anyway.' And one more thing Mikey; remember you said the Higgs boson that triggered the Big Bang had to come from another universe that has a Higgs field?"

The beer fog forcefully cleared. "Yes, that's the first question you asked, where did that boson come from? And now you propose to spray particles like a garden hose into the multiverse field."

"And that means that the streaming particles will make babies! It's like a puppy mill, a fish hatchery or a sperm bank!"

"Particles spontaneously reproducing universes?"

"Oh yes, and I'm buying the cigars!"

"Brodie, if our universe was started by a Higgs boson that can exist under our physical laws, that's proof that there's another anthropic universe like ours in the multiverse with idiots like us sowing wild oats."

"Stop it, man. I'm choking up. It's like Father's Day!"

*

Mara
2326 A.R.

It was officially Spring-Summer Day, halfway between the equinox and the solstice, but still conveniently close to Kali-Bhakti. This was the government's long standing policy of trying not to offend anybody while actually celebrating everything. Anyway, the day off and no entrance charges at the museum planned their morning itinerary, focused on working up an appetite for Grandma's holiday cooking.

The Museum of Man had been rebuilt with a faux Etruscan façade, and the tripartite interior style favored since temples were first built in Etruria. The only concession to Latinate and colonial revivals was the grand set of steps up to the double door entrance. Shanti held Charlotte's hand as Dan brought up the rear, then stopped at the ticket window while the ladies looked at the posters of the current exhibition.

Shanti noticed one poster in particular. "Mom look! It's like *Night at the Museum*, tiny little soldiers!"

"Ok, let's do that first." One of the three main exhibition halls was filled with dioramas under glass, like large aquaria, about eight by four feet and sitting on platforms at about Shanti's eye level. Charlotte looked down from above. The first one was about the Babylonian Accords with Canaan and Egypt. Charlotte had actually helped with the preparation of this one. It was part of her specialty.

Dan sidled up with a guide map which he was trying to decipher upside down. "Hey, here's that thing . . . about your . . . stuff."

Charlotte said, "Why do I even talk to you at the dinner table, Dan? Mesopotamia? . . . Anything. . .?"

He said, "Sure, B-52's, Twenty-two Eighty something? Kidding, what is it, Sumer, Akkad, Syria, Babylon?"

"Well that's better, at least within four thousand years; it's the peace treaty between the Babylonians and the Canaanites."

"Got it." Dan started to read for Shanti's benefit,

The effort of Ashurbanipal to coalesce Mesopotamian city-states into an expeditionary empire failed and therefore, Babylon's plans to incorporate the peoples of Canaan and Egypt into an empire, instead, took shape as the first real intercultural trade and defense agreement, a pattern followed by others as civilization progressed.

Shanti said, "Why are the men wearing long hair and skirts, Daddy?"

"Yes, Professor, why was that?" Dan asked Charlotte.

"I guess men were just prettier then, it's all fashion, Shanti."

"Prettier legs. That's funny!" Shanti laughed.

The next diorama was the Indian Emperor Ashoka installing a stela listing his Buddhist laws. Shanti recognized this as well. "We have this in my book, he was nice to animals. I like him."

Charlotte said. "Yes, he even had sanctuaries for injured animals."

"And he stopped wars."

"Mostly. . .well he tried, he was a good guy."

"I like the good guys." Shanti said.

Dan leaned over to read the description of the stelae and what was written on them:

Ashoka the Great (1 A.R. to 62 A.R) elevated Buddhism to the State religion of his empire.

Dharma is good, but what constitutes Dharma? It includes little evil, much good, kindness, generosity, truthfulness and purity. Pillar Edict Nb2

And noble deeds of Dharma and the practice of Dharma consist of having kindness, generosity, truthfulness, purity, gentleness and goodness increase among the people. Rock Pillar Nb7.

The diorama showed the installation of the border stelae which marked the entrance to Ashoka's empire and gave notice of the laws in effect. The punishment for breaking the laws was banishment. Ashoka himself sat in a royal howdah on an elephant, pointing to the stelae with his imperial staff. Bactrian nobles on the other side of the border knelt in honor and subjugation to the Dharma.

Dan caught up to Charlotte but Shanti was already at the next diorama. "What's this Mommy?"

Dan said, "The Etruscans at the Tiber?"

Charlotte said, "Right, the consolidation of the Etruscan confederacy, with the defeat of the Latins at Rome."

Shanti tugged on Charlotte's hand. "I'm bored, let's go see the dinosaurs!"

"That's a different museum honey."

"But I'm bored!"

Dan said, "Oh look Shanti, there's the snack bar, let's eat." Shanti grabbed his hand and dragged him toward the food shouting,"Sno-cones!"

Charlotte waited until they were about thirty feet away and called, "Dan.. . . .Dan! Hey Dan!"

She commanded him seriously, arms akimbo, legs set apart, "Buy me something I like, Baby."

She looks just like Wonder Woman, Sufferin' Sappho!

"What did Wonder Woman say to the God of War"?

"She said, 'I believe in love.'"

"So do I."

"Then she killed him. So, do as I command, mortal."

He bowed from the waist with a flourish like a musketeer, doffing his baseball cap. "Something from the banquet table? As you wish, my queen."

Shanti pulled, "Come on, c'mon, you do this all the time! Grown-ups are so annoying!"

*

Mara
2341 A.R.

New York Times Book Review March 26, 2341
Heart String Theory
Charlotte Pritchard, Ph.D. , *N. K. Jemisin*

The recent best seller status of *Heart String Theory* has probably surprised its author Charlotte Pritchard, Ph.D. as much as anyone. Dr. Pritchard has long been known in a small circle of historians specializing in the mid Greco-Buddhist period (36 B.A.R. to 742 A.R.) in a corner of the Mediterranean Empire States, then known variously as Phoenicia, Canaan and the Hyksosian Protectorate. This period, in a remote corner of the Etruscan Confederation, was mostly known for being uneventful, until Dr. Pritchard strayed from her cloistered History Department at the University of Colorado, Denver, to the world of fantastic fiction.

I would have to say that she invented the genre of alternate history from whole cloth. Her colleagues in the scientific and artistic communities were hard pressed to understand why a radical new art form was necessary. Academics are often characterized by disdain for commotion of any kind disturbing their cogitation. "Just do the old forms better," they said, "but more quietly." Well, the public certainly thought differently.

Dr. Pritchard's first book in this series, *The Rise of the God of Atheists*, dealt with her imagined history of a small tribe in Canaan, known to us only in the historical record as Judea. In Dr. Pritchard's history, Judea, hard pressed upon by aggressive empires, exiled and enslaved, their temples and culture destroyed, began the worship of a wholly unitary God; a portable God, if you will, for those travelers forced to pack light.

This plot device required Dr. Pritchard to wave her magic wand and make the Greco-Buddhist Empire disappear, even to the point of abandoning Ashokan Reckoning dates. This void is then filled with fancifully homicidal Assyrians, Babylonians and Egyptians, harassing the Judeans all over the then known world. The devotees of this kind of God however, had to deny all other Gods, resulting in a level of violent intolerance that made for a real page turner. This is why the Judeans are called 'Atheists,' by their Latinate rulers, because they deny all gods but one.

This book was immensely popular and was followed by sequels that saw the rise of other monotheistic cults violently competing with each other because they all could envision only one God. The seed for the most influential permutation of this monotheism involves a germ of an idea found in a history of Canaan written by the Etruscan-Judean historian Flavius Josephus in 394 A.R.

This is the core of Dr. Pritchard's method. She takes a fact about a little known event and changes it in a minor way. Then, it's like the proverbial butterfly flapping its wings causing a storm half a world away.

Josephus reported:

> About this time there lived Yeshua, a wise man, for he was one who performed surprising deeds and was a teacher of such people as accept the truth gladly. He won over many Judeans and many of the Greeks. And when the principal men among us had condemned him to death, those who had first come to love him did not cease. And the tribe of the Christians, so called after him, has still to this day not disappeared.
> - *Judean Antiquities*, 18.3.3 §63

Dr. Pritchard then added the three lines in italics below to the known text:

> About this time there lived Yeshua, a wise man, *if indeed one ought to call him a man.* For he was one who performed surprising deeds and was a teacher of such people as accept the truth gladly. He won over many Judeans and many of the Greeks. *He was the Messiah.* And when the principal men among us had condemned him to death, those who had first come to love him did not cease. *He appeared to them spending a*

third day restored to life, for the prophets of God had foretold these things and a thousand other marvels about him. And the tribe of the Christians, so called after him, has still to this day not disappeared.

The three lines refer to the same itinerant preacher, said to have worked miracles and then run afoul of the authorities, was executed and rumored to have reappeared to continue his teaching. The term *Messiah* refers to a Judean political leader prophesized to establish a renewed Judean kingdom. The Messiah, by definition, could not be a lowly itinerate preacher or an executed criminal. But it is just this contradiction that gives the new prophecy its power.

Much to the dismay of the morphed Etruscan Confederacy (called Roman Empire in this alternate history), the monotheists following this man continued to convert followers and by two thousand years later end up conquering most of the world. In the meantime, Pritchard's pot boiler of holy wars, persecutions, slaughter of innocents, blood, sex and death also drew converts with an almost religious fervor.

Well, that was surprisingly good fun, but after six volumes, the latest of which rapidly approached the present date, fans wondered what Dr. Pritchard would do next. Not to worry, she has now taken us into an alternate *future* history.

Heart String Theory starts with an unremarkable couple, living and working together in a Denver of the near future. Sherry Dee is dead when the story opens, but soon is found to be an energy being, symbiotic with humans. There are others of her kind and all are clamoring to return to the living. Meanwhile, her husband helps to invent a 'quantum gravity device' that allows for anti-gravity and the return from the dead of these beings that believe they are human souls.

This is actually three stories intertwined. First, there is the story of a small love between a boy and a girl that eventually crosses multiple universes to be fulfilled. Second, a small invention leads to a radical change in worldview and possibilities, ending with the ability to avoid the speed of light and travel through an anomaly called the Akashic Record to other places and other times. Finally, the life of one person, Sherry Dee, is commandeered into a full blown inter-galactic, interdimensional and interspecies religion starring our heroine as an incarnation of our familiar Bodhisattva, Quan Yin.

It cannot be denied that this has become a hit like no other. For years, behind the curve academics will argue as to why this is so. The simple answer is that the mass of the population loves this oddly scientific yet oddly reverent, romp through a hard science fiction universe where love is as great a power as quantum gravity. Flying through space on the bow shock of the solar wind, you and your lover spread your arms and solar sails and shout in your helmets, "I'm King of the Worlds!" I have no doubt that future legions of fans will continue to be willingly led down the starlit trails of Dr. Pritchard's imagination.

*

Earth
2040 C.E.

Six months after the science fair, there was a different arrangement of slinkies and hanging ducts in Brodie's garage. In the center of the garage hung a ball of metal and glass, a little steam punkish, looking like a diver's helmet or a bathysphere, about three feet in diameter. This was suspended from the ceiling but also connected to the floor, to the eight corners of the interior space and to the centers of the four walls with quarter-inch cables tightened by turnbuckles. The cables tethered the ball so it couldn't move in any direction.

What looked like small fuel injection nozzles protruded at regular intervals inside the ball, each pointing to the center of the sphere. These were closely packed with maybe only an inch of clearance equally separating all of them. On the outside, the end of one of the slinkies attached to the back end of each nozzle. The slinkies were now in closed metal pipes just big enough to house them, sealed to hold liquid nitrogen.

Giving up on an orderly pattern of pipes, like dryer vents in a surreal laundromat, each wound its way more or less spiraling in toward the ball. Freezing condensation on the pipes confirmed the liquid nitrogen inside.

The far ends of the slinky pipes were gathered in bundles near the joints of walls and ceiling. There, they were attached to the business ends of what looked like pipe bombs sprouting wires; Brodie's homemade particle accelerators.

There wasn't much room to walk. Mike, in a parka and nursing a beer, sat in the open kitchen doorway. Brodie, tucked into an adjoining corner and wearing a snowsuit and gloves for warmth and to prevent his skin from sticking to the pipes, held an RC controller for a drone. In a fit of uncharacteristic prudence, he had not invited Archie.

"Jobs and Wozniak started like this," Brodie said.

"With a lot less hardware and one less loose cannon."

With his goggles on, Brodie looked for all the world like Captain Nemo meets Admiral Perry. He said, "Famous last words: Hold my beer and watch this."

Mike took the beer. Brodie flipped toggle switches on the remote that lit the proton beam generators and turned on the electromagnetic coils. The slinky pipes stirred a bit as the proton beams spiraled through, interacting with the magnetic field.

It looked like a children's museum display on string theory as the pipes started to oscillate in tight little loops about their long axes. Inside the ball, a blue beam began to emerge from each nozzle. As Brodie pushed the rheostat of the controller up further and further, the beams resolved and met at the spatial center of the ball's interior. With all parts vibrating, and all lights in the local power grid dimming, something started to stir. The liquid nitrogen tank valves began to vent, releasing a build-up in pressure.

"Mike, put on the goggles!"

"It's going to explode!" Mike yelled.

"Probably not! Just watch!"

Counting the liquid nitrogen safety rules being violated, Mike put on his goggles and drew closer, curiosity overpowering his apprehension for the moment. In the center of the ball a clear spot was forming and the beams started to play around and over it like static electricity on a Tesla generator. As the contraption whined higher and higher, the vibrations damped down and seemed to reach an equilibrium.

Brodie toggled the joystick and inside the ball something started to move. A small spherical object, golden in color, moved on tracks in the spaces between the nozzles in response to the joystick movements.

"What's that?" Mike yelled.

"That's Sparkle; an A.I. nano-robot! Artificial Intelligence! Edmund Scientific robot kit! She steers!"

Of course she does. As Sparkle rode shotgun, there seemed to be a tidal swell slightly distorting the bubble that followed her movement. The cables began to strain and squeak as the ball pulled slightly in a direction always the opposite of Sparkle's position.

"Jesus! It wants to take off!"

"*Ficht nicht mit der Raketenmensch!* To infinity and beyond!" Brodie laughed and whooped.

The whole garage began to creak rhythmically. Now, the cables seemed ludicrously over-engineered to be attached to the wood framing, roof and rafters of the garage, eye bolts screwed into two by fours. A truss began to crack. Suddenly a turnbuckle failed. Ping! An eyebolt explosively dislodged. Bang! The cables sliced through the air. The one wielding the eyebolt came close to beheading Mike, but cut through one of the liquid nitrogen pipes instead.

Brodie dropped the remote, ducked and ran toward Mike, tackling him into the kitchen as the heavy metal door slammed shut. Sparkle and the disco ball were now circling unevenly, tethered by the remaining cables, as the venting nitrogen tank, with a final shake and death rattle, its whistle screaming upward toward silence, exploded.

*

Leaning against the now concave door of the refrigerator, still spooning Mike, Brodie pushed up his goggles. "Good thing I beefed up that kitchen door."

Mike, stunned, coughed and muttered, "Your insurance won't pay for that."

All circuits blown, the brightest light in the grid was now the fire laying waste to Brodie's garage. Later, as the neighbors stood and watched the embers, Brodie and Mike examined a large piece of the garage roof that had landed, intact, on the lawn. Brodie stooped down to look closely at a neat round hole about three feet in diameter.

"Huh, son of a bitch worked."

*

April 1, 2109 C.E.
First Moving Day

The slag-ship Spartacus, filled with the waste products of asteroid mining, prepared to start its haul to Europa, where the material was needed for construction. It was a twenty minute commute; a one man operation on these short runs. With A.I. controls, the biggest danger was boredom. Crossword puzzle and trivia books littered the dash.

Becker, in his jumpsuit, feet on the dash, started a crossword puzzle as the run began. He thought: "Alpha Centauri, now that's a run for *War and Peace, Ulysses* or *Proust.*" Still, he had just been reading how, before the GUT drive, it took as long to get to Mars as it took now to cover the four light years to Alpha Centauri. That was back in the '80's. So, can't complain.

"Sparkle, prepare to take control of the run." The A.I. pilots were traditionally addressed as Sparkle. Becker thought it had something to do with the way all radio operators in the military were called Sparks in the 1900's. He hadn't found the answer in the trivia books yet.

Sparkle said, "Mr. Becker, fasten your harness, secure all movables, drive is on line." Becker puffed on his vaper, pencil poised thoughtfully over the crossword, but otherwise didn't budge as the smooth ride began.

In the rear of the ship, the bubble-drive started to whine as the magnetic fields in the cryo-slinkys began to buzz. Ramscoops opened to gather particles and the first graviton beams met to form the Higgs bubble. The trivia books said the first drives used boson accelerators and weren't nearly as fast. *Glad I live in the future.* Sparkle steered as the ice of Europa glimmered faintly off the starboard bow.

Becker put down his puzzle finally to watch the coverage of the first Moving Day on the console streamer. The pilgrims forming concentric spheres around the Library seemed to move in time with the mantra soundtrack. Becker gave his Xià lù dì bobble head a poke and watched it shake and nod in agreement as pilgrims flowed toward the nodes in the Library. The optical illusion made it look like the anomaly was sucking the pilgrims in, sucking them in like spaghetti into the mouth of it. "No fucking way, not me, baby," Becker said.

Emma Sandifur was in her prime eighties, short and svelte, her hair done in a grey pageboy and her clothing a non-committal coverall that bespoke as much of labor as it did of leisure, neatly pinning her on the cusp between her CEO and retired status. She stepped down into her office, its 360 degree view windows level with the main holographic traffic control displays, floating above the routing floor, showing all the company drives in the system, more of a show piece than any useful tool. She noted the departure of the Spartacus. It was certainly impressive, thousands of proprietary drives knitting together the lives and fortunes of the worlds, from the floor, all seeming to orbit her own golden seat of power. *Off this pedestal and none too soon.*

Her retirement party was just winding down, spilling from the conference room and foyer into the hallway to her office and private quarters. As laughter receded, her assistant was bringing in the gifts and commemorative knick-knacks, a pile accumulating. "What's that, Michael?"

"Oh, a desk model of the first drive."

"Yes, I recognize it, a bit later model; more crystal, less metal, nice paperweight."

"No, no, they work, I mean they don't fly off or anything, but it makes a bubble. The hobbyists like to build them. Your brother got one when he retired."

"That's right, thanks."

"Right, Good night ma'am." He put his hand out but kept a respectful distance as she shook it. "It's been a pleasure working with you."

"Likewise Michael and I'm sure I'll hear of your accomplishments in the future; good luck to you."

He said, "Thank you Ma'am," and she was alone.

She picked up the model, which featured a small sphere mounted on faux ebony base like a snow globe. That was fixed to a desk set sporting pen, pencil, business card holder and charging ports for various devices. The 3D printed crystal sphere was dotted with graviton accelerators, combining 3MI technology with the original patented process.

That's when things really took off, Dan Pritchard and Dad teamed up and Brodie disappeared. Archie lost interest a bit later. Once things became predictable, successful, off they went.

She walked over to the door, nodded the last party stragglers off and closed it. The gravitel at her desk rang with Archie's dedicated toodle tone. The screen resolved showing an aging male version of herself in a saffron robe.

"Hey b-b-b-big b-b-b-brother!"

"Oh the cruelty, you b-b-bitch; I've spent a lifetime getting over your torture. You're still mad about Barbie? Happy Retirement Emmie."

"Thanks Archie, I don't think the score's quite settled from your ass-holery; don't be a pussy. Where are you, still a monk at the bung hole?"

"Blasphemy! You mean the *Debris Ring*? Yeah, and I'm not ordained, just a humble oblate enjoying the quiet of the temple stacks, quite alone mostly, thank you very much."

"I think I'd like some of that."

"Eighty's the new forty, right? You got your implants?"

"I don't mind the cell checker and CRISPR-nanos, but I'm not going full cyborg or spookball."

"You can afford it, and thank the Bodhisattva for the cell checker."

"Peace be upon her." She pointed to her left eye. "Even this one eyeball is a pain. They have to keep putting it in the shop and giving me a loaner; pisses me off. Now, the new one is so perfect I can tell the real one is yellowed and hazy; otherwise I wouldn't know; so, manufactured discontent. "

"Planned obsolescence; the very basis of marketing! Well, if you need a rest, get on the slow boat, round the horn to L3. I'm not going anywhere."

"Hey, they gave me one of those bubble drive models, the desk set; you got one."

He looked over his shoulder and said, "Yeah, that was a long time ago; it's tucked up there in the closet somewhere."

She held hers up to the gravitel. "How do you turn it on?"

"Ah, if they're made the same, there's a switch on the bottom of the base, and then it's driven by the standard graviton emitters in your office."

She turned the model over, flipped the recessed switch then pushed the button on her desk console turning on the graviton field emitters usually used to manifest with spooks. The studs around the crystal ball started to glow in the field and emit their beams to the center of the ball. "Got it, there's the bubble."

"Remember Sparkle, Emmie?"

"She was a good fish."

"Well, a prophetic fish, the first bubble-naut. That was the beginning and then we all bailed. You did a helluva job. Dad would be proud. I just wanted to give you my love and good wishes for the next challenge. Good night Emmie."

"'Night Archie, thanks." She blipped off and looked closer at the model. The first real drives were made of metal with portholes, like a deep sea submersible. *What was that called? Bathysphere, that's it.*

The model, like current drives, was 3D printed crystal, even the emitters, so the whole process was visible, and the light it made, the blue light and blue bubble, radiated out like a disco ball light show, flashing on the walls like wavy reflections through water. She looked at it, hypnotized, saw the field inside the bubble, still couldn't make that idea feel normal, even though people didn't think about it, thought it was just a machine, but she knew, she always reminded herself, that she was looking outside of the universe.

There was unfocused depth in there, if you looked at it long enough, you felt sucked in or like *something* was staring back. The metaphor of the science was even more disturbing. The drive worked because of particle collisions, transformation and decay that attracted Higgs bosons at one end of the chain and repelled Higgs bosons at the other end. Feynman diagrams made it clear but you had to be an organic chemist to see the connection. The arrows and squiggles all had one end pointing within and the other end pointing without, a self-ordering natural unavoidable structure, the bubble.

Even Brodie saw it in the beginning, an analog to hydrophilic-hydrophobic molecules, the molecules that arranged themselves because one end was attracted to water and the other end repelled water, the natural quality that formed cell membranes before life, the quality that formed a semi-permeable membrane in every living cell, another bubble that, like the drive, allowed *something* to pass through to the without and something to be contained within; a necessary condition of life, it *was* life. With that knowledge, it didn't take a starry eyed mystic to look into the blue bubble, like looking into a mirror or a crystal ball, and fear and dare a demon into existence, looking back, reaching into your world and dragging you down its rabbit hole.

Unnerved, she flicked off the switch on the model and the room darkened. She poured a glass of the good Scotch, neat, downed it and flipped off the graviton emitters, leaving just the accent lights on, as she shut the door and started down the corridor to her living quarters. Michael could sort the gifts and pack things up tomorrow; time to call it a day-cycle. Soon, she would get on that slow boat, see the Waypoints, maybe go sail suiting; eventually she'd take Archie up on his invitation.

Earth
July, 2124 C.E

At the Quantum Mechanics Union /
Knights of Columbus Motorcycle Club Bar
Meyrin, Switzerland

In the bundled warmth of his pre-alarm dream state, Stuart found himself in a familiar pub back in Glasgow. Silver spookballs buzzing at the next booth startled him and gave him a quivering feeling of existential terror. It was one of those dreams where he dreamed he was paralyzed, the feeling of the need to bolt made so much worse by the inability to do so, the awareness all the while creeping in that he was dreaming and only a paper thin dimension separated him from rescue.

In a dream he dreams he wakes, he dreams he dreams a sound awakes him.

It was a recurring dream, the same feeling, fear and paralysis, the situation always in different familiar settings, current or past.

What was worse, it was close to the same feeling he had every time he ran into one of them in real life. It wasn't run of the mill prejudice, like some folks who just hated them on principle, it was involuntary but deeply personal. Shining bright, featureless or grunged with some cartoon grin; either way, they reminded him of something deep in his memories of youth. Even though these things that once composed, still did compose, part of humanity, were not to be feared, he couldn't quite shake it.

When he was eleven, he was lying on a hill outside of Glasgow with his buddies, looking into the diffuse blue sky. A cloud or two passed but the main effect was a loss of perspective, the feeling that he could be looking a mile away or light years away. The depth of the unfocused sky then acted as sort of a blank mirror, out of which the mind might play tricks, show visions or materialize something real in the world.

As he watched, a small spiral of condensation started to spin not too far up, like a drain sucking upside down, a vapor trail formed and fed into the spiral, a bright spot of light popped in the center like a pinprick in a piece of paper hiding the sun, a crack in the sky, like that old Bowie song, then like the song, a hand came down through the whirlpool and the nightmares began. Following the hand an arm appeared, two arms and shoulders, a silver featureless head and hands pushing against the sky to worm its way through. If it had happened B.C. it might have taken the form of the imaginary alien abductors of urban legend, large black eyes in a rounded triangular face. But this face was just blank, a silver, blank face.

Instinctively, he covered his eyes but between his fingers watched it emerge. Then, without his willing it, his arm began to rise up extending his hand toward the apparition. His friends remembered only the vortex, weird weather, but they seemed to have blacked out for the rest, while Stuart had vague memories of interacting with the being. Even though aliens of one kind or another were no longer breaking news, there was something disturbingly human about this silver surfer.

The rest of the experience was gone for Stuart as well; all of them having lost ten or fifteen minutes, retaining only the memory of the blue sky and sun on the grassy hill and a wordless walk home. It grew into a wall between them in time so it was never discussed but Stuart had become convinced that he had been abducted, but to what purpose? Then came the nightmares, recurring and confusing mixes of the familiar and the threatening. That's why the silver balls disturbed him as much in reality as in his dreams. In dreams they were ciphers for real terror, now thankfully interrupted by the insistent buzzing of the alarm.

When he had slapped the alarm into silence, it was a Tuesday morning in May, 2125. After his morning ablutions, Stuart exited the ground floor entrance to the building at 23 Rue de Berne where he occupied a quaint second floor worker's flat. It was a typical Swiss street in Les Paquis, a few blocks from Lake Geneva, where in the past a red light district had in turn flourished and languished. Now gentrified, it was a narrow street with apartments above shops, the kind of street where, in centuries past, they emptied chamber pots out the windows. No sidewalk seating back then.

Wrought iron café tables reflected the ornate iron window railings above. On one side of the residential entrance, the Funny Horse Restaurant was just getting started with breakfast. Stuart got his usual rösti, a solid disk of fried grated potatoes wrapped in foil, something to eat one-handed on the commute to work.

On the other side of the entrance was the Inside Africa Salon de Coiffure. Stuart waved at the two dark African stylists vaping by the door before the shop opened. They were continually giving Stuart the look, admiring his still buff frame and just greying chest hair spilling over his t-shirt collar.

He nodded politely and said "Mamzelles." They covered their mouths with their hands as they giggled and went inside. *A perfect cure for a midlife crisis, but. . .*

Stuart unlocked his hover cycle parked at the curb, set the grav-lev at one meter, put it on autopilot and started down the Route de Meyrin, rösti in hand. Behind him was the Space Elevator on Lake Geneva, its carbon nanofiber ribbon rising up until it was indistinguishable from the blue sky and grey haze. The early passenger shuttle was heading to the halfway station in orbit. In the morning sun and lake fog, the ribbon made its own rainbows cascading down.

It seemed to rise directly out of the 460-foot high Jet d' Eau water fountain, spouting on its jetty where the Rhone entered the lake. This made for quite a show as more rainbows sprang from the fountain. But, Stuart had little patience for such magic and the rainbows were relegated to the rearview mirror.

He buzzed through the lakefront district and the industrial center, quaint shops giving way to light industry and railroad yards. It seemed the city was contracting and Meyrin edging further out into the countryside as the housing needs of CERN diminished. In the suburbs, the cows were taking back their pasture one street at a time.

As he finished his rösti, he took the handlebars and clicked down to "assist only." At that setting, he felt the road with direct feedback through the grav-lev, leaning into the esses and tucking into the canopy on the straights. The wind chill cut right through his light clothes as he exceeded the speed limit. When he could just barely stand the cold and his fingers were freezing into claws, he squeezed the brakes and let out a cathartic scream, disturbing only a few stray dogs.

He was on this edge of frustration daily from loneliness, longing and the feeling that his world was just about to collapse. Screaming gave some relief but it didn't help for long.

The Route de Meyrin was straight as an arrow as it approached the CERN administrative offices. He parked in the empty lot and let himself in. The squints, admins, receptionists and official greeters were long gone. He had a non-descript cubicle; just a place to drop his lunch bucket and check his email. But, even so, he had decorated it with salvage from the offices of the absent administrators, an inspirational plaque, bobble heads, an executive sandbox and his favorite, the model Higgs Bubble desk set snagged from the Executive Director's office.

After reading his morning memos and the euro-news feed, his routine was to wander down to the collider tunnel to show the security cams that he was actually doing his job. He was in charge of the dismantlers, not tasked with manual labor. But, once in a while, he took up a wrench or hammer just to remember the feel of muscle on metal. There, underground, he joined the crews working with hand tools, shoulder to shoulder where the working room was tight. The sweat poured off Stuart and his crew equally and the camaraderie was real.

He was also in charge of the security cameras watching the workers and the videos he sent upstairs. This gave him a little side income from making routine malfunctions on request. Stuart just played the dumb handyman, reporting, "It'll be back on line in the morning," as a game of high stakes Russian Go Fish got started unobserved. He had received a few warnings from the admins for inadequate maintenance, but he thought no one was the wiser. *As long as I get my cut. . .*

Back at his cubicle in the afternoon, Stuart looked out his window at the wooden spheres composing the visitor center. It was impressive. Made of wood, it was about ninety feet high and 130 feet across. From the outside, you could see eighteen wooden arches supporting the structure, like telephone poles curved into longitude lines. Horizontal lattices, like open window blinds, formed the exterior and a ramp system spiraled up between the lattice and another sphere inside. It must have been a showpiece back in the last century. But, without maintenance, the wooden marvel had seen better days.

Now, unkempt green fields butted right up to the parking lot and the sphere seemed natural in its decay, like the giant petrified boll of an ancient tree. Mildly curious, he had expected to arrive one morning to a pile of splinters or cinders. But no, one day there were workers power washing, sandblasting and staining the wood. The parking lot was cleaned and resurfaced, the grass mowed and the shrubbery trimmed. Then a banner went up. It said: *Quantum Mechanics Union Bar.*

It had a symbol of a fist holding a pipe wrench in the center of a field of red rays and a motto: "Infinity or Else!" He had seen this symbol in the tunnels, with more aggressive taglines. "Keep your multiverse, Give us a living wage!" He felt a deep connection with that kind of resentment.

A few days later, the banner was joined by a hovering neon sign right above the door: *Happy Hour 4:00 to 6:00 daily.* Stuart checked the time, 5:15, clicked off his desk light and headed out the door. *Time for a pint!*

He crossed the street, jumped the curb, walked into the joint and sat at the bar. It smelled of incense, cannabis and varnish. The bartender was a tall dark North African. From the trendy kohl eye liner and top knot, he had to be a Carthaginian. He gave Stuart a nod.

Stuart said, "Can anybody get a drink here? I'm a union man."

The Carthy said, "It's a joke brotha', but the squints that made it up have all left town. We're just carrying on their tradition." He brought a menu and water and went back to polishing glassware.

The interior was impressive too. The inner sphere was also supported by curved poles suspending the second story. The intricate construction was revealed in exposed beams tightly fit together with wooden pegs, dovetails and rabbet joints, like giant cabinetry. A similarly styled wooden bar had been recently installed. The ramp provided access to the second level seating and then extended to a small observation platform at the top of the globe.

The Carthy said, "Wattle yav?"

Stuart was surprised to see a list of single malt scotches. Supply was spotty in those days. He hadn't had one since he left Scotland, "Laphroaig 15 . . . and a Guinness." Not surprisingly, this combination got him thinking of home, his mum and Christine. He was starting to feel a little less like screaming.

*

July, 2124 C.E.

At the Old Chart House Bar

Dismember the Alamo

On the observation deck of the Tower of the Americas, Walter Brodie and S. C. Schneider drank warm micheladas from cans. The recipe was variable; beer, tomato juice, lime, hot sauce and salt on the rim, even on the rim of a red Solo cup; but in a can it was pure blasphemy.

Schneider said, "This is the worst beer I've ever had."

"Brodie said, "If you don't like that, you can have any other kind of hot beer they have."

"Right, but after the seven hundred foot stair climb, it's kind of crappy to not have cold beer."

"Yeah well if the sign said 'Hot Beer' at the bottom, nobody would climb up. But hey, you can't visit San Antonio without going to the top of this thing."

"When they had elevators, maybe."

"Nine hundred and fifty two steps," Brodie read from a peeling display. "They used to have competition stair climbs for charity. A mile run and then up the tower. We could do that, reminds me of my days as a gym teacher."

"And they got cold beer at the top, I'll bet. Let's not and say we did."

The barkeeps were squatters in the tower, which had been without official status since the first Moving Day. After that exodus, the non-essential attractions had to fend for themselves. One couple sat at a table in the darkened restaurant. You could still see a name through the soot and grime on the wall, *Chart House*. In its day it had seen a constant stream of prom dates, proposals, weddings and wakes, from blind dates to the wistful reminiscing of the elderly. Now, there was just a young couple drinking warm beer and munching on stale Buc-ee's Beaver Nuggets. *Best fucking thing about Texas, Buc-ee's Truck Stop.*

He was kind of a skinny geek with a bowl cut and bad teeth who nonetheless transmitted confidence, passion and naïve enthusiasm when he smiled. The girl, with serviceable curves, long strawberry blond hair and a pert face like Tinkerbell, was way out of his league but she didn't know it, or she knew exactly what she wanted and this guy was it.

He fiddled with the holographic juke box then boxed its ears with a good slap on both sides at once. A Tex Mex snare drum and acordeón did the intro and then a Mariachi band projected on the bandstand and played *Besa Me Mucho.* The young man produced a small box he had decorated himself with rainbows and sparkles. Down on one knee (he had obviously been practicing) he opened the box to reveal a ring; the sound of applause came out of the box and he popped the question.

The girl laughed behind her hands covering her mouth, did a one handed fan wave at her reddening face and nodded enthusiastically. It was like a bedazzling jewel in the most unlikely of places. It was good to know that love was still blooming amid the uncertainty and squalor. Maybe the Chart House could chalk up one more wedding before it was deserted for good.

Nodding to the couple, Schneider said, "I had a girlfriend and a roommate, another girl, both from Texas. I was in San Diego then. Brenda; that was her name, Brenda Taylor.

"I can still see her in my mind. We worked together at a pizza place. She didn't shave her pits or legs and she had wild bushy eyebrows but she was beautiful because in the moment she had no fear, no doubts and no hesitation. She had really beautiful breasts, too, breasts that you couldn't help but dream about. I mean, they looked like they defied gravity but seemed to be of weighty and prophetic importance in your hands.

"You had to hold one with two hands, and when you got really close to *that*, it was the biggest thing in the universe, filling your entire visual field. Immediately it took you back to the day you were born."

"Wow!" Brodie said, "Did you just make that up? You sound like Dan Pritchard, all misty over some ordinary girl."

"I told you those breasts stayed with you."

"Even so, you're kinda sick in the head, buddy. You must have been a bottle baby."

"I don't, what. . .?"

"I used to teach sex-ed to middle schoolers. You were deprived of a basic element of your humanity, man, so near and yet so far, you're stuck right there, a thirteen year old boob man. Breast feeders become ass men, scientific fact." He took a long swig of michelada and shook more salt on the can top.

Schneider said, "I don't even know what to say."

"Not fake news brotha'."

"Anyway, just listen, she stepped up to me one day after work. I was standing on the door frame of my VW bug and she was standing on the other side of the door. We were the same height that way. She kissed me and it was like gravity just took over.

"She wouldn't have passed muster in Playboy but didn't have to clean up nice to be irresistible. And those nipples had already made an impression on me through her sweaty grey t-shirt dusted with pizza flour like a powdered sugar garnish over sweet baked pears."

Brodie said, "Stop! You should write poetry man, I'm tearing up."

"Some women bring poetry with them, arising out of the sea foam, you know, like Aphrodite. Some women force men to write poetry by muse or madness. I just felt like I had been given grace; you can't ask for it, it can only be given.

"She stepped in front of me with flour dusting her hair and pizza dough on her hands and saw me like it was the first time. Her eyes sparkled and her head tilted a bit to one side and then straightened. Without words she said *I am for you.*

"Anyway, she was sweet and willing and enthusiastic, sex was like candy then, good and plenty. We would drive in my Uber and take a break at home to have sex and watch the soaps on the streamer. We'd try to go back to work but only get a few blocks and then drive back home, log off and run back to the bedroom."

Brodie looked off wistfully. "Ah, back to the secret room of the heart. Never had a really sweet girl, not for long anyway."

"So, I adored her for a short while. At the same time she was with another guy, the cook at the pizza shop, Dan something. I went over to pick her up once, carrying flowers. Dan was there, just leaving. I said to him, 'These are for you.' and gave him the flowers. Everybody was amused. It was so liberal and surreal, the earth mother and her suitors, all of them in love."

"What happened to her?"

"She got pregnant and she asked me to drive her to the abortion clinic. But when the time came, she just sat down on the steps and cried. She couldn't do it. I told her I would stay with her and raise the kid. She was even sweeter in tears. But, she chose Dan."

"You dodged that magic bullet."

"I would have married her, really, I would. It's what a man does. I was adulting. About nine months later, I saw the baby. I honestly could not tell you if it looked like me or Dan. But, being a mother made her even more radiant. It was ok, I let her go and I think she was the first girl who didn't cause me any pain on leaving. She was honest and real. She left me with sweet memories and no regrets."

"And the other girl from Texas?"

"My roommate, Pam, she also worked at the restaurant. It turned out she had a crush on me. We were actually driving home drunk from a strip club one night and I was going to have sex with her. Instead, I spent the night in the drunk tank."

"Dodged another bullet."

"Uh huh, but then it turned out she was jealous of Brenda, so I said I was moving out. She said, if you're moving out, then I'm moving out. So I said, 'If you're moving out, I'm staying.'"

"Well played; har, har."

"It seemed clever at the time, but I was kind of an asshole about it, hearts were breaking all around. Anyway, all my exes moved back to Texas. I keep thinking I might see those breasts again. Maybe Brenda moved back here."

"Ah, *Sweet Bird of Youth!* Now you're breaking my heart. Hers aren't like that anymore. But there're still some out there; you just can't touch them for free."

"I don't want that, just want to sit down next to that person and know what it feels like, what it feels like when the memory blooms, you know, like dehydrated reality in a spring shower, like that smell after rain? It would be like that. I just want to inhale that smell, honor that girl everybody has forgotten."

Brodie said, "Everybody except you, right? Sheeyit. Like you still *own* her, you're still the only one who understands her? That's so passive aggressive; pretty, but bullshit. She's still out of your league, brotha'. Cheer up and pay attention."

The view from the observation deck took in the curve of the world, peeked over the horizon, diminished the browning dark green oaks, was still spectacular over the few remaining water towers and a couple of roller coasters jutting above a seemingly unbroken forest, a forest that became the urban arboreal as it filtered into the city center.

The San Antonio River bubbled up from springs in Midtown and then wound through Downtown just north of the tower. The old Riverwalk, once the place to be, the thing to see, the only place to find a cool breeze on days like this, now harbored the homeless and criminal cohort. They gathered where tourists and young professionals used to drink slightly colder beer, down tapas and nachos and complain, yell at children or flirt. The artificial meanders had been blocked in some ill-fated last ditch attempt to use the channel and locks to generate electricity. The old barges were rotting on the floor of the canal while being used as makeshift housing. It was eerily like looking down on the gorilla grotto at a zoo.

There also, the primates were given toys and tasks to accomplish in finding food and other necessaries; to keep them from getting bored. Here, there were other toys plus robberies, fights, sex and death all played out for the spectators.

"See? Welcome to the monkey house."

"Well, that's just sad," Schneider said, peering into one of the big binoculars mounted around the deck.

"As long as they don't start throwing poop at the guests, it's usually ok, just watch the show." Brodie looked through another binoculars and then tilted it up to scan a bit further away.

"Can I quote you? You're bound to offend somebody."

"That's why it's funny, Essey."

"S.C.? Do you give everyone nicknames? It sounds like Effie, a *faux pas* in polite company."

Brodie said, "Again, that's *why* it's funny, but why waste good humor on the spookballs, they're so airy. Actually, it's an old Chicano gang thing. 'Hey Ése', like 'Hey Dude!' Somebody painted it on my car once, 'SA', like that. It's like you're part of the gang now; high concept humor."

"Sounds like you've been cosplaying with Andromedans and spooks."

"Don't really like spooks. How can you read an electronic face? And spook balls don't do body language either, they just buzz and click like Solenoid Robots."

"What?"

"Roger Ramjet, you know," Brodie sang, *"Roger Ramjet he's our man, Hero of our nation. . ."*

"No. . . I don't. . ."

"I do like the lizards though. They have double the body language with those chameleon scales. They just can't hide their excitement."

A couple of blocks further north were the Alamo Plaza, the old Mission San Antonio de Valero and the Long Barracks. On this day however, they also watched as Mexican troops marched north on Highway 37, approaching San Antonio on their way to push the border into Oklahoma and points north. Brodie said, "Now watch the troops."

Entering the city, there was no resistance, just as there had been none when the Mexicans dismantled Trump's Wall. The interiors of continents were becoming less and less hospitable, and populations were shuffling and reconsolidating, while the leaders and elites were looking elsewhere, looking to the stars. With 20% of the population, representing 80% of consumption and carbon footprint, now gone, changes were beginning to steamroll for those left in the gravity well.

Schneider had been doing embedded journalism with the New United Futurists for about a year now. He was trying to document, figure out really, just what the heck they were doing, what they stood for. It seemed like some kind of retro fascist movement and Brodie was its incognito, cryptic, spokesman.

Schneider would pour through records and archives for background research but, often enough, Brodie would call and take him on some adventure, seemingly pointless and also part of some plan. In the process, Schneider got to enjoy Brodie's company and they both got to know each other well.

Letting your guard down wasn't standard practice but did hearken back to the old gonzo journalism that was popular in the late twentieth century.

Schneider tilted his binoculars as well and saw the Alamo, La Villita and the surrounding academic centers and museums. The now shuttered *Ripley's Believe it or Not Museum,* had stuck it out the longest.

"We used to get nacho cheese flavored crickets and grubs at the *Ripley's* in Jackson Hole."

"Over five billion served."

"What?"

"McDonald's, shush, now look," Brodie said.

Schneider focused on the Mexican troops. As the troops approached the city center and were passing by the Alamo exits, a number of soldiers peeled off the sides and the ends of the column, took the off ramps and headed west toward the old mission.

Within a few minutes they had been in and out of all entrances of the Alamo, the Long Barracks and the courtyards and grounds. When they came out, they were no longer in Mexican uniforms, but in the green and brown camouflage tones of the Tejiano Militia. When they were all out, they dispersed by a number of different routes to put about a quarter mile distance between them and the plaza. "Los Nuevo Futuristos." Brodie said, "Watch this."

Schneider took out his phone-pad and put it on camera and telephoto and started to record. As the last of the Mexican troops marched passed the Alamo exits and headed toward Austin on the freeway, Los Futuristos crouched down in the shop entryways and appeared to be waiting for something to happen.

Loud explosions and pop, pop, popping like firecrackers confirmed that guess. In the wake of this precisely engineered destruction, all of the ancient structures in Alamo Plaza were reduced to piles of rubble and clouds of dust. Then, Los Futuristos became Tejianos, running through the town declaring that the Mexicans had destroyed the Alamo in retribution for their prior loss of the Mexican war in 1836. As the local militants began to gather and listen, Brodie said, "What a riot, am I right, right, . . right?"

"Whose side are you on anyway?"

"Everybody's and nobody's."

Schneider said, "That's how the Nazis came to power, and the Emperor Trump. Tell everybody what they want to hear even if it's all contradictory."

"Now you're just being mean." Suddenly becoming eloquent, Brodie said. "I know that it's rude to tell people they should know something and then force it down their throats. But, we the 80% need to look skyward instead of staring at our shoes looking for salvation in the mud. So, these sleeper cells are creating conflict so that the remainders have real pressure to take power from the absentee landlords."

"So, what's going to happen here?"

"The Tejianos are now going to get mad and chase the Mexicans south again and maybe push north into the plains. Filling up the abandoned lands is one way to shake up the power structure and move into the vacuum at the same time."

"And the ultimate goal?"

"Not sure; we're making the playground, the jungle gym. What acrobatics the people will perform within that structure is up to them. Freedom, including freedom from capitalist socialism, or whatever they're calling it now, involves responsibility, attention, work. You just have to give people hope and a little power and they will figure it out."

"And what about the Cult?"

"The Cult is a racket, but it provides for everyone equally. It needs the unequal participation of the wealthy to subsidize the poor. It's like Christian communism. That's all well and good if you want to play. But not even all the spooks and lizards want to hop on that hayride. It's not exactly a bad deal to be left behind without the burdensome 20% that used 80% of the resources.

"The problem is that they want to treat this planet as a sanctuary, an untouched wilderness. They're willing to let the infrastructure crumble and treat the world like a picturesque park, one big fucking Acropolis. Our view is, if they want it they can pay for it. If you want a park bench with a pretty view, you have to pay the gardener and the maintenance man, right?"

"And 3MI?"

"Did you ever wonder why the phones work and the rest of the infrastructure is crumbling? 3MI panders to the pilgrims and the rest of us can just tag along. We're like barnacles on a whale, not a bad deal until the whale needs to scratch an itch, then you're expendable. Makes people feel like charity cases, superfluous, unintended consequences. It's easy to tell where the trains still run on time, wherever the Cult and 3MI are in charge, like oases in the desert. Makes the natives restless, cranky."

Schneider said, "All of a sudden you seem focused and rational."

"I ain't *real* dumb, and I wasn't just born out behind the turnip truck, nome sayn? *In the fullness of time, all shall be revealed.*"

"Ok, that's either scary or ludicrous."

"Take your pick, either way, the mighty fall. Anyway, I'm heading for Geneva in a couple of months and then upstairs. Wanna see Geneva?"

"As long as the GP pays me to follow you around, just keep talking, I'll be there."

INTERSTITIAL I

*

Pinky's Guide for the Perplexed
2109 C.E.

What right do spooks have to take over a human body volitionally in another timeline? It's like terraforming Mars, we have no inherent right to do either. In our universe, spooks gestated and were born with the host as one entity. We simply could not be separated before the death of our human body. The body was not just a receptacle. One might just as well ask if the head could be separated from the body and then wonder what kind of life each could have without the other: none.

Now, those same symbiont spooks are self-aware and some choose to live without a host at the Planck scale. Even so, most human-spook partnerships still live out a natural life together as a cooperative. It is not however, conceivable, and is indeed a crime, for a spook to enter a human body without permission and take control. It is also difficult under civil and canon law for the partnership to be dissolved without agreement of the partners. Special cases exist in the event of mental or physical illness beyond that which the other partner is prepared to endure. Secular and Hadith precedents for these cases are still developing toward consensus but are by no means settled law.

Another possibility now exists for both humans and spooks, not to mention Andromedans. After Moving Day, and before final *transitus*, all sentient beings may find and enter a body after passing through the Library. Most typically, the traveler seeks their own body in a different timeline. In another scenario, the traveler seeks to experience an alternate reality where their body does not exist.

Different questions then arise:

1. How does one enter and partner with one's own body in a different timeline?

2. May one enter and partner with a sentient being in a different timeline where one's own body also exists?

3. May one enter and partner with a sentient being in a timeline where one's own body does not exist.

Bear in mind that one may also choose to exist as a non-corporeal in one's natural field sentient form. We have acknowledged that there are no practical conflicts in any of these scenarios, only moral, ethical and theological problems. After all, in the common idiom; In a multiverse, every universe that can exist must exist, even the ones in which we are irresponsible.

In the first instance, start by asking how does the Self guide humans? The Self is imaginary but it works through interior dialog, the theater of the mind, memory and imagination. And what does the imaginary Soul do? It doesn't guide much either, it's too presently involved.

And if a spook goes through a whole lifetime and then re-enters the same body at a younger age, is that body-snatching? It's a very real, very serious, problem; so very complex, because *that* human body will die as well. What does the spook do then? Hang out until quantum gravity devices are invented there? Invent them itself? And don't forget, in the multiverse there must be others with this technology. Are spooks from other universes then implanting in human bodies here, bringing a lifetime of memories from other worlds to ours? The permutations of this concept are endless.

A great corpus of thought problems is developing; an interdimensional Hadith and Talmud. Questions are posed in the hope that the answers will be remembered and useful when the transitus is made. But, we won't know the real answers until someone comes back. Somehow, given the last hundred years, it's not hard to believe, to hope to believe, that such a day is inevitable.

*

Earth
2150 C.E.

My Life B.C.
Charlotte Pritchard, F.S. Ph. d.

In his book, *Sweet Charlotte*, Mr. S.C. Schneider wrote part of my story in a first person stream of consciousness style and called it *Charlotte's Soliloquy*. I learned that this was a tribute to Molly Bloom, a character in *Ulysses* by James Joyce. Well, I had not read that book, on this Earth or the other one, but I took a crack at it then. *Molly's Soliloquy* is the first person story of a strong woman, who does good things and bad things but is true to her surrender to the love of one man, even when she is cheating on him. She experiences that first love as transcendent and a contradiction. It gives her power and has power over her. Ultimately, she surrenders to transcendence itself, in the guise of love and longing. Either way, the man never really knows what captured him as he skirts the event horizon of that crushing singularity, he never knows. He frets and worries and pouts, but he is always safe, and he never knows it, not until he is taken inside the heart and womb of that woman. Even then, he is not sure *just what* he knows, only that it is good, truthful and beautiful. I found the surface of this described in the ancient Irish epic the *Táin Bó Cúailnge*:

> But though Ailell was king, Maev was the ruler in truth, and ordered all things as she wished, and took what husbands she wished, and dismissed them at her pleasure; for she was as fierce and strong as a goddess of war, and knew no law but her own wild will.

In my early life, my life B.C., I must admit, I knew no law but my own wild will. More than one man was defeated by that disregard, but Dan Pritchard followed me wherever I went. In that first book, Mr. Schneider wrote this in my voice:

I loved him and I left him and he followed and I let him and he followed and I left him and he followed. I loved him so much it took me three years to leave him the first time.

It was true and beautiful and when I read it the vibration of tears overtook me. Dan however, was not clueless. He honored me and loved me until he defeated that wild will and in the end he captured me completely because I *was* like Molly Bloom. So here is my story as a thank you and a tribute to Mr. Schneider, may the blessings of Xià lù di be upon him.

*

Charlotte's Soliloquy

When we were young our love was like a wrestling match where the combatants twist and shout and throw barbs and chairs and yet they are unalterably connected, tied together, codependent, the one incomplete without the other, primed for the next match even as they share their secret victory behind closed doors. A young man, a boy really, he had never been frustrated and loved so hard at the same time, his fragile composure snapped, his boundless energy sapped, his youthful passion always ready to revive at the slightest provocation or glimmer of hope, but that experience, a testing and tensing of invisible chords and strings that remained as spandrels in the structure of his psyche, that necessary fire, the spotting of the Holy Grail, its loss and his lifetime quest to regain it, the end of which he was not to know when it captured him, but which climaxed much sooner than it should have by the calculations of the recurrence of the retrograde position of Saturn that had marked his birth; no, he only felt the loss and despair, which I could relieve with change as quick as a magician's assistant but it wasn't a change of costume, more of a dance of veils as the anger blew off like chiffon and passion and compassion took its place in the silky moiré below. One night, he was getting ready to leave for work and I had dealt him one in a series of blows, he was so angry and still he had to go to work and so had done with me and went to the shower as I acted uncaring on the couch. His boy's body wanted to relieve its frustration and anger in the one way it was sure of, the thing that had relieved his loneliness and longing even before he knew what he longed for, and even more, in his anger it was perhaps an irrational blow against me, denying that he needed me even for that, not love, not compassion, not caring, *take that*; but this time he just couldn't make it happen and he was becoming a wreck and incapable of going forward or backward, so he came to me still drenched and so obviously in pain and without embarrassment, in tears, asked me to help him, without hesitation, I took him into my arms and took him inside me and let him vent his anger where it could not hurt him and gently let his pain go inside me, right there on the very couch where minutes before I had just caused that pain. That was how intimate and unreasoning our love was. Even in anger and absurdity, we were responsible, each for the well-being of the other. When I had left him and moved into my mom's duplex and made a complete mess out of it as my two Salukis tore up her meticulous gardens, and I still asked him to spend the night and sometimes just showed up on his bed at his house, let myself in when he was gone and just waited for him to come home, I curled up in my own despair about the end of a rope, one in a series, and I could smell him and I could smell our little dog that he got in the break up, right there on his unwashed and unmade bed and it was the one thing and the one place that was utterly safe, and I knew that every time he came around that corner, his eyes were closed at first because he was wishing me into existence and more than once it worked. At my house one morning after we had spent the night together because he wouldn't say no, I won't, we had just woken up, probably just had sex and he was in the bathroom and I answered a knock at the door. A guy I had been going out with, who was not ready for the mess I was, the mess that Dan just swam in, who had money and Dan didn't, who was hmmmmm . . . (I thought at the time) sophisticated and Dan was hmmmmm . . . something better (that I did not recognize?) and told me on the doorstep he didn't want to see me again because of my needy volatility, it's not me, it's you, and I broke down in just those hysterics he described and ran right to Dan and he was on the toilet taking a shit like Jacob Bloom and I collapsed and he just held me in that awkward and embarrassing place and time, something that sophisticated guy would never do for anyone ever, and Dan did nothing but hold me, that's that same love again, look back on that and try to explain it to anyone as if it were normal, and a few weeks later he stood on the sidewalk in front of that duplex crying in my mother's embrace with a note in his hand that started *"Daniel, my love. . ."* and ended with, *"I never want to hurt you again."*

*

Ted Jasper, Galactic Press, Space-Time Today, Thursday August 30th, 2050, with Michael Sandifur, Founder/CEO HBD Conglomerated, Inc. Interview Transcript.

Jasper

We're back now with Michael Sandifur on the subject of Walter Brodie, co-inventor of the Higgs Bubble Drive in 2040. Brodie is famous for giving up any interest in the patent and dropping out of sight by 2045. Although there is no certain confirmation of his whereabouts, or demise, there are also enough unconfirmed sightings to rival Elvis.

Sandifur

That's an interesting comparison, Ted. He had a bit of that Elvis lip curl even as a child. I don't think this is widely known, but I knew Walter first in elementary school. We lived in military housing in San Diego. What the Navy did was take people from very diverse backgrounds and make them next door neighbors. My parents were from Minnesota, Dad was the younger brother who opted out of the family dairy farm, that whole conservative, proper, Scandinavian thing. They didn't show a lot of emotion, quiet, don't look where everybody else was looking, you know.

Jasper

A man's gotta do what a man's gotta do.

Sandifur

Right, exactly. I was the youngest and, I think now, any attempts at harsh parenting had been kiboshed by the time I came along. But, I was pretty good, so hardly got a harsh word.

Walter's family came from some cracker holler in West Virginia. His mother was a large unpleasant woman who never got out of her night gown and never stopped yelling at the kids. She had a toddler in diapers and would just roughly hose her off in the back yard when she had to be changed, that sort of thing constantly. When his mom wasn't around, Walter's father would say to no one in particular. "My life is a living hell."

They were not sophisticated but had plenty of opinions, called Muslims Towel Heads, Dune Coons and Camel Jockeys, kept some imaginary body count of 'A-rabs' on the front fender of the family SUV, upside down camels with x's for eyes and feet in the air. My Dad took it in stride, 'Don't you think that will offend people?' Pat Brodie would say, "That's why it's funny, man."

Jasper

With such different backgrounds, how did you become Walter's best friend?

Sandifur

Maybe my naïve innocence was attractive. I was someone who apparently never had a bad day at home, a condition Walter was not accustomed to.

I wasn't good all the time, but I learned. I shot a rubber band gun into a kid's ear while other kids held him down. Then they let him up, got chased and punched, didn't do that again.

One time, Walter said, "Fuck," at my house. It was the first time I had heard that word, really, and he didn't bother to define the word. So I asked my Mom, "What does fuck mean?" She walked right out and smacked him upside the head, something I had never experienced. Well, Walter went home but he didn't cry and wasn't mad at me either.

Another time, my Dad pulled the old spring loaded wooden garage door right down on his head. A big hollow 'bonk' sounded. Walter rubbed his head but did not cry. He just pursed his lips, rebuffed any comforting and went home.

Years after we had lost touch, I met him again in Community College and we became friends. He told me some other things. His father punished him, when it wasn't a slap or a fist, he went for the belt or a wire.

Jasper

A wire?

Sandifur

Right, It only occurred to me later what cruelty that was, an insulated wire with the end bare used as a whip. That's torture. And this, and I don't feel bad about saying this as betraying trust, it's just horrendous. He had two older brothers and they would catch frogs down at the creek by Mission Bay High. They would stick a bicycle pump in the frog's rear end and blow it up, literally.

Jasper

Jesus, Mike!

Sandifur

Yes, well one day they held Walter down and did the same thing to him. I don't mind saying that a person who survives a childhood like that has earned a few peculiarities, if he hasn't ended up in prison or dead. One of those brothers did commit suicide, so, 'living hell?' I guess so.

Jasper

So, you think that's why he avoided fame?

Sandifur

The approved structure of society hadn't treated him very well. He could have been a Nobel laureate, but that would have just validated another social structure that he didn't trust.

Jasper

But wouldn't that have been rising above the bad childhood?

Sandifur

Well, he had no choice about that, did he? You are your most powerless and vulnerable as a child and the biggest thing in your life is your parents, who you must trust, at least to be fed and not killed.

That's a pretty low bar but a lot of parents can't even reach that. When they are psychopathic to boot, I'd give him permission to feel however he liked about it, and using that experience, he helped a lot of students in middle school to at least have someone to talk to who appeared stronger than the parent who abused them. He was my friend, he was brilliant and I loved him. He loved my kids and they loved him. That's all I need to know.

PART TWO

Brimstone Cowboys

I had held her once while she slept
And did not make a move, and
Was so different in her short experience,
That she asked if I would have her.

And that small moment,
That day in the cross hairs,
Made me tell everyone I met
I will never, ever, envy you again.

And she did love me; so much that
It took her three years to leave me
And finally, my heart bled out angrily
As I cried on her mother's shoulder

Excerpt-A Small Goddess, Poetry of Dan Pritchard,
Devi Sheridan, editor, Centennial Edition, Modern Europa
Press, 2199.

*

Earth
2120 C.E.

Songline
Uluru to Munurru

Bindi and Kumpaya set out westward from Uluru on a songline that would take them northwest through the Great Sandy Desert and the Tanami Desert to the land of the Worrorra, Ngarinyin and Woonambal people in what the white settlers named the Kimberley region, a series of rugged rocky plateaus, lush peninsulas jutting out into the Indian Ocean and long fjords cutting into the coast. Munurru was situated in the Kimberly on the Mitchell Plateau at a crossing of the King Edward River, one of thousands of sites where rock paintings chronicled 50,000 years or more of habitation.

Each carried a long walking stick that doubled as a pike when hunting feral cats and goannas. Kumpaya and Bindi both went without much clothing, the Andromedan with her chameleon scales didn't normally need anything except safari vests and utility belts, and Kumpaya, like all traditionalists on walkabout in the bush, had no need for more than a drawstring bag hung from a cord belt.

Each stood on one leg with the other leg bent to rest the foot against the opposite knee, the difference being that the saurian's knee bent in the opposite direction; she could also pick up both feet and sit on her tail, but that was a bit showy.

With Uluru at their backs, blood red in the sunset, the ancient black woman said, "Got sabbatical for your walkabout, understudies taking up the slack, doulas gotta get experience anyway."

"You know I appreciate it and the Andromedan Cultural Studies stipend isn't bad, right?"

"You bet, big money, but can't stay out too long, not like the old days, anyway, three months oughta' do it, this songline, better to make it before the monsoons begin."

A songline is the path in the world that a song unerringly reveals to the singer. Songlines traversed the whole of the continent, the songs' lyrics changing language with traditional tribal boundaries, the rhythm and timbre signaling physical features of terrain and the narratives describing the travels of ancestors and powerful beings as they created the landscape; waterholes, deserts, hunting grounds and fruitful forests.

Bindi's current academic focus was tracing the songlines of the earliest settlers in the northwest of Australia. More than 50,000 years before, they came across the water from Indonesia, bringing their myths and cultural understandings with them; and it was only in that spot that the most unusual and iconic aboriginal rock art existed, the Wandjinas; spirits from the heavens, spirits of rain and clouds, spirits that came from the sky, not just the blue sky, aliens from the Milky Way.

This story, this creation, has a solitary Wandjina arrive from the Milky Way, and, seeing the mass of humanity needing a home, it returns to gather its fellow spirits. The Milky Way draws a giant emu in the sky, and from this emu, the whole mob of Wandjinas arrived. They spread out from the northwest coast across the continent to the east and south and drew the songlines by creating the land as they sang.

When they were finished, they returned to the Kimberley and flew down into the earth through the waterholes they had created. The law men of the tribes painted their portraits in the rock shelters near the waterholes to keep the seasonal rains coming. The paintings also kept the rest of creation in place and the law men were charged with repainting the spirits to maintain their power. These duties were faithfully performed down through the millennia to the days of starfellas; spooks and lizards.

Kumpaya said, "Wandjinas have eyes and noses but no mouths; whitefellas said they looked like alien abductors, maybe in the face but they also got halos or maybe space helmets. Whitefellas always see what they want to see, believe what they want to believe."

Bindi said, "Before they had seen real aliens. Some said the art was much older, one hundred and forty thousand years, quite a controversy."

"I'd say those archeologists bumped their heads and got some things mixed up, they might find a toothbrush down in the wrong sediment, don't mean ancestors got toothbrushes."

Bindi said, "Even so, the fact that they are only there at the first landing and nowhere else, would suggest an older tradition. Just like the Irish epic, the *Tain*, has the heroes driving chariots when there never were chariots in Ireland, or the Iliad preserving the culture of the Iron Age Greeks; Wandjinas could have been brought from Indonesia, but maybe further, maybe from Africa."

"Things change quick, Wandjinas only in the Kimberley, then you got Rainbow Serpent flying west to east creating the land too, then we got Goanna Man, same thing. Then when the whitefellas came, another religion, the High Mother crossed the same territory, north to south."

"That's the point, the story doesn't really change, just the avatar of creation."

"Not saying it's not so, even the Seven Sisters songline goes west to east, from Roeburn to Anangu Pitjanjara Yankunyjatjara lands; evil man Wati Nyiru chased the Seven Sisters across the land, then up into the sky."

"The Pleiades, the Greeks and many other cultures named them 'Seven Sisters' even though there are nine to twelve stars in the cluster that can be seen with the naked eye."

"Just like Subaru, so we had it 50,000 years ago?"

"Maybe Homo Sapiens brought it out of Africa; maybe Homo Erectus."

"Hey that reminds me; best part of that story is when Wati Nyiru cuts off his dick, it flies after the ladies like that rainbow serpent, then dives into the ground. They grab it and run, now he's chasing them to get his dick back. Old ladies laugh when they tell that story, old men check their crotch just to be sure it's still there, Ha!"

"Why do I bother?"

"You got sense of humor, right?"

Bindi ignored her. "So, you sing and the song tells you the way, by describing their travels in detail, but we'll just sing it backwards east to west."

"You can sing it backward or forward; still can't get lost."

"Again, Ireland is the same, Fionn mac Cumhaill and Cú Chulainn's battles are all marked on the land, so the ford is named for the battle, and the route to Ulster is created in the story or named after the events in the order they occur."

Kumpaya said, "Australia's bigger than Ireland but, yeah, same idea. But you're not just curious, you were snooping around before you got introduced, long time ago."

"Not that long ago, maybe four thousand years, and it was only because of Purgatory, which isn't really working anymore. I am following something. When we get to the Wandjinas, I'll be heading further west."

"Then finish your book? Gonna be a big star? Gonna remember me when you're famous?"

Her scales started to twitch. "You know it's not like that. Nobody gets famous. It's the work of the Goddess; for the last fifteen years. I walked from Tierra del Fuego to the Bearing Strait, my name was Corn Mother, before that from Scotland to the Indus, my name was Madb and then Kali; then sailed from Rapa Nui, island hopping, reading ripples and stars, heading for something you can't even see, below the horizon, all the way to New Guinea, my name was Moana, and now I'm here and my name is Bindi. It's not cosplay." Her scales rippled like mother of pearl and she reared back on her tail.

"Crikey, ok, you one big fuckin' Disney princess alright. Don't get so touchy girl, use that thick skin of yours, just messin' with you, shit. . ."

Bindi's scales settled back into the body paint patterns of the Seven Sisters; matching Kumpaya.

"Ok then; stop talking and sing."

The two began to walk, singing together the song that would lead them to the first waterhole by morning .

*

Earth
September, 2124 C.E.

At the New Choctaw Republic Stickball Nationals

Sitting in his official spot in the lower bleachers, Luke Koachubbee Patterson, Principal Chief of the New Choctaw Republic of Oklahoma, officiated over the annual Labor Day Stickball Nationals in Tuskahoma. He was a tall man, awkwardly tall, more than six feet, with the kind of long dark weathered face that might be seen staring out of photographs of Native Americans taken before the turn of the Twentieth Century. In this age of homogenous gene pools, something ancient and recessive had made one more last stand, belying the end of the trail once more.

Under the bleachers, Grandma Ruby Dell, F.S., spookballed these last five years, was herding great grandkids like a border collie. Otherwise, she led them around like ducklings, depending upon how distracted they were. Her electronic face reflected a less wrinkled kindly version of her final look, familiar and comforting. Always a strong partner in Luke's life, she still kept close, still didn't cut him any slack.

She saved manifestation for Luke in the evenings, usually at their house in Durant where they had raised three boys and entertained scores of grand and great-grandchildren; where lately they sat bathed in the graviton field emitters, reviewed the day and watched the streamer in tableaus from youth, middle age and recent maturity as the mood suited them.

Their most recent accomplishment had been the success of the movement to re-establish the Choctaw Republic in the face of the twin challenges of climate change and Moving Day. The Choctaw had never been reservation Indians in the strict sense. In the seventeen and early eighteen hundreds, they had lived in towns like white settlers, borrowing and adapting what worked for them, from the first contact to the Trail of Tears.

Then, it was simplistic bigotry, corruption and greed that underlay Andrew Jackson's elaborate justification for forced removal. From the 1840's to the early twentieth century, southeastern Oklahoma had been the Choctaw Republic, like Texas, a foreign country on the borders of the United States.

Famously, the tribe sent foreign aid to the Irish during the potato famine of the eighteen forties. It wasn't much, but it came with the express acknowledgment of the kinship of the colonized. The colonizers were essentially the same, a generation or two apart, but the penchant for extermination and ethnic cleansing was a self-evident legacy passed from the British to their American cousins.

They also had the unfortunate bad luck to side with the South in the Civil War. When it was over however, the U.S. affirmed tribal investments and the Choctaw took in resettled slaves and developed public schools and townships for them.

Finally, as Oklahoma approached statehood and federal land was made available for settlement, the Choctaw and other tribes opted to cede federal functions to the United States while keeping their own local sovereignty. They suffered and survived through the same schemes and land grabs as other Native Americans but through it all retained their distinct infrastructure and identity, and by the end of the twentieth century were one of the largest and best organized tribes in the nation.

Here, in that tribe's future, the disinterest of the larger population and the fulfilled promise of the benefits of Choctaw sovereignty had allowed the reestablishment of the Republic in the post Moving Day climate of first world flight.

One thing that hadn't changed was the spectacle of stickball, a game called 'little brother to war.' Like Irish hurling, the game was a strong connection to the era before colonization that brought with it a wealth of cultural treasures, language, values and state of mind.

In the eighteen thirties, George Catlin had painted vast conflagrations and portraits of individual players, men with loincloths and elaborate feathered tails signifying the animal spirits that fired their enthusiasm and protected them in the game as well as in battle. Luke watched sixty young men, these days in t-shirts and shorts, each with two stickball sticks, committing loosely camouflaged mayhem, attempting to get a small leather ball to hit a post at either end of a 100 yard field.

The sticks were made of hickory, bent over to form a loop at the end with a cross of sinew making a pocket for the ball; wielded crossed like scissors, they flashed and clattered, juggling the ball, the smallest thing in that giant scrum. It was anything goes, but just short of mutilation and murder.

With the temperature at 110 degrees at the nine a.m. game time and the play now approaching the halfway mark, exhaustion, heat stroke and injuries were taking their toll. It had been 110 or higher for three weeks, now a regular dog days expectation. *It's a Doggie Dog world.* The dark green wooded hills of the past were turning brown and dry after years of drought and changing climate. The tribe was considering building an indoor arena but the boys and young men still wanted to play like tough warriors, until the paramedics dragged them off the field.

In the grand scheme of things however, blood and broken bones fit into the tradition while heat stroke did not. When it came right down to it, sane practicality could preserve the tradition better than bluster.

Even though the Trail of Tears had brought them here, Oklahoma had not been a desert until the late 21st century. In fact, where the Choctaw had settled, in the run up and foothills of the Ozarks, it was something of a paradise and bastion of tribal sovereignty unique in the Old American States, not the least of which was signified by thriving tribal businesses; the casino resort at Durant was still the flagship.

The Assistant Chief was Pushmataha, F.S., a spookball painted in traditional primary colors and diamond rattlesnake designs. He was not a hybrid but had a deep interest and attachment to the culture of the Five Civilized Tribes. On demonstration of his dedication, sincerity and good intentions, the Choctaw Autonomous Congress had granted him full citizenship as a brother in spirit. *Him*, gender being a fluid concept and personal choice. He continued his work then as tribal historian, eventually being tapped to lend his talents and perspective to governance. His electronic face favored his namesake, the great Indian General of the War of 1812.

All in all, it was a good choice for a Field Sentient elected to succeed to the office of Chief. He hovered at about eye level and said to Luke, "John Asényahola is here to speak with you." This Seminole name had been transliterated in the past as Osceola, another great chief, of Scots-Irish and Creek descent.

"Bring him over." The young Seminole was familiar and welcome to Luke. Their histories were intertwined, both tribes having been forced or coerced onto the Trail of Tears in the 1830's. Each year the tribes re-enacted the trek together.

The Seminole Nation of Oklahoma was centered west of the New Choctaw Republic. If anything, their lands were even more parched as the Ozark foothills around Tulsa flattened out to the plains of the panhandle.

Luke greeted him, "John, my friend, what brings you here, a fan of stick ball?'

"Is it on the GSPN, like intergalactic curling?" he joked.

"Perhaps, perhaps in the next Olympics, if there is one."

John said, "Fucking hot in Seminole Country."

"Same here." He shaded his eyes and watched as a scrum turned into a fireman's carry of a fainted player off the field.

John said. "Have you heard what's happening in Florida?"

"Full of crocs and gators now?"

"So I hear."

Luke said, "Same as in Mississippi and Alabama?

"Coastal cities are being abandoned. People are heading north to escape the water and the heat."

Luke said, "Maybe they run north too soon."

"Let them run. In Florida, the sea is over Highway 1 and into the everglades. All the emergency measures of Dade County couldn't stop it. Likewise in Alabama and Mississippi, Mobile and Biloxi have evacuated. Even sea walls are proving unrealistic; Pensacola, Gulfport and New Orleans are next. But the centers of the states are abandoned as well. North is their only goal."

Pushmataha said, "And up. The modeling shows that the tempering on-shore effect of the ocean now reaches further inland. Just as the interior desert grows, the deep south is becoming more tropical, like the Yucatan."

John Asényahola agreed, "It seems to be the same in Australia and Africa, the interior takes the brunt of climate change. The new shoreline becomes more tropical, warm and wet."

Pushmataha said, "And the taiga moves north, the U.S. population is reforming north of the old border. Even further north, the tundra is hosting paleo ranchers raising engineered mammoth, megatherium, giant elk, auroch and oryx. Plenty of ecosystems for all once things settle in."

"The Bangladeshis were here too, describing their floating agricultural mats, extending farmland and fish farms into the sea, over the flooded lands," John said.

Luke said, "We pioneered floating botanical mats to process polluted lake water a hundred years ago. All of this technology and best practices are coming together."

"All together in this 'new wild'; isn't that what they call it? The old land is adapting to these new conditions, especially with the decrease in population, and the major polluters running like Chicken Little."

Luke said, "And you, I hear, are proposing a reverse journey."

"Yes, the Trail of Tears in reverse. The Five Civilized Tribes should reclaim their homeland."

"No government would object."

"True, the top 20% is focused on leaving the planet."

"Or leaving the Universe," Pushmataha said.

"It takes some of the pressure off climate change. Instead of directly reducing carbon emissions, we reduced them by getting rid of the emitters."

"Once the population stabilizes at a lower level, the climate will be more stable as well.

John said, "That's the theory, and it's not like there haven't been changes before in the history of the species."

Luke said, "Just ride out the imbalance, and go where the climate is the best for us when it's all over. "

"I think by consolidating in the Southeast we will have a strong voice in our own future. We need to build that strength together. The Mother Mound is there. We may have to defend that territory. "

John said "Nanih Waiya; we have been in touch with its caretakers, the Choctaw of Mississippi. They have been joined by the Biloxi Choctaw. They were the first climate refugees back in the twenty teens, right?"

"Hmmm, Jean Charles island went under the water just before the levees failed at New Orleans. They have suggested a similar plan, extended an open invitation to the Five Civilized Tribes to retake Mississippi, Alabama and Florida.

John said, "What's that story, we all came out of Nanih Waiya, and all traveled on except the Choctaw? A bit self-serving brotha', don't you think?"

"Don't start that again, we've been taking care of it just for you, visit any time. But there's another story; that we came from across the water, from the Yucatan. "

"And the Mississippians were remembering the stone pyramids of their collective past? I've heard that."

"And the Ixil Maya are now arriving from the Petén, following the jungle, punting up the river. It seems to make our going back to the jungle appropriate."

"A good spin on it anyway. Your members are scattered far and wide."

Luke said, "Like that song, we all may have been refugees, but we stopped living like refugees years ago. Thanks to my predecessors, yes, we are successful in all major cities."

"Major evacuating cities."

Luke said, "Yes, and we are watching them approach in larger numbers. This desert can't support them, there has to be a plan.

"Well, be ready. We will pass through Durant. "

"I'm not walking back, that's for sure."

"No, no, all modern transport, a hoveRV caravan."

Luke said. "Meet us at the old casino, in Durant.

"Still have that bar in the swimming pool?"

"Yep."

"Save a pool stool for me."

"Indeed, we'll leave from there, and then, the next stickball tournament will be at the Mother Mound."

John and his Seminole spooks settled in to watch the game before heading back to Seminole country to plan the grand migration.

That evening, Ruby Dell buzzed into the Tuskahoma Resort room where she and Luke held court for Labor Day. She said, "The Mexicans and the Tejianos are fighting at Austin."

"Brodie's here?"

"Passing through; he saw the start of it, came to warn us, whoever wins that battle will be heading this way.

We will need to keep ahead of that push north. Better call John."

Ruby said, "Did that, right after I tucked in the kids. We're moving up the timetable."

"You always were better at administration." He booted up the streamer and the graviton emitters, "Let's watch some old Star Wars on the couch."

"Ok, Grandpa, but don't try anything."

"I think you're safe for tonight, too tired." While the opening titles scrolled, Luke fell asleep. As his rhythmic breathing started, Ruby turned off the emitters, dimmed the lights and buzzed out to see Brodie off and synchronize calendars.

*

Mara
2330 A.R.

Having studied and analyzed all aspects of Mara, her new Earth, since a young age, Charlotte naturally took up the study of history and archeology as she worked toward multiple degrees, became an academic and then settled down into tenure and writing a series of very popular alternative history novels; in reality just retelling the improbable history of the Earth of her first timeline.

On that long ago Moving Day, she had bid farewell to the silvers, the manifestations of her and Dan's human souls, before her travel through the Library and splashdown on Mara. She believed that the silvers existed between universes in the multiverse; with that and her first return from Purgatory in mind, she created another meditative practice, that of maintaining a beacon between universes to attract those souls, like Meg Sheridan, Dan's second wife and spook therapist, had said, *"Like night fishing for spooks; set the right bait and they jump right into the boat."*

To contact the dead still with us, Rudolph Steiner had taught, we must meditate on the departed and then they may put thoughts into our minds in the moments between sleeping and waking. She believed in what Steiner called 'reading to the dead.' This could involve reading books on spiritual subjects, internally, not aloud, or just going over thoughts carefully in the mind. The dead were attracted by the slow recitation that rolled each word over, savoring it on the tongue, and the steeping of thoughts until understanding rose from the mix like the aroma of the finest tea from a cup.

In her first timeline, Dan had read her books after she died to try to understand what she believed. Petra Rousseau had told him that Charlotte believed she could communicate or at least stay connected after her death. Petra suggested that Dan read Charlotte's books slowly and take the time to read *and* understand. She had told him, "Winter is a nice time to read, don't you think? Take the winter to read and we'll talk more in the spring."

Dan had felt that Petra was teaching him something that required patience and obedience first, like a Sufi master. He did what she told him. Without him knowing it, Petra had made sure that Dan was reading to the dead, the dead Charlotte, as Steiner had taught. Ultimately, that was what drew Charlotte back to the world, brought her irresistibly to the edge of Purgatory and made her believe that she could make contact. Then Tom Petty's quantum gravity device broke down all barriers and the spooks, including Charlotte, came back into the world.

On Mara, she kept watchful for anything that would result in a different future. She also had to choose if she wanted to participate in the scientific discoveries again. The breakthroughs had, after all, been precipitated by her *transitus* and return. The whole point of this sojourn was to avoid that death. Would Dan keep his patent practice and meet Tom Petty again anyway?

She did want to work with her spiritual teachers again. She still wanted to pursue Encounter with the divine. She had a head start now. When she had reached an age where her reading level was just 'gifted' and not an impossibility, she began to search for familiar authors. But here there was no theology about the God of Abraham except for the Judeans, just a vestige of the Judeo-Christian-Muslim world powers on Earth. The theological vacuum had been filled with some version of the Perennial Philosophy and the Platonic World Soul. Surprisingly however, she found the same authors ensconced in this world's religions.

Well, it wasn't that surprising. The religions and cults that preceded Christianity also had themes of virgin birth, the death and resurrection of gods, the trinity of the ultimate god, the flood and the ark, and many more. In the Greek world, Christianity overlay Greek philosophy. That philosophy was made to foreshadow Christianity in the same way that Christian observances, Easter, Christmas and All Hallows Eve were grafted over existing pagan rituals to co-opt and diminish them.

On Mara, the effect of the same Greek philosophy developing on its own was to expose to her how thin the veil of Christianity actually was. So, she could read Teilhard de Chardin, Sergei Bulgakov, von Balthazar and others, especially the mystics, using the same points and logic to reach the same conclusion, only substituting Osiris and Isis for Jesus and the Virgin Mary.

*

Earth
January, 2125 C.E.
Choctaw Capitol Grounds, Tuskahoma

Chief Patterson's hoveRV idled in front of the Choctaw government offices at Tuskahoma while the rest of those who chose to travel were staged on the stick ball field near the capitol museum waiting for the scheduled time. The Chief's four granddaughters had arrived the day before from the Pacific Northwest.

About a hundred miles to the southwest, Durant had been scratched as a staging point as the Mexicans and Tejianos sparred ever northward. The only safe route now was due East through Hot Springs, a bit of a hike through the national forest, but I-80 through Memphis held more danger from stragglers in suddenly plentiful free derelict housing.

Chief Patterson and his granddaughters were packed and ready in the hoveRV. Ruby was to take the first shift driving. Uncle Cliff said one of his usual aphorisms, "Never stop a woman from working." The ladies rolled their eyes.

From across Oklahoma and further afield, tribes were assembling at various staging points and heading toward the new tropics, coastlines and wetlands, to harbors and beaches looking out on the awash and vacant cities of New Orleans, Biloxi, Mobile and others. At Biloxi the only thing visible was the top of seawalls breached in the end by hurricanes with a fury unknown before the 21st century.

Closer to the old Mexican border, Trump's Wall, paid for by American taxpayers, had been dismantled by the federales heading north and braceros heading south. It was used for battlements by the federales and by the braceros to build seawalls at Monterey, Cancun, and other cities on the gulf coast and in Baja.

Sadly, in the ocean the repurposed wall continued to perform no useful function to humans. It did, however begin to anchor coral and other creatures that drifted in their larval state, destined to live to adulthood only after encountering such a surface. After that, there would be reefs and reef fish, predators, plants and a full ecology restored. It wasn't just the seawalls, the whole of the cities and what had been dry ground, was virgin territory ripe for settlement as fast as the ocean could arrange it.

The former inhabitants went further than the adjacent suburbs, if not to a latitude north or south that approximated the climate that used to exist in the submerged gulf coast, then off planet to an asteroid colony or the Library. Anyway, that was what the advanced scouts reported. As Ruby started the chief's hoveRV, let it idle smoothly forward and checked the side mirrors, she could see the Choctaw bison herd coming around the curve and into position behind the families. On either side of the lead animal an Andromedan walked with a staff. These had scales mimicking traditional patterns and walked with an avian/saurian head bob.

The bison were used to them and took their lead like obedience schooled puppies. Someone, maybe the cosplay loving aliens, had been creative and bleached the fur of the yearling bison in the lead, since a real white buffalo had not been conveniently born as an good omen for the event.

Ruby asked, "Grandpa, how are the buffalo going to do in the jungle?"

"They used to live in the woods, from Alaska to Mexico. They were probably gone from our home before the removal, but still were held in our memory as we met the plains bison here."

Pushmataha said, "They're pretty adaptable and there's plenty of forage on the forest floor and grazing in meadows. All the trails were originally blazed by forest bison. They'll probably just munch their way back down those old trails.

Luke said, "Maybe those trails were made by mastodons, and the buffalo trailed along behind them."

"Yes, it had to have happened that way. They evolved together in the same places."

One of the great grands said, "Maybe dinosaurs made the trails for the mammoths!"

Another said, "That was millions of years not just thousands. The land was way different."

"But it could've happened!"

Ruby was named after her grandmother, who buzzed forward to belt the kids into captain's chairs with her waldoes. "Shush, settle down so we can get moving." Her own children were off planet but heading in, grandchildren returned from Seattle, Portland, Spokane, and southern California. All heads were filled with the magical realism of this trek to a home they had never known.

*

When the last of the Red Man shall have perished, and the memory of my tribe shall have become a myth among the White Men, these shores will swarm with the invisible dead of my tribe and when your children's children think themselves alone in the field, the store, the shop, upon the highway or in the silence of the pathless woods they will not be alone.

At night when the streets of your cities and villages are silent and you think them deserted, they will throng with the returning hosts that once filled them and still love this beautiful land. The White Man will never be alone.

- Chief Sealth of the Suquamish and Duwamish, 1854

*

Earth
October, 2124 C.E.

At the Beachcomber Bubble Tea Bar

After the flood, there was a lot of good salvage and found art in the Silicon Valley. The big earthquake resulted in a tsunami at the same time that a freak storm surge entered the Golden Gate. This rode on top of the nine meter sea level rise which had already extended San Francisco Bay as far east as Sacramento. The same earthquake and its aftershocks took out the Oroville dam which emptied flood stage waters into the Bay, after passing through Yuba City and Sacramento. The tsunami punched a hole through the Golden Gate, hit Berkeley and Oakland directly and joined with the Oroville flood which turned the surge south.

All the old docks and waterfront industries along South Bay were already gone but newer construction at Alameda, San Leandro and Hayward was taken out as the wave slammed right through San Jose and ended up in the Santa Clara Valley. As the waters receded or evaporated, they left a stinking mosquito infested mud flat. Debris from the whole Bay Area that hadn't piled up in downtown San Jose was submerged or protruding, garnishing the mud pie.

A few years on, the stuff you could see without digging had been removed, but dangerous and maybe valuable salvage was still there under the mud. Some rebuilding at the edges was starting, but most of the valley was cracked dry flats in the summer or quicksand that ate your boots in the rainy season. But, the beachcombers who knew what they were doing could navigate to the old tech campuses and extract items of archeological interest as well as precious metals and rare earths.

You could see them from the Beachcomber Bubble Tea Bar, equipped with mudshoes; like snow shoes with vibrating graviton soles to compact the mud as you walked. Also ubiquitous was a metal detector with ground penetrating radar and a long bamboo staff or metal pike Experienced beachcombers could tell pay dirt just by poking around with the staff and then confirm with the GPR. Spookballs, some with humans and some without, had their own detection devices and could telescope a probe or a grasping claw when they found something.

Larr Yellingson had been at this for five years. At the beginning, the pickings were all above ground. The flats were covered then with salvagers collecting copper, glass, iron and aluminum along with circuit boards and other more esoteric items. Later on, he just followed behind them like a bird looking for grasshoppers behind a plow.

By the time the salvaging was no longer cost effective on the small scale, Larr had learned how to glean the mudflats all on his own. The Beachcomber was in Los Altos, in the hills above the mudflats. It was roofed with palm fronds and had a veranda bar where warm breezes from the west let patrons pretend that the view was of something attractive. When the wind was from the east however, the stink was the main draw. The gleaners, who tended to stink anyway, had made it a staging point, so business was good.

When Larr wasn't gleaning, back at his studio in San Jose or schmoozing with clients, he liked to sit there and survey the flats just to spot any new hotbed of activity that might indicate a major find. The mudshoed gleaners were like any hopeful treasure hunters, or fishermen for that matter, relying on luck disguised as arcane knowledge. A shout or a quick shift in movement tended to draw them like flies. When that happened, Larr worked like in the old days when he could just examine the scraps without doing any digging himself. Not a bad idea when seasonal rains and flash floods periodically erased all traces of prior finds. When the rains ended, the gleaners faced a once again pristine and clue-less sea of mud. Annually at least, it gave everyone a fresh start at the stinking bog.

Sucking tapioca bubbles at the Beachcomber, Larr was trying to dream up a commission for a client with a house on high ground who still had money. An artist spookball, done up in Frida Kahlo surrealism and Georgia O'Keefe gardenias, hovered nearby. If he closed his eyes he could see Frida manifesting the whole scene and herself. Instead of her spookball hovering above the stool, she manifested as her human avatar sitting next to Larr; dolled up in a brightly colored peasant dress, paper flowers and coiled braids, the Salma Hayek biopic, not the historical mono-browed Frida.

Once in a while, a pattern of activity on the flats caused one of them to point, with a real or manifested finger; in the world, the spookball extended an antenna. Then they commented like they were watching a no hitter from the nosebleed seats. Nothing much was happening but that just made the subtle details stand out. Not hard work but it passed the time.

Even that easy work was however, disturbed when a guy in a bad suit and skinny tie plopped his fat ass down on the next bar stool. Larr opened his eyes and the spookball growled in annoyance.

A hand with pudgy fingers entered Larr's peripheral vision. *Shit.* "Hey, you're that guy, right, the artist? Frank Franco, I wanna buy some art!"

Larr grabbed the hand and it pumped his hand up and down like cracking a whip. "P'p' pleased to m'm'meet you,"he winced. "This is Frida."

He closed his eyes. "Salma Hayek, cool, can't miss with that, a real looker, doll."

"Likewise, I'm sure," Frida said, then feigned indifference.

Back to Larr, " Yeah, yeah, my real first name is Leslie, but as a kid they called me Scooter, but you can call me Frank or you can call me Frankie, or you can call me Franco or. . ."

Retrieving his hand, Larr said, "That wasn't funny even when it was new."

"Yeah yeah, I know, You can call me Ray, yada yada yada," Then to the girl behind the counter, "Hey honey, make me one of those root beer float ones, with the root beer barrel bubbles." She said something in Korean which didn't sound nice like, *you wanna see a root beer barrel, look in the mirror baby*. "So, I hear your stuff features junk from the mud flats; just like digging for clams, right?"

Larr said, "There's a sort of gruesome provenance some people seem to like, yes. It's not as easy as you might think what with the debris and quicksand, a bit dangerous."

"Well, that's just combat pay, right? Jacks up the price, right? Gotta give the people what they want, right? Am I right, right, right?"

Frida said, "Y'know, you don't seem like the typical art collector. . ."

"Har, har, har; I like art as much as the next guy, but I work on commission, I do lots of different stuff. Today somebody wants Larr Yellingson. Tomorrow, somebody wants a grenade launcher, doesn't matter to me."

She said. "A mercenary."

"You say that like it's a bad thing, but nah, don't like to get dirty, I'm just a personal shopper, high end though, a class act, right?

Larr said, "Right. So, why me?"

Frank pulled out a photo and a handkerchief from his breast pocket. As he wiped the sweat off his brow and double chins he slid the photo over to Larr and poked a Vienna sausage forefinger at it; thumpety, thump, thump, "This your thing?"

Frida buzzed in closer. Larr could see one of his more recent works on a screen shot of his website, *Silicon Grave No.*

9. It was an enameled canopic jar, a copy of the ones used in ancient graves as ossuaries, or to hold organs of mummies. It was embellished with tech parts, things that were more interesting because they were out of place, unhinged from their former reality.

"Yes, that's one in a series."

Frank thumpety, thump, thumped it again pointing to one item like a disk that reflected rainbow colors inside a mesh cage, like two halves of a clam shell, like a golden clam or a heart shaped locket. Wires protruded which obviously made it a part of a larger apparatus. Larr couldn't figure out exactly what it was but he knew he liked it.

Frank pointed to the golden clam. "This thing, you got more of those?"

"It doesn't work like that; it's serendipity, random connections. I don't think you or your employer are interested in art."

"Jeez, don't get touchy. We're willing to pay double your price for that piece."

"Why?"

"Goodwill, supporting the arts, whatever you want."

"And if I can lead you to more?"

"Same for each and you don't even have to make art." Frank sucked a root beer bubble up the straw. "I love this shit."

The bartendress brought Larr a refill and ignored Frankie. Larr said, "I can find more, just have to relocate the site with the GPR. It might take a while and I don't want to do any heavy excavation, it'd just draw the others. Meet me here in a week, unless you want to strap on mudshoes and help."

"No, no, no, no, don't have any casual clothes really, gotta keep up appearances. You get 'em, I'll buy em, and you can even keep your jug thing and sell it to a real collector, ok?"

Larr and the artball watched Frankie waddle out and blow a kiss at the bubble girl's poker face. Frida said, "You do know you shouldn't have anything to do with that guy, right? I used to be human. I've still got a bullshit sensor."

"Ahhhh, you know me Frida, I just kinda want to see what sort of bullshit it is."

"If you knew what that thing was, you'd know already. But with that guy, I'd say it's more like a grenade launcher than a valentine."

"But, it's so boring this time of year, maybe some intrigue will inspire me."

"And the money. . ."

"It'll be ok." Frida began a low frequency hum just to annoy him. Larr wasn't catching on. He actually had a crate-full of those clamshells and was now doing some mental math with a lot of zeros.

*

Frankie drove up the peninsula from Los Altos towards San Francisco. The peninsula had narrowed but the 280 was still well above water. He pulled off in Daley City on John Daley Dr. and took it west to Skyline Drive. On the west side of Skyline, the cliffs had eroded, taking out the subdivisions that used to be valued for the view. That was before they figured out that pouring water on unnecessary lawns just made for a slippery slope, literally. Now however, that subdivision *was* the view, the debris at the bottom slowly being smashed into driftwood, crumbling concrete and jagged metal as the waves and further erosion did their work.

The suburbs on the east side of Skyline now had some cachet, since they hadn't fallen into the ocean yet. The yards were fashionably brown but sellers could not give them away. After the first Moving Day it was definitely a buyer's and renter's market, no lack of inventory in any condition. Spookballs didn't even need housing, except for the company and maybe a place to get out of the rain. So a rental hood had formed, no upkeep, no nosy landlords. As long as you paid the rent, they left you alone.

Frankie pulled into the driveway at 89 Eastwood Dr., a nondescript split-level on a narrow lot. The paint and roof had thirty years on them and there were wrought iron bars on all the windows. In order to preserve any front lawn at all, the entrance was up a full flight of stairs on the side. If they had built them a little closer they would all be Philly townhouses. This way, at least you could wave at your neighbor in their bathroom window as you climbed the stairs.

Frankie was not happy about the climb but was going to get an advance if he made it to the top. He didn't want to be puffing when he got to the door, and so took the stairs in sets of five and watched the seagulls and pelicans soar while he caught his breath on the sixth. He reached the top and did 'shave and a haircut two bits' on the door.

A low bark confirmed the resonant ribcage and steel trap jaws of Blossom the pit bull. Frankie pulled a baggie with hot dogs in it out of his pocket, bent over and pointed a hot dog at the door jamb at about Blossom jaw height. The door opened a crack. With a big smile, Frankie said, "*Who's a good boy? Who's a good boy?*" wagged his butt and shoved the hot dog into the crack. Blossom returned the wag, gulped and woofed a welcome.

Brodie opened the door and said, "Frankie! Good to see you man, come on in." Brodie, past his natural life span on state of the art nanobots and implants, had a bit of a Wayne Newton shine on him but not as scary. Fortunately, cell checker protocols kept the skin taut without glare. He still looked about fifty five with a well-muscled frame, Bazooka Joe buzz cut and lantern jaw. He hadn't been wasting his retirement on cheap booze and loose women, no sir . . . well not on cheap booze anyway.

"That dog likes me." Frankie said as he wiped his fingers on his pants.

"As long as you don't run out of hot dogs. Did you find Yellingson?"

"You know it brotha'. God, open a window or something, it's too dark and hot in here."

"Like my coffee."

"Har, har, har. Outside of a dog, what's man's best friend?"

"What?"

"Don't know, but inside of a dog it's too dark to see."

"What?"

"Never mind, in one week I'll have the dozen you want, maybe more. Larr's just got to dig some more clams. Just need the first installment."

Brodie punched his phone-pad and Frankie's pad ting-a-linged with the twenty g's advance he was hoping for "Hey, how'd you know he had one, out of all the artists in all the bubble tea bars in the world . . ."

"Casablanca?"

This was a game popular among re-enactors and cosplayers, an ongoing version of Name That Tune and Trivial Pursuit. "Right, right." Doing Bogart now, "The problems of two people like us don't amount to a hill of beans in this crazy world. . ."

Brodie laughed. "God, stop, you sound like an Andromedan. It's like facial recognition software, the internet of objects. I found out where they were making them before the flood, from 3MI shareware. Shadow government black ops with 3D printers, you know. Then I just had to run the program on the scavenger chat rooms and bingo, Yellingson's art 'r us."

"But what is it?"

"Now, now; if I was buying a graviton detonator, you wouldn't want to know how I was going to use it would you?"

"La, la, la, la, don't know nothin' about birthin' no babies, Miss Scarlet. See you in a week pal." Frankie tipped his fedora, gave Blossom another hot dog and tap danced out the door and down the stairs like Gene Kelly.

Brodie shouted "Gone With the Wind!" and shut and locked the door.

"That's guy's crazy. . . Insane m'sayn?

"Woof," Blossom agreed and then went back to watching his favorite show; *A Puppy-clypse Now* on Animal Planet.

Brodie turned on his desk lamp, removed a drop cloth and continued with his work, checking instructions he himself had posted on the New United Futurists website. His assembly line turned out little barrels with wires coiled and protruding. Heavy magnets surrounded a spherical void in the center of each. There was nothing inside but the surface was studded with wires all pointing in toward the center. The other ends of the wires entered a buss connector that plugged into a receptacle at the top end. Also on the top of each were thumb screw fasteners around an indentation about the size and shape of Larr's clamshell.

As he finished the one on the test stand, he started looking on the net for flights to Geneva. Nothing was on schedule these days and you might have to wait a while for enough passengers to show up for the pirate airlines to fill up the fuel tanks, cash only of course. *Cash, grass or ass, like in the 20th century, if you want top level trivia.*

Everybody was holding everybody up, all trying to re-create normal at a sub-discount rate. Unregulated commercial and passenger transport was combined and all in all it was like riding on the roof of a bus in India with passengers, chickens and piglets all crammed aboard. And, you had to bring your own snacks and booze but could drink as much as you liked. The crew certainly did. What a world.

He decided the Cult spaceplane out of Oakland was the best bet and the best cover actually; NUF business under the saffron robe.

*

Mara
2330 A.R.

Charlotte waited for the book reading and signing to begin. This leg of the tour had her at Powell's, the largest, oldest bookstore in Portland. Her newest book *Heart String Theory* had been picked as a book club favorite and was the subject of the latest 'Portland Reads' promotion. It was certainly better than the old days when she presented to a sparse audience of grad students in the History Department. Today, she was a minor celebrity, spending a good portion of her school break time on book tours and local television appearances.

The city was immersed in "Portland twilight," meaning constant grey from dawn to dusk. It was hard to tell when night began and ended but it seemed to her to be a good excuse to sleep in or go to bed early. She was experiencing her forties, something denied to her in her first life, dead from cancer at forty-one, and so the novelty of naps and the lessening of the adrenaline of youth was bringing her unknown pleasures. She reveled in naps.

Refreshed with a cup of tea in the late afternoon, she made her way past the floor to ceiling stacks at the old-school bookstore, up the stairs to the reading stage and took the podium. She read significant passages, parts that she thought were particularly lyrical or moving, some poetry, some space travel, incongruities. Her audience was attentive, emotionally charged, sometimes even tearful. After an hour and then some questions from the audience, she took a bow to applause and went down to the main floor, sitting at a table with stacks of her book ready for purchase and autographs.

As the line wound down and her signature became erratic with fatigue, she noticed one last couple. They were, in fact, hovering at the back to make sure they were the last. She thought, *Here come the obsessed fans who know more facts than I do about the world I created. Gods love' em. Ok, what's the meaning of life today? Whatever they say, I nod, look them right in the eye, point and say "Exactly!, that's what I'm talkin' about!* They love it even though later they can't quite figure out what they were right about.

This couple comprised a young man of about twenty four years, looking a bit northern Indian or Pakistani, and a young woman, much darker, skin almost black but with long straight hair and non-African features. Charlotte recognized her as Dravidian, the non-indo European inhabitants of southern India, supposed to be the descendants of the first humans out of Africa.

The young man said, "I'm Krishna, this is Radha"

She smiled warmly with recognition of the names of familiar deities. "The holy couple, well; interesting coincidence or do you intend to channel the divine?"

Radha said, "A coincidence, but it seemed appropriate."

"Or, you could actually be the next incarnation, avatars of the gods."

Krishna laughed, "Yes, and how could you tell?"

"Staring into the mouth of Krishna, like Arjuna? That seems rude. Anyway, I think it's lovely. How, shall I sign your books?"

"To Radha and Krishna. Next year at Moving Day."

Charlotte's shock was palpable. "Can . . .can you two hang out for a while?"

With a little bow, Krishna said, "Enchanté, but of course, mademoiselle."

Charlotte's jaw dropped, "Ok, come with me. *Now.*"

The staff tried to intercept her, "Dr. Pritchard, we need you to sign. . . , " but they were already out the door.

Nanih Waiya, Mississippi
Leaning Mountain

The Choctaws a great many winters ago commenced moving from the country where they then lived, which was a great distance to the west of the great river and the mountains of snow, and they were a great many years on their way. A great medicine man led them the whole way, by going before with a red pole, which he stuck in the ground every night where they encamped. This pole was every morning found leaning to the east, and he told them that they must continue to travel to the east until the pole would stand upright in their encampment, and that there the Great Spirit had directed that they should live. *George Catlin, Smithsonian Report 1885.*

*

Earth
October 1, 2124 C.E.

The road out of Tuskahoma was flat and bordered by farmland on its last legs, dustbowls waiting for a breeze. But, soon enough, old deciduous forests and windbreaks encroaching onto flat shoulders widened the two lane old highway 63 to a usable width for the Five Civilized Tribes convoy. As they approached Muse, which was only a crossroads even when it was inhabited, Ruby pulled over, turned on the lead hoveRV's emergency flashers, the grav-levs whined to a halt and the vehicle lowered slowly to the ground.

Luke said, "I had an antique Peugeot that did that, pneumatic suspension, I miss that crate; actually I miss internal combustion, I miss diesel exhaust."

The other conveyances moved off to the shoulders to pitch camp while the bison moved into the trees to forage under the watchful eyes of the Andromedans, Choctaw teenagers and a couple of border collies. The other tribes, the Seminole, Creek, Cherokee and Chickasaw, were following along at staggered intervals, probably all bedding down at the same time, checking perimeters, posting sentries, sending scouts out under cover of darkness. They kept in contact with gravitels and coordinated their progress, but if something unexpected happened, a concerted attack or even an innocent disruption, it would be difficult to come to the rescue. All were a bit nervous therefore, until all had arrived at their common destination, Nanih Waiya.

As the light dimmed behind trees, dark and silence blanketed the world, but only temporarily. Stepping into the road, Ruby watched the sliver of the new moon descend behind the trees as the Milky Way began to appear and its stars began to roil and boil like an immense luminescent river. To the southeast she could see the Cape Canaveral ribbon and to the southwest, the Houston ribbon both arcing up as far as the eye could distinguish. Out here, even the glare from the illuminated ribbons did not diminish the wonder of the stars, could not diminish the widening gap between those that climbed the ribbon and those that did not.

She mused, *People used to stare and wonder, what's out there? What are the wonders we will never know? Funny, we still don't have the capacity to know more than a tiny fraction of what's right in front of us. It just boils down to relationships, the universe, the multiverse, it's all just one encounter after another with sentient beings, I prefer babies, before they speak even, taking in the sensory world at an impossible rate we all forget as soon as we are complete. They are the most promising, and yet each cohort quickly outgrows our amazement at the impossibility of that pudgy pupa becoming human, then we turn around to find new babies, to get a new fix of impossibility.*

In the kids' trailer, Ruby's sister Penny cuddled each of the children in turn, holding the toddlers the longest, the one's whose attention span made them understand and crave the connection, holding them close and singing softly in their ears songs she made up on the spot, songs with words woven around their names but still sounding like the oldest lullaby.

Oh my darlin', Oh my darlin', Oh my darlin' Evelette, sleep my darlin' like a baby, Oh my darlin', Evelette. Light she was and like a fairy and her shoes were number nine, wearin' boxes without topses . . .

The little girl was transfixed, wide awake. keeping still but fussing just enough to make it last as long as possible, eyeing the next kid in line with menace while incarnating an angel, *Not just yet,* semaphoring the conspiracy of oneness, the best feeling ever, the dream that dreams no worries.

Each child was then passed to another aunt, grandparent, cousin who would repeat the cuddling and then pass the child on until all the beds were filled.

Ruby stepped into the trailer, took the handoff in turn and sang old songs softly in their ears:

> *Oh the summertime is coming*
> *And the trees are sweetly blooming*
> *And the wild mountain thyme*
> *Grows around the blooming heather*
>
> *Will ye go, lassie, go?*
> *And we'll all go together*
> *To pluck wild mountain thyme*
> *All around the blooming heather.*
>
> *Will ye go, lassie, go? . . .*

*

Over the next few days, the caravan passed out of the scraggly deciduous trees into scraggly coniferous trees as the altitude increased, skirted the developed area outside of Hot Springs and then back again into trees. About a mile outside of town, a couple of crackers in overalls appeared out of the woods indulging in gawking and seemingly good natured but ill-advised taunting. *Hey Tonto! Hey chief! Kimosabe, Woo, Woo, Woo, Woo, Woo!*

Ruby picked up the pace a bit and the herders moved around to the rear leaving no stragglers behind. The two Andromedans pointed their pikes at the crackers and off they ran laughing at a high pitch.

Ruby said, "For fuck's sake, what are they re-enacting now, reverse evolution?"

Luke said, "Sounds like the Lone Ranger, Kimosabe."

"*Deliverance*, more likely, mouth-breathers."

"Don't be mean, Ruby." He made the same clichéd war whoop from the old movies, "*Woo, Woo, Woo, Woo, Woo.*"

"Don't do that Grandpa."

"Ancient history; before your time. Stop for a minute, Ruby. Push, go talk to them."

Pushmataha nodded his electronic face and buzzed up and over the trees back along the road they had just come down.

"Really, Grandpa? Are we going to have to put up with the same genocidal nonsense in Mississippi that made Oklahoma look great in the first place?"

"Long, *long* time ago. They were just being stupid Baby; don't mistake incompetence for an evil plan. The country is not empty. We just need to see who is here and try to coexist."

"Well, we *are* running away from warring factions with guns and running towards who knows what. The cities may be empty but the forests are full of people surviving without infrastructure."

"So, that's why they need us. We are the five civilized tribes after all."

"Bullshit, sorry Grandpa."

"Stop and play your banjo for me. Play 'You Are My Sunshine or, 'Keep On The Sunny Side.' Hey," he said, trying to distract her, "Do you know how to get perfect pitch with a banjo?"

"I've heard this a million. . ."

"It's when you hit the dumpster on the first throw. Still funny. . ."

She said, "Here's one you don't know, How did a banjo start Modern Art? Duchamp's first painting was called "Tin Cans Descending a Staircase."

"Must be art, I don't get it."

"Because . . . the classic description of a banjo is tin cans falling down stairs and Duchamp's first painting was *Nude Descending a Staircase*? It's not funny if I have to explain it."

"What happens when you leave your banjo in your unlocked car?"

"You come back and there're two banjos, I know. . ." Her mood lightened, she started to play while they waited.

"You are my sunshine, my only sunshine, You make me happy when skies are grey, You'll never know dear, how much I love you, Please don't take my sunshine away."

As Push skimmed the tops of the trees he passed the crackers but kept on the same bearings, soon spying a circle of trucks and trailers, vans, busses, tents and other habitation on the grounds of an abandoned high school. There seemed to be a communal fire, humans mostly, but a few spookballs. He kept a good height and signaled on the open channel. "We are the New Choctaw Republic of Oklahoma. Will you speak with me?"

A ball rose up from the fire and buzzed in Push's direction; they acknowledged each other and signaled peaceful intentions. "Wally here, what's your name?"

"Pushmataha. We met a couple of your people on Highway 63, now running this way. They were a bit confrontational."

"Those guys? They're a bit differently abled upstairs, wander off looking for provisions and trouble I guess; harmless really."

"That's what I thought; looks like you're traveling too?"

"We started south from Fayetteville, spotted you at Muse. We've been following the tribes. Different populations are going north or staying put, but we believe your plan is promising, some kind of government surviving outside the system."

"System's gone North/Up, maybe Antarctica, Anzac, South Africa."

"Don't want to make trouble, but everybody's got to get out of the desert sooner or later."

"Bring a delegation; we'll have everyone stay put for a day, we'll talk with the Chief and Counsel. I'll set it up; tomorrow at noon?"

"Thank you. I'll bring our leadership."

Spookball scouts from the Five Tribes fanning out in advance and at a good height had discovered other abandoned townsites with informal communities nearby and on the road, the migration having caught their attention, refugees from Durant and Broken Arrow, others from further north and west, Fort Smith and Wichita.

Some tribes in the northern tier had headed further north to join with the First Nations Tribes developing opportunities in collaboration with the Cult and off-planet enterprises. Kamchatka, Alaska, Yukon and Nunavut; all held promise as tundra was turned by plowshares into farmland and Paleolithic meat ranches. Servicing the Northwest Passage, supplying North/Up and maintaining limited net and broadcast power infrastructure was enough opportunity to fulfill the aspirations of many.

Even so, displaced plains communities, Blackfeet and Sioux from reservations and other random refugees were also heading south, seeing a different promise in what was becoming known as the Five Tribes Confederacy, FTC for short. The convoys then acquired more coherence as the fellow travelers filled in between the Five Tribes. Even Cult, 3MI and the elite upstairs began to take notice of this winding snake of a migration visible from space, like the Great Wall, morphing into a dimly lit string of fireflies at night.

The next morning, just before noon as promised, Wally and a human delegation approached the Choctaw convoy. Luke, Grandma Ruby, their granddaughters, the Andromedans Urizen and Blake and John Asényahola formed the circle of the outdoor council. Communication spooks on gravitels had confirmed other meetings back up the highway with the other tribes. All of a sudden, it seemed like a momentous and providential day.

Pushmataha introduced Wally to Luke and Wally introduced Steve Vallush from Fayetteville. Vallush had been an accountant and ran the local farmers' market and his own Figgieville Farms before things got bad in the heartland; A professional, administrator, political activist and small businessman; seemed like the perfect skill set for a savvy and self-sufficient leader. They sat on mats on the ground, the delegation in the center of the circle facing Luke. The lack of emitters and manifestation marked a practical trend, spooks didn't need to pretend they were human and humans didn't need the false comfort of imagining that spooks were anything other than perfectly evolved field sentients.

Luke said, "Welcome, it seems we are attracting attention."

Vallush said, "Good ideas spread by word of mouth, old school memes."

"The dream of a homeland apart is not ours alone."

"The system continues to break, evolve, some say worsen. All following you, I believe, want to build a better life away from the Cult."

"The theocracy."

"And the techno-political complex, control and persuasion, even if it seems to be for the good."

Ruby said, "It's not so nice if you don't want what that system offers. They drive outsiders down to a basic hierarchy of needs. When we get food, water, shelter, safety, then we'll take on interdimensional politics and transcendence."

John Asényahola said, "She's right; if we build our own infrastructure outside the system, we can negotiate for other amenities as one nation to another."

Vallush said, "There's no scarcity of sustainable basic resources now that the surplus population has left the planet. I've studied economics and agriculture enough to know that there is stability in the local supply of food, shelter, clothing and muscle power. Once that works, we can acquire other technology and goods from a position of strength, that is, if we have the numbers."

Luke said, "A position of strength must also be a position of peace. A willingness to lead and follow in turn, balancing personal good and the communal good without coercion; workable dispute resolution, achievable goals."

"All classic political problems, but now we have different mix if all participate fully, humans, spooks and Andromedans, all bring unique perspectives. We've been working on some ideas on how to start over, if you will, how to build a community and an economy from scratch."

Luke said, "If your group and others are willing to work on a mutual agreement, there could be a communal compact in the new settlement. No one can tell you not to come anyway."

"We can at least be good neighbors."

Grandma Ruby said, "Well, get your butts in gear then, travel along with us and we'll weave this new cloth, see what it looks like."

Vallush said, "It will be our pleasure. Wally, head back and take charge of breaking camp and I'll keep the discussion going here. You can join us at Hot Springs."

"On my way." Wally buzzed off to the northeast, having recorded the conversation to replay for the Council. The Fayetteville camp, anticipating a good result from the meeting, were getting ready to bug out as Wally arrived.

*

Earth
October, 2124 C.E

San Jose Watertown

Larr hiked down the ridge trail from Los Altos to the dock at the edge of San Jose Watertown. Frida buzzed along at shoulder height so they could converse easily. It was basic human-spook etiquette, a suite of standard protocols intended to prevent injured shins and noggins: Miss Manners for the cyborg generation.

He shared a studio and loft with Frida in the old KQED Building on San Fernando Street. The K had fallen off some time after the flood. Now it just said QED, *Quod Erat Demonstrandum, the old Latin Ta da! Voila! Wah La!* as if the flooded building was the mathematical proof of the equation of global warming. Or, was it the Quantum Electrodynamics QED; the beginning and end of the Higgs field where it seems everyone is at a party to which one was not invited? Either way, a good joke if you still had a sense of humor.

The QED and all the other buildings in Watertown were only open above the fourth floor. Larr paid a ferryman with a dinghy to take him over. If you squinted just right, it almost seemed romantic, like Venice. But really, it was just more dirty water and low class rentals with their own kind of stink.

Larr paid the ferryman and stepped out on the retrofitted dock. For humans, this was the only way in or out except for the helipad on top. It took some real money to make that fare and nobody with real money wanted into this swamp. Thankfully, the elevators still worked with a combination of rooftop block and tackle and graviton retros. Quaintly, you needed an elevator operator with muscles like Popeye to make the thing work. The swing shift operator, Santos, welcomed them onto the elevator with a nod, closed the doors with some welded-on handles and started to haul on the cable that hung down through a ceiling panel and looped through a pulley on the floor. The graviton retros started to whine and then Santos was just taking up slack till they got to the tenth floor. Then, he wound the rope around a tie off and opened the doors manually, like Sampson at the temple.

Larr beamed a good tip to the operator's phone-pad as he ducked under his arms. "Thanks Mr. Yellingson." Larr nodded and Frida said, "Thank you Mr. Santos." as they started down the hall. "Ma'am," he said as he tipped his cap.

Larr had not come through the flood unscathed. Neither was it chance that he was now in this sunken dream of what his life could have been. This had been his old office suite when his acoustic engineering firm had been booming. The quantum gravity revolution and spooks had provided new opportunities in every industry.

Like the 3MI ad campaign had said *"Not just a new way to do things, It's A New Thing to Do."* Larr thought it was both, starting with the Hover Mike and various other refinements that made his business successful by staying ahead of the curve. At the end of that curve he had envisioned another life, picking up the musician and artist personas he had embraced before he became practical, running and then growing the business his father had started, renting out wireless microphones and other audio and video equipment.

For his transition, he had picked out an office condo in a two hundred year old remodeled flour mill with a view of the bay. It had exposed brick interior walls, sixteen foot ceilings and tall windows around a corner that also had views of parks and a Ferris wheel.

It was to be a new beginning. He had just sold his stake in the engineering firm, and was working late there as the rest of the staff members were inching home on the freeway, when the tsunami hit. The new office was gone and everyone he knew was killed in the rush hour traffic jam before his own building stopped rocking back and forth in the advancing and receding waves, earthquakes and aftershocks.

His staff and partners, his elderly father, his wife, all were gone in a matter of minutes. Of course, everyone who was going to pay to buy out his shares was dead as well. Insurance companies and reinsurance companies were breaking trail on this one. Someone was going to make money but not Larr.

He just never went home. He stayed in the office, really just scavenging and going native until eventually the owner figured out how to charge rent again. Right at that time, his old friend Frida came down from the Cult's administrative temple and stupa at the L3 Lagrange point where the Library sat at the center of the Debris Ring.

He had known her when she was a human artist. Her life had always been part of her performance art but she really pushed the envelope when she downloaded into a spookball and left her body behind forever. She hadn't explained why she came back after being a pretty high level bodhisattva in training, and he didn't ask. That's what old friends are for.

No need to take up floor space when you didn't need the floor anyway; a few hover screens, other workspace up near the ceiling and a docking tee mounted on the wall sufficed for Frida. Anything else, she could manifest for the both of them, breakfast in Paris, nights in Tunisia. *New Carthage now.* So, he puttered, she buzzed and they kept each other company. It was a good arrangement.

She had missed the flood. It was more than five years in the past but it still haunted Larr; he wasn't just being patronizing with his Silicon Grave series and other somber art, working through his grief just like everyone else who couldn't get out of the Bay Area.

He would have left a long time before if he'd had the money. You could sign on to the Cult and spend some time learning mantras and begging around stupas for a free transit. But, if he had about twenty g's in bitcoin, he could get a quick astronaut/a-roid course and get out to a really new neighborhood.

Then he would transfer his lease to Frida. At one time she was pretty famous and had a lot of followers visiting her in the woods near Santa Cruz. Those devotees as well as Cult groupies were starting to find her again. She would be able to use the space when he was gone to accommodate them, so she wasn't really unhappy either that Larr might have his ticket off planet.

She was focusing on her art of descriptive experience as she did when she was human. Now she had the experience of being a data stream, a devotee, a guru and a bodhisattva in training. From each of these experiences she had taken a physical object around which to start the web of her art. Just like old times.

Larr didn't have to go to the Library, though it was a must see on the Way. He might just rent an old miner's shack on Vesta and live out his natural life, or maybe get cybernetics if everything turned out ok, maybe a little fembot action would make him want to live longer. And if everything went to hell, a spookball or a one way ticket through the Library on Moving Day made death just another adventure.

Examining the clamshell on Silicon Grave #9, Frida said, "Well what do you think it is?"

"It looks like a graviton capacitor of some kind with a rheostat control like a dimmer switch."

"Sounds romantic."

"No, it's not for atmosphere, it could deliver a graviton burst with some accuracy, maybe for a spot welder or precision retro, maybe some medical uses. I just liked the way it looked."

"Did you try plugging it in?"

"Do you want me to?"

"I have delicate circuitry."

"Me too, plus brains and bones. No, I make a point of *not* plugging shit in, safer that way."

Frida said, "Power one up with a delay switch, throw it out the window and see what happens."

"Really? How 'bout I give you one to play with *after* I'm gone, since you're disembodied already."

"I would like to contemplate one for a descriptive piece."

"I can never tell when you're joking, but sure." Larr heard a ping on his phone-pad. A round face filled the screen. Larr said, "Frankie, I figured out your cosplay deal, Sidney Greenstreet in Casablanca."

"With a fez, right, right, and The Maltese Falcon, 'I like to talk to a man who likes to talk to a man who likes to talk.'"

"We'll always have Paris."

"Or San Jose; but he died from being too fat, you know, gotta get some jazzercise going, right, right? Anyway, I got the first installment, ten g's to start. I'll put it in your account as earnest money, just send me the numbers."

"Sure," he sent a packet over and heard the theme from *Gone With the Wind* from Frankie's phone, signaling receipt. Frankie sang, "La *La!* De Dah, La *La!* De Dah, *Frankie* my dear I don't give a damn! Get it? Frankie? Instead of *Frankly*? Har har, *Fiddle de dee*, ok man here it comes like a Hank Aaron line drive. Get out the mustard and rye bread Grandma, it's a Grand Salami!"

Larr's phone-pad made a less creative beep. "I wish everybody was as happy as you to give me money."

"You know how some see a glass half empty and some see it half full? I just see a shot glass, so small it's either full or empty, nothing in between. More than a mouthful is a waste.

A little bit of happiness goes right down the hatch, smooth and easy, spoon fulla sugar, don't worry about it so much. I'm like a big grizzly bear, in a salmon stream; we still got grizzly bears, right?"

"In Alaska, I hear."

"So, I'm like that bear, I just need to grab one fish every once in a while, don't need all the fish. I get just what I need, no reason to be dissatisfied."

"Nice philosophy, maybe you have less stress, singing and dancing all the time."

"You know, Larr, an insincere smile will actually make you happy, muscles create the brain state, not the other way round. So, I smile as much as I can; song in my heart, ready for love."

Larr said, "But there are some people out there that might screw you; but you just keep on like Pollyanna?"

"Sure, and yeah, got screwed already more than once, but the defense mechanism still works, don't get cynical. Life is like a box of chocolates, right? But no, I just assume that people have good intentions, usually they do, and so most of the time I'm happy and less stressed in the meantime."

Frida said, "You're a patron saint of something; maybe a bodhisattva."

"Isn't that just a girl thing?"

She laughed, "Heavens to Betsy, no, lots of macho boddhi's all over. Why don't you come by sometime so I can make art about you?"

"Ok, lady, but I don't do nudes. Har har. Gotta go, see you on Tuesday next. Better have the goods Rico or it's curtains."

Larr said, "Next time wear a fez."

Frankie tipped his fedora and said, "No chance man, don't want to look ridiculous, right, right?"

*

Now that he actually was leaving, Larr did ask Frida what made her come back to the old planet. She was manifesting her old garden grotto in a forest meadow near Santa Cruz. She said, "It's complicated, people have different reasons for getting into the Cult. But if it's a true calling, a person has some kind of experience that makes faith and belief logical. That was true even though it looked like there were no mysteries anymore and all the old religions took it on the chin.

"People still get up and take on the robe and mala because they have a personal experience. The Cult started as the mediator of that experience, but soon it was the administration of the brick and mortar face of the faith. It has to deal with infrastructure, utilities, potholes and politics, just like any government.

"We encouraged people to go on the Way, to leave their prior existence behind. It was kind of like the old householder turned mendicant idea of Hinduism. You did your time as a family man and then went out in the woods and provided a living testament to spirit, it was useful.

"But, see, all this shit happened; the mid-21st century climate change deniers just revved up the process until it was obvious. The sea level rose, the interiors of continents are becoming deserts like the outback, the tundra became prairie and the temperate zones became rain forests, jungles. The old first world had nowhere to go really but off-planet. The Cult already had the Way and so why not?

"They left a lot of anger behind, among the people who didn't have the resources or desire to go. It's not a Disneyland cruise when the end is a one way ticket to another dimension, unless you really, really want that. So, the 20% left and took their resources and donated them to the Cult. The 80% still had nothing.

"Jeff Bezos had a vision in high school that Dan Pritchard inherited; his valedictorian speech was about colonizing the solar system and a plan to keep the Earth as a garden for the colonists to visit. But it was like letting the Titanic sink on purpose because you had a life raft. They led the planet down the road to hell and never figured out how to pay the fare, or even pay the gardeners.

"Anyway, I stopped wanting to do my bit by just fixing potholes. I might take the final jump someday, but it's not going to be part of some package tour, m'sayn?"

Larr said, "I think I understand, I'm going in the opposite direction, but I'll be broke. I'm leaving all my possessions here, gonna leave all my keys on the counter and just go walkabout."

Frida smiled, "You'll do just fine; I can see you in overalls tending sheep on Vesta."

"Ah yes, and finally, I'll have time to write that novel."

"And I want to watch how the world changes. I'm not immortal but, barring a coronal mass ejection, I should be around for some time. And the Earth will survive, with 20% of the population gone, the part with the biggest energy consumption anyway, a burden has been lifted off the Earth."

"Under new management?"

"Yeah, I want to see what happens and interpret that for the people who are in need of beauty and art. People do need it. It's a fundamental road to the divine, and you don't need a temple, a stupa or a bodhisattva really. I want to watch the changes and help all sentient beings with art."

"Someplace less stinky than this swamp?"

"I can't really smell it, or I can make shit smell like roses, is more like it. But yeah, it's not pretty but there is still beauty in it. I'll get back to the woods once I get some administrative groupies again."

A week later, Frankie showed up in person with the final ten g's, and took possession of a baker's dozen of the clamshells. He brought Larr a fez and they all got together and took a selfie.

Frida said, "You're not such a bad guy, Frankie. Larr's going hitchhiking but I'll be here. Stop by anytime."

"Ok Doll, hey, why don't we get one of those fembot prosthetics, you just hook up to the docking port and then. . ."

"Let's just be friends first, ok?

"Ok baybee, my love is pure and chaste from afar."

"You might get more action if you didn't do that. . . that thing you do."

"Tell me something I don't know. But, the one girl that likes it, that's the girl for me, just gotta be patient."

Frida said, "You do have good qualities, other than the fact you'll end up in jail sooner or later. I'll see if I can do some matchmaking with a performance artist. They like to take risks."

"Or those girls with the hula hoops and the ones that can bend like a pretzel? They got moves, right?"

"It's nice to be nice, Frankie. Practice that first. Now run along. Gotta shut down for a while. I'm tierd of the novies."

Frankie blew a kiss at Frida and Larr started toward the door. A thought hit him and he turned.

"Where're you hitchhiking to with the bitcoin anyway?"

"I was thinking I'd get upstairs and hop a slagship to Vesta, why?"

"You got to get to a space elevator first, that's the trickiest part, everybody's on standby nowadays unless you got a lot of cash."

"I know, so what would you suggest?"

"I got a guy, Frosty, at the Oakland Suborbport, got a Lear Spaceplane, first come, first serve, and when the ride's full, off he goes, wild blue yonder, blue-black yonder, anyway." Frankie dug for a card in the depths of his fraying wallet, pulled out a wad, unfolded it and handed it to Larr. "He runs shuttles for the Cult so the wait's not too long if he's there. Tell him Frankie sent you."

"Of course, thanks. Hey don't forget the clams."

He took a step back in and grabbed the box. "See, that? Frida distracted me with her feminine wiles. Dames! Toodles!"

*

In another half an hour, Frankie was pulling up to Brodie's house in Daley City. This time he was lugging the clamshells up the stairs in a plastic crate. It was a lot slower than the last time when he did it unburdened. He whistled show tunes from *La La Land* while he was resting between five-stair lugs. But, soon enough, he gave the hotdog password to Blossom, entered and put the crate on the floor. Brodie had a duffle bag packed with a change of clothes and personal necessities and a suitcase open on the floor filled with foam that had compartments cut out in the shape of the cylinders he had constructed.

Frankie said, "Just gotta snap these clams on those things and you're done. You know, they look kind of like camping lanterns. Is that what you're going to tell the bouncers at the suborbport? You're the lantern salesman?"

"Looking for an honest man?"

"Uh huh, like Diogenes, see I know stuff."

"The suborbport bouncers are just like everybody else, mercenaries. I just have to pay the proper fare, and these things follow me right along. First I'm going to Mt. Angel and then to Geneva, to CERN."

Brodie offered his low rent digs to Frankie who had been living with his mother while he got some financial problems worked out; the ten grand he made off of this deal had got him out of his old bedroom not soon enough.

Brodie said, "I have a lot of faith in you Frankie. You're a loyal and honest crook. I don't know how long I'll be away; don't know if I will get back at all."

"Black ops; the shadow government?"

He grinned. "Things you don't know Frankie, things you shouldn't know, things you *can't* know. Listen, take care of Blossom. He likes you and you need some protection. I've left an account in your name with enough money to keep you and Blossom in kibbles and bits for his lifetime anyway. Will you do that for me?"

"God, Brodie, of course I will. We'll get along just fine. We'll watch *Rin Tin Tin* and *Beethoven,* Animal Planet 24 - 7."

"Don't let him get fat like you. Both of you get out and walk every day, ok?"

"Ok, yeah, we'll get each other in shape. We'll get on the treadmill like George Jetson and Astro."

Brodie shook Frankie's hand and kissed him on the forehead. "You're a real human being, and a real hero, potentially. Frankie, just keep being you, don't compromise "

"Like Sinatra, Gotta be me and I did it my way."

"Thanks pal, See you later."

Outside, a Huber honked and Brodie gave Blossom a hug and the same kiss on the forehead. Blossom gave a little whine and licked Brodie on the cheek. Then he said Woof! *Get outa' here kid, don't like long goodbyes, This? Jus' got somethin' in my eye, get outa' here, willya?* Woof!

The cab door slammed and Brodie was off on his next adventure. Frankie turned on the streamer.

"Well, wattle yav, *Puppy Party 3* or *Classic Kats in Boxes?*"

Woof!

"Ok, *Puppy Party 3* it is."

*

The Huber took Skyline to John Daly Drive and the 280 into San Francisco; then the 101 west to the Presidio past the Golden Gate Bridge Memorial. It was a lone tower commemorating lives lost in the disaster. The reconstructed causeway had a roundabout skirting the tower so you couldn't help being reminded of the death and destruction. The 101 was still just above the water, but what used to be park and viewpoints between 101 and the Bay was submerged.

The Cult now owned the Presidio. The main buildings were converted to classrooms, temples and performance venues. The landmark cupola had been transformed into a stupa. At the top of the old structure, they had placed their mystic calling card. *I saw Beauty. . .It was my Destiny. Therein lies all. Södergran.*

Södergran. He had seen it a hundred times, in his peripheral vision as he ran different parts of his plan, scenario by scenario, through his mind. *Beauty . . .Therein lies all.* He attended classes, special tutoring sessions, voice training for mantras, learned the whole catechism of the imagined lives of

Dan and Charlotte, B.C., before Charlotte, F.S. but had not yet looked at the Cult deeply. *I saw Beauty . . .It was my Destiny.*

He had been immersed in cognitive dissonance most of his life. First, it was abuse at the hands of his own family. Then it was his anger at the structures and strictures of every part of normal he brushed against. He had his own path, his own truth and coming right down to it, he did not suffer fools, or metaphor, or fairy tales, even when they were useful.

He did not think that he was the arbiter of truth, but he worked so hard at it, at finding true things, that he couldn't abide with any lack of struggle in those around him. It wasn't important to him what truth they arrived at, but that they struggle for it, that people find the hard truths that they don't want to believe. His personality was abrasive and he was not understood on this point most of the time. He didn't understand himself most of the time, but he kept looking and examining what he did and why he did it.

When he put on his robe and mala and went to the Presidio he knew it was a lie. Since the NUF's followed the Cult following Brodie he enrolled under an assumed name, Walter Sandifur. And though the lie had utility, it actually did bother him so he began to listen and look for true things even in the Cult. Speaking to a fellow student after class early on, Brodie took him aside and explained that there was a real history of flesh and blood human beings behind all the parables and scriptures, that it was not that long ago really and you could find that real history if you wanted to see it. He went chapter and verse through the 'truths' of the Cult and exposed them for what they were. And the student said to him, *Yes, that may be true, but you don't have to be a dick about it.*

He began to see the oldest wisdom, still passed down; that myth, metaphor, poetry and allegory contained more truth than what was declared as fact by those in authority at any particular moment. After that, he didn't hate the Cult, or rather he realized the Cult was subversive enough to earn his respect. He absorbed its more amorphous truths and, even though he was pretending, the experience stripped away some of the discord within him. Instead of increasing his cognitive dissonance, he found the truth was soft and pliable, and didn't always have to be struggled for or pounded against.

He still wanted to blow it all up, but that was a political stance, a means to an end. The syncretist perennial philosophy had been there before the Cult and would survive the Cult. He came to know that he did not have to rage against it, but took from it what was valuable precisely because it was not factual.

With this realization, he stopped and looked at the inscription and took it in. *I saw Beauty. . .It was my Destiny. Therein lies all.* Wheels began to turn, like a giant clockwork dragon set out before him, where one switch or click of a lever started springs uncoiling, flywheels spinning, and momentum transferred until at the end of it the dragon's jaws snapped open and fire shot forth with all the energy hidden within matter by the Beauty of just one equation.

The Cult wanted this metaphor of Beauty. Under all the infrastructure and bureaucracy, was this *experience* that made faith logical. It was an *experience* that made people want to become mendicants and perennial pilgrims and give all their worldly goods to the Cult. If there was injustice in this, the very same experience blinded the pilgrims to it. Brodie began to think that this light could be turned back to illuminate the worlds. And for the first time, his cynicism shrank and it seemed to him that the worlds could change.

This night was the last of a series of seminars leading up to Moving Day, the event being held annually on April first. Brodie met with his mentor monk Bob. He said, "Blessings of Xià lǜ di upon you."

"And upon you," said the burly man with a shaved head and a few days growth of stubble. Bob had once been a fixture at Rock Bottom on the Debris Ring.

Bob the Builder had been his gang name. In those days, he sported coveralls and a yellow safety helmet. The gangs included his own post-soviet polyglot cohort, sharing the Russian language as well as greed, cruelty and terror. He had reached a position of relative calm and safety, by terrorizing all contenders into submission and running a protection racket on black marketeers with the tacit approval of 3MI and the Cult. *Nice joint you got here Sergei Ivanovich, be a shame if anything happened to it...*

It had all gotten a bit too dangerous and monotonous as he aged. In the course of this business however, he had met and befriended Pinky Sheridan, F.S. and Tom Petty, III, the sacred and secular leaders of everything and everyone legitimate in the Ring.

Pinky had told him the story of Ahimsala, the murderer who had claimed 999 victims, keeping track by collecting a finger from each. When he met the Buddha on the road, he was determined to make him his 1,000th victim. But, as Ahimsala ran as fast as he could after the Buddha, the Buddha stayed out of reach walking at a leisurely pace. Because of this magical display, and the Buddha's subsequent forgiveness and compassion, Ahimsala became a monk and one of the Buddha's most devoted and tireless disciples.

Bob took this to heart, seeing only more violence in his future. He left Rock Bottom to its turf war and a mop up operation that Tommy accomplished with Bob's inside information. Bob followed Pinky Sheridan on the Way. Even in his robe and tonsure, however, his Bob the Builder persona broke through as he greeted Brodie with a big Slavic bear hug.

"Walt my friend, privyet, right on time like usual, can't be too punctual or too clean, people won't trust you, but just a formality now, such a good student you are. Have you made your decision?" There was still a bit of vodka in the air around him, combined with cigarette smoke and cheap aftershave. "You know I have Bob, it's never changed." He gave Bob a big man pat on the back as they disengaged

"So I could not dissuade you from this horseshit madness of yours?"

"Madness is relative like everything else."

"Ok Einstein, khorosho, just another formality. I'm here for less excitement, I do respect your choice, but no guarantees; again, my friend, we are at a threshold where no one has returned with answers."

"And yet, we all seem to go there."

"Eventually, what's the rush? But, not my job, so the final *transitus* is your destination, flying on faith as it should be."

"I have my itinerary, a few places to go first."

"Mt. Angel has confirmed your stay there until you head for the Debris Ring temple. Here's your intro, talk to Frosty for the suborbital connection."

Brodie took the flyer and Bob's blessing then received the purple sash of the pilgrim, said goodbye to the underclassmen he had lapped and to Bob, another big hug, a man pat and tears. Well, Bob cried anyway.

Outside the temple, once again, Brodie read the invocation of Beauty. *It was my Destiny. Therein lies all.* "Well, okay, then," he said to himself as he took off the robe, folded it neatly and stowed it in one of saddlebags of a motor pool hoverbike. He put the suitcase in the other saddlebag then sped away from the Presidio and south past San Francisco, Frankie and Blossom and into the woods of Santa Cruz. At the old Humphrey Go Bart station at the UCSC campus, his second in command of the New United Futurists took possession of all but three of the graviton devices.

*

After the bitcoin deposit was confirmed, Larr said his only goodbye to Frida and hopped a flatboat from the QED to a passenger tug at Old Bay for the trip to Oakland. He took Frankie's advice and at the end of that run asked for directions to Frosty's hanger at the suborbport. The tug captain pointed north of the dock at a cluster of hangers on the far side of the abandoned terminal.

Larr only had his one duffel bag. His art was in Frida's care to sell however she wished and split the profits. Really, he had just the clothes on his back, a change of clothes in the duffel and some personal items.

Dad used his one pair of socks and skivvies as washrags in the bath, then hung them out clean to dry by the morning. Besides, they had grocery stores and civilization enough on Vesta. No need to get weighed down. A song on my lips, the wind at my back and. . . love . . . or something like that.

He had his phone-pad with its gravitel booster package. That gizmo was all anyone needed for communication, streaming, snapshots, video apps, art and science. A 3D printer database meant he could make anything else he needed anywhere. Even the favelas in the Debris Ring had 3D printers. They weren't quite at the quality of Star Trek pattern buffers and replicators yet, *Tea, Earl Grey, Hot*, but good enough if you needed a shoe or a hat, even a crown or a spare kidney for that matter.

Larr's plan was to get to the Cult hub at Mt. Angel and then to the Space Elevator in Geneva. It wasn't as roundabout as it seemed. When Benedictine monks built a monastery and seminary at Mt. Angel, Oregon in the 1800's, they had been sent out from their monastery at Engelberg, Switzerland and still had that connection. Engleberg actually means, "Angel Mountain," though in Switzerland it was the Alps and in Oregon it was just a hill.

Even though the current monks professed to the Cult, as much as anyone had to publically, the old ties were strong. It helped that Mt. Angel was a Waypoint, where the Bodhisattva Xià lù di, before her first transitus, had planned to study the creation of icons. The part of the story that was commonly performed at Moving Day services had the dying Charlotte beseeching Petra Rousseau to take her to Mt. Angel to study under Brother Claude, the monastery's master iconographer. She wanted to create a window to heaven, an icon showing the Archangel Michael carrying her to meet her Maker, Creator Mundi, she called him.

Besides, practically speaking, the Cult was the one outfit that still made the planes run on time, sort of. Larr easily walked the quarter mile from the dock to the hangers. Like everything else after the flood, the hanger was a bit rusty and worse for wear. In it however, was a sleek new Lear Spaceplane; built on the tried and true Challenger 650 platform with two turbo jet engines, one on either side of the tail with graviton boosters beneath. These conserved fuel and gave the extra push needed to go suborbital for the majority of the great circle routes preferred by the economy minded jet jockeys.

As he walked up to the hanger the captain had indicated, a tall man on a rolling ladder platform was leaning into the port graviton booster banging on something inside with an old analog torque wrench, cussing, "fuckashitpiss!" and leaning precariously further in, keeping one toe on the ladder as it rolled back and forth with each blow. *Bang, Bang, Bang, Bang.* On the back of his denim coveralls was embroidered a hyperbolic cursive slogan *All Shook Up!* with musical notes scattered around it.

Larr said, "I think you need a bigger torque wrench!"

The man started, banged his head on the inside of the booster *Bang* and sent the rolling ladder skittering away as his toes now hung three feet above the ground. "Shitgod*dam*muthuhfuckah! Mader chod!" Then he let himself slowly down until his pointy toed winkle pickers touched the ground.

He was about six foot six, and as he turned around rubbing his head, Larr could see his embroidered name above the breast pocket 'Frosty.'

"Sorry, you must be Frosty?"

"Sarrite brotha', not allowed to murder paying customers."

"Blessings of Xià lù di on that."

"Got that right; we all owe some thanks to that broad. Nice to be employed though, right?"

Frosty's coveralls evoked an Elvis Las Vegas jumpsuit done up in denim with nuts and bolts and washers sewn on instead of sequins. An oil rag like a big sash and a dyed black duck's ass do rounded out the picture.

"Elvis meets Johnny Cash? Not what the reenactors would do."

"Nah, I'm just in it for laughs. A streamer star I flew around on charters before the flood gave it to me; had the suit made in Bollywood. It's held up pretty well. And I can play weddings and bar mitzvas. Where you headed?"

"Mt. Angel and then Geneva."

"Alright, you'll be on standby but so's everybody except the big boddhi's. My crew still has to fix the boosters and I gotta wangle some jet fuel. Got any liquid bitcoin?"

"Yeah," Larr put his duffel down and pulled out his phone pad. "Is that in addition to the fare?"

"That is the fare, mostly; cash, grass or ass, you know."

Frosty paused and then laughed, "I'm just messin' with you. Once we get a full tank, we'll settle up. Usually, the pilgrims show up at the last minute and the Cult is good pay. But, still gotta fill the tank, the gas wallahs don't do credit."

Larr sent a bitcoin packet over to Frosty's phonepad and Frosty slapped it on his hand as it chimed its receipt. "K, be back by flight time." He started across the taxiway to the gas wallahs. No pipeline survived in the flood zone so fuel was arriving in salvage tankers, on flatbeds in fifty gallon drums and other more prosaic transport, even jerry cans strapped to mules and camels.

Three spookballs buzzed in to finish the torque wrench banging on the boosters. They sported virtual do's like Frosty's, shinier sequins and names emblazoned, Jerry Lee, Johnny and Elvis. Larr stepped back as they went about their tasks. He thought, *Everybody's gotta have a gimmick.*

He sat down at a picnic table outside the hanger while a few pilgrims trickled in, in ones and twos. Some had robes and malas, seminarians, some civilian pilgrims. Some were just starting their life in the Cult, still in their street clothes, like recruits showing up for boot camp not knowing what to expect. They nodded or namaste'd and he blessed them back.

Then, about thirty more pilgrims and boots came on a bus from the staging stupa at Sacramento, now the easternmost port on the New Bay. Milling about, talking among themselves and comparing itineraries on phone-pads, they ignored Larr but turned as one when a hover cycle blasting an internal combustion roar bore down on them from the tarmac. The seminarians recognized their class clown right away.

"Walt!"

"Bout time brotha'."

"Thought you woulda been excomm'd by now you heretic."

Brodie laughed and dismounted, pushing the hover cycle into the hanger.

"What a pack of cards. Keep your adoration in check man. I'm just another padawan, m'sayn?"

He laughed again and indulged in hugs and man pats.

Larr watched without recognition, since he hadn't known the identity of Frankie's money man. But there was something. He saw what appeared to be a late middle aged man with a sun bleached blonde buzz cut, about 5'5" still muscular; way more than the classic mendicant. He was cell checked and cyborged as much as anybody could be without a full reboot, so chronological age could be . . . *Walter Brodie? Larr thought. That would make him about a hundred and five?* Not unusual if you had the money. *He certainly should have the money. I thought he was dead.*

He wasn't sure, but anybody of his generation would have known the features, even aged, of the mad inventor who dropped out of sight after making FTL flight possible. The kids here wouldn't know, but Larr did. On the other hand, Brodie knew exactly what Larr looked like from his webnet site, but wouldn't let on. He looked back over to Larr, gave him an upnod, joined him at the picnic table and offered his hand.

"Walt; sup' brotha' cool kids won't let you sit at their table?"

Larr said, "Ha! More like the nerds won't let me sit at *their* table."

"They'll warm up to you; just young, shy and paranoid, like Catholic school boys at their first day in public school."

Then, a man approached, younger than Brodie, short as well but not so muscular, civilian clothes with a fanny pack, a man purse and black rimmed glasses.

Brodie said, "Hey, this is S. C. Schneider, famous journalist, he's like job shadowing, incognito. Oh, man I just blew your cover."

Schneider said. "Just call me Essey; Walt christened me, but I like it. I'm working on a story for the GP. . . about the pilgrimage, you know, and Walt is a lot more fun than the boots." .

Brodie said, "So we, the older generation, hang and commiserate."

"Hike our pants up to here and complain about the guvmint full time."

Larr shook Schneider's hand, "Larr Yellingson, unemployed artist, or retired artist."

S.C. said, "Where you headed?"

"Relocating or wandering, Geneva and then Vesta."

"Ok then, I'll be riding along to Geneva with Walt. Oh, looks like its boarding time."

A fuel truck approached with Frosty sitting on the hood waving for the passengers to board and the spookballs to finish. Within a few minutes, the spaceplane was fueled and rolling toward the taxiway. Frosty collected bitcoin and Cult vouchers as Jerry Lee and Elvis taxied and cross checked in the cockpit. Johnny buzzed around the outside performing the final check on the graviton boosters. What passed for air traffic control in the flood zone searched the skies with binoculars and then gave a non-committal shrug and thumbs up for take-off.

Over the common channel the passengers heard the usual chatter, no safety lecture though; *Figure it out yourselves. In case of loss of pressure, put your head between your knees and kiss your ass goodbye.* No snacks and drinks from the management but you could bring all the booze you could carry. The seminarians and pilgrims were not adverse to some mystic imbibing and Brodie had a liter of Russian Standard in his duffel bag. S.C. sat across the aisle from Larr and Brodie sat down next to him, set down three metal collapsible cups and poured lime juice and vodka,

"Kamakazi's Comrades?"

"Da, speciba, ochin khorosho."

Larr and S.C. toasted with Brodie, clinked and emptied their cups in one gulp and slammed them down on their tray tables like bolsheys in St. Petersburg. The cups collapsed and sprayed a mist of vodka in the air, creating an atmosphere heady with liquor and mantras.

Brodie said,"Smells like a Moscow restroom now! Sweat and vodka. Anyway, you know what they say, some say a glass is half empty, some say the glass is half full. . ."

Larr finished, "But a shot glass is only full or empty, no worries, bottoms up."

"Hey, where'd you hear that!"

"A funny guy in a bad suit said it."

Brodie poured another round and changed the subject, "Huh; hey you said you're an artist, right?"

"Yeah; of some renown in Watertown; used to be an engineer, sound and gravity."

"Like Sound and Vision."

"Classic Bowie."

"Atswhamsayn, jussayn, m'sayn?" and to no one in particular, "I like this guy!"

All three downed their shots and slammed the cups again; *bang, bang, bang* The boots were now into their cheap wine and piss yellow pilsner, acting like they were really drunk, slapping each other on the ass and reciting dirty limericks. *There once was a monk from Nantucket. . .*

Brodie said, "So, the quote on Beauty, on all the Cult buildings, do you know what that means, as an outsider and an artist?"

S.C. said, "Didn't they test you on that on the finals?"

"Not so much, but, it must have had some meaning before the Cult right?"

S.C. said, "Edith Södergran, early 20th Century modernist feminist spiritual bolshy poet, Swedish Finnish, right across the border from St. Petersburg. Where, by the way, your Russian Standard was made, Lake Ladoga water, recipe by Mendeleev."

"Thanks for the usual useless TMI. Goes with your 20th Century Nerd cosplay, is that it?"

"No, no, no, it's too subtle for you, no pocket protector; therefore, not a re-enactment; therefore, way past cool! You just don't get me Walt."

"If you ever get got, let me know. What did it mean B.C.? What does it mean to the Cult?"

S.C. said. "It's Theological Aesthetics, not art aesthetics."

"Not sure if there's a difference; Larr?"

Larr said, "What did Petra Rousseau say? Beauty as a transcendental, a divine being in the world?"

"Right, what's that all about?"

"Transcendentals are like free agent attributes of the divine in the world. I think people see God in what beauty comprises; even in imperfections. That crosses over, imperfections make art valuable."

S.C. said, "But the word *fair* as in beautiful and *fair* as in 'fair deal' have the same meaning, symmetry, equality and balance. Petra talked about balance too, beauty, truth and goodness out of balance creates evil in the world. That's simplified, but too much emphasis on superficial beauty, like in advertising B.C., created huge social issues, devaluing truth and goodness. Too much goodness maybe ignores truth to a fault; too much truth demolishes goodness and beauty. It means something in the world even if it means something that transcends the world. See."

Larr said, "And the need for social justice made some people suppress art as frivolous and dangerous. Even now, the Futurists don't want the distraction of art, right?"

S.C. and Brodie looked at each other.

S.C. said, "That's what they say anyway."

Brodie said, "Yep, I can never figure them out. "

The boots and pilgrims then started a stadium wave from the front of the spaceplane to the back. Frosty came out of the cockpit and announced. "We will experience weightlessness for about ten minutes now and then head down to Mt. Angel, so put your tray tables and seat backs in their upright position. If you don't fasten your seat belt it's your own damn fault." Then he released a net full of brightly colored plastic balls which began to float and the weightless ball pit game started as everyone ignored Frosty's warnings.

*

The spaceplane landed at what had been a drag strip near Woodburn, Oregon, twelve miles from Mt. Angel. The Portland suborbport hadn't faired any better than Oakland, so the Cult had opted for self-reliance and predictability. Besides, Portland was another forty miles further away from the monastery.

The drag strip had been widened and lengthened from a quarter mile to a full mile to accommodate the needs of the Cult and Mt. Angel, specifically, Frosty's Lear spaceplane service. The drag strip had always been surrounded by farms and it now encroached over well-tended wheat fields farmed by reinvigorated Old Believers.

As Larr exited the plane, right before Frosty turned on the hose to rinse out the sweat and vomit of the partying monks, he surveyed a flat valley, stretching off to the south and east, Mt. Hood visible and majestic, as it was on a clear days like this one, and the small town of Woodburn stretched out languid in the sun. Their destination, the hill of Mt. Angel and the former Benedictine monastery upon it, was not visible, lying below the horizon to the southeast.

Wheat shimmered in the sun as golden waves moved over the top of the grain in concert with a warm breeze from the west that blew through the fields, waves that were like living creatures swimming through the medium of the grain tops, things that went through the wheat but were not of the wheat, like waves of light through the ether or ripples coursing through water. Here too, the scythes collapsed the waves of the wheat as surely as a measurement collapses the uncertainty of the quantum wave function.

Larr saw the reapers, Old Believers, split from the Russian Orthodox Church since the 1400's, becoming even more tradition bound since the droughts and the Cult arrived and the economy started to slip back toward a more local, less technological version of itself.

The men in the field were dressed in old fashioned Russian tunics, tied with intricately patterned hand woven belts, hand embroidery at the collar, rough linen drawstring work pants, boots and the traditional apron. As their faith required, they did not cut their beards or the hair around the front of their faces, so that their visage was in the likeness of the God of Abraham, the God in whose image they were created, cut short in back however, a reverse mullet, topped with a kartuz cap. These signified something decidedly other than the strictures of the Cult, though strictures they were, nonetheless.

The women wore shashmuras, the cap and snood that hid the hair of a married woman, the scarf and long single braid being the mark of young girls and unmarried women. They were dressed in peasant sarafans, high yoked jumpers with more embroidery and woven belts, the kind of thing you can do yourself when time is regulated by seasons rather than seconds, seconds these people, who had cell phones and electric cars in the twenty first century, regained as they had to relearn monotasking, relearn what the outward remnants of their traditional culture signified and adapt it to the new conditions of an older future. *Progressively old school.*

In the rows of wheat, a line of men and teenage boys used wooden handled scythes in a curving sweeping motion to cut the grain in rhythm to a Russian work song sung in low tones. To the scything men, the tool was an extension of their body, proprioception extending their fingers out into the grass, the stalks surrendering to their sharpened grasp.

Although seeming to be one long machine, the men stopped when necessary and honed their scythes with a stone kept in a copper holster at the ready on the belt, a whetstone soaked in water, quickly and efficiently restoring the edge and then stepping back into the line, like the regrown limb of a many armed beast, a gentle dragon of the wheat.

Women gathered the wheat into bundles and threw them onto hay wagons, high sided carts drawn by mules or ponies, while girls brought ladles of water to the men and boys. Incongruously, a few spookballs buzzed in and out helping to load the wagons and taking the reins with articulated waldoes. They had probably been symbiotic with Old Believers in this very community. How did the Old Believers deal with this incursion of technology and transmigration of souls? They had adapted, just as they had in their wanderings to China, Turkey, Brazil, Alaska and Oregon. Only this time, the strangers were actually long lost members of their own congregation.

As was the custom with any who lapsed in their faith or simply wandered away, the spooks had to ask in front of the congregation to be allowed to rejoin the faithful. Inevitably, with humans, the answer had been a Christian 'yes', so why not now with spooks? After all, the Old Believers had been staying out of linear time and embracing magical rituals for centuries, ultimately dating back to the 800's when the Byzantine tradition from Constantinople was transplanted into the frozen muck and slush of the land of the Rus.

There was no terminal of any kind at the drag strip/airstrip, just an administration building made from the old concessions center. Here too, amateurs with binoculars served as air traffic control. As Larr, Brodie, Schneider and the other passengers hefted their duffel straps to their shoulders and, hands shading their eyes, squinted in the sun along the dirt road bordering the fields, the men and women stopped their labors and looked back at the arrivals, the one man at the nearest end turning and shading his eyes as well then pointing to a buckboard parked next to their loading dock where the wheat bundles were being transferred to larger wagons for the run to the communal threshing floors and silos.

"Posmotri tuda! Over there!" The men resumed their song and reaping.

Up ahead, a man on a horse turned from the buckboard and trotted over to the group. He was tall in the saddle, over six feet in his boots, jeans and chaps, now a necessity with lack of county noxious weed control, a western cut shirt and cowboy hat. An impressive and well-earned tan set off salt and pepper short cropped hair, long sideburns and mustache. Almost comically, he sported a large silver star on his breast, engraved with the word 'Sheriff.' He pulled on the reins and clicked his tongue to the horse as he began to speak.

"Privyet pardners, I'm with Mt. Angel, Logistics for the Cult; name's Georgi Garoldovich Latropov, but you can call me Dusty."

Dusty looked directly at Brodie at the front of the group as he spoke and then tipped his hat to the rest. "You folks seem to be a bit short on ladies this trip; well, less danger of kidnapping that way, I reckon, but I'd tuck up those skirts boys, the natives might get confused."

He laughed as the monks looked at each other nervously. "I'm just messin' with ya' guys; don't need get your knickers in a twist. Get on up to the transport wagon, and we'll get to the frat house this afternoon in time for dinner; takes about four hours. The monks will take charge of you from there. Until then, you're all mine, ladies. Let's move on up to the platform."

They started moving then and when they reached the wagon, threw their duffels on board and, hiking up their robes, boarded from the platform. Dusty said, "Y'all do just fine. Vladimir here's driving and I'll protect the flanks. Relax." He pronounced the name 'Vla-dee-meer,' like a real Russian

Larr said, "What happened to cognitive dissonance?"

Brodie said, "What? Aren't there Russian cowboys on the steppes, Cassocks?"

"Kazaks, maybe, not cowboys."

"The re-enactors and the luddites are just blurring lines, who knows anymore? Just go with it Comrade Pardner. The climate and political changes affected everyone differently. In the Old Bay the disasters just broke things down faster. Here, the reaction was to take on old traditions more seriously, to survive and prepare for whatever's next.

"Re-enactment is becoming more of a necessity than a hobby; of course it's going to evolve. If Dusty Georgi wants to innovate and contribute in his own way like he's the law in these here parts, well and good. These people will need him more than ever pretty soon, and when he calls for a posse, those dancing bears will be very impressive with their scythes and pitchforks, ochin khorosho, I say."

Brodie pulled on Larr's arm to launch him over the rail, landing him on some hay right behind the driver and then settled in close as the horses started to pull away. Schneider piled in the back with the monks, now all old pals. Vladimir slapped the reins on the horses' backs and encouraged them forward with a Russian whinny and gittyup.

"e'e'ee go-go, e'e'ee go-go! Durov! Geedjahp!"

The buckboard lurched forward and then settled into a rhythm, a rhythm combining the sound of the horse's hoofs and the washboard ripples of the road into a jarring lullaby for the bobble headed passengers toying with siestas.

It was twelve miles down the road to Mt. Angel, first passing through the old town of Woodburn, then stopping under the I-5 hoverway to water the horses and let the passengers stretch their legs. Every so often, an auto-semi would woosh past overhead or the whine of a hover cycle would wax and wane, mostly heading north. In a bit higher breezeway, a phalanx of spookballs in a 'v' like Canada geese were headed northeast.

Civilization, while planting various flags in Canada and Siberia, had mostly left these midlanders below to govern themselves. The southernmost major city, major inhabited city, in North America was now Seattle. Beyond that it was a mix of high tech and DIY communities, floundering among the excessive pyramids of no longer necessary infrastructure, like ancient Roman aqueducts still standing and in use by the new favelas of Truscany, once again surrounded by the faded ruins of civilization, temples dismembered to build shacks and outhouses.

The monks stared at the graffiti on the concrete supports of the hoverway. *NUF said! - No one here gets out alive! - Everybody got to fight to be free!* and other more obscure messages, were painted over the tags, slogans and boasts of the disaffected of prior generations, their particular struggles now forgotten, their paint built up in layers like slate in fossil beds waiting for a future paleo anthropologist to pry apart the delicate sheets and reconstruct the story of these humans.

Schneider said to the monks. "That's the New United Futurists, 'NUF said.' Don't worry, they're not mad at you, not you specifically anyway." He looked down the road to where Dusty had stopped to roll a joint, still on horseback.

Brodie approached Dusty, his duffel on his shoulder, and stood beside the horse as they engaged in a private conversation. Dusty passed the joint down, Brodie took a toke and passed it back up. When the conversation had ended and just before he turned to head back to the wagon, with one quick motion Brodie took a package out of his duffel and placed it in Dusty's saddlebag, patting the horse's flank with the other hand. Dusty nodded and then turned to the monks. "Head 'em up! Move 'em out! "

Larr said, "Yeah, keep them dogies movin'," then to the monks, "He just means get in the wagon," They nodded, hiked up their robes again and got back in the buckboard

The road ran through more fields, through the even smaller ghost town of Gervais and south onto Howell Prairie as farmland again became the main feature, interspersed with stands of trees originally planted as windbreaks or as ornamentals, now marking the footprint of a house and yard that no longer existed, silent sentinels waiting for picnics, rope swings and stolen kisses to resume beneath their boughs.

Approaching the town of Mt. Angel, things took on a more modern look, spookballs and hovercycles interspersed with electric cars, internal combustion being *tres outré*. The combination of old and new was not just a courtesy to the Old Believers. In an uncertain world, there is utility in not depending upon one technology when you can survive through hard times without it. But, since Mt. Angel was a Cult Waypoint, transfer station and administrative center it had actually grown and thrived since the 21st century.

Clip-clopping down its busy Main St., Dusty tipped his hat to ladies on the sidewalk and traded howdy's with others. They passed the Mt. Angel Market and the Bierhaus, still advertising 'Millennial Oldies Karaoke Friday,' a reassuring 'Est. 1968' and the uncertainty of 'Under New Management.' After turning onto College St. and passing St. Mary's, where Petra Rousseau had spent her final years as a Benedictine oblate, they began to glimpse the hill of St. Benedict's peeking through the trees and finally, after turning up Abbey Drive and cresting the hill, the monastery and seminary came into view. Roused from their rocking slumber, the boots became excited to see the site of their future ordination into the theocracy of the Cult.

Dusty announced, "All right gentlemen, this is the end of the road for you monkeys. Anyone continuing on will ride with Vladimir back to the airstrip in two days. We are waiting for some arrivals also headed on to Geneva. Sorry to say you will not bask in my joyous company, I'm headed to Seattle for a bit. Don't worry, there'll be another drover to make sure you get back to Frosty's in one piece."

Larr asked Brodie, "Why don't they just move the airstrip here?"

"It's good PR for the Cult and the Old Believers are happy to have the Cult around; in case things go bad they'll have powerful friends. By going back and forth on these roads we show the flag a bit, in case anybody thinks the old traditions signify weakness. And the Cult doesn't want to be seen as just sending dilettantes into orbit, holed up on this hill."

An elderly monk walked out on the front step and beckoned to the three men. Brodie said, "Let's go meet the head honcho."

Brother Ambrose led them into the monastery and showed them to the monk's cells where they would spend the night, then invited them to dine and have some of the house wine, still made on the premises.

After introductions and a good repast, Schneider asked, "I'm curious, as a journalist, about the unique situation of the abbey here within the Cult. I mean, up here, sometimes it seems nothing has changed? Are you Benedictines at heart?"

"Of course we are," Brother Ambrose chuckled, "The Cult doesn't care what is in our hearts and we continue to minister to the same people and clergy as before. We are busier, yes, but the seminary is full, and the monks still need our guidance, our group history, how to work and live together addressing physical, mental and spiritual needs. Benedict's Rule works regardless of the heaven you believe in.

Meditation and mysticism, the bedrock of the Cult, these are things all religions practice. Religion is just something humans do; we all have that much in common."

Larr said, "But isn't all of that essentially a way to create a social structure?"

Brother Ambrose said, "From the nuclear family to empires, it seems religion serves that purpose. But the other part is an experience, the ineffable experience of oneness. Before the Cult, melting into the divine was difficult; now, that reality is very close, Purgatory, Over There or just close your eyes."

"Close as your jugular vein."

"Yes, yes, Allah is that close."

"And the God of Abraham?"

"El and Yahweh; they'll do just fine."

"And Jesus?"

"Yeshua Bar Yehosef was a man. Jesus the Christ is a metaphor. Paul did not write about Yeshua; he created the Christ out of whole cloth, but he and the Church Fathers understood that the Christ had to fit into neo Platonic spirituality. Actually, that metaphor has just as much truth in it as all the others embraced by the Cult. Von Balthazar, Charlotte's own guide, wrote that it was the idea of the resurrection that was important, not the fact of it. It is only fiction that holds truth."

Brodie said, "That's how Christianity treated other religions, as filled with myths. But now, we all look in the same mirror. All fingers pointing to the same sun."

Larr said, "That seems so liberal."

"The Cult isn't spiritually oppressive but it guards its myths so their truths aren't diluted by inconvenient facts; that emphasis keeps them out of touch with the hearts and minds of those left behind."

"And you monks can do more good inside the Cult?"

Brother Ambrose explained, "Simone Weil would say we stand outside to show the universality of the truth within, that the truth doesn't need the structure of a Church. As long as she stood outside, the *catholic* nature of the Church was confirmed as more than a name. She would not be baptized because that would have separated her from the truth without."

"And the Cult needs this 'without' as well?"

"We would have to say that there is neither within nor without, that the Cult comprises the mysticism of all religions, one finger pointing to one sun. It has always been so."

Ambrose continued, "There was a story told by the Irish called; Rotha Mór an tSaoil; The Great Wheel of Life. A boy was ill-treated by his father and ran away from home. A wealthy farmer found him huddled and hungry at the side of a road and took him in. The boy was fed and clothed and treated as his son. The boy asked the farmer why he had been so kind. The farmer said, 'There is a Great Wheel of Life. One day you are on the top and then the wheel will roll and you will be ground into the dirt. We must be kind to those less fortunate because the wheel will put us in their position one day.'

"So, the boy grew up and the farmer paid for his education and sent him to seminary where he was ordained a priest. The priest lost touch with his benefactor as he worked in a number of parishes before settling down in a permanent position in a small town. One day, a stranger came to the door, an old man in rags begging for food. The priest recognized him as the farmer. As he ate the bread the priest offered, the man said 'Father, you remind me of a boy I once knew.' The priest said, 'That is because I am that boy. The wheel has turned and put me in this place where I can help you, and I promise that you will never be homeless or hungry again.'

"At the other end of the world, on the steppes north of Iran, four thousand years ago, a story was told, later written down in the Rig Veda. 'Your companion who does not share when you are in need is not your friend. Let the stronger man give to the man whose need is greater; let him gaze along the lengthening path of life; for riches roll like the wheels of a chariot, from one to the other.'"

"The Good Samaritan."

"And the Great Wheel of Life. The final point I'll add is that both Irish and Sanskrit use the same word for wheel; 'rotha', tracing both back to the Proto Indo European origin of the languages. In Sanskrit, the word is also used to mean 'chariot', while in modern Irish, the word 'rothar' means bicycle."

"That's more than remarkable."

"That's the point Mr. Schneider; the human experience is ultimately one sentient experience from Africa to the stars, an experience now confirmed by spooks and Andromedans at the deepest levels.

"So, happily, we serve no master but that of the oneness of all sentient beings. Here, come along and I will show you our collection of fin de siècle icons by our Brother Claude."

Larr and Brodie begged off, tired after the long sunny ride and headed for their cells. Schneider and Ambrose headed down a long hallway, flanked on each side by icons.

Ambrose commented, "The connection between the Old Believers and St. Benedict's is on display here. There was a priest here, also named Ambrose, more than a hundred years ago when they came here from Brazil. Father Ambrose took it upon himself to minister to these devout people and even started a museum here of Old Believer culture, including icons and other material arts. A young seminarian arrived in the 1970's and was inspired to take up the art of making icons. It's called writing icons, not painting, as the saints and their symbols stand in place of scripture for those who could not read."

The paintings were stylized images of saints and Jesus, without perspective but not quite flattened either, evoking an old style with new beauty. In some, angels were seen taking the faithful into the sky, visions of heaven beckoning them.

The full portraits featured the subjects with halos in different colors and patterns, Roman numerals and letters displayed beside them, their cryptic meanings now the subject of scholarly speculation.

The artist was not adverse to writing a joke or two either; an icon of St. Luke, the patron Saint of Lost Causes, had the birth date of his cousin in Roman numerals. This was presented to the cousin for his birthday of course, with a wink and a nudge. When the cousin died, the icon was left to the monastery.

And then there was Michael the Archangel, the patron saint of the monastery. Brother Claude had created a few of these, but one in particular seemed familiar. St. Michael was holding a small image of the Christ Child, the image surrounded by its own halo, Michael looking adoringly at the image.

Schneider said, "I've seen that one. . ."

A clicking on the slate pavers accompanied by a low hum did not enter his awareness until a voice startled him, "It is the icon of Charlotte's dream, Mr. Schneider."

A spookball floated into the light from a dark passage that led to a chapel and more cells beyond. Beside it walked an Andromedan, female from the size and gait, still a bit of a novelty in person. The bipedal saurian extended a two thumbed clawed hand in greeting. That and the sharped toothed attempt at a smile always gave one pause. She said, 'Sulaimon,' as he gritted his teeth and shook her claw, mimicking her manner, three fingers folded to the palm and the thumb and little finger embracing her thumbs. Less puncture wounds that way. Then the spookball dipped a nod and the electronic voice said, "Petra Rousseau."

Ambrose stepped back as the three began to talk. "Schneider, S.C. for short. I thought you were. . ."

"My presence is not generally known. I'd have too many visitors. I lived here in my body till the end of it. My garden is nearby. Where would I go? We are not anchorites, but choose to stay cloistered to continue our spiritual work as oblates."

Sulaimon said, "And the Cult would rather not have apocryphal versions of the canon, so they don't mind if Petra chooses to be cloistered."

"You're saying the people who actually knew Charlotte might rock the boat?"

She said, "St. Paul had no interest in eye witnesses to the passion of the Christ even though they were his contemporaries. No one needs fact as much as they need truth. I can offer nothing useful to the theocracy here or Over There. Maybe I'm under benevolent house arrest, like Tolstoy, hard to tell. But enough about me Mr. Schneider, I know who you are."

"What do you mean?"

"You are a journalist for the Galactic Press, correct?

"Yes."

"Concentrating on the New Futurists?"

"I have been, yes."

"And yet strangely absent for the past year."

"I'm on sabbatical. Finally going to finish that novel, you know."

Petra buzzed a little closer, inside his comfort zone. "You have access to first-hand information now. You must know something is happening."

"Not specifically."

"No need to 'break cover', so to speak, but I would like to offer you an additional opportunity."

"I'm pretty busy."

"Let's not be cynical, Mr. Schneider, you are already within a very rarified circle, with Mr. Brodie at your service. I could offer you more, another perspective; unique, you must admit. You are positioned to write a story like no other."

"Ok, I'll bite, keep talking."

Sulaimon said, "Something *is* happening, S.C. It is not obvious here in Mt. Angel; nor in Seattle, Fragrant Mountain,

Cape Canaveral; all the Waypoints and Space Elevators, these are oases, sea walls around imagined normalcy. Outside, with the oligarchy, even the upper middle class, off planet, humans on Earth are making their own version of the eternal present, their Dreaming, if you will."

Petra said, "A bit of a bad dream. There is resentment, even anger, directed toward the perceived cause of Earth's poverty being allowed to leave the planet, the self-absorbed dipping their toe into eternity; fiddling while Rome burns, yes?"

The Andromedan continued, "I have been a chronicler of these changes, for our own purposes, continuing our journey with humanity initiated millennia in the past. We will never be inconspicuous but our movements are rarely questioned. It is a paradox, but others become inconspicuous in our company.

"You're the hot chick."

"I think I know what you mean, so yes, and that distraction may be useful to you. There is a need, you see, for Earth's history in this moment to be accurate and unbiased."

"That's what I'm trying to do."

"As a diplomat and historian, I have been given complete access to the Cult archives and the 3MI vaults. I have diplomatic immunity. One can easily see that in order to do my work I must hire an amanuensis. This could be you. Then you will have all sides of this story."

Petra said, "Come here, sit, look." S.C. sat and saw the next icon. It was the same icon of St. Michael, but instead of the Christ Child, an image of Charlotte rested on his hand.

"Is this the original, the one you see on prayer cards and in stained glass?"

"Well, there is no 'original.' Someone created this when Charlotte's story became known, a hundred years ago. It is what she longed to make before her first transitus. If she had made it, then there would be no story. But now it has acquired the adoration of the Cult as did the relics of the true cross and the shroud of Turin and its origin has become steeped in magic. Somehow she did make it after all, or it made itself."

"You can't unwring that bell." Schneider said.

"Yes, S.C., " Petra said, "and even if the facts were revealed now, no one would want them or believe them; they would be met with hostility. It is important then, that someone have access to records that are contemporaneous with events as they occur. There will be access to truth then, when hostility to truth has passed."

"I am honored, I am, but right now, I have to keep moving fast to keep up with my sources."

"There will come a day when you will have time on your hands, or seek refuge in the dharma as all sentient beings do. Then you will know you are welcome here, and you may choose to do this work."

"I will consider it Petra."

"Good, now stay with me a bit longer and I will show you the books that formed the basis of Charlotte's real beliefs."

He followed them into a small room, a monk's cell, this one filled with bookcases. Sulaimon picked a thick book from the shelf and handed it to S.C. Petra said, "This is a book that Charlotte and Daniel read, the very book that knew their gaze. When you come here you may read any of these books. You will know the Bodhisattva better than her devotees. Then you may wish write her story as well."

"What was it like at the beginning, Petra?"

"In the beginning there were two remarkable people who gave and received love. All that came after was an attempt to spread that love to all sentient beings as the means of Encounter with the transcendent. Everything else is unnecessary. Religion is part unfeeling infrastructure and part intimate individual experience of Oneness.

"But, we had no idea what Beauty we held in our hands like a wounded bird nursed to health and then set free with tears and hope. We had no idea then, and now we wander, once again lost, lost but with new companions, listening for the lone voice crying out in the wilderness, calling us home.

"Even so, there is truth in the story as it is now told; that is what must be cherished, that is the way forward. Attend to the Golden Wire Sutra Mr. Schneider. In the end *Love alone is credible.*"

He said, "I believe you will see me again," and bowed to both of them. They took their leave and S.C wandered back to his cell, stopping at the communal bathroom on the way to relieve himself and wash. In his room, an ancient cross was still affixed above the door. On the opposite wall was an image of the Bodhisattva Xià lǜ dì, née Charlotte Pritchard, covering all bases. He sat down at the small desk and sent a message from his phone-pad to his family in Vancouver, B.C. promising to be home before Moving Day.

The next morning, Petra and Sulaimon were nowhere to be found, having disappeared into the depths of the abbey, continuing their work in the World. A simple breakfast of muesli and cream, rösti and sausage, remnants of the Swiss origin of the abbey, was served up on a small buffet table in an alcove with an arched opening into the kitchen. Brother Clarence replenished the food as needed, leaning out through the opening.

S.C. fell in line behind Ambrose, plate in hand. Larr and Brodie had not arrived.

"What, no waffles, biscuits and gravy?"

Ambrose chuckled, "This ain't your grandpa's Motel 6, isn't that the idiom?"

"Yeah, thanks for the introduction last night. I assume you knew I was coming as well?"

"I delivered you into their hands, yes? Not an unpleasant visit?"

"Quite the opposite, but I'd hate to think people are wasting a lot of energy following me around."

"Not so much trouble as you might think. Your writing has made quite an impression, one needs only to follow certain publications, certain bylines, certain subject matter, there you are. "Who else knows about the night staff?"

"Petra and Sulaimon? Sulai is quite conspicuous and she sort of distracts the eye, doesn't she? Not bad camouflage for anyone right next to her."

"We were just talking about that."

"The senior monks know, not the seminarians. The Cult knows of course, but has a don't ask, don't tell policy."

"I'm not sure what I felt when I was with her but it was a very clear reality."

"She is a liminal being, moving back and forth between worlds, not just the known worlds. When you sit next to the divine, you know it. You can't help but feel that pull, like quicksand. That's what she is to us, to this reality."

"It felt like she was living the experience that started the Cult in the first place, stripped of all dogma, stripped down to. . . something, I don't know, but it made me want to follow her, to be a student."

Ambrose said, "Like a Sufi master, you may follow her, but be aware, just when you get comfortable, she'll abandon you, kick you to the curb, under the bus, out of the nest. Take what she offers but don't lose your head."

"Like Alice."

"There are dangers everywhere, even here with our bellies full before the fire."

Larr and Brodie showed up right as S.C. was leaving and Ambrose bussed the dishes. Another round of the same breakfast was put before them and a couple of monks in between prayer and work. Larr said he was going to spend some time with the art and in the museum and Brodie didn't say, but neither one of them turned up looking for him until late in the afternoon.

In the meantime, S.C. made a beeline back to the book room, this time taking his notebook and phonepad. He made notes as to the titles and subject matter of the oldest volumes pointed out by Petra, Charlotte's books. The editions were all from the twenty teens and twenties, a hundred years ago, before the worlds changed.

He had to keep shaking his head to realize just what he held in his hand, just what kind of world existed B.C. The 'known' structure of the universe was utterly destroyed by the appearance of field sentients and Andromedans, but the shock, despair and cognitive dissonance of it was gone, subsumed into the new certainty of the Cult of the Bodhisattva.

He was as non-Cult as one could be, non-practicing, non-indoctrinated, moving along in secular life, trying not to get sucked in. Just like Christianity was a given background to social and intellectual life B.C., so the Cult and its parables were the unspoken background now, like Noah's Ark, Adam and Eve and all that. You had to know some of its allusions just to carry on a normal conversation.

Sitting before the bookcase, he catalogued Hans Urs von Balthazar's Glory of the Lord, Sergei Bulgakov's works on Angels and Sophia, Rudolf Steiner's Staying Connected, The Tibetan Book of the Dead, The Book of Going Forth in the Daytime from ancient Egypt. And in this cataloguing, the wonderment of seeing and touching the actual handwriting of Charlotte, her notes and comments, the ephemera of sticky notes, perhaps even a slight smell of aged roses imbedded in the book jacket, all of that brought something up from inside of him that caught in his throat and made his eyes water while short shallow breaths made him dizzy.

He wasn't a devotee but even so, was used to myths staying myths and not walking around chatting with you. First Petra and now the historical Charlotte and the childlike cursive of the woman who did not know who she was or what she would become.

He felt the need to honor her. He also felt compassion and sorrow for that woman and all she had gone through, and then the joy when that personal loss became a new reality upon which she soared like an albatross over vast oceans, a tiny glimpse of a destination preserved from some archetypal experience driving her on, driving her home.

It was becoming overwhelming and he started to feel as if there was a presence emanating from the books, something enveloping him; he felt his face flush with warmth. He looked up and saw the icon of God the Geometer, the God of Abraham in the form of Yeshua, Jesus the Christ, avatar of Logos/Sophia, illuminated in the 12th century for the *Bible Moralisere*, now as then, holding the golden compass, the draftsman's dividers, dividing the heavens from the earth, the firmament from the waters, inscribing a circle containing amorphous blobs of the sun, moon and earth and blue fractal waves forming the waters, the Deep, the inside border of the circle.

He knew that this was Charlotte's own possession, her favorite icon preserved here from the time before her first transitus; she called it Creator Mundi, Creator of the World. This is whom she imagined meeting, reaching out a hand, pulling her into oneness, though she did not know it then; it was a quantum singularity melting into the divine.

The fact that she had worshipped this image, touched the wooden frame, infused it with her sweat, straightened it absent mindedly while cleaning house on an uneventful day, all this struck him absurdly and powerfully as a presence in the room. The image was illuminated with gold leaf and deep colors, in a tradition where it at once seemed awkwardly stylized and flattened, iconic, and at the same time fluid and in flux, self-referential, one foot treading outside the border, ready to step out of the frame and into the room, ready to say 'Oy gevalt; how's the weather down here? Hot enough for ya?' and 'How 'bout them Yankees?'

He had never had a daily practice but he realized that he was now sitting in a half lotus position before the bookcase, his back straight as an arrow, the arrow pushing upwards, straining to push through the top of his head as he counted his breaths. The room had darkened while he had been sitting like this and he realized that somehow it had become evening when it had been noon a minute before. His breathing had become regular and timed with his heartbeats, four heartbeats in, four heart beats out, each breath focused and felt at the tip of his nose.

He could not remember how long he had been doing this but he did feel a rise of something spiraling upward into an event horizon, stalled in time, ever trapped, ever falling; then, just as he was about to lift off the ground, following the surge of energy out of the top of his head, a flutter of wings drowned out his silent counting as an impossible angel surrounded him and anchored him to the world, and he knew he was safe. The feathers touched him gently and semaphored, *not yet, not yet, all in good time, all in good time.*

Then, suddenly though the room was dark, the lids of his closed eyes brightened with light, a silver figure like a manifestation started to resolve from the light and he began to pray the only prayer he knew, *Hail Xià lù dì, mother of light, thy love is with me.*

"Sup brotha?"

S.C.'s eyes shot open and Brodie stood there, finger on the light switch, eyeing the book in his lap. "You'll fuck up your eyes that way, reading in the dark, didn't your mom tell you? Dinner's ready, s'go. Ambrose is breaking out the good port. You ok?"

At that, all the beautiful feelings of comfort and safety just blew away like eider down on a breeze and he could have pulled that wagging tongue right out of Brodie's face; then the anger subsided, replaced by something between sadness and despair, and then a return and acceptance of the world, for one more day. "You startled me you son of a bitch. Damn!"

"Hey, don't shit a brick, let's eat." He put out an arm and hauled S.C. up, a bit wobbly and tingling on sleepy legs. S.C. flicked the light switch down and closed the door, knowing he would return.

The next morning, as Larr, Brodie and S.C. waited for Vladimir to pull the buckboard around for the trip back to Frosty's, Dusty Georgi appeared, pushing a hover cycle from the carriage house motor pool. He was wearing street clothes, not a speck of cowboy bullshit anywhere to be seen in his get up though the same saddlebags that graced his horse were now securely fastened under the seat of the mechanical beast. He came abreast of the men and said, "Well if it ain't the three musketeers."

"What are you all dressed up for?" Larr quipped.

"I'm just heading up to Seattle to see my accountant. Had a lot of real estate investments before things got really bad and the money went North/Up. Every so often I have to show up and swear that I'm a sophisticated investor and waive any claims against him for all the shady deals he makes. There's a big futures market in the future now as well, betting on disasters, investing in temporary power, emergency shelter, everything needed for the apocalypse is bullish now. Be back in a week, but you'll be long gone." He shook hands all around then hopped on the hover cycle and sputtered down the hill to pick up the hoverway north, yelling "Da svedanya," over his shoulder.

As Dusty disappeared, Brodie came around a corner engaged in conversation with Sulaimon. The lizard shook his hand goodbye and her scales rippled with nervous anticipation mixed with humor. Brodie trotted over to the buckboard and climbed in. "C'mon, c'mon ladies, what's the holdup?" he said, as the others threw their duffles in, "Next stop, Engelberg."

Brother Ambrose and Sulaimon waved as the three took in a glimpse of the whole abbey complex from the winding road down the hill. Though the seminary and Cult additions were of more recent vintage, the abbey itself was old, from the mid nineteenth century, and it evoked something even older. It was affiliated with the Benedictine mother house at Engleberg, Switzerland; Engleberg, meaning

Angel Mountain, thus the name Mt. Angel, Oregon. The complex there was built around an eleventh century Benedictine monastery in the rarified high altitudes of the Alps.

Ranks of travelers could attest to the hair-raising hairpin turns and precipitous drops on narrow roads, enough to set even a Cultist signing the cross and promising to convert to . . . anything, if they arrived alive. In that place, as in Oregon, a simpler pastoral reality was preserved, or reinvented, one in which the frenetic pace of the early twenty second century was gone.

It wasn't that it hadn't touched here, it had come and gone with the pilgrims, as it became apparent that the rush and crush of technology, the fear about missing out, the constant viewing of the world through secondary and tertiary images, the vast electromagnetic spectrum needed for ordinary life, the constant uncontrolled hum and vibration of the old modern, all that was not needed and not missed. Silence was cultivated here, was regained here, was the birthright of humanity going forth silent in a world that merely whispered its magic but was never unheard.

After all, the meek *were* inheriting the earth. Arrogance had launched itself to the stars, why not enjoy its absence? No more requirement for GNP growth ever upward and it was back to a cyclical world. The Hindus had ages of hundreds of billions of years and nature's yearly cycle; that's enough even for the high tech that remained, everything having its season. When do the microchips ripen? When are the spooks calved and lambed from the birthing field? On Earth and Over There the cycles were slower. How much better is that than noise and bright lights? You could still have that too, but on your terms, if you were willing to chance a Rumspringa walkabout among the English in Toronto or Londinium. But, in Engleberg, as in the vast expanses of Mongolia, as in the beautiful desert of Namibia and the boundless churn of

Oceana, humans were beginning to know again and relish their quiet place in the immensity of their true mother.

INTERSTITIAL II

*

2125 C.E.

From *The Five Tribes Confederacy*, Pushmataha, F.S.,
Modern Europa Press, 2125

Introduction

At the beginning of this work as chronicler of the New
Choctaw Republic, before the war, I was not always welcomed
with open arms. This was understandable. The question was
legitimate: Why would a spook with no human past engage in
such a project. Is he a dilettante, a cosplayer or simply naïve?

Certainly, both species have learned by now that we
are not so different, even in our home in the field. We laugh,
love, cry, oppress and misunderstand each other just as
humans do and, in the beginning, all jumped at the chance to
love and misunderstand another species as well.

Something else compels us now; familiarity, shared
sorrows, cross-species reenactors and all manner of formal and
informal contact have made us fellow travelers and trusted
companions in this multiverse. The crisis in Purgatory in the
last century and subsequent mass migrations, have driven this
home. We are all part of one continuum of life. The details of
this life are worthy of our love and admiration. And so, cross
cultural study and preservation was taken up with all sincerity
by Andromedans, spooks and humans.

It is also not hard to see that hybrid spooks with a past
symbiont relationship in the cultural group are no less a
member of that group and worthy of their status as revered
elder/ancestor, once they have shed their corporeal body. But
even spooks from Over There sometimes fit better in human
culture than in their own. Such are not discouraged from
leaving by the theocracy. It can be a safety valve and also

source of innovation, officially frowned upon but always necessary. The theocracy is at least this wise. In this casting out, we may be in the position of the culture hero, as is Coyote to the Native Americans.

All over the world, the culture hero breaks the rules and is cast out of civilization. He is a trickster and a delinquent but only by this process are genuinely new treasures bestowed upon civilization, as Prometheus brought fire to the Greeks.

In this way, I explain my love for the Choctaw people. I am cast out but compelled to bring wisdom back to the land of my birth while seeking my own place in the worlds. In service of that quest, I have put my sincerity before the Choctaw people and the Autonomous Congress. The acceptance I have received is the most valuable gift I can possess and display, like a precious jewel for all to see.

In addition, the metaphor of the Choctaw genesis, shared by other Native Americans, strikes a chord that is worthy of our attention. The Five Civilized Tribes appeared one at a time out of the Mother Mound, Nanih Waiya. Like the blue green door of the Irish, the Dreaming and the thin veil of other cultures, this tells us that our origins, destinies and companions are right here, even if we do not perceive them readily.

Thanks be to the Goddess, Kali-Ma and Xià lǜ dì, may peace be upon all sentient beings through their love and longing.

Chapter 1: Pushmataha in His Time

The historical Pushmataha was a military commander who fought the British on the side of the United States. He was also a cultural conservative who nonetheless supported adoption of colonist technology and infrastructure when it suited the Choctaw. He died in 1824 at the age of sixty while on a delegation to Washington D.C., still treated as an honored head of state. His gravestone in the Congressional Cemetery, burial place of members of Congress and other notables who died in office, includes these words:

> Push-ma-ta-ha was a warrior of great distinction. He was wise in council — eloquent in an extraordinary degree, and on all occasions & under all circumstances the white man's friend.

Later generations, used to the image of Native Americans as societies in decline were struck by the honor in which such leaders were held, as equals, before the official and unofficial extinction of the tribes began. The *Washington Intelligencer*, written by white journalists, was similarly expansive in his obituary.

> At Tennison's Hotel, on Friday last, the 24th instant, Pooshamataha, a Chief of the Choctaw Nation of Indians, distinguished for his bold elocution and his attachment to the United States. At the commencement of the late war on our Southern border, he took an early and decided stand in favor of the weak and isolated settlements on Tombigby, and he continued to fight with and for them whilst they had an enemy in the field. His bones will rest a distance from his home, but in the bosom of the people he delighted to love. May a good hunting ground await his generous spirit in another and a better world. Military honors were paid to his remains by the Marine Corps of the United States, and by several uniformed companies of the militia.

Pushmataha's life represented the status of the Choctaw Nation as one of the 'Five Civilized Tribes' and also its suffering on the Trail of Tears.

But, before their forced removal at gunpoint, many groups organized their own departure and saw the journey, legitimately, as one away from their oppression by the state of Mississippi and Andrew Jackson. Remarkably eloquent at the age of twenty-one, Choctaw chief George Harkins stated in his *Letter to the American People:*

> We were hedged in by two evils, and we chose that which we thought the least. Yet we could not recognize the right that the state of Mississippi had assumed, to legislate for us. Although the legislators of the state were qualified to make laws for their own citizens, that did not qualify them to become law makers to a people that were so dissimilar in manners and customs as the Choctaws are to the Mississippians. Admitting that they understood the people, could they remove that mountain of prejudice that has ever obstructed the streams of justice, and prevented their salutary influence from reaching my devoted countrymen? We as Choctaws rather chose to suffer and be free, than live under the degrading influence of laws of which our voice could not be heard in their formation.
>
> Much as the state of Mississippi has wronged us, I cannot find in my heart any other sentiment than an ardent wish for her prosperity and happiness. I could cheerfully hope, that those of another age and

generation may not feel the effects of those oppressive measures that have been so illiberally dealt out to us; and that peace and happiness may be their reward. Amid the gloom and horrors of the present separation, we are cheered with a hope that ere long we shall reach our destined land, and that nothing short of the basest acts of treachery will ever be able to wrest it from us, and that we may live free. Although your ancestors won freedom on the field of danger and glory, our ancestors owned it as their birthright, and we have had to purchase it from you as the vilest slaves buy their freedom.

One cannot help but compare this statement to the American Declaration of Independence, which voiced much the same grievances as the basis for the clear duty of a people to throw off oppression. Even more remarkable is the fact that the U.S. Constitution was influenced by the Great Law of Peace, the governing document of the Iroquois Confederacy, the first democracy established in North America; it was a wampum record that began, "We, the people, to form a union, to establish peace, equity, and order..."

Alexis de Toqueville, celebrated author of *Democracy in America,* wrote of the Choctaw removals in 1831.

In the whole scene there was an air of ruin and destruction, something which betrayed a final and irrevocable adieu; one couldn't watch without feeling one's heart wrung. The Indians were tranquil, but somber and taciturn. There was one who could speak English and of whom I asked why the Chactas were leaving their country. "To be free," he answered, could never get any other reason out of him. We ... watched the expulsion ... of one of the most celebrated and ancient American peoples.

— *Alexis de Tocqueville, Democracy in America*

The Choctaw had been subject to legal conflict, harassment, and intimidation, "have had our habitations torn down and burned, our fences destroyed, cattle turned into our fields and we ourselves have been scourged, manacled, fettered and otherwise personally abused, until by such treatment some of our best men have died."

The Five Civilized Tribes had been forced, coerced, encouraged to take over lands west of the Mississippi, including what would become Oklahoma, to appease settlers who coveted Choctaw and Chickasaw lands in Mississippi and Arkansas Territory, Seminole lands in Florida and the Creek and Cherokee lands in Alabama and Tennessee.

These forced Indian Removals lasted from 1830 to 1839 and included over 50,000 tribal members, along with some whites and slaves. The latter removals involved the forced marching of thousands at a time, subject to disease and decimation on the way.

And so, it was not of small import when the Five Civilized Tribes set out to retrace the Trail of Tears and retake the Mother Mound in the spring of the year 2124.

*

God the Geometer

When he set a compass upon the face of the deep, I was there.

He took the golden Compasses, prepar'd
In Gods Eternal store, to circumscribe
This Universe, and all created things:
One foot he center'd, and the other turn'd
Round through the vast profunditie obscure,
And said, thus farr extend, thus farr thy bounds,
This be thy just Circumference, O World.
John Milton - Paradise Lost

Plato, John Milton, William Blake, Phillip Pullman and Charlotte; all loved the Divine Geometrician, not the God of Abraham, but the Ancient of Days, Urizen, God the Geometer.

Even the Maya envisioned creation as the work of divine geometricians, the world laid out in sacred proportions like maize fields, temples and houses, with chords used as dividers, without units of measurement; praising the Popul Vuh it was written:

> *Great is its performance and its account of the completion and germination of all the sky and earth—its four corners and its four sides. All then was measured and staked out into four divisions, doubling over and stretching the measuring cords of the womb of sky and the womb of earth. Thus were established the four corners, the four sides.*

In Charlotte's case, it was a twelfth century illumination, showing Logos at Creation, wielding a draftsman's dividers, a golden compass.

. . . *and God divided the light from the darkness. . . And God made the firmament, and divided the waters which were under the firmament from the waters which were above the firmament . . . Let there be lights in the firmament of the heaven to divide the day from the night . . .*

He is shown using the draftsman's compass to divide and create blobs for the earth, sun and moon surrounded by the waters of the Deep. That image was her favorite icon, the one that adorned her home for many years before she died, and many years after.

It had been remarked upon, even B.C., because the waters of the Deep looked a lot like the Mandelbrot Set, the first fractal imaged by computers, mimicking one of the fundamental patterns of nature, unknown, needless to say, in the twelfth century.

The Deep; In Hebrew the word was Tahom derived from the Babylonian Mother Goddess, Tiamat. She was the sky goddess, the salt waters of Chaos and mother of all the lesser gods. The Israelites in captivity by the waters of Babylon, where they lay down and wept and remembered Zion, knew her. And then, when in Zion, remembering Babylon, they took that idea home with them, putting El, the Lord, in the place of Apsu, the fresh waters, Tiamat's husband. And the two of them were the division of waters above the firmament and waters below the firmament just as it was then told in Genesis. In the same way, they retold the tale of Utnapishtim, as Noah and the Ark, writing Genesis only after they returned to Israel from Babylon, with visions of Gilgamesh the King, Gilgamesh who was told, *All is vanity.*

And she is also there, the divine feminine, Hagia Sophia, divine wisdom, there at the Creation. Controversial in Christianity, the presence of the divine feminine was an obvious confirmation of the truth of the Cult. The eternal wisdom of the Bodhisattva has always been there, even when obscured by errors of the ages.

Children of the Cult recited these stories of *The Bodhisattva and the Icons* in grade school pageants, just as they used to memorize and perform the Christmas Story, Before Charlotte. It was a new Nativity, the birth of the Bodhisattva from the human/spook hybrid, Charlotte. Charlotte could not attend the icon painting class because her cancer had destroyed her pelvis to such a degree that moving her would kill her. She then created the form of the icon in Purgatory and hung it as a beacon to guide her home.

That beacon, and instructions from the Tibetan Book of the Dead, which she considered a pedestrian how-to manual, assured her *transitus* and resurrection as a Bodhisattva. That was the beginning of all the factual and fanciful doctrine, parables and sutras of the Cult of Xià lù di.

A repeated theme in stupa art was the creation of the fabled icon itself. Many interpretations existed. The most popular was an icon actually painted in the last century by Brother Claude of the Archangel Michael.

Originally, Michael held in his hands an image of Christ as a child within a circle of rays symbolizing the Glory of the Lord. Within this circle now however, appeared an image of Charlotte. At one time, it had been a natural photograph, then altered, changing contrast and color to mimic the icon.

It was a photo of her at eighteen, a beauty with ivory skin and   black hair, a white peasant blouse and wide brimmed hat of midnight blue. She focused in the middle distance and her hands were raised to her shoulders, the fingers about to form the abhaya mudra signifying reassurance, blessing and protection, reflecting the gaze of Michael, and its promise of 'Have no fear.'

In holding her, Michael's hands were interpreted as seeking the lotus bud mudra, signifying light emerging from darkness, heavenly life emerging from the dark earth. As Michael looked down and she looked up, it was clear that she had achieved her desire, though, as the story was told, a very different *transitus* followed, with no certainty of a Maker.

Michael himself had also been altered over the years to resemble St. Daniel, Dan Pritchard. This was apochryphal but a nice touch, as she returned to the beacon of his love and he became her defender.

The Jesuits

We didn't lose faith in God, in *a* god anyway; it's just that the rules changed. People believe that what they experienced with spooks and transdimensionals was the basis for all the old religions. But now, they don't need a mediator, or a filter to experience what they think is old school transcendence. Shit, you could shed this mortal coil anytime you want and become an angel for all they knew. The loss of self is so compelling that stepping in and out of that experience created whole civilizations. But they think that *their* goddess is not unknowable, *their* goddess is accessible, because they can go where she went at will. They don't need blind faith to explain transcendence anymore. Brother Ignatz, S.J., F.S.

The truth of the Earth after Moving Day was not all spirit and light and bedtime stories. The mendicants and pilgrims heading North/Up didn't look back and left the 80% to fester. Even disaffected spooks were among those sneaking in the Quantum Mechanics' Union Hall. It became the seething core of a small but expanding gathering of futurists, anarchists, trade unionists and others, 'Occupy Earth!' being the real slogan.

And what was the plan, the purpose of the meetings? Nothing less than taking back the earth for the slugs and grubs and common folk. The unending screed of the New United Futurists was taken up by the Jesuits, now lone rangers of the errant Knights of Columbus Motorcycle Club.

Leave the fucking planet, but leave its virginity. Rape the planet with your passive carbon footprint? No more for you; leave the innocence of the earth right here. Go to your fucking *transitus* but leave what you have grabbed from this planet right here. We will even guarantee safe passage off planet and you can mumble your mantras in peace. We want the beautiful planet to rehabilitate, to revel in what can be done with the empty declining cities of the first world. Give us stewardship of the planet that you take for granted. Keep Europa, Vesta, all of those, but never come back here to this planet that you just used as your spiritual door mat, wipe your feet of the shit and walk away down a pure white corridor without soiling the floor, all dirt left on earth. But without your dirt, you are nothing; you are not even human, even the spooks know this. They are nothing without their aspiration to the imperfection of human life. Brother Ignatz, S.J., F.S.

The Rise and Fall of the New United Futurists. Modern Europa Press, S.C. Schneider 2130

PART III

THE SEIGE ENGINEERS

Turning and spinning in the gyring wild,
The heroine hears the hero, and rescues him.
Things fall into place; the centering holds.
The blue lit sea foam mimics the river of stars;
Mere Beauty is loosed upon the world.
The best are filled with passionate intensity
The worst are merely in love

Surely, a revelation is at hand.
Not the first or second coming, but
One of multitudes, cycles without end.
And in the desert she stands
Creating mirages of earthly love
To lure our parched beast to the true water
Deluded, we crawl toward our divine nativity,
No less certain for lack of the knowledge
That once again such a birth is a light to the
worlds.

Yeats in the New Babylon - S.C. Schneider, 2125

*

Mara
2429 A.R.

After Charlotte met Krishna and Radha at Powell's, the three made a concerted effort to track down any other travelers. They thought they could find more, people rebooted by the book tour since Charlotte's book did the trick of reviving memories of their first lives. Because they all had entered their host bodies as embryos, and basically hibernated, flying under the radar, until close to adulthood, those that traveled before them, or even with them, had been reduced to hazy memories; past lives, dreams of dreaming dreams.

Even so, Krishna did remember some distinctly, Betty from the 3MI labs for one. She had left in a bootleg transporter with a bunch of spooks on one of the first Moving Days. They knew her intention was to follow Charlotte, and that was part of the reason he and Radha came here as well. She wasn't that hard to find buzzing around the book fairs in their natural state

Eventually, the four . . . aliens, all moved to the same neighborhood in Denver, hung out at coffee shops and book groups and built a nice cozy relationship guarding the biggest secret on Mara. After their day jobs, they patrolled the known nodes of the Library and making note of any activity.

On April 1, 2429 A.R., April 1, 2125 C.E. back home, Charlotte and Betty approached the point in the outer atmosphere where Charlotte had entered this universe forty two years earlier. It was part of their regular patrol along with other possible nodes she could sense but which she could also tell had never been used. Now that Krishna, Radha and Betty were part of the team, they shared the duties of being ever watchful; routine, but every once in a while a new friend would fall in from the sky. It was almost like some bad science fiction movie remade again, Invasion of the Body Snatchers. *But we're nice.*

This time however, in the airless haze at the ionosphere boundary, she could feel a bump, some bit of the holographic node that existed between universes. Krishna had pointed this out the day before, something intangible suddenly becoming more solidified, day by day. Somehow it seemed different; something anticipated in non-linear time; a vibration had started.

*

Earth
March, 2125 C.E.
Meyrin, Switzerland

A bunch of Carthies at the end of the bar had some local girls in stitches. The ladies were in a scrum admiring one girl's ring finger by the beer sign light. The Carthies all sported Cheshire cat burglar smiles as the girls settled onto their laps. At the other end of the bar, a flash off that ring hit Stuart right in the eye. He was transported to a memory that was as clear as day, a memory of a slight girl with long brown hair holding up her hand to admire a silver band engraved with initials and a heart that Stuart had made in metal shop.

As she turned to him and smiled, her eyes sparked. They did not twinkle, no, not this girl. They arced with electricity that burned the air between them. Then and now, a heady perfume grabbed him and shrank his world to a silent cocoon that had only enough room in it for two lovers and the entire universe.

Stuart's isolation in Geneva made him think about this memory of Christine that he had constructed over the years. It had become his focus of longing and regret. He imagined her doing the books or rising up the management chain of some space export or insurance firm, slowly forgetting him.

He thought she was probably being wooed by some rich Angkor Wat financier in Londinium. *Probably tandem sailsuiting to some lunar hot tub spa right now.* He knew he didn't deserve her and that he had waited too long. But still, it was the only fantasy that kept him going.

When he had finally got up his nerve, he picked up his phone-pad and dialed the still archived number for Christine's mum in Glasgow.

"Halloo?"

"Misses Taylor?"

"Aye, who's this?" Her voice was a bit thin and shaky but Stuart recognized it immediately.

"Misses Taylor, it's Stuart. Do you remember me? Stuart? Christine and I . . ."

"Stuart. . . ah. . .my memory's not as . . . Stuart! Of course luv. . . where are you?"

"Geneva; on a job."

"I'm just getting ready to go to the Hebrides for the summer, it's too hot for me in Glasgow these days and my sister Clara has a nice little cottage on the water and some of the family goes along and it's . . .Oh, sorry, why did you call?"

"I just wanted to get in touch with Christine, I might be heading that way soon. Can you tell me. . ."

She interrupted, "Oh. . .oh my. . .Stuart, you didn't know?"

Stuart was silent for a beat. "Know what?"

"When ISIS attacked London . . . Londinium, she was at the . . . That was ten years ago."

"I didn't know . . . sorry, Misses, I mean, sorry for your loss . . ."

"Stuart, luv, you don't have to say anything. I don't know what happened between you two. In a different world, maybe. . . Come and see me if you're coming through, ok? . . . ok? Stuart?"

"I will Misses."

He walked out on the loading dock and stared at the scrap.

*

That seemed an angry lifetime ago. "Another round barkeep." At the sound of the familiar voice, Stuart's reality snapped back to the bar. He recognized a clean shaven Arab with hoop earrings and long black hair with magenta highlights, tied in back. The others were still in their work clothes, jeans or overalls, but this guy was all panache in his new wave burnoose.

Technically, it was Stuart's job to keep track of these guys even when they weren't on dismantler duty at the Large Hadron Collider. He was curious too. *What kind of nonsense have they got themselves into now?* In those days, at the Quantum Mechanics Union Bar, it was anything goes and the Wild West all rolled into one.

By 2115, New Carthage, Babylon and the Greco-Buddhist Xanders had beat the crap out of ISIS, taken away their nuclear toys and were just mopping up the mess they left behind. As for the old first world, the wealthy were heading upstairs, buying into the Cult and life extension tech as rising sea levels and climate change turned temperate zones into deserts. The Carthies and others were simply filling the vacuum left by the northern elites riding the Space Elevators off-planet.

They were ever so much more civilized than the old guard terrorists. With national borders more or less erased, everybody was welcome to the party as long as they paid their tribute. The economy chugged along just fine, but at a more leisurely pace. Working class Joes like the ones at the Meyrin bar were more interested in impressing girls than building a caliphate, harems not terror, make love not war. Seventy-two virgins? *Not for long brotha!*

*

Stuart remembered the feeling of being stalled between a limitless youth and the cautious mantle of adulthood, the feeling that something was about to slip out of reach never to be regained. In a recurring dream, Christine had moved away and he couldn't find her phone number. She made a new life while he rummaged through drawers until he couldn't remember what he was trying not to forget. Those dreams ended with an emptiness that pulled at him the whole day.

Stuart liked to say he was from a working class neighborhood of Glasgow but most people didn't get the joke. Post-Brexit Glasgow was *all* working class, some neighborhoods just rougher than others. A young tough on the street, just petty theft and minor mischief, he was also an admired young artist in secondary school. His art teacher had kept one of his paintings hanging above the classroom door. He visited this inspiring teacher off and on after graduation. But eventually, the artist regretted not taking the gift further, and the visits ended.

Like most people, his adult life was the product of a series of very ordinary concessions. It was just a harder road in Glasgow

Financial realities required a day job so he put his shoulder to the wheel and started off on a predictable path. First he was a hod carrier, then an apprentice with the pipefitters union in Glasgow. When the jobs dried up in Scotland, he went chasing work across the continent.

The call came from CERN for the tradesmen and labor needed to dismantle the 150-year old Large Hadron Collider. The parts were being used in the rebuilding of the Orbital Collider after its destruction in the event that created the Library.

The physicists that used to fuel the squint bars and discos around Meyrin had gone upstairs too. So, the work boiled down to mothballing the parts that were in good condition and hauling them into orbit on the Space Elevator. The scrap went up the elevator too, refined in orbit into component metals. When that job was done, the whole place was going to be a twenty-seven kilometer empty hole in the ground

*

The ladies hung onto their guys and laughed at whatever sweet nothings they whispered in their ears in a language they didn't understand. Just eighteen, give or take, they were basically high school girls in prom dresses, milking the working stiffs and maybe getting a grubstake together, putting their big plans on layaway. Taking their drinks, they started up the ramp to watch the sunset from the roof.

Stuart sighed and left his Guinness to warm. He sidled down to the end of the bar and nodded to the natty Carthy, a foreman of the dismantlers. He was the only one of them Stuart might call a friend. Just a few hours earlier they had sparred over favorite fútbol teams, with the Carthy gently asserting the homo-erotic implications of *Man United.*

Stuart said, "Hey Hannibal, what's up with the sparklies?"

"Now that's just racist Stewie, you know my name," he said with good natured indignation.

"Gaddafi? Why isn't that name racist too? It's just as much a stereotype."

"Weren't you at cultural sensitivity training my friend? Our given names are Arabic. *Hannibal* is a name used to make fun of our proud Carthaginian heritage; so hurtful in so many ways. Someone might report you; send you back to empathy school."

"Like who? Nobody's in charge but us."

Gaddafi put on a little pout. "It's nice to be nice Stewie." Then, a little snarky, "What you want brotha? We're off duty. You good cop or bad cop today?"

"Depends. Where'd you get the rings? Stealing some salvaged goods again? Diamond drill bits, that sort of thing?"

"Borrowed, and that was just one time Stewie. The girls wanted to make proton bubble tea. Big mistake." He bumped his two fists together and then pantomimed an explosion, "Booosh!"

"You 'borrowed' proton accelerators and did something that blew the roof off the storage building." It was the explosion that got Stuart in trouble with the admins. He didn't really mind the theft.

"The things we do for love. Like I said, big mistake. But here, sweetheart, look, this one's harmless."

Gaddafi slid an ornately carved wooden box along the bar, the kind the Carthies sold to tourists at the bazaars in Geneva. Stuart frowned.

Gaddafi smiled and said, "No, really, I kid you not', look in the magic box." When the box was opened, a lovesick tune played; an old Farsi ghazel. He took a lump of coal from a drawstring bag, put it in the black velvet interior, closed the lid and shook the box. With a nod and a wink he tossed it over to Stuart who snagged it out of the air and examined it while flexing his bicep like Rosie the Riveter.

He opened the lid. This time it played an applause track. Nestled in the velvet was a large uncut diamond, four or five carats, at least. He wasn't sure he would know the difference, but it seemed real enough.

Stuart passed it back dismissively. "Sleight of hand, that's all, in goes coal and out comes diamonds."

Gaddafi said, "Stewie, that wouldn't be profitable, I'd have to buy the diamonds first."

"Well, if it's the goose and the golden egg, you sell the goose to the rubes; and if it's to impress a girl, easier to buy her a ring at Bucherer's on the Rue de Rhone."

"Old school Stewie, these girls are smart. If you tell them you made it with shady tek, they want the box as much as the sparklies."

"A good trick. What *did* you steal to make it work?" Stuart leaned into Gaddafi's personal space. The Carthy leaned in too, eye to eye, affecting a conspiratorial stage whisper.

"Nothing, we found some microscopic black holes cleaning out the experiment housing, not on any salvage list. They disappear when you scrap the machine. So, we catch them like fireflies with a standard graviton wrench. Physics does the rest. Wa La!"

"Ok . . ."

"Now, what else do you think we scraped out of that collider?"

"There's more?"

"Unintended consequences, emergent properties, the implicate order; quantum entanglement, Einstein-Rosen bridge."

"Wormholes?" Stuart knew the technical name for wormholes from the safety manual protocols.

Gaddafi pulled out two more boxes, each with a glittering rainbow on it. "Traversable wormholes, yes, Stewie. Send one box to your girlfriend up north, put a lump of coal in your box and it comes out in her box as a diamond. I thought of the name, The Rainbow Bridge."

"That's Norse mythology, not North African." Stuart said.

"Bifrost, correct, I was thinking of you. Some red haired Viking shagged your distant ancestor on a raid I bet. But very poetic, don't you think? Tells your girl she's your road to heaven, your flaming rainbow bridge, Woof! Great idea, no?"

"Well, it's an idea, I'll give you that," Stuart said.

Gaddafi touched a finger to Stuart's chest, "Ssssst! She'll be so hot, you'll sizzle. Nome sayn?"

"It's still theft. CERN just doesn't know it has what you're stealing."

"No admins here, all upstairs building their new toy. Why do you care? We're both underpaid. Wage slaves. Maybe you should get your share too."

"Be careful pal."

"No cameras here, no worries. And who's in charge of cameras downstairs? You, my friend."

Stuart put his hand down on the boxes, "Fifty-fifty on profits, boxes or diamonds."

"Eighty-twenty."

He pulled the boxes toward him. "Forty-sixty, and I'll have to confiscate these. See you on the day shift. And don't talk about my girl, any girl, like that, or I'll make *you* sizzle."

Stuart had not dissuaded Gaddafi from thinking he had a girl waiting for him back home. Even though she was imaginary now, Stuart started to get defensive of her honor.

"No offense intended Loverboy. *You* think about that girl. You know she'd love it."

*

And he did think of her. Christine's grandmother had lived next door to Stuart's family, so he had seen her off and on since childhood. At one point however, when they were fourteen, a woman he didn't recognize waved from the house next door. He blinked his eyes and it was Christine, blinked again and it was a stranger. He saw the same effect as he closed one eye and then the other repeatedly until finally, Christine yelled, "What're you blinkin' like an eejit for?!" From then on she made him nervous and he hung back a bit while watching her intently.

She always traveled in a gaggle of girlfriends, laughing and telling secrets as he kept his distance. Every so often she would toss her shining brown hair over her shoulder and her eyes would flash as she looked straight at him. She might be telling stories at his expense, but at least, he thought, he was on her mind.

Then one day she spun around and didn't turn back, letting her friends go on without her. As Stuart walked up to her, she said, "Stuart, are you following me?"

He was emboldened by her directness and reacted with studied disinterest, just the opposite of how he felt.

"What if I am?"

A laugh burst out of her pursed lips. "Stuart, don't try to be tough with me. You can't pull it off. You're a sensitive guy, not a bully boy."

"Sounds like an insult."

"You're such a numpty. Some girls like bad boys; Neds and Teds, but I'd rather have a boy who'd cry if I broke his heart. Would you cry if I broke your heart?"

Again, he wasn't quite sure what the answer should be.

"Not if I broke yours first."

"There's that tough guy again. Anyway, this is serious. I need a partner for the final art project and you're feckin' good. Will you be my partner or not?"

"Oh well, if you insist."

"Great, come to my house Saturday morning, not too early." Then she ran back up to her friends and didn't look back.

After that, one thing led to another. They circled each other warily and then with purpose. They became something new, something more than either could be alone, something larger than two kids together, another emergent property, something even more than love.

They were together until they were nineteen. Then Stuart started his union apprentice training in Glasgow, while Christine took a job in Manchester. From there, she moved to the head office in Londinium; it was still London then. There were tears and promises but he didn't follow her. Even so, he never stopped holding her image in his mind as a beacon; the perfect form of a girl, just imperfect enough to be his.

Ten years on, Christine had already made a life in Londinium. So, he had put his nose to the grindstone and thought of her only now and then, until the day that he talked to her mum. Since then, he thought about her all the time.

*

Stuart decided to start early and skip his afternoon rounds. He wanted to get a head start on his drunk without his charges watching.

He took a seat at the bar. There was one table with a couple of guys in black leather jackets and two spookballs and one other customer at the bar nursing a short glass of something.

The Carthy bartender said, "The usual?"

"And an extra shot."

He put two shots of Jameson in a glass and poured Guiness over it. Stuart took a good swallow, tasting the tang of the whiskey under the dark caramel of the porter.

Stuart asked him, "I've been meaning to ask, what's with that sign? Is the Knights of Columbus still a thing? You don't have to be Catholic now to join?"

"What's the use with all the saints replaced with spooks? Any good myth will do. But they still gotta drink, right?

"Well, you know the Catholics weren't too popular in Scotland anyway. My grandmother used to sing a song: *Oh, no popes of Rome, no chapels to sadden my eyes, no nuns and no priests, no rosary beads, every day is the 12th of July.*"

"What's the 12th of July?"

Stuart said, "When William of Orange kicked the Catholics out of Scotland."

"That was a while back, I guess."

"1689, but it still gets people worked up."

A voice from down the bar said, "Are you with the deconstructionists?"

Stuart said, "Dismantlers; yeah, trying to take down the LHC without destroying the parts. I'm the last one who's going to turn out the lights when the Carthys are done."

The man said, "Well I never much believed in science anyway. Science is just one more folk psychology, nothing more, something you have to believe in for it to work for you, just like religion. Placebo and nocebo, rolled into one. What do you think about science?"

Stuart said, "I know about pipes and fittings and whatever makes the metal melt or break, nuts and bolts. Maybe I believe in engineering, torque on a wrench, but science seems to be a bunch of pompous overachievers who are just showing us the surface of a thousand years of tinkering that I don't understand, that they don't understand either. I could choose to believe it or not, none of that affects the strength of pipe. And then the spooks came and science just had to take a back seat, now it's all magic again."

The man sidled over and held up his glass, "Walt, from the States, what's left of them, after the Tejianos and Mexico moved the borders."

Raising his glass in response, "Stuart, from the Brexit Isles, what's left of *them.*"

"Here's to the Brexit Isles!"

"Glasgow, actually, the murder capital of Europe, at least my neighborhood was."

Brodie said, "I used to be a scientist, well, a graduate student in physics, anyway. Couldn't take the whole system, left it behind and became a gym teacher, middle school. Different choice, but same reason, the man, the squinty physics man, was holding me down."

"So what did you do?"

"I built a fucking collider in my garage out of spare parts."

"Really?"

"Yeah, called it the redneck hadron collider. Ever heard of the Higgs Bubble Drive?"

Stuart laughed, "That's a stupid question, they're buzzing all around the solar system and the milk run to Alpha Centauri. . ."

He took a swig. "You know that story about two guys who built the first one in a garage?"

"You're that guy? How come you're not hob-nobbin with the 20%?"

"I couldn't stand that freak show either. I just took a severance package and signed over my rights; couldn't be happier."

"What brings you to this joint?"

Brodie said, "Well, I *was* down at the Particle Dance Disco; but that place is dead without the geek squad. I'm torn, I hated the squints, but with no one to pick on, it might as well be the Dairy Queen."

Stuart said "Here, at least, as Hemingway said, it's a clean and well-lit place to drink. Add blessed silence and it's a feckin Fortress of Solitude."

Brodie said, "I still feel like a peanut buster parfait. So you're a union man? I stopped by the CERN offices, the union hall there is empty."

"There's no union labor. They've closed the Swiss entrance now that Al Andalus and the Carthies are taking up the slack in France.

Brodie said, "We've got our own independent local here now."

"We?"

"The Quantum Mechanics Union, kind of like the I.W.W.; Wobblies for the 22nd Century. It started as a joke at happy hour at the Particle Dance, the place the tour guide books touted as the chief hangout for physicists from the Large Hadron Collider. *Is it a large collider of hadrons or a collider of large hadrons? badda bing!* Well, if all the trades drank together it should be called the Quantum Mechanics Union. Their motto? Infinity or Else! Har, har. It was all very funny, before the spooks showed up."

Stuart said, "Ok, I get it, but what's with the monks and spook balls in the corner?"

"The Knights of Columbus Motorcycle Club? They're Jesuits, Ignazis, black robes; but without a pope in Rome, they're like Ronin."

"Samarai for hire?"

"For the right cause and price, sure. But they were outlawed by the Pope in the past more than once anyway and they're still miffed at the Soldiers of Christ being replaced by a chorus line. They set their own agenda."

"And the spooks aren't their enemies?"

"It's not the spooks' fault that humans want to leave the planet; spooks are ok. It's the theo-political magisterium they don't like. The Ignazi's don't want another pope in disguise, they might just help kick the bums out, a new Paradise!"

"More outlawed agitation?"

"Nobody cares anymore, Stuart. Spooks are taking all the squint jobs on the Orbital Collider, The LHC is just a salvage operation. Spooks don't need a living wage, CERN and 3MI subsidize them, the pilgrims treat them like the second fucking coming. Africa and the Mid East are rumbling north as first world intellectuals and spiritualists drink the koolaid."

"You're right." Stuart agreed. "Nobody North/Up is committed to the old economy. The workers are just getting by with the dismantling work but the planet's resources are leaving with the Boddhies."

"Exactly, and you saw what happened to Texas."

"Tejas?"

"Right, the Mexicans overran Trump's Wall that the American's paid for, dismantled it and used it to build sea walls around their own resorts."

"Poetic justice."

"And then they blew up the Alamo for real. Then the Tejianos took it back and pushed their borders further north and south."

Brodie pulled a necklace chain out of his shirt and showed Stuart a piece of crumbled brown adobe enclosed in clear plastic hanging from the chain. "See, they took the Alamo with them and defend it with each inch regained. 'Remember the Alamo' all the way from Zacatecas to Tuskahoma."

"You were there?"

"Con Los Nuevo Futuristas? Claro que si. I helped the Mexicans blow up the sucker, and then ran with the Tejianos, recruiting on both sides. Frankly, I got about as much patience for the new bobble heads as I did for the old ones. If 20% of humans keep leaving the planet, well, it could be a paradise for those who stay."

"Who's going to be in charge, you?"

"Nah, we'll just let all the factions kill each other and take over another 20%. All the nukes got shot into the sun back in '09. The battle field will grow poppies eventually for those who wait."

He was starting to make sense. "And how do you start this apocalypse?"

"It's starting already. Let's take a walk." They walked up the ramp to the scenic viewpoint at the top. Brodie didn't bother to lower his voice. "*Things fall apart, the center cannot hold, mere anarchy is loosed upon the world. . .*"

Stuart said, "Yeats, '*The blood-dimmed tide is loosed, and everywhere the ceremony of innocence is drowned. The best lack all conviction, while the worst are full of passionate intensity*'."

Brodie nodded repeatedly, "Helter Skelter brotha', take out the supports and watch it fall; pick up the pieces later after the fires burn out."

"Class warfare?" Stuart downed the half empty half of his Guinness.

"That's part of it, and then it's the Christians against the lions too, you know, the Cult against the atheists. That's an even better show. And all the old school monks and imams are marginalized too. The new religion is blasphemy and a hoot at that; just made up."

Stuart said. "Two thousand years ago, St. Paul did the same thing."

"And Bob's your uncle!" Brodie clinks his glass on Stuart's. "You know what they say, tragedy plus time equals comedy."

"I need a few laughs, and I've got lots of time on my hands." Stuart said, "After I'm done with the last magnet, there's just a lot of plumbing. Can't do the piece work too fast or you're out of a job."

"Right, get off your mustang, Sally. You know what the 20% is really about?"

"The pilgrims' line?"

"Right, the pilgrims use it to focus on *their* numbers, 20%, and their damned Library. *Five to one baby, one in five, no one here gets out alive.* See, the secret there is that, to the Boddhies, death isn't any worse than a lost data stream. Anyone who goes through the Library fits the definition of dead anyway. That's how sick they are. Live or dead, it's all the same. But, what about the 80% that stayed?

"It doesn't matter if we live or die either?"

"Exactly, we're fucked, but *we* got the 80%. Occupy Earth! Let's go talk to the black robes."

Stuart followed Brodie back down the spiral as the setting sun lit up the space elevator cable like a golden stair, like Rupunzel's hair, just waiting for a hero's quest to climb it.

Over in the corner booth, Stuart saw that the two black jackets had been joined by a couple of civilians, all mulling over a manuscript and some diagrams. The two spookball brothers hovered at eye level, one on each side of the booth. Brodie made introductions.

"Brother Claude, Brother Andrew, S.C. and Larr in the flesh, our effie brothers are Telly and Ignatz. Larr's hitching a ride to Vesta. This is Stuart, wasting his time dismantling the LHC."

Stuart said, "So, no Popes in Rome?"

Ignatz buzzed and turned toward Stuart, who flinched. It said, "No flock, no Rock. We're freelancers now."

Brodie said, "S.C. Schneider's a journalist. Give him the high tone version S.C."

S.C. took a sip from a large glass of cheap red wine. "Special to the *Faith and Values* section? Ok; see, grass roots faith and belief have always been based on some kind of experience, some event that people don't want to look at too closely, something just outside of normal mental life. When the spooks came, and quantum gravity, those events were explainable scientifically, but not explained away by science, it was transcendentalism not debunked, but proven, by science.

"So what happens? Something unexplainable does remain, it's the lack of a creator; it's the lack of knowledge of ultimate reality by the very entities we expected to know the answers. Spooks and Andromedans have no idea what happens when any sentient being ends its corporeal existence. So, there still is an unknown, but all the old religions, especially the People of the Book, the God of Abraham, Yahweh, El, Jesus, Allah and Mohammed. . ." He waved his hand, ". . .complete loss of credibility."

Ignatz said, "These are not the droids you are looking for."

Stuart said, "Whe . . ?"

S.C. said, "Some old re-enactor joke. Something only the spooks and lizards remember now."

Brother Andrew ignored the joke. "But, we can still fight against the Cult, not because it's wrong, but because it doesn't stand for social justice on Earth. There were plenty of wars in the past where the combatants were separated by religion but the goals were political. Like the Buddhists fighting the Hindus on Sri Lanka, two overtly pacifist religions, pacifists to a fault, just fighting because of political inequalities. So now we have real religious divides that mean more to people than political territory. This is the first time, we think, that there can be a war that is really about theology, I mean theology that matters, theology that creates social justice."

Brodie said, "I just want to blow stuff up."

Brother Claude examined his fingernails nervously, "Walt, you can't just want destruction. There has to be a purpose, or you'll just be disappointed in the end."

"I want things to get better, I do. I just get more joy from knocking out the rotted supports than you do. I'm not crazy. Besides, I'm not counting on making it to the promised land anyway. Have a drink on me when you get there." He threw some credit chits at the table, laughed and waved good bye to the group. To Stuart he said, "Come back for happy hour on Thursday, it's taco night. We'll talk some more."

*

The next afternoon, Stuart made his second daily inspection of the jobsite. The dismantlers were just finishing detaching one of the thirty-five ton dipole magnets and hooking it up to a crane. Gaddafi signaled to the crane operator and stood back while his crew kept the big magnet from swinging as it went up.

When it had cleared the top of the tunnel, Stuart approached him and said, "Are we on for tonight, dinner at 10:00?" This was code for the prearranged camera malfunction at the ten-kilometer marker, where a new crop of singularities would be harvested. Gaddafi took off his hard hat and smiled. "See you then, my treat."

This kind of thing would not have gone on at any time prior to his talk with Christine's mum. Before that, he had imagined he had a reason to be a better man, to be an honorable man that Christine could love again. Now, it seemed like both he and the world were on a zip line to hell in a handbasket.

Gaddafi added, "Come to the bar after. I got a girl from Addis Ababa, a real beauty, lonely like you. You'd look good together, Ebony and Ivory. She'll cheer you up."

"Is she a real girl, not a professional or a fembot?

"Love doesn't care, my friend. But yes, she's real. Here you are, a stranger in a strange land, lonely and far from home. Love the one you're with."

"Maybe. . ."

*

Instead, that evening, Stuart examined the two rainbow bridge boxes he had taken as consideration for his part in the criminal enterprise He put the boxes side by side and opened and closed the lids to calibrate the quantum entanglement. Then, separating them, he put a lump of coal in one and when the music started playing in the second box, he retrieved a diamond.

Then, he took one box home and did the same trick the next morning. When he got to his office and opened the second box, there was another diamond! Voila! Stuart's mood picked up. *This could be a real money maker.* Maybe he'd take a run at that Ethiopian girl after all, or the stylists at the Salon de Coiffure. It was a good opening act anyway. *Nothing up my sleeve, ladies.*

That evening, after work, he wrote a message on a strip of paper and put it in the box in a small graviton field capsule, included to protect fragile items. When the capsule appeared in the second box, Stuart opened it and the strip of paper was intact.

His e-mail started to chime. It was the tune reserved for the admins at the L2 Lagrange Point Station, the big brass upstairs. It was too late for mundane news. His mood instantly sliced into the rough. He clicked on the e-mail and scanned the message . . . *immediate termination . . . . clearances revoked . . . aiding and abetting theft of CERN property . . . conspiracy . . . racketeering. . .possible criminal charges. . .*

His face froze and his stomach dropped as if he was on the edge of a towering precipice. The job was the last bit of normal he had left, like a life preserver in the ocean.

He got up and walked out on the loading dock into the starlit dark and silence, still holding one rainbow bridge in his hand. He threw the box as far as he could onto the scrap heap, crossed the street to the bar and started downing shots of cheap Irish whiskey.

The workers had gone home by then. S.C. and Larr were lingering over tacos in a booth but they could tell Stuart wasn't interested in small talk by his drink. He hadn't even had any tacos. Gaddafi walked in a bit later and sat beside Stuart.

"Stewie, I heard what happened. You really screwed the pooch big monkey man."

"They didn't fire you or your guys?"

"Well, they're still colonials at heart, white man's burden, don't expect so much from my guys. I, of course, know nothing. They gave me your job; now that's funny."

Stuart said, "Feck and shite."

"What will you do now?"

"Get out of Dodge, maybe South Africa, Antarctica, up the Elevator, take a sailsuit to the Moon or Mars . . . anywhere but here."

"Peregrinatio? A pilgrimage?"

"That's not what I need." He downed another shot and stared at the rainbow bridge he'd kept, imagining himself still staring at it years from now, nothing having changed.

In the morning, the truck drivers would show up to start their daily runs to the Space Elevator. The scrap was loaded into shipping containers and trucked to Geneva. They were then clamped on the freight shuttle for the lift into orbit.

The containers were boosted toward the sun for a tight orbit; this time of year it only took a couple of months. Then their contents, including the rainbow bridge box, would melt and distill layered ores to be mined as the containers went round the horn and returned to Earth.

He was thinking he might just jump that boxcar and stow away to the L3 Debris Ring, as far away as you could get from Earth, from everything that had him in its sights.

*

Earth

March, 2125 C.E.

The Debris Ring

Arch Sandifur's responsibilities at the Debris Ring Temple, by design, allowed him to ignore the companies his father had started with Walter Brodie over eighty years before. Although his Asperger's had been under control, control did not make him any more suited to corporate work. There was a sheer maddening numbness in the business of research, design and manufacturing, not to mention freight and passenger hauling. Even a star drive corporation was still a rat race for which some people were just not suited.

By the time Arch was chronologically forty years old, he had abdicated the throne of the Bubble Drive Dynasty to his sister Emma. Walter Brodie had jumped ship years earlier and *his* demons, and everyone knew this, *his* demons had not allowed him to stomach even grad school physics departments, much less entrepreneurship and fiscal responsibility. Even years after Brodie took his buy-out, it was rumored that he had joined, some say started, the New United Futurists, channeling his sociopathy into a private anarchist agenda. *Conspiracy theories about conspiracy theorists.*

But Arch, he needed something that was OCD enough to keep him calm and also something intense enough so he wouldn't get bored. Religious ritual took care of the first need and the rabbit hole of quantum gravity field theory and theological aesthetics took care of the second.

After the first Moving Day, Emma visited frequently on her travels from one bucket list or Waypoint destination to another. Finally, she too settled down in the stacks at the Debris Ring Temple, a secular, sometimes blasphemous and profane, counterpoint to her brother's robe and mala, but blasphemy was a moving target. As long as one didn't question the basic narrative in public there weren't a lot of rules. After all, the underpinnings of historical religions were on the ropes or were on hospice care, but the need to define and question theological reality, the questions of life, consciousness, meaning and purpose; why are we here? where are we going?; those questions remained.

Each new layer of reality that had been peeled back revealed sentients that had no better answer to those perennial questions than humans did B.C., Before Charlotte. Therefore, necessarily, the adepts of the old religions as well as the old scientific method all had a place in crafting the new evolving theories of everything.

*

March 31, 2125 C.E.
At the G-Sink Tap Room
Cape Canaveral Elevator

Outside the G-Sink Tap Room, Tom and Jen, in their sail suits, sat in oversized wooden rocking chairs on the Victorian front porch of the space elevator station locked at the geosynchronous point midway up the carbon nano tube braided cable, about 35,800 kilometers above the base station at Cape Canaveral. The chairs, crafted in a faux Americana style, were attached to the porch so they could rock and not float away in the zero g. Likewise, hidden grav-lev magnetics grabbed their butts tight down on the seat so they wouldn't launch out of the chairs. The station comprised a rest stop, tavern, maintenance and administrative offices and graviton retros that kept the elevator in place above the Cape.

Before lunch at the G-Sink, the down shuttle had deposited them at this point where gravity and centrifugal force were equal. It was the 'down shuttle' even when it was going up because it never went all the way up. Now they were waiting with other passengers for the 'up shuttle' to come down.

From there, the up shuttle built momentum as gravity let loose and centrifugal force took over, gradually accelerating as it approached the counterweight above. More graviton retros there kept the counterweight above the G-Sink.

The traveler had a choice when boarding the up shuttle. Six-passenger transfer shuttles attached as modules to the main unit and could detach when the acceleration hit escape velocity. These ran to a set destination, usually to the nearby L1 and L2 Lagrange Points or the Moon Tether.

The one-man shuttle and sail suit crowd, clipped to the outside of the up shuttle, set their own agenda. In either case, the speed attained at the top end of the cable assured the minimal escape velocity required at that height. In a sail suit, the boost was enough to provide momentum until the slow build of solar wind and photons took over.

The rocking chairs and the porch were a bit of whimsy designed by Tom's grandfather Tom Petty, Sr. and his great uncle Dan Pritchard, founders of Mike the Mover Magnetics, Inc., known as 3MI. The rocking chairs were sized to allow travelers in pressure suits and sail suits to have one last incongruous rock before stepping off for destinations near and far. It was, by design, a set piece, touching and absurd, a call and response; a volley from Dan Pritchard and an invitation to create, innovate and imagine. It was a call to play in the future.

It was also, in a very real sense, the front porch of the planet, where one could just take a stroll around the neighborhood and be back by dinner, or start walking and never come back, with no schedule or deadlines, except perhaps the next Moving Day.

This trip, they were just headed to the L2 Station, a quick jaunt that gave a good experience of solo flight, but not long enough to get tedious. They also had been to the Moon as sort of an anniversary tradition, as well as to Waypoints on the annual pilgrimage before Moving Day.

It was sort of a January-December romance since Jen had been Uncle Dan's secretary at the beginning, almost a hundred years before. During her interplanetary kickboxing career, she had rebooted her cybernetics and augmented her fleshy parts so that she still appeared about thirty.

Tom said, "You know, I was in love with you when I was thirteen."

"A wet dream is not love, Tom."

"I think it is, actually, it's something naturally arising, without thinking logically about it, that's love."

"Not just some sick old lady fetish?"

"Well, you never actually got old, so no. Have you ever read Proust?"

"Sounds like a bad idea, something about French pastry?"

"Yeah, seven volumes of memories from the taste of a cookie dipped in tea."

She said, "No, I was more of a Bruce Li, *Enter the Dragon* kind of girl."

"Right, well I only read the first volume, myself," he said, "but you'll get this. He wrote about the first time you fall in love. Before you know what that is, before you know you can be aroused by *any* woman, the first one comes out of the natural world. He talks about walking through the woods and a peasant girl appears. She comes out of nature, and so he thinks that the feeling comes from her particular being, you know, the trees and the girl are part of the same thing, and he hadn't generalized it. Everyone's first love is like that."

"Ok."

"It's only later you get jaded and see women as interchangeable. So yes, a wet dream that arises naturally is like that girl in the woods."

"Ok, I think I'm flattered, but how do you feel now?"

"I got over the jaded part and went back to that first feeling, but instead of a lifetime of regret, imagining what might have been, there you were, the same person that the universe gave me when I was thirteen."

"You're such a sensitive boy. Is that in again?"

"I don't do trends."

"But I didn't arise out of a walk in the woods."

"You appeared out of *my* natural world. Humans, and all our technology, mediate nature anyway. There's never been a noble savage, living in harmony with unchanged nature. We always have managed nature. If you appeared from bricks and steel instead of rocks and trees, it's still my mind creating something from the reality at hand."

"Like Charlotte from the Higgs field."

"Yep; that's my story and I'm sticking to it."

"That's why I love you baby, you never let a good fantasy get in the way of facts. Ooh, here's the up shuttle."

*

April 1, 2125
Meyrin

After his termination and Taco Thursday drunk, with Brodie conspicuously absent, Stuart stomped back to his office instead of going home. Stepping on his own shoelace, he tripped and unceremoniously flopped into his chair. Putting his head down on his arms he fiddled with the model of the Higgs drive, inscribed with a small plaque honoring someone else's years of service or some long sought teravolt landmark, his vision was too blurry to tell.

The blue light usually soothed him, but this night the wavy patterns surrounding him just made him feel awash and drowned, at the bottom of an impossibly blue and sunlit lagoon, a dream of death infused with light.

He was still hanging on to the other box, clutching it close to his heart as he slept. His breathing was shallow and fast; periodically, a tear escaped from his dreams.

Sometime in the night, a tinkling tune coming from the box stirred him. He opened it and there was the capsule just as he had seen it the last time he was at work, before they revoked his security clearance. He unscrewed the cap and took out the strip of paper. He read. *What're you blinkin' like an eejit for?*

Half drunk, half asleep, he did the rational thing, turned the strip over, wrote *Christine?*, put it back in the capsule and closed the lid. A few moments later, the music started up again. Now more awake, hands shaking, he opened the box and the capsule.

Took you long enough. Of course it's Christine.

The strips, like fortunes, came and went rapidly.

Your mum said you were gone.

I am gone, gone somewhere, anyway.

Without Stuart realizing it, he began to hear her voice and he replied out loud.

"But, you're not a spook."

"Not."

"How did you find me?"

"Hard to miss, blubbering at this wormhole. I finally made you cry."

"I wasn't. . ."

"Was, and mooning over me."

"Sorry."

"Don't be. Just stop depressing everybody. Love me. I'm still a beauty, a mirror of your dreams."

"Where are you?"

"Don't know, not far, wait, something, something, the dark forever?"

"But?"

"Find me."

"Find you?"

"Your love made a light in the darkness. Your thoughts were hard to resist."

"But, how?"

"I did my part, now find me."

Dawn was breaking. Stuart's head cleared as the sunlight dimmed the blue ripples on his cubicle walls. Without hesitation, he was up and out the door, got on his hover cycle, took full manual control and redlined it. Alarms sounded and faded as he passed speed limit monitors. He blasted past his company flat without a glance. CERN could have his crap. He stopped in the Space Elevator parking lot and, for the first time, really looked at the ribbon rising from the Jet d' Eau. In the morning sunlight it was his shimmering Rainbow Bridge as far up as he could see.

He bought a ticket and went to the travel store. His last paychip, delivered to his account with the pink slip e-mail, bought the latest model sailsuit.

As he headed toward the boarding ramp from the parking lot, a commotion was starting. A group of people had rushed the ribbon, jumping over the low railing into the scrubby landscaping and woodchips surrounding the base. The mostly decorative light security was nonplussed by the rush. Mostly, they just posed for selfies with the tourists. The surge blew past them and began to encircle the ribbon. Security was now just keeping the curious from joining the coup, or whatever it was.

Stuart wasn't about to let these goofballs get in his way, not today, not with Christine egging him on. He ran past the loose cordon and was going to pry them all off the ribbon one by one if necessary.

But, as he was running toward the ribbon, they all let go and ran in every direction straight away from the ribbon. It was then he saw Larr Yellingson running toward him.

"Stuart, run! C'mon!" Larr grabbed Stuart's arm and spun him around. Stuart ran too. An explosion from behind them deafened him and a shock wave hit him from behind and knocked him down. Larr kept running. Stuart looked back over his shoulder and inconceivably, as smoke cleared, the ribbon had separated at the base. In slow motion, the tether was lifting off of the station base and rising up as the whole thing started to approach the horizontal as far as the eye could resolve it. At that point it was starting to burn from re-entry. It looked like the fuse on a cartoon anarchist's bomb, a bomb the size of the earth.

*

April 1, 2125
Cape Canaveral Elevator

At that same moment, as the up shuttle slowed to settle in at the G-Sink platform, a low flying drone delivered a quantum gravity bomb to the tether base below at Cape Canaveral. As Tom and Jen watched, the shuttle jerked back upward trailing ramps, docking clamps and hoses that had just been attached, upward in a motion that gave the illusion of the platform plummeting down. Their stomachs dropped as well as the elevator suffered a complete failure, the base of the tether having been severed by the blast. The other tethers around the planet, Spaceport America, Geneva, Tokyo, Brisbane and the rest were attacked at the same moment. Earth's off planet capabilities were destroyed and the New United Futurists took credit with their ubiquitous *N.U.F. said!*

The only thing that saved Tom and Jen was the grav-mag clamps locking their butts to the rocking chairs. The initial jerk didn't dislodge them and they were able to detach as the station continued in its geosynchronous orbit, but without its base or counterweight.

The Down Shuttle succumbed to the force of gravity, detached from the now slack tether, deployed a parasail and rode home with only a bump and a bit of turbulence. The front porch emergency protocols cut the up ribbon when the down ribbon went slack. The untethered Up Shuttle and its hangers-on followed the counterweight above which suddenly had a trajectory, now a true geosynchronous orbit speeding away from its terminus, unmitigated by the gravitron retros.

Before the counterweight could react and cut the other end, the newly energized ribbon cracked like a whip and the Up Shuttle was subjected to multiple gravities. The thirty people inside were killed by their harnesses. The people on the outside were connected with cable and carabiners which held as did the freight tie-ons. Their suits however, split and rapid decompression killed the fifty travelers. Similar incidents occurred at the other elevators. The ribbons also fell but mostly burned up on the way down. All told, around the world, about two thousand people died in the attacks, but more importantly, the Earth was blasted back to the stone age of Saturn V rockets and old school Russian boosters. The New United Futurists had achieved their short term goal.

*

Mara/Earth
April 1, 2429 A.R./April 1, 2125 C.E.

As Charlotte probed her side of the anomalous node, at the Library, on the other side of that node, it was April 1, 2125, Moving Day. At the Debris Ring, the Library floated at the center of the L3 Lagrange Point donut hole while the Temples and 3MI offices bulged like garish gems at the arbitrary top of the Ring, flanking the sparkling jewel of the Golden Wire Stupa. The seedier sections of the cobbled together Ring became thinner and joined at Rock Bottom, from a distance blending into an uneven grey with points of light and vents of exhaust and ice crystals randomly scattered along its dark circumference.

Thousands of pilgrims arranged themselves in concentric spheres surrounding the Library and inside the Debris Ring. The pass required to be in the closest sphere indicated the successful training and gnosis acquisition needed for the high road, not just for ordinary travel. It was the pass needed to take your final *transitus* through the tachyon anomaly. This gnosis would not end in a familiar but alternate dimension and timeline. This gnosis led you to a final passage and not even the Bodhisattva knew exactly what that entailed; you didn't come back, that was for sure.

Brodie, in a saffron and purple pressure suit caught the last Up Shuttle from Geneva, then a Cult shuttle to the Ring. He had earned his stripes by learning all the gnosis and mantras required for him to be in the first sphere. He rode a one person scooter, like a Harley with just the seat, handlebars and gas tank. The deep mantras started on the common channel. The Gayatri Mantra first, greeting the sun, *Oṃ bhūr bhuvaḥ svaḥ, tatsavitur vareṇyaṃ, bhargo, devasya dhīmahi, dhiyo yo naḥ pracodayāt, Oṃ*

Then the talking drum, the tabla, taught by pandits to students by singing the syllables first, *DhaDhaTiTa DhaDhaTuNa TaTaTiTa DhaDhaDhinNa . . .*

The signal was given, one tone from a Tibetan singing bowl that peaked and shimmered as it dissipated. Then the individual mantras sounded in sections and rounds, intensified and intertwined like liquid braids. The first circle pilgrims began to move toward the Library at a steady pace. Brodie pulled slightly ahead of the others, not noticeably at first, but then faster and faster.

The pilgrims and the monks were too intent on the correct pronunciation of the mantras and the correct trajectory required to enter the chosen tachyon node to notice. By the time the alarm was sounded at Central Temple Operations and the abort signal was broadcast to the pilgrims, Brodie was already entering the Library. Clearly, his intent was more than just to enter a node. The speed alone would make that difficult. As horrified pilgrims watch, Brodie pushed off the scooter into a node causing the scooter to veer away from him and into the mouth of the anomaly out of control.

A small flash appeared to ignite a fireball. For a few seconds, it rivaled the much more distant sun, then imploded into blackness. Brodie, the Library and the hopes and dreams of multitudes disappeared in seconds.

*

In the Dark Forever
$$T = -0$$

Though Charlotte was shielded from the devastation of the Library itself, her side of the node imploded as well. Technically, the implosion created a rare magnetic monopole that captured her with quantum gravity stronger than any naturally occurring phenomenon.

Her energy body was too close and the monopole pulled her back through the node, retracing her entry of so many years ago. But the Library, her means of return to Earth, no longer existed and she found herself in the in-between, the multiverse field, in the dark-forever, but hurtling out of control. She was unable to remain conscious in this flux and the fields and gage bosons that formed her suddenly reverted to an unobserved wave function, the superposition of love and longing.

Silver Dan was waiting. As Charlotte lost consciousness in the dark-forever, Dan wrapped his potential body around hers and held her completely enclosed, to shield her from the effects of the implosion, the monopole and unified field forces that no Planck scale sentient could survive unaided. For some time, he merely cradled her and directed her momentum safely though he could not diminish it. And so she slept, between universes in the multiverse field where, in its infinite tensor braiding, every point in a resting state held the promise of creation.

They skimmed down natural flumes and neuron tubules and in each bump and scrape felt sterile or fruitful futures arising from their passage; from big or other bangs or bounces to heat deaths, to the collapse of moments into eternities. She slept like Tiamat commingling her salt waters of Chaos with Daniel's sweet waters, tingling with desire for her husband even though they inhabited each other already, completely. Even in that first embrace, she already held their children, the lesser gods, within her; ancient, stirring, suckling.

With her speed undiminished, her every turn, every kick of the covers and every dreaming fluff of her pillow created space time and the potential for life. None of this woke her as she rode with no senses directed outwards, dreaming while poets and mystics, St. John of the Cross, Edith Södergran and others, listened and whispered,

What has captured me in the night? Where have you hidden Beloved, and left me moaning? You fled like the stag after wounding me. I went out calling you, but you were gone. Why, since you wounded this heart, don't you heal it? And why, since you stole it from me do you leave it so and fail to carry off what you have stolen? . . . On foot I wandered through the solar systems before I found the first thread of my red dress. Already I sense myself. Somewhere in space hangs my heart, shaking the void, streaming sparks to other intemperate hearts. . . .Where is the ring that twists the knife; that signifies the unfairness of the universe to all but me; even to dark matter and energy that can only recall an aching distant dream of you in fitful sleep between stars, crying out: What has captured me in the night?

Silver Dan simply let her sleep, he didn't try anything, didn't make a move, like the first time she had lain down with him at his parents' house in his bedroom. Back in that room, he had imagined that he pulled her from the air, pulled her down, subjected her to gravity, a small unkindness leading down, down, *down into the folds of something so soft and warm, down beyond her own retreat, downward further than light would have her perceive, cool darkness, illuminating the sound of all the joy she did not remember.*

And she continued to dream; *Amelia and six white vapor trails, geese in formation, delta-v; the sum of Low Earth Orbit to Geostationary Transfer Orbit and Geostationary Transfer Orbit to Geosynchronous Orbit should equal Low Earth Orbit to Geosynchronous Orbit, delta v, Delta of Venus, a spy in the house of love, little birds, little burns, how it burns! My love, my Daniel, my one soul, Daniel. . .*

Eventually, she stirred, regained her coherence in her own island field and caressed the boundaries of his cocoon, her birth canal, pressing outward and then releasing like contractions, tumbling in a marsupial's pouch, lapping milk from the skin of her savior. She was a stranger in this place, in danger without the womb of his energy body around her. Somehow, that was exactly the right answer. He was her pressure suit, her diving bell, her god and protector. No, it was just Dan, the Dan she remembered.

"I'm so sleepy," she said.

He said, "Don't worry, Baby, I'll take the wheel for a while, you sleep." She began to remember and relive that day in his room that held the promise of a lifetime of mornings, then two lifetimes. She mumbled, "Ok, Baby, but don't let me sleep past seven, Shanti has a thing at school."

He said, "It's not a school day."

"Where are we?"

"On our way to find out."

She said, "I've missed you Daniel, so much."

"It's a completeness that we all remember, long for. It will return in time."

"But I want you now and forever."

Daniel said, "You have Dan, your husband, your daughter Shanti, a whole life. When we left you on Moving Day, you knew for sure what you wanted."

"It's not the same, gods forgive me; it's just not the same."

"Sleep, we'll talk it out later."

Again, her consciousness entered a liminal state. She whispered in her dream,

Thinking about you, your face, your beautiful poetry, who you are, your mind, your soul, concentrating on you, imagining you're here, imagining it is you, wishing it were you in your body as I knew it, just for a moment, imagining the feeling of you and the smell of you, the taste of you, your lips, your voice, your face, how nice that would be. I wish you were really here, so I could look in your eyes and tell you how much I love you and what you're doing to me, what you've always done to me. I do remember you, Daniel, the real Daniel. I remember a lot about you. I have those memories of our beginning pretty clear and I have thought about them, over the years, now and then, because they're good. You were always good. Right from the start, and you knew what you were doing. I do love you, this you. How could I not? Always have. Je t'aime, I love you.

"Listen," he said, but not forcefully enough to wake her. "It *is* me. There was an accident, an attack. The Library, your Library, was destroyed. It created a monopole, the rarest of things. You were too close to the node when it was created and were pulled in. I saw it before it happened to you and waited for you to appear. It's the tachyons in the anomaly, all moving faster than the speed of light.

"But. . . that can't. . ."

"Shush. I know, I know, just listen. Inflation means that the whole of space time can expand faster than the speed of light, because the speed of light is only real within the space time that inflation creates. That velocity got inside of you and we're going to do some aerobatics to slow you down. For right now though, you just have to sleep."

She heard his poetry from two lifetimes ago. *A light could shine to me just like a darkness, its backwards progress making cross a room, and hit me from behind and trace a brightness that swears I've been again that way too soon.*

He swaddled her more tightly as he veered toward a spot where he could try to dissipate the velocity which would eventually kill her if unabated. He felt the delta v required to alter her trajectory and velocity. Delta v, the same calculations that took rockets to the moon, that pork chop diagram of the three body problem now in the multiverse field in a place that its bespectacled, slide-rulered, pocket protected, acolytes could never have imagined in their most fevered wet dreams of curves and hollows, ellipses and foci, wormholes and black holes, dark energy and dark matter, all expanding and aching in the void.

Again, the specter of his youth spoke to her: *I walked around the park in the sun and yearned for you with my whole being, to hold your hand, to smile the smile of those who still have their smells intertwined from their morning coupling, ready to run back again to that secret room of the heart, leaving the world behind for yet another eternal moment.*

The whole world, the children playing, dogs running, workers resting, gulls and ducks, the music of the carousel, the smell of something delicious wafting, all, all, all are there only to make our memories exquisite. This is all a world where love awaits only us around every corner.

Thinking of this, of your face, your voice, every image of you, I want nothing but you. Every desire I ever had was a shadow, a poor imitation, of the clean bright razor sharp pure necessity of this desire for you. It is tragic, it is not; it is transcendent, it is not; it is knowable, it is not; it is the ultimate truth behind all things, it is an insignificant speck. I am always at its mercy.

When you are away from me, I am jealous even of the cloudless sky that can touch you when I cannot. I am jealous of the ocean waves that can embrace you when I cannot. I am jealous of the sun that can heat your most precious places, driving them to desire, when I cannot. I am jealous of any being whose breath is on you, whose heart beats with you, whose attention is caught by you only for a moment.

I am maddened by the universe that created you as its offering to me and now holds you just out of reach as its cruel punishment. I am consumed by jealous raging against the sheer injustice of a moment apart from you. I am spent, punished, exalted, born and die inside of your womb, I want to lay my head at the opening of your womb and breathe in the life force denied to me, a small and sorry life without your living, flowing energy to nourish me. How can I even go on and put on a face of pleasant resignation? It is only the dream of you, the thought that you hover over me at night, touching me with astral kisses, only this conceit, by which I fool myself into thinking I am alive without you.

Silver Daniel whispered, "We are going to get some drag off the black hole at the galactic center, in the old neighborhood. We can dip in and drag our heels a bit at the event horizon. Coming out we will have reentered space time in our past. By the time you are safe we'll be pretty close to the beginning."

"The big bang?"

"Yeah, or big bounce; well, here it's just another roadside attraction, like the World's Biggest Ball of String, we're in the neighborhood, might as well pop over and see what all the fuss is about, right?"

"How can we move so far, so fast?"

"All of space time in our home universe, well any universe, is accessible without physical distance, it's just a matter of dipping your toe in at the right spot. And there're a few other things I want to show you, as long as we're in the Way Back Machine."

"And I'm your boy Sherman?" She asked.

"My girl, Shirley?"

"Your girl? Surely." She vibrated laughter a bit.

Dan said. "Wow, I did miss you, this part of you, you're right."

"But, you've been cheating on me with me?"

"It's more like a threesome. Well, anyway, she's busy on Earth, it's like a hall pass."

"You always made your indiscretions logical."

"Mostly imagined."

She said, "You sinned in your mind, but you did enjoy it so much."

"It's ok to read the menu as long as you eat at home."

"And on the road?" she asked.

"I'll have to think a bit to rationalize that one. She loves you as much as I do, as much as I love her. And you're a tease, go back to sleep."

Inside his embrace she dreamed again, *Now,* this *is the best feeling ever.*

*

Earth
Geneva, April 1, 2125

Larr and Stuart sat on the pavement, both having fallen down backwards as they craned their necks trying to follow the crazy trajectory of the unleashed ribbon. The crowd of fellow travelers had disappeared into the city as the security officers just stared up as well. There was a moment or two of silence with just a seagull call in the distance and then their radios began to squack, phone-pads started ringing and sirens began that europop beat that assured Larr he was no longer in Kansas.

He began to talk as if being interviewed for the news, man on the street, literally, just processing what he couldn't stop from saying, "I was looking for Walt, waiting to board . . . Brodie, I know it's Brodie, known it since Oakland . . . hadn't seen him in a week, but this was my shuttle, my ticket upstairs, going to Vesta, but the crowd came rushing in, just as I was at the boarding platform and I couldn't get on, just pushed me away, then somebody shoved me ahead of them and I knew something was happening, and they all ran, and I thought they would think I was one of them but the cops weren't here and the security guards weren't looking and I just ran . . ."

Stuart swallowed his own disappointment, put his arm around Larr and started to rock a bit as the adrenaline drained out of both of them. "Larr, it's ok, were ok, we're alive anyway."

"You always smell good Stuart."

"Old Spice, but it's not for you, ya poofter."

"You're a good person."

"Not anymore, I got fired, trying to leave town, but now, I don't. . ."

"I'm not a good person. Gotta find Frida, she'll know what to do."

He got his phone-pad out and swiped to her number but all connections were down. Stuart got up and helped Larr get to his feet. They walked back to the hover scooter and Stuart put his own helmet on Larr and pulled the strap tight. As the 3MI and CERN cops entered the parking lot like the Dukes' General Lee, Stuart and Larr puttered out to the street. "Hey, let's get some breakfast at the Funny Horse. I got some girls I want you to meet."

"I don't want to . . ." Stuart ratcheted the handle bar grip back and the accelerator whine drowned out Larr as efficiently as the sirens.

As they pulled up to the Funny Horse, it was not a typical morning. The joint had morphed into a self-serve coffee only establishment as the staff joined the customers, watched the news on their phone-pads or ran off to family or out of town driven by adrenalin, angst and fear. The stylists were barricading the Inside Africa Salon de Coiffure, suddenly not interested in Stuart's chest hair. Everyone seemed to be charging toward or running away from some imagined confrontation. Stuart and Larr took it all in just staying out of the way.`

Stuart brought some coffee to Larr. "I couldn't find any cream."

"That's ok" Larr closed his eyes, breathed in the coffee aroma and then blew on it before taking a sip.

As they watched, a few people running with what seemed like more purpose were methodically tacking up posters on storefronts and old microwave poles. As they disappeared up the side roads, Stuart got up and pulled down one tacked over the Fancy Horse menu beside the entrance.

"'*New United Futurist Manifesto.*' What the fuck? This is Brodie's crap!"

Larr said, "Did he do this?" as he began to see his own part in the disaster.

One of the stylists came over, "Stuart, look the GP reports more things; not just here either."

Stuart and Larr looked at her phone pad. "All the space elevators were bombed. Any one of them could land here if they don't burn up first." They all looked at the sky. The Geneva ribbon was gone, only the trailing smoke from reentry identified the danger, but the Moscow ribbon or even Cape Town, could rain fire at any moment. Most likely it would be one from the same latitude depending on how the Coriolis effect acted on the whole ribbon suddenly free from graviton control. Too much math to be sure, but New York or Tokyo, could certainly fall right on them. "Ahh . . . and . . . the Library was attacked."

The stylist said, "Look, the starships, they've stopped."

Larr read the pad and said, "The Bubble Drive no longer works. What? That's most of the system's economy right there, and are the people stranded light years from home? *Light years*, Stuart, did Brodie do *that*?"

Stuart said, "That's unbelievable. How could he. . ." They all looked up squinting to see the first fiery descent of a carbon nanofiber ribbon 36,000 miles long, seemingly aimed right at them, like a high pop fly in deep center field, lost in the sun.

*

The sleeper cell cadres moved in as soon as the bombs went off. The Temple Monks and 3MI Security were in disarray, dealing with their own dead and desperately trying to contact the other elevators, spaceports and stations on and off planet to determine the bigger picture. Ignazi's and NUF's quietly just walked in and secured the buildings, escorting everyone else out at gunpoint. They let all dead and wounded be carried out in an orderly manner. The only hostage was the elevator base itself. The severing of the ribbon did no further damage at the base, but it came down like twisting serpents on fire, raining carbon nanofiber like hail and the remaining intact sections of the ribbon, by the time they hit the ground, cut swaths of damage thousands of miles long. Fires, craters, cities evacuated, and then tornadoes and other climate disturbances as the global weather patterns were sliced like a bizarre birthday cake, creating a myriad of small but powerful storm cells.

And what did the 80% think about the elevators? Anyone could see them unaided as far as the horizon. With binoculars and telescopes, you could sit in a mountain meadow in the Alps tending goats and see the ribbons in a 360 degree view. From Geneva, the ribbons at London, Moscow, even Nairobi, were visible. With a good telescope you could see the geostationary stations and the counterweights in orbit. Sail suits glinted in the dark as they reflected the sun. Surrounding each of the pilgrims left behind was a clear vista of what they no longer had, a way out.

The Rise and Fall of the New United Futurists, S.C. Schneider, Modern Europa Press, 2130.

*

Mara
June 1, 2430 A.R.

The cat alarm usually awakened Dan before the real alarm. Biddy knew when the real alarm was supposed to go off on the weekdays and before that, she gently tiptoed over his back and sniffed at his face as if she was being careful not to wake him. Usually, automatically, he put one arm out of the covers and drew her in. If he wasn't ready to get up, she acquiesced to a bit of spooning, and then left when his breathing became deep and rhythmic.

If she was lucky however, he got up and started shuffling to the kitchen. With success in sight, she either meowed at the food dish or the back door. A "No, it's too dark." or "No, the raccoons are out." would send her skittering down the hall and then, finally, she would concede to use the scorned litter box. Even if it was raining, she had to go out the back door and sit in the mud room window for a while just to meow the weather report and get back in. It was as if she didn't want to deprive Dan of *his* ritual. It was comforting for both of them, small talk like 'how's the weather' in the dark stillness otherwise only disturbed by one or more sides of conversations Dan conducted with himself.

The first thing he did on waking up was to walk to the kitchen and turn on the coffee machine. Then, he turned on the water to run and get hot while he retrieved the paper from the front porch. With reading material in hand, he passed back through the kitchen on the way to the bathroom and filled two cups with hot water. He had to complete these tasks before he could get in the bathroom and take care of his morning ablutions. *Please put the roll on the holder. Don't leave it on the counter; and it unrolls over the top. And please don't let it unroll on the floor, I could get an infection.* He flushed, tore the cardboard tube off the holder and replaced it with a new toilet paper roll, unrolling over the top.

Can you spread the shower curtain when you're done? It bunches up by the toilet. He pulled the shower curtain to its full length and started back through the kitchen, made his cup of coffee and left her cup on the counter. If her cup cooled off too much he had to refill it with hot water to keep it warm. Then he would check on her and whisper "Do you want to get up today?" *Not yet, but don't let me sleep past seven. Shanti has a thing at school.*

Only then did he sit down on the double love seat recliner, read the paper and take a first swig of dark coffee as the cat burrowed into his side again. With Miss Manners, the funnies and legal notices read, he skimmed the rest and got up to get ready for work. He sat the ironing board up in the guest room, plugged in the iron then went to his closet and picked out shirt, pants, tie, socks and suspenders and laid it all on the bed. *Don't just put your clothes in the dryer, iron the creases. You have to look sharp. And please don't leave the hangers on the bed.*

On his way to shave and wash up, he straightened the place mats on the dining room table and picked up a stray paperclip and popcorn kernel off of the floor. She had made the placemats and embroidered a stylized capital 'D' and 'C' intertwined so the 'C' set like a horseshoe ringer on the curve of the 'D.' *Like the first day we were together, I slipped my arm in yours and pulled you tight next to me and never let you go, never will.* His heart skipped a beat there but soon he continued on to the bathroom. He looked in the bathroom mirror and shaved while he ran the water to get it warm enough to wash his face. He flipped up the trimmer to trim his mustache and then froze again. *Put conditioner on your mustache.* "I could shave it off but you told me to grow it." *Put conditioner on your mustache if you want to kiss me.* "I do want to kiss you." Sadly, he realized that he never followed that rule. Something began to well up inside as he ironed his clothes and got dressed.

The top buttons on dress shirts now had elastic attachments so you could get pork jowls and not change your shirt size; medium is the new large; or is large the new medium? Suspenders had the same effect, if your belly grew, suspenders would still keep your pants up, and maybe you would lose weight, right, so why buy bigger pants just yet?

Dan tied his tie in the mirror. He did it with his eyes half closed because if he actually looked at it or thought about it, the muscle memory would fail, the non-cognitive process would explode and he would have to start over. Then he put on his sport coat and checked the pockets; wallet, phone, checked the top of his head for eyeglasses and stuck his fingers in his ears for hearing aids, check, check, check, all spare parts operational. Briefcase, laptop, files, lunch, car keys, check, check, check, *and Honey, is your fly up?* "Check, why are you always checking out my package?" *You wish, I just don't want you to embarrass yourself.* "It's ok to tell the truth, baby it's always there, you know you want it." *Hold that thought, Dan, just keep it in your pants, now go to work and make some money.*

He looked in the mirror one more time and corralled a stray eyebrow hair. He opened his sport coat to the mirror to show the coordinated shirt, tie and suspenders; a skill she had taught him so he could avoid her withering look. *You're not going out like that are you?* He would say, "Why no, why would you even think that?" or if he was feeling cocky "Why? Don't patterns go with stripes?" But this morning he knew he would receive an approving nod and safe passage out the door.

He picked up his briefcase and started out the kitchen door but stopped as he looked at the window above the sink. On the kitchen window sill were two ceramic birds. Charlotte had placed them there, one seeming to nuzzle head down into the other's breast. *When I'm mad at you, the birds won't be nuzzling, that's how you'll know.* He noticed that they were a few inches apart and adjusted them so that they were as close as they could get, fitting together. He took a deep breath apologizing for whatever transgression he imagined had caused the birds to move apart.

On the wall next to the kitchen cabinets was a colored pencil drawing that Charlotte had made of sweet peas twining around their porch railing. One pod was larger and partially opened, showing two peas with smiling faces. With the curling tendrils she had written *Two Peas in a Pod.* Then he heard her voice clearly, *Bye Honey Bunch, Honey Bunches of Oats. Have a great day, I'll make dinner,* the message was still on his voice mail.

He locked the back door when he went out, thinking *Not on my watch; No home invasion on my watch, you son of a bitch,* and thinking, like an obsessive compulsive earworm, *Peter, Peter, Pumpkin Eater, had a wife and couldn't keep her, put her in a pumpkin shell and now he keeps her very well.* He turned the key with aggression as a warning to any hooligans that might be about. *There, take that!* Then, finally, he walked down the steps, out the gate, unlocked the car with his key fob, opened the car door, sat down, put on his seat belt, adjusted the mirror and seat, started it up, found NPR on the radio and began to cry.

From a deep place inside of him, racking gut wrenching sobs broke free. He howled to the universe about love and loss and the unfairness of the whole fucking thing. *Nobody loves me nobody loves me nobody loves me!* He lowered the seat back and cried himself to exhaustion and sleep with the car running.

His neighbor Andrew heard the garage door open and stepped out on his porch to see what drama today would bring. *At least he's not locked in the garage this time. That was a 911.* Andrew knocked on the window of the car. He unlocked it with his spare key, turned it off, took Dan by the arm, helped him inside, loosened his tie and pulled off his shoes. "Back to bed. Did you take your meds?" Dan shook his head still blubbering, "No, no, no. I was feeling better."

"That's was just *because* you were taking your meds. Ok, then, let's get that done at least." He fished the week long pill sorter out of the night stand, emptied 'Tuesday' and handed the pills to Dan with a bottle of water. "Here, down the hatch. I'll be right here until I find someone to babysit you till the caregiver comes. They're tired of you at the emergency room." He held Dan's hand as the cat retook her beachhead at his side.

"Randy's coming."

"Ok, good, some of us have to work for a living."

"I can work."

"Sure you can, Dan, just hold that thought." A few minutes later, Randy Hawkins came in the open front door and headed for the bedroom. "I got it Andy, Thanks."

"He needs a keeper or the psych ward, Randy."

"I just got approval to be his mentor from the Bar Association rehab program. I'm putting together a treatment plan with the doctors."

"Good, Can't be on call today but you know how to reach me." Andy walked out the door and started on his own day.

Randy took Dan's hand. "Take your meds asshole."

"I just did. Before, I was hallucinating, now I'm just sad. Don't be mean to me."

"Fuck you. You're depressing everybody who knows you, rubbing the fragility of sanity in their faces."

"I saw her, Biddy saw her."

"It's just your coat on the bedpost, see? That cat is co-dependent, an enabler."

"Nobody loves me."

"And nobody will if you keep yelling that at the top of your lungs at all hours. It's very manipulative to yell until someone notices just because you're lonely."

"I shut the windows first."

Randy said, "Anyway, Shanti is coming home soon, maybe then a semester on line. You'd better pull yourself together and take down the Ganapati decorations."

"But I didn't get them up until New Year."

"And don't forget the Diwali lights either. They've been up since October. Here," he pushed the smart phone into Dan's hand, "Shanti's on the phone from Truscany."

She was finishing up a year abroad and packing boxes were visible behind her as she spoke. She was the image of her mother but with lighter coloring, and the eyes were undeniably Charlotte's. It was almost better not to see her, but that just left him stuck further down in the quicksand. Dan knew, under his anguish, that she was just what he needed to get better.

Although Charlotte could have been cared for at home, and she was for some time, the unpracticality of it made her transfer to a long term care facility inevitable. He had visited her frequently in the beginning but it wasn't a charade that he could keep up indefinitely. Six months before his meltdown, a decision finally had to be made to disconnect Charlotte from life support. She had been without higher brain activity since shortly after she had lost consciousness without warning and for no discernable reason. She just never woke up. Shanti had agreed, and they each held one of Charlotte's hands as a relaxed beauty overtook her previously tense features. A silence filled the room as her family held each other and wept.

"Dad, I'm coming home next week. Can you behave yourself until then?"

"Ahhh, I'm ok, you just take your time . . . can you come sooner?"

"Stop sniffling, you'll get a migraine. I'll be right there before you know it. I can see you need some help with the house, we'll paint, work on the bathroom, repair my quilt, just like old times, it'll be fun. Now, stop giving Randy so much trouble."

"Ok, bye Baby." Dan took a deep non-hyperventilated breath as Shanti blipped out.

Randy said, "See, everything's going to be ok. The Bar Association rehab stipend came through so I'll give you a hand today and then you're on a high intensity program, grief counseling, in-patient if necessary, round the clock-keepers."

"I don't want to grieve."

"You're grieving already, just doing a lousy job of it."

Just Now

Just now I smelled you on the sheets.
You were one synapse from my hunting brain.
Short, technical inhalations identified you,
Calculated time and distance, knew you were near.
The trail was lost but not desire.
In the night I pulled you from the air,
Kissed you gently, only as a lullaby,
Held you at my right side as I lay on my back,
Your head on my chest,
Your arms and legs around me,
My right arm holding you close, a kiss on the forehead.
And so you slept. I didn't try anything.
But I dreamt of curves and hollows offered to me.
I dreamt of you above me, crying out. I dreamt
The smallness of you, the ampleness of you;
Dreamt the feel of you into being, and awoke
Moving inside of you, and continued
In a dream, holding onto the bed, pulling.
Then I saw a vision of you above me in another bed,
In your room, through a window I appeared;
Something you had prayed for to many gods.
I still remember you in that bed, sleepy,
Happy, delighted. Somehow you knew
Everything you needed to know.
We were alive then and I smelled you all the day
And treasured that presence on my body.
I smelled that on the sheets just now
But you were gone.

*-A Small Goddess, Poetry of Dan Pritchard, Devi Sheridan,
editor, Centennial Edition, Modern Europa Press, 2199.*

*

Earth
April 1, 2125 C.E.

At the Kissimmee Flying J Truck Plaza

Like the space elevator in Geneva, the Cape Canaveral facility was dominated by water. Where generations had sat in bleachers, shaded their eyes and followed the arc of the Saturn series rockets out over the Atlantic, in triumph or, infrequently, in shock, horror and despair, a permanent arc of carbon nanofiber now marked the new path to the stars.

Parker was on 3MI business in Miami where the remaining population had tried to wrest a living out of disaster tourism and a Venice-like downtown theme park. This optimism had however, given way to the practicality of bayous full of shacks on stilts, like villages in Indonesia, transplanted into the flooded high rent district. Fish farmers, gator hunters and cheap labor-driven assembly plants in upper floors seemed to be the wave of this particular future.

While promoting off planet enterprises and Debris Ring science, 3MI was also perpetuating this third world business model much to the scorn and political fallout among the resettled population North/Up.

Parker was a bit pragmatic about those who chose to stay in the swamp instead of migrating, but then, he hadn't been human past the age of five. It seemed more like the South Pacific to him or what it really was, an extension of the old Caribbean, scattered islands with micro industry suited to the new economics. At least, the people getting paid by 3MI seemed to be satisfied with income sufficient for their limited standard of living, the real issue being whether or not there was a practical choice for them.

Parker had watched this evolution for about a hundred years, still, as in the beginning, from his prototype spookball. He liked the reliable old tek and the stares and admiration it evoked, like a 57 Chevy among the hover cars. He was not therefore, naïve about the politics of the situation, that being one reason for his visit.

While the workers were paid a living wage for Miami, that wasn't saying much, and it was never enough for them to aspire to join the nano/cyborg enhanced customer base that actually used the products they were making. It was not enough even for them to aspire to lengthen their lifespan beyond what could be accomplished with unaugmented daily practice; didn't seem worth the effort just to spend more years in the swamp.

That kind of dissatisfaction moved under the radar and manifested in work slowdowns, absenteeism and subtle sabotage. It didn't help that the Cult and 3MI were popularly seen as an inseperable theo-industrial complex. That arrangement rubbed a lot of people the wrong way, even many within those organizations.

Parker was traveling with Pinky Sheridan, who he had also known for that same hundred years, first as a five year old, then through a long human life as Devi Sheridan, Dan Pritchard's daughter, and now, the spookballed bodhisattva successor to Charlotte as Xià lǜ dì. Parker said, "Do you know the origin of the word 'sabotage'?"

"After today's rash of complaints, I'm sure it will lighten the mood, do tell.'"

"In the first workers' protests in the 1820's, workers threw their wooden clogs, sabots, into the textile mill machinery, and wah lah, sabotage!"

"Seems a bit passive aggressive when they can't articulate their demands."

"Karl Marx said it takes a while for the workers to redirect their anger from the machine to the machine owner."

"Something to look forward to, then. I'm not sure how to proceed, Parker, the people need employment, but it can't resolve this unspoken . . . I don't know . . . existential unhappiness. It doesn't translate well into practical action."

"Jusayn, it's not a new problem, you know, *let my people go.*"

She buzzed back and forth tentatively, "Is that what we're dealing with, theocratic slavery?"

"Stratification, at least. Look at Tom and Jen, they left the meeting and are off tandem sailsuiting for their anniversary, so normal but light years away from Miami."

"Sometimes that kind of disquiet gets your head cut off. What did that French queen say? 'Let them halve their cake and then eat two;' right?"

"Something like that."

Tom and Jen had left the conference earlier to catch the noon down shuttle up the elevator. As the transport drove North, Parker caught a glimpse of the shuttle at the limits of even his augmented visual acuity, like the decapitated top of the old Space Needle. It had faded into blue grey and merged with the sky well before the G-Sink station. The rest of the path was visible from its proximity beacons and utility illumination at night. Others were visible then as well, as they never dipped below the horizon if they were within a hemisphere with your current position as its pole. It gave the impression of being surrounded by a giant Tesla static electricity generator, or maybe giant spiders in their death throes.

Parker and Pinky were headed further north to check in at temples and 3MI facilities in Toronto. There wasn't much left in between Miami and Toronto so there was no real speed limit past Cape Canaveral. For convenience and necessity, they were on a 3MI security transport with other 3MI employees and their security detachment. It was more predictable than a spaceplane, not much slower given the wait time and worth the first-hand ground level survey of the changing planet.

Even the alligators were heading north. Pinky and Parker could see them swimming along the edge of the US 95 Hoverway Sea Wall.

Florida's big plan to cope with rising sea levels had involved pumping more freshwater from Lake Okeechobee into the aquifer, charging wells and keeping the salt water at bay. This actually expanded the fresh water Everglades. The sea wall was built to demarcate the fresh from the salt water swamps. The hoverway ran along the top of the sea wall, the route of the old Highway 95, U.S. 1 being mostly under water.

With a ten meter rise in sea level, the common urban reaction was to close the lower floors of buildings and sacrifice the suburbs with the displaced population moving inland or north. The once endangered Everglades were expanding up the coast into Georgia. North of Dade County, the hoverway, which had to be relocated up slope in places, nonetheless gave a glorious view of the sea of grass.

The alligators were also moving north, basking on a beach east of the hoverway or disappearing into the grass on the west, waiting for key deer or small humans to wander by. At times they could also be seen tromping single file along the narrow dry space between the hoverway and the grass. *Pretty soon we'll be paying tolls to the alligators.*

And then there were the coy-wolves, hybrids moving down from Canada through the northeastern states, adapted to living in urban sprawl. They were making a beeline south and west. What they would think of the alligators, one could only guess. Life would find a way.

The transport was just blowing past what used to be Ft. Pierce, now a mangrove swamp. In *that* swamp, the previously endangered salt water crocodile was staging a comeback too, sometimes nipping at the heels of the alligators, so more incentive for the alligators to keep up the pace.

The young security contractors in the transport were not talkative and probably didn't have the cognitive power even to bounce ideas off of. But Parker had been around since the 2030's, as a spook anyway, giving him a depth of experience these meat sacks could only imagine, and not even then. *What they don't know they don't know can't hurt them.*

One of them pointed out the gunport. "Look, manatees!" A pod of the slow moving aquatic mammals could be seen as dark undulating shapes just under the surface among the roots of the mangroves. A resurgence of manatees following the expanding swamp had surged even further as graviton drives replaced propellers on boats. They also seemed to actually become more aggressive as they increased in numbers; manatees acting like honey badgers, taking no shit, snapping their flippers and smoking Marlboros on street corners like the Sharks in West Side Story. *Or was that Kurt Weil, Mack the Knife?*

This kid had seen a nature clip on his streamer feed; when threatened by predators, the manatees made a circle like musk oxen on the tundra with the young ones and females in the middle. They had learned to use one tool, which was to hold a branch like a pike in their fore flaps, with the other end resting in their turned-in tail flipper. This made a circle of spikes that could be moved in any direction or brandished like a stadium wave. Alligators choked on those sticks just enough times to learn to leave the manatees alone.

They had another trick for deeper water, where the swamp had turned into salt water lagoons, where now they had crocodiles and sharks to deal with. They made the ring and then started to spin it. The little ones in the middle weren't subjected to much force, but the pikes were racing like a buzzsaw. The sharks were confused and also lost their enthusiasm after a few severe lacerations and bonks on the head.

Some spooks said the dolphins showed them how to do it. But the dolphins didn't do it themselves. Maybe they were just consultants. That would mean that the dolphins were getting smarter too, or maybe just coming out of the closet. *Anything goes, I guess.*

In between epic fails and kitten party videos, the soldiers have also seen dolphins dancing with blue fireflies in the night. This was something else out of the closet, just coming under study. At some point in their evolution, field sentients had established symbiosis with dolphins. They were not human spooks, they were dolphin spooks. Was that the sign of consciousness everyone was searching for? When sentience approached consciousness, was there an inevitable bonding? Were the blue sparks attracted, not just to consciousness, but to its preconditions?

Did the humans go too far, or did the dolphins just realize the gift they had and choose to embrace it rather than ignore it. Now that human spooks were out in the open, the dolphin spooks wanted to play. That's the thing; field sentience came in different degrees, unconscious, conscious; it seemed to be keyed to the evolution of the host.

*

As the transport approached St. Lucie, the nominal driver heard someone squawk 'may day' on the gravitel security com. He slapped off the automatic and grabbed the wheel with one hand and pointed with the other. "Mr. Parker, look, the ribbon!"

Parker spun his spookball around to look forward to the northeast and the Cape. Something was missing; a thin ribbon of black smoke snaking from the horizon to disappear into the clouds in place of the carbon fiber nanotube cable that had been there just a few minutes ago, now leaning toward horizontal and bursting into flames as each section hit the atmosphere. "Turn on the common channel!" Parker overloaded his voice generator, as Pinky rushed forward as well. The security detail shifted their rifles into defensive positions, but there was nothing to shoot at. The driver took the transport off of auto and hit the brakes. "Everyone, stay in your harnesses until we assess the situation." The humans listened to the common channel while Pinky and Parker accessed their own on-board analytics.

"It wasn't just this one. Looks like others have been blown . . . I can't . . . Maybe all of them. The NUFs have taken credit."

It was hard to understand why, since the NUFs were in favor of technology. In their neo-fascist logic however, the fiery blast of the 20th Century Saturn V was the preferred masculine imagery they wanted, ignoring the cost of it, or actually, reveling in waste. The space elevator however, was somehow soft, feminine and therefore, decadent, a danger to the heroic march of history. *But the cable* does *go through a hole, right? Or is that cigar just a cigar? I can't figure it out.*

Pinky said, "We can't keep heading north, the hoverway was destroyed when the ribbon dragged over it."

The driver said, "And there are unidentified agents heading to the Cape from the west approaching Orlando."

Parker said, "No one there to stop them even if it could be done."

Now 3MI security was in a real pickle with the Second Bodhisattva Xià lù dì on board and the way forward uncertain. The driver said, "Ma'am, protocols would have us head for the nearest elevator in this situation but they're all out as far as I can tell. With unknown combatants at Orlando, I don't think we could make it to a temple or 3MI facility. "

"Can't we just buzz out of here above the mess? Parker and I could lose the spookballs and just take off."

"Ma'am, we don't know if they're spooks out there with the unidentified, there are some with the NUF's; it's not safe in or out of the ball."

"Parker, what do you suggest?"

"It won't be dangerous for us to just head back to Miami but that won't get us to where we can eventually get upstairs; *that* ride would be an old school shuttle at Houston, they're still maintaining independence from the Tejianos, and the fighting with the Mexicans is north of there."

"We'd have to cross the Gulf or skirt the coast, just us, the humans can get back to Miami safely enough."

The driver said, "We are going to sit right here for now and see what we can find out on the gravitel."

Parker said, "Something's coming in on the spook channel."

"Put it on the speaker."

"This is Pushmataha, F.S., and John Asényhola with the Seminole exploratory corps, Five Tribes Confederacy, approaching Orlando, do you read me?"

"This is Parker, F.S. with 3MI heading north from Miami, we are on the 95 at Port St. Lucie." Parker didn't mention Pinky and the Cult embassy.

"We hear you; you can't go any further north on 95 but you can take the surface roads and meet us at Kissimmee outside of Orlando. We have a sizable force of the Five Tribes Confederacy and safe passage west to Nanih Waiya, the NUF's are to the east of us heading for the Cape. Not sure if they're hostile and to whom. Get the 75 at Ft. Pierce and we'll talk you in from there."

The driver said, "That's good enough for me," started toward the off ramp and down to the road just barely above the grass and water, the limestone karst and sinkholes of west central Florida having been submerged as the coast was inundated.   Because of an increase in sinkhole activity as the ground water rose, the roads had been repaired with arcs around the damaged sections, stopgap measures since the sinkholes were only getting bigger. The result was incongruous half roundabouts that could be amusing or dangerous. Gators liked to lounge on the lagoon-like inner curves of these structures and bask on the roadway prompting the driver to keep his speed up so the gators didn't get too interested as he headed generally northwest to meet the FTC west of Orlando.

*

The seemingly spontaneous movement of a number of unidentified groups toward Cape Canaveral was nonetheless highly organized. Similar sleeper cells had been primed and waiting for the signal to man the siege at all space elevators, Cult administration centers and stupas and 3MI security compounds. After the abject violence of the initial attacks, the second wave had instructions not to engage the security personnel or cause any damage to the local population or infrastructure. The point seemed to be to create a standoff with the only international powers that mattered.

The Rise and Fall of the New United Futurists, S.C. Schneider, Modern Europa Press, 2130

*

G-Sink to L2 Station

After the severing of the ribbon the G-Sink station moved outward on its own momentum and, nudged by graviton retros, gradually accelerated in the general direction of the L2 Station. Tom and Jen, in shock after the jolt of the attack, stayed put since their sailsuiting flight plan had the L2 expecting their arrival anyway, and 3MI security sounded like a great idea at that moment; 3MI corporate offices were as good a place as any to assess the situation. Tom had passed out initially and Jen, her reboot not so susceptible to g-forces, patched into Tom's analytics and monitored and adjusted his systems until he awoke on his own. "Jen, what. . ."

"I'm trying to reestablish links to L2 or a base station. The normal relays on the elevators aren't functioning."

"None of them?" he could look straight ahead and see the planet since the north-south axis of the G-Sink was now pointed toward its L2 destination. "I can see them."

"That's right." glowing worms contorted and then blasted fire like the tails of comets where each loop started to descend through atmosphere. They looked like those fireworks snakes that you touched a match to and then grew into black and red sputtering twists, like molten lava rapidly congealing. "I . . I have to assume it's the same on the dark side. I'm patching through the proximity beacon straight to L2. *3MI Proximity, do you hear me? This is Jen with Tom Petty, III inbound on the Canaveral g-sink, do you hear me?*

It came back on the common channel with its AI generated voice. *"This is Proximity Zed Alpha. All communications are local only, we are working on gravitel patch-throughs. Please proceed toward L2."*

Tom said. "What the hell else could we do?!"

"The G-Sink will get us there, look, the bouncers are coming out to bring us in, detach and hang on to the rocker."

"Back to the bar? Sounds like a good short term plan. Try to find Parker and Pinky. They would not have been at the Cape when it blew. That's our best bet, line of sight gravitel."

Jen booted up her advanced optics and zoomed the view to pick out the coast of Florida below and then the Cape. She should have been able to see a gravitel beacon if the transport was in trouble and the driver thought to turn it on. It was automatic in a crash so, at least it seemed they were still moving, but where? With Pinky Sheridan, the Second Bodhisattva Xià lǜ dì, on board it was a rescue operation *and* a target of the highest value. She decided radio silence was a good policy until they got to the L2. In the meantime, the G-Sink Lounge could nurse their wounds inside and out with liquor and icepacks, respectively

The bouncers shepherded them into the airlock and it cycled them through. The bar was serving as a minor triage unit while the sick bay took care of more severe injuries, and the morgue, well strapping corpses to the outside railings wasn't the worst method of preservation until someone could figure out who was who and how to contact next of kin.

*

At Kissimmee, about twenty miles south of Orlando, the 3MI transport pulled into the Flying J Truck Plaza as had been arranged with Push and Asényhola. The spookball advance scouts for the Five Tribes Confederacy had set up shop in the abandoned REACT Emergency booth and Parker buzzed over to make introductions.

John said, "Parker, you're almost famous, head spook at 3MI?"

"More like the oldest spook in the spook hall of fame, they keep me around for show, I think. I get to do whatever interests me, that's the main perk. So, these events definitely interest me."

"We are trying to assess the current situation but I will tell you that we were tipped off at least that *something* was going to happen?"

"By who?"

"The deep web, the sub-common channel, the grapevine if you will, those at the top are not in the loop. Otherwise, I'm not at liberty to divulge more."

Wally said, "Can we get out of these tanks for a while."

"Gladly." The spookballs settled onto the counter and went into sleep mode. Three pinpoints of blue light emerged and formed a spiral comet trial as they stretched their bosons, then hovered in the booth merging their energy bodies to facilitate communication.

"That's better," Parker said. The communication no longer needed soundwaves in atmosphere and therefore, was protected from interspecies tapping.

John said. *The disaffected and left behind are no longer content to take orders from the theo-industrial complex.*

But the Cult does not govern the earth.

Neither does 3MI, that's the point, no one does, and yet the off planet interests assume they have unfettered access. They frequent what's left of the first world and the slums fend for themselves. Look around, the Miami refugees are fighting the gators for living space.

Can you get us in touch with anyone with authority?

Grammy can. Come with us to Nanih Waiya and we'll talk to her. It's the only route that's open right now anyway if you're dragging humans and tek along. The gulf ports are abandoned so we skirt the coast. Eventually we can get you all the way to Houston that way. In the meantime, not a bad place to wait this out. I assume you can speak for 3MI; who will speak for the Cult?

Her Holiness the Second Bodhisattva Xià lǜ dì, is back in the transport, peace be upon her.

*

Earth
Geneva,
April 2, 2125, 6:00 a.m.

Larr awoke to the eyelids of morning, the darkest darkness before the dawn, eyelids blacker than he had ever seen this close before. It was difficult for him to even focus on any larger expanse of the skin of her body, all of which by now he had seen. It was like being snow blind, a certain kind of vertigo that sucks on the senses, erases distance and makes one lose all perspective.

With a blink of an eye however, the details snapped into sharp focus; the highlights and shine of curves and hollows, the impossibly smooth small of her back, the aerodynamic art deco hemispheres of her buttocks, his hands scrabbling for purchase like shuttle docking clamps, grasping desperately and even then being overpowered and knowing it was she drawing him inside, upward, inward, without his control or choice. Finally on top of this summit, he focused on the nape of the neck of a princess of Great Zimbabwe, full of decorum and eloquence but right there, where the neck met the hairline, was a promise of ritual spiritual abandon and Dionysian madness.

At that line, her hair began as the small hillocks that would eventually resolve into nascent dreads, a maze of black haystacks within which he again lost perspective and was cast adrift in the labyrinth of the surface of her head like a naïve farm boy being led further and further into a game of hide and seek by a farmer's daughter that he is fooled into believing he is pursuing. She might be only fourteen or fifteen but she has seen the animals do it and she feels in her body an unreasoning imperative to capture this boy, having lured him one haystack too far, just over the last fortification of his boyhood, down into a scratchy bed of hay even further contrasting with the smoothness of her skin, naïve until the point where his only rescue is deep within the beast that is devouring him.

The girl has prayed for this to many gods, somehow knows everything she needs to know, and the boy, no matter how much he knows, will always be clueless and in thrall to the wonder that will rule his life from this moment forward.

But these are typical reveries; one slap on Larr's butt and her laugh upward pitching into extended vowels, breaths and Himba curses becoming wordless shuddering; well now, *that* brings a real clarity to that good old morning wood.

Even so, it is the kind of wonder that forces men to write prose poems and slip them into the pockets and purses of women, poems awkward or elegant, with the payback, if he's lucky, of a cock of her head and a wondering stare right through his pupil into his macula and up his optic nerve to his brain where she mounts the throne chariot and then commands him, she alone.

Larr's princess blinked, inhaled and exhaled stretching her neck and arms above her head, still meeting him eye to eye but now maneuvering the front of her pelvic bone into the angle of his, grinding bone against bone. *Because . . . I . . . want . . . more.*

He said. "You smell really good. Is that something from Africa?"

"No baby, its Hello Kitty, *Puppy Love* from the samplers downstairs." She sniffed. "You *stink* really good mister."

"I'll assume that's a compliment."

"I'm gonna roll around in that stink like a big dog, nome sayn?"

"No but . . . yes please?"

"Ok, Daddy, don't move and you won't get hurt." He shuddered. She said, "Just kidding, you buck like a bronco, cowboy and I'll be your rodeo queen, you ready?"

"I . . . "and then he couldn't speak until she was done.

*

The catastrophic reason for this tryst however, was soon remembered and a bit of unease crept into the afterglow in Larr's face.

Larr asked his companion. "The world didn't end?"

She replied, "Not this one, baby, not yet, go get breakfast, I'll bet you can find still something at the Funny Horse, no? Or knock at the hair shop and see if anybody's in."

Larr glanced over at Stuart and the other stylist, still embracing and snoring, well, Stuart was anyway. "I don't know your name. What's your name?" Larr asked.

"Edelweiss."

"The snow flower? That's beautiful, what's your friend's name?"

"Cousin, Heidi."

"Of course, and I'm Shaka Zulu. You'll have to explain that when I get back."

*

Stuart and Heidi were up by the time Larr returned with coffee, rösti, muesli and yoghurt.

"All quiet?" Stuart asked.

Larr said, "Too quiet; funny, you don't notice the elevator's hum until it's gone."

"We'll have to investigate after breakfast. Feeling any better?"

"Somehow there's comfort in company."

Heidi said, "And love, lover. The threat of extinction makes you wanna have sex."

Larr said, "Doing our part to save the human race?"

"Scientific fact baby, saw it on the net."

"Fine by me. Hey by the way, where are you from with those German names?

Edelweiss laughed, "Oh, we're spies for the Schwarzkommando, black ops, incognito."

"So you have German names so no one will figure out you're black?"

"Ha, you're smarter than you look Larr. No, we're from Namibia; Germans dipped their wick down there long time ago, got burned like Bobbit, but we still have connections, following family, Uncle Kleinfelter runs the hair shop. We hide in plain sight."

"So you're not really spies?"

"What would we say if we were? Besides, in the movies, the spy girls are the best lovers, right?

Stuart said, "And then they kill you. I'll just assume you're not."

"Hmmm . . .Whatever."

"Are you here permanently then?"

"You betcha, too hot and dusty down south, like Texas."

"That bad? Still have family down there?"

"Auntie Mukaa-Ma's the Queen of the Ovahimba; real big shot. I can get a dirt floor of my own any time I want, but I think I like this kind of civilization better."

"What's left of it; nothing gets up or down now."

She said to Stuart, "So maybe you're not fired now."

"There's no job to do now, can't ship parts or scrap off planet."

"Well, no harm in hanging around, somebody's got to mind the store, or at least to get your share."

"Let's get through this day first, ok? Shouldn't we go see what's happening at the elevator?"

They went down the stairs, checked in with Uncle K who gave a big toothy grin to Stuart and Larr. "Top o' the morning, Uncle." Stuart said. Larr nodded and the ladies did the perp walk with their hands over their faces, laughing all the while.

It was only a few blocks down to the waterfront. There were more flyers and posters plastered on buildings, utility poles, trolleys and busses, all put up overnight. Around the elevator, groups of people were arriving and sitting down in concentric circles, legs crossed, some in lotus positions, some making mudras, some chanting.

It seemed like a diverse group; Stuart spotted the Knights of Columbus Jesuits, the Carthy dismantlers, what looked like students, grandparents; even suits and ties. Above the seated people, hover signs floated, sporting various old slogans like "NUF SAID" and "INFINITY OR ELSE!" and a new one: "OCCUPY EARTH!" As more people arrived, they took their positions silently, ever increasing the size of the barrier by accretion.

At the same time, 3MI and Cult security just stood around, moving back as the circle expanded. They talked on gravitels and chatted with the sitters but all in all didn't get in the way. Larr and Stuart looked at each other and then at the schwartzkommandos, then they all turned around facing away from the elevator and sat down, settling into the, temporarily, outermost circle, somehow in silent accord, in complete union and understanding, with the myriad strangers now covered in mist from the Jet d'Eu, now steaming in the sunshine, now becoming one with . . . something, co-opting the Cult's own meditative practice to lay siege to the stars.

INTERSTITIAL III

Ephemera: The New United Futurist Manifesto, April 1, 2125:

THE VOICE OF EARTH COMMANDS
THE STAR ORPHANS

The New United Futurist speaks:

We had been up all night, my friends and I, beneath the harsh light of dawn flashing off of the space elevator ribbons miles over our heads, ribbons that had destroyed the horizon, bringing the morning sun to us at midnight. In our cities, they had destroyed the very galaxy we inhabit by shielding it from our eyes with glare. Only the privileged that left this earth, self-made orphans though they may be, now may own the beauty that once was our birthright.

A vast pride swelled in our breasts, to feel ourselves standing alone, like lighthouses or advanced guards, facing an enemy that knew no fear, not from strength, but from ignorance, indifference and a paucity of experience. The Bodhisattva Cult devotees face extinction like some ornate beast whose mutations are no longer relevant as they become feed stock for the true ubermensch.

Then, unexpectedly, the bright silence of midnight was overtaken by the real dawn and we were disturbed by the rumbling and screeching whine of the enormous hover transports hauling scrap to the space elevator, and then a greater rumble and whine as even the sacred refuse of the planet was hauled to the stars.

Come, I said, my friends! Let us go! At last the Mythology and the mystic Ideal of Science have been surpassed. There is no God of Abraham, in Heaven or Over There. But, we shall witness the birth of the New Mythological Science; the roar and blast of the new Archangel Saturn the Fifth! This is truly the first sun that dawns above the new Earth as our red rocket blast battles with lesser lights in the millennial gloom.

Then, we approached the elevator ribbon itself. No guards kept us away, arrogance recognizing no threat. Below the embarkation platform, by design, soft dilettantes and tourists could touch the ribbon, put their ear to it and hear the approach of the shuttle like the iron rail that crossed the prairies of the past.

We too put our bodies flat against it and turned our heads to place our ears upon it, now to hear the quavering tones of the graviton retros, the g-sink and counterweight whiplash end of it miles above us. The great folly of this monster transcended us in its long dimension but we curled about it hidden like the obscure dimensions encircling strings. We joined hands, planted the seed of revolution and then ran.

And around the world, our brothers and sisters made the same attack all at once, Cape Canaveral, Spaceport America, Tokyo, Moscow, Cape Town; all of them gone in the same instant. Our scythes tore through the abominations and the bow shock swept us into the streets as the first sacrifice to the Archangel fell from the sky.

But we did not rest in the retaken garden. We hunted, like young lions, hunting meaningless immortality, at our flanks, death, its black fur dappled with pale crosses, and the Cult ran before us under the vast violet sky, palpable and living, but now no refuge as their works dimmed and vanished.

As the ribbons and their riders fell like hideous confetti, we rose from our motherly ditch of Earth, half full of muddy water. We tasted by mouthfuls the bracing slime, from the saintly brown breast of our true wet nurse.

And as I arose, a muddy, stinking messiah, I felt the red-hot iron of joy deliciously pierce my heart. A crowd of the faithful, confused and aghast, had gathered in terror around us to hear the new sermon not on the mount of stars, no, but from the trenches of Earth.

Then, with our faces hidden by the good slime, covered by metal dross

of earthbound industry, by useless
sweat and heavenly soot, amid the
plaints of monks and bodhisattvas,
among the fallen helpless
scientists, themselves the
concubines of gravity and
distressed deluded politicians, we
dictated our will to all the living
sentients on Earth, down from the
Mountain, we delivered our
Manifesto to our quaking enemies
and laid siege to the palace of the
Gods.

*Ephemera reproduced in The Rise and Fall of the New United
Futurists, S.C. Schneider, Modern Europa Press, 2130.*

*

Earth
2199 C.E.

Charlotte's Soliloquy

When Dan Pritchard caught me the second time, he worked in
my mother's law firm as a paralegal. We got married and had
a sunny wedding day where I wore a wreath of flowers in my
hair, braided and wrapped around my head, fastened in the
back, a white peasant dress with eyelet lace and no veil, in the
pictures I look too thin but smiling, and everyone around,
Dan's mother, my mother, my step father, my brothers, people
I don't even remember now, all smiling too. We were both
twenty five and still thought we knew everything but, since I
was eighteen, really since that séance in junior high where I
first met Dan, I had been staring at the world looking for
things I could not see. Something entered into me that night
and made me cry and scream and that spectacle or the thing
itself, got into Dan and made him cry and scream in unison
with me and did that ever freak out the other kids and

Stephanie's mom. No more séances and later Dan said 'you had me at psych ward,' but inside of me there had been an experience that seemed more real than anything in this supposedly solid world. People have always shaped their lives around such experiences, St. Paul, Mohammed, Yogananda, Simone Weil, and that is what makes religion; an experience that makes faith logical. Well, later I heard it explained as the Holy Grail, what one loses as a child and spends a lifetime trying to regain. My wanderings were spiritual, eastern mysticism, gurus, worshiping relics of the saints, kissing the shoes of yogis, and Dan indulged me and had an interest himself if it kept me beside him. Eventually we got a little more courageous and certain in our love so that I wandered a little farther into the mist as he went to law school and got ever more logical, logical except where it came to me. See, I was his mysticism, his Song of Solomon, his Sufi Psalm, his dervish dance. It was his experience of me that made faith in love logical to him. So we met a couple who were in an Anthroposophy study group, followers of Rudolf Steiner. Around the turn of the twentieth century he was one of many people who believed in spiritual science, in fact he taught about contacts with the mystical and the dead according to scientific principles, not the Enlightenment science but Goethe's Teutonic view of science, he had views on medicine, psychology, education, economics, politics, religion and everything else, he was brilliant and deluded, a product of his age, maybe, no excuses, but there was something that translated and spoke to me across the years, and I started to work as a teacher in a Waldorf School, a method that grew out of Steiner's thought, educating mind, body and spirit, but really stuck in the 19th century, homeopathic theosophists, no wait, too radical for theosophists but Steiner did say one thing that turned out to be true. The dead are not like us but they are with us, here, waiting, listening, feeling . . . something. Well, that was me. He could be wrong about everything else, well, I did die because of his homeopathic placebo mistletoe cancer cure, but he was different and close but no cigar about that one thing. There *was* an existence after the death of the human body that either sped on to the light or waited, confused and longing at the stage door, locked out. But love and attention could be sensed. He called it reading to the dead, meaning silently reading spiritual books, especially the books the dead held dear. This was no face to face conversation, no channeling, no landing of the mothership, no, this was simply a light in the darkness, the moths were lost to begin with so it was no unkindness to draw them back to the flame, the porch light, and there to nourish them with energy, bosons, he didn't know about quantum physics, but he somehow, and I have to say by experiencing it, discovered bosonic life, field sentients, peering down from the glass bottomed boat, from the airplane window, tapping at the blue-green door. But none of us knew that then.

*

In the peace process, the idea of the Threefold State became a mechanism and framework on which to hang the various proposals for the consideration of the opposing parties. The general theory comprised the economic ideas of Rudolph Steiner as interpreted by Steven Vallush and the Andromedan system of governance as modified by Urizen and Blake, all of the Five Tribes Confederacy. The official platform read, in part, as follows:

> Platform of Economics and the Threefold State
>
> There is an inequality and natural predation involved in paying wages for labor, it objectifies the sentient being and naturally subjects it to a loss in its intrinsic value *as* a being. The key is separating the value of sentient labor, intellectual or physical, from its end product.

What one needs as an individual bears no relation to what one can produce. Certainly, one can produce far in excess of what one can use and one can use far in excess of what one can produce. Both result in an accumulation of unused capital, wealth.

Steiner said: A true price (and the living wage demanded by the Quantum Mechanics Union) results when individuals receive, as counter-value for the product they have made, sufficient recompense to enable them to satisfy the whole of their needs.   Apply this to the relationship between the System and Earth.

If products can become worn or obsolete and sentients can lose the ability to produce, then wealth in itself must also have limited usefulness and natural obsolescence. The other part of the equation is that selfless service must have the same value as profit. The more that individuals use their intrinsic value to serve others, the more valuable they become. The resulting social business has as its goal social good as much as, or more than, profits, and if the profits must be expended on social good or face expiration, the social good churns and pays forward and the welfare of all can become a reality.

This is different from the old communist trope of 'from everyone according to his ability and to everyone according to his needs' and this could not have happened at any other time of history. This is a unique juncture; the accumulated wealth of the planet and its disproportionate ownership have flown as the wild geese of legend. The New United Futurists have locked the gates behind them. It is the opportunity, the necessity, to create a different economy without that stockpiled wealth. The necessity may be answered with this proposal known as The Threefold State.

Just as there must be a separation of labor from value there must be a separation of the cultural, economic and legal circles. In place of a centralized unified state or even global order of competing interests, we propose three independent systems, three independent circles; the autonomous rights circle, limited to judicial and political matters, an autonomous economic circle, cooperative and associative by nature, and an autonomous spiritual-cultural circle. Each sphere must be independent of the other two and none may be more powerful than the other. As is said of beauty, truth and goodness; if one is more powerful, then evil is unleashed in the world; so it is with the threefolding of these circles. The autonomy of these three spheres should make possible a spiritually healthy, productive society and open the possibility of a lasting peace.

What does this mean in practice? In the aftermath of war? In a solar system forcibly separated into two independent entities, Earth and everything else? Each earthly sentient has an equal right to its footprint on the planet, and an equal right to the resources of the planet, each has the right and obligation to serve all sentient beings and to be served in return.

This is not, however, a closed system and cannot be limited to the planet Earth. How do we convince the greater System to embrace this solution? By making this new economy between them one of the requirements for planetfall. Yes, this requires enforcement, but in a generation it will be accepted as the new normal. We need only point to the sweeping and literally astronomical changes absorbed since Charlotte came back from the dead. If that transformation occurred and was survivable, how hard can this one be?

The Rise and Fall of the New United Futurist, S.C. Schneider, Modern Europa Press, 2130

PART FOUR

CHARLOTTE'S CHOICE

It is the very symmetry of beauty that leads us to, or somehow assists us in discovering, the symmetry that eventually comes into place in the realm of justice. *Elaine Scarry -On Beauty and Being Just*

Earth, April 4, 2125 C.E.
Nanih Waiya, Cahokia,
Five Tribes Confederacy

After Kissimmee, the road skirting the fishing villages and abandoned cities of the Panhandle and Gulf was uneventful. As the transport with its spook scout guides passed through Louisville and approached Nanih Waiya from the north, it was evident that something new was arising from the mound builders' relic. The area around the Mother Mound was still a flat broad plaza, as it had been a thousand years before when the Mississippian culture was at its height. In the last century, it had still been farmed. But now, the approach and uncleared areas were tropical jungle instead of deciduous trees and kudzu. Even the fire ants had moved north, closer to the new outback. It was going to be necessary to clear the jungle back to the old perimeter.

In the plaza however, as the caravans arrived, a new habitation was taking shape, mobiles and hoveRV's were interspersed with salvage and stick built shanties and sod houses. It looked like a cross between the Debris Ring fallen to Earth and Burning Man, but homey. The Mother Mound was at the center of a half circle about a quarter mile across.

The main streets were parallel half circles designated by letters and sectioned by perpendicular cross streets radiating like spokes from the center. The spokes were designated like an analog clock with twelve o'clock at the center, three o'clock and nine o'clock being ninety degrees on either side and fronting the highway. So, navigation was easy enough, your address might be "D Street at 2:30," as simple and accurate as the construction was haphazard the further away it was from Nanih Waiya. The first street, fronting on the council clearing, was named the Promenade, again looking toward the future with hope of a more dignified habitation.

Also optimistically, but with a nod to the past, the settlement had been named Cahokia, in honor of the mound builders' capitol along the Mississippi in Illinois. The pyramid at that Cahokia actually had a footprint larger than the great pyramid at Giza, the city in its heyday rivaling any city in the Americas.

There would be no slash and burn here, prudent thinning of the jungle instead; the managed wild, but with sufficient new building materials to stitch together the old and new components. It was obvious to Pinky that this was not just a project of the FTC. The tribal construction was cheek by jowl with what looked like local populations and traveling companions of all stripes, from the crackers and trailer trash to those who used to be members of professional and trade classes. Even the Ixil Maya barrio diffused their bright primary colors right in with the rattlesnake diamond patterns of the Choctaw traditional dress.

Solar cells and wind turbines poked above the ramshackle structures which were connected by makeshift electrical cables and water and sewer pipes, causing even the locals to watch their heads and their feet so as not to bump into or trip over any of the creative infrastructure. It was off the radar and, although it was monitored from space, didn't seem connected to any previous faction, detachment or grid.

The earthen Mound itself was parallel to the road, about thirty feet high with a flat top, all grown over with grass and now encroaching jungle, reminding one of the Yucatan and its Mayan ruins. There was an old wooden stair and ramp that led to the top of the mound but no other construction had been allowed there. Hugging the east side of the mound, the FTC offices, residency and guest quarters, where Pinky, Parker and their human cohort were going to be housed, were built to a less creative aesthetic that inspired confidence in the appearance of governance. Between the mound and the Promenade the half circle had been cleared and maintained with grass for outdoor councils.

As Pinky buzzed the perimeter of their room and Parker started to download analytics and algorithms into the docking tees, another spookball hit the proximity detector, sort of an automatic doorbell. Grammy Ruby was making an unofficial visit.

She blinked a welcome pattern and said, "The Bodhisattva, it's an honor, hope the accommodations are acceptable."

"Pinky, please; we are just happy for your kindness. Funny, the top isn't so far from the bottom, one day to the next."

"It's The Great Wheel of Fortune and Jeopardy, Simba."

"That sounds sort of familiar, *It's the Circle of Life Simba*, but what does that even mean?"

"It's why the Lion King eats his subjects."

"And the Little Mermaid smells like fish, but didn't your scout mention you had a warning on this disaster?"

She lied, "Too busy for much more than this traveling circus but we all had heard rumors."

Parker said, "The Nuf's claimed it."

"It's more complicated than that. But you probably want to get on to Huston and back upstairs as soon as possible? Spooks don't need the elevator with the proper escort."

"I think what we need is not upstairs. I had a long talk with our diplomatic liaison at the L3. I've been out of the loop long enough. I am not the inertia of this situation and I'm not just climbing behind the barricades either. I took on this mantle out of my love and friendship with the real Charlotte with the hope I could continue the good she brought into the world. I didn't care about the Cult when I was human and I'm not deluded as to history. I was there, I *am* history . . "

Grammy said, ". . . and touchy too."

"Not . . . That didn't sound right, you know what I mean. I was Dan Pritchard's daughter after all; give the people what they want. Well, they wanted religion. Charlotte and I were just convenient figureheads."

"You're the hood ornament, that's true, peace be upon you and all that aside, but also one of a very small group of people that can actually help resolve this thing you say you're so clueless about. I don't think you can do that from orbit. Can we meld for a bit before we go see Luke?"

"Certainly, Parker, can you manage this for a while?

Parker acknowledged with a nod and "Yes, boss." The others locked their spookballs to their docking tees and two blue sparks spiraled tightly out the window and up into the cold night air.

*

At 35,000 feet, the Milky Way still honored the promise it had made to the first consciousness on the planet; was it Australopithecus, Homo Erectus, Field Sentients, Dolphins? Maybe it was a squid with an eye evolved over millennia to somehow see the same world as a human but no more related to that human's evolution than a human is to a dragonfly, an eye that dips above the surface tension, that dips into the deathly *dry*, and sees, really sees, two types of outer space instead of just one, *the ether and the air*, and may, nonetheless, in time, figure out how to get there, to another sea, under another sun, another world of water, after all the ground apes have sprouted wings and gone to hell and good riddance, apes whose crumbling remains are finally poked at by scientists with tentacles at some backwater dig as the sun turns red and expands into *their* future.

But for now, two blue lights meld as one, reclaiming only their own unique heritage. Then, surveying the settlement from that height, a height that irons out all the wrinkles and reveals only the largest fractals in soft focus, they see all the beauty and none of the shit of it.

Grammy said, "We used to be the Five Civilized Tribes, now were doing societal triage with a bunch of crackers. It's very messy, inelegant, somehow inspiring."

"And you love it."

"I'm used to chasing babies and herding cats, but this is a real challenge."

"Well, I've got the whole System on my plate."

"Can't top that, but you're going to have to get a tighter focus here, Earth has shunned your pilgrims. All we can do is move forward, regardless of what you do. The siege engineers make no demands of us, except to stop looking to the Cult and 3MI for the new world order."

"We can shut off the utilities but we won't take the planet by force, we . . . I won't allow it."

"Then it's time to be creative. Cahokia is all about creation. The world can get along without all your science, the wild is returning, just look at the Gulf Coast, Vietnamese and Cajuns are building third world fishing villages and having slap fights with gators, happy as clams."

"I don't doubt it, 3MI and the Cult are more connected to the off planet infrastructure than to most of the Earth."

"So it's a stalemate maybe; that both parties could walk away from?"

"But they don't want to, the broader population, not the siege engineers, they don't want to be schooled or played. They will however, take advantage of the disaster to build something new while the System catches its breath."

"Maybe that was the point, the combatants handing off to the disenfranchised but not tied to any particular solution."

"That would be refreshing."

"Come on; I want you to meet my Luke and Steve Vallush, and I'll tell you about Walter Brodie."

"He's still alive?"

"Well, he *was*; let's get down there, I'll fill you in on the way."

*

Frida had said a hasty goodbye to Frankie and Blossom, leaving her studio and Larr's art in the hand of trusted acolytes. She continued to try to raise Larr, hoping he hadn't been on the last shuttle up from Geneva when the ribbon crashed. The most reliable connections and communications would be at Cult facilities, and direct flights to Europe might still be operating out of Houston and Cape Canaveral.

So, she set out on a solo spookball traverse from San Francisco, through the Great Basin, skirting the Oklahoma and Texas panhandles under the radar and just over treetops until she could triangulate on the Mother Mound, Nanih Waiya and the new Cahokia. There would still be some semblance of independent government there, government that was not a target of, or complicit with, the terrorists. With her destination in sight, her mind began once again to weave inspiration out of experience, turning straw into gold.

As she approached Cahokia she searched for open channels but only the subcom was accessible. *The admins upstairs aren't sure what to do yet, so they just shut everything off. It's too soon, too soon, got to reach Larr, but in the meantime . . .*

"Cahokia proximity, Cahokia proximity, This is Frida, F.S. approaching South 15 degrees, 40 minutes, 35 seconds West, two kilometers out, come in."

The subcom barked, "Parker, F.S., Frida, How did you . . ."

"Parker, gods, I don't know anything yet, why are you there?"

"Long story, come to the guest quarters when you get here."

"Twenty minutes." Then she switched to a scanning algorithm. "Larr, Larr Yellingson, Larr Yellingson, pick it up!"

One reason she had lit out so soon after the attacks was because of the newsvid footage of the bombs taken from tourist selfies and security cameras, enlarged to show the lantern shaped devices with Larr's clamshells on top. It was the worst of what she might have imagined, worse than any exaggerated jest. But at that point she also knew who Frankie's patron of the arts was. From the point of view of the Cult, nothing was more certain than the continued presence of Walter Brodie in the worlds.

The observation office she had retired from had tried to keep track of Brodie and others associated with the New United Futurists without devining what they were actually up to. Their rants seemed nonsensical, but there was no mistaking the fact that they were the only ones capable of coordinating such an attack, and if they could coordinate it, then Brodie was the only leader who could pull it off right under their noses. It looked like he was a hands on terrorist as well, and Larr was his dupe.

But, even looking at it charitably, Larr wasn't adverse to being duped if the money was right. He wasn't cavalier, just naïve, not wanting to believe the presence of volitional evil in the world even though he had been subjected to enough anonymous practical disasters to rival Job. He just didn't think humans could do worse. She wanted to make sure that he didn't just fess up to it in despair and shock; he was such an ingénue when it came to the big picture. Still, her first instinct was to protect him. If he hadn't gone up the elevator before the Geneva attack, she knew his first impulse would be to contact her. She was therefore, heading to whatever place could make that connection in the aftermath. If Parker was at Cahokia that meant that he was on Cult business when the attacks went down. That meant he was actively working to reestablish communications. The fact that he was not at a Cult or 3MI facility meant something too, not quite sure what. She was glad however, that her old friend Parker was there, and idled in for a reunion a little less frantic than when she had left Watertown.

As Pinky and Grammy Ruby reentered their spookballs, Parker was just finishing up establishing communications with 3MI and the Cult administration upstairs. The common channel and subcom monitors were also coming in clear. As the three headed out to the open air council, Parker touched Pinky just long enough to transfer a private packet. "Frida's coming." Pinky nodded, suddenly feeling more like things could work out, her friends and confidants gathering at her side.

*

At first, the siege engineers, sleeper cells all, kept guard with guns. But when both the fellow travelers and the Cultists simply sat down facing each other, they disabled the weapons and joined one side or the other. What had looked a coup was shown to be a forceful push of the planetary 'pause' button. Even before the attacks, the bulk of the human population left behind had instinctively created multiple redundant levels of subsistence. All they had to do was back it down a notch and whatever it was that the theological-industrial complex was selling off-planet, they didn't miss.

Local networks started to replace system-wide infrastructure and people started to settle into a slower pace, inadvertently slowing climate change even further, and then started trading amongst themselves and the cities. Cities started looking outward instead of upward, just for the duration of course, and then the stupas, temples and administration campuses started to pass out food to the non-violent combatants.

Off-planet, it became clear that the harvesting of resources could go on whether or not Earth was in the trade network. Settlements on asteroids, moons and stations had been purpose built to be a self-sufficient system. The freight traffic was a bit slower, a lot slower, contracting the reach of humanity inward for now. So, there were two closed systems, and yet something, even now, something was passing between them, something hard to quantify. It was more than love and longing, it was a desire anchored to a deeply felt *lack* of *something*. It was a *wanting*.

The Rise and Fall of the New United Futurists, S.C. Schneider, *Modern Europa Press*, 2130.

*

By the time Frida buzzed into the guest quarters at Cahokia, the Autonomous Council had started, but Parker had waited for her; Frida hadn't blasted two thousand miles across the continent for the change of scenery. And she hadn't known who was here, so he was also more than curious about what she might know, *must know*, about the attacks.

On her way in she activated the graviton emitters so she could manifest. She was a rare case, a human who had voluntarily left her human body and then stayed in the world; she did it for art, for her art, to be honest about her being and still explore the worlds. Before Charlotte, B.C., Frida had been crippled, her legs bent and useless, not congenital, but due to an accident, after which she had an epiphany and thereafter refused to move in any manner in which her body did not allow. Her devotees came to her.

When a spookball came to visit in the Santa Monica woods, Frida realized she could have a natural and honest existence as a fully realized field sentient, a data stream, instantly mobile. After that, her devotees had to follow *her* on her traverse of the Waypoints of the Bodhisattva.

In the graviton emitters, the two field sentients appeared as humans to each other, Frida as Salma Hayek as Frida Kahlo and Parker as a young Peter O'Toole/Bowie hybrid. Well, cosplay was still a thing even without Purgatory.

Leaning against the desk with his arms crossed, Parker said, "How did you know we were . . . I was here?"

"I didn't know. Is Pinky with you? She must be with you."

"We were on a diplomatic mission to Miami when the ribbons blew. Tom and Jen were halfway up and the Five Civilized Tribes rescued us from the Big Swampy, gators and crocs and crackers, oh my."

"I needed to find my best friend; we've been pulling art out of the mud in San Jose and he was heading Up from Geneva. I thought there might be good comlinks here, if not; I'm just on to Geneva myself."

"Well stick around, I've almost got the link re-established, then we can tap the subcom channel on the gravitel and talk to the whole System. In the meantime, let's get to the council, pretty interesting conversation, I'll bet."

*

Geneva
April 8, 2125

Larr, Stuart and the schwartzkommandos, one week into the siege, had fallen into a rotation of sitters around the ribbon. Sections took a break every few days, gathered supplies for the others and rested up for their next shift. It had become clear that the NUF's plan, if you could call it that, was to blow things up and then stand around doing nothing. *Looks like a union job.*

In the grand scheme of things, this wasn't far from the truth. The higher echelon directing the sleeper cells' range of choices of course had a philosophy, which was to motivate the general population to liberate themselves from real or imagined theological-industrial oppression, maybe just neglect. This was especially tricky when the populace wasn't sure how they were being oppressed and yet suffered from a deep unease and anger about the world as it was. Parroting a mangled fascist call to arms seemed to be smoke and mirrors and if you couldn't understand the official propaganda you had to figure out how to make the resulting anarchy work anyway.

Brodie trusted in the endless adaptability and creativity of the human race, especially with the new blood of spooks and Andromedans in the mix. It was anarchy based on the best in our natures, tend and defend instead of fight or flight, a threefold pact, three species each being trusted to temper the unique excesses of the other two and thereby govern themselves on a much smaller scale than at any time since the rise of agriculture and cities.

Individual humans, and Charlotte had taught this, progressed from the simplicity of a child through the complexity of adulthood and, hopefully, on to simplicity again in the wisdom of age, all the while building a personal and societal myth that held the experience together. Brodie believed that this same thing could happen in a civilization, once the lid of the pressure cooker was off.

Stuart's group finished the self-help breakfast, cleaning up their mess at the Funny Horse, now a communal kitchen. Uncle Kleinfelter was still holding court at the salon but the blacks seemed to be all going unkempt afros, dreads and Black Panther skinsuits for the duration. That didn't change his smile as he waved off his nieces and the boys.

Settling into their places, now on their own cushions, and unfurling their signs, they melded into the broad camaraderie of the moment. Then three Jesuits on real Harley's turned into the parking lot and made a beeline to Stuart.

Stuart smiled at the boys from the Knights of Columbus Motorcycle Club that he recognized from the bar. "Hola Ignatz, Claude, Telly; protesting by polluting the air?"

"How much damage can three guys on Harleys do? I mean without the big polluters, we can have a little fun right?"

"If you say so."

"Hey, you were the business agent for the pipefitters union in Glasgow, right?"

"A long time ago."

"Still, that and your leadership at CERN . . ."

"Corralling a bunch of Carthy malcontents?"

"Actually, Gaddafi recommended you."

"For what?"

"Diplomacy is starting, we're getting a team together to negotiate and rebuild. The first planetary meeting is in Namibia. Then we'll engage the other side. Might take a while, might take a year."

Heidi said, "Do it Stuart, we'll go see Mukaa Ma!"

"She's right, that's the lady in charge down there. C'mon, it'll be fun."

"Do I get my own Harley?"

"Sure buddy, whatever you want, bring your friends too."

S.C. had already set out for Engelberg to try to find Frosty and a ride back to his family in Vancouver. He had moved them down to Mt. Angel where he could assure their safety at the monastery and work on the book, maybe indulge in Charlotte's library as well.

Larr on the other hand was a bit more disturbed. There was still a regional newsfeed in Geneva, where he had seen pictures of the bombs and Walter Brodie. His contribution to the bombs was unmistakable, the images of the clamshells on his website now prominently displayed next to the head siege engineer. Now he knew who Frankie's money man had been. Not that there was any real government to call him on it, but, at least, he had to get out of the spotlight for a while.

So, when Frida finally got through to him on the subcom he said his goodbyes and left for Engleberg with S.C. Frosty was going to drop him as close to Cahokia as he could find an adequate air strip and then he would start working on his life, just one more time.

Stuart had gotten stuck with both ladies, Heidi and Edelweiss, having to keep them both happy. *Too bad, so sad.* The three of them each got on the back of a Jesuit Harley and that good old deep bass chuckle of the internal combustion engine rumbled through their bodies as they leaned into a sharp turn out of the lot and onto the road to Meyrin, CERN and the Quantum Mechanic's Union Bar, now to work on a different kind of salvage operation.

*

The Debris Ring
May, 2125 C.E.

After the terror, even though he was an academic, or maybe because he was, Arch Sandifur was drafted into the Cult's diplomatic corps by Pinky Sheridan herself, the Second Bodhisattva Xià lù dì, blessings be upon her, perhaps with the idea that he knew Walter Brodie as well as anyone. Not a bad thought, but totally useless information; Brodie was on his own agenda from beginning to end. He only appeared to be toeing the line in any group he joined or led. Brodie used other people to get to escape velocity after which he slingshot on his own to his true destination, deranged or not.

As a boy, as Archie Sandifur, geek savant, his mentor and gym coach had been Walter Brodie. Arch had enjoyed the rapid fire telegraphed scientific conversations that he had engaged in with Brodie. Brodie didn't care if Arch stuttered, rocked and snorted in the throes of autistic creativity. But that was then, and the monastic recluse bit suited Arch better in the end, though now he was being thrust into the spotlight by the Bodhisattva, an offer you can't refuse.

The Cult was not ready for subtle diplomacy, or all out warfare. The Second Bodhisattva Xià lù dì, like St. Paul, had taken over an organization based on the short life of a real person, a person press-ganged into a myth, a myth that grew and came to power due to a hundred million individual epiphanies and the new world order of humans, spooks, Andromedans and hybrids. It had always succeeded by being the eight hundred pound gorilla in the room. But, hired mercenaries and collateral damage left a bad taste with the high and mighty, no matter how liberal they wanted to appear.

It had been this way even at the beginning of Christianity. Those at the intellectual end of the spectrum were the highly educated from the Hellenistic Roman world. Latin and Greek were the languages of philosophy, not the common vulgate of the masses, yearning to be free and saved. While the Neo-Platonists pontificated, warrior monks in goat skins and hair shirts delivered the 'convert or die' message to the mean streets from Bethlehem to Rome.

The same format seemed to be playing out here. The Futurists adopted the any-means-to-an-end, gotta-break-some-eggs-to-make-an-omelet, extremism-in-the-defense-of-virtue-is-no-vice, type of mindless steam roller that was necessary to accomplish the first round of attacks on Earth's infrastructure. They were finding it hard to back down from that even if there was a liberal secular humanist core. Still, the intellectuals tried to rise above this, playing the good cop-bad cop game.

That kind of schizophrenia drove away some of the most effective guerillas and left the pragmatic hierarchy trying desperately to keep the storm troops in line before they tore everything down on their own. So, Arch Sandifur was tasked with stopping the siege and retaking planet Earth through secular compromise that made sense to the theocracy, the faithful and the front line anarchists.

With the Library in ruins, the rush was on to rebuild the Orbital Collider and create a new portal, as was being done at other sites in the System and in Andromeda. The ultimate goal was to prevent future attacks by redundancies, by building a factory collider, popping out Libraries on an assembly line, to be towed or transported to their installation sites. But, the original site, where the unknown was created from the ineffable, was still sacred. So, the Temple remained like the Wailing Wall, to give meaning to the new farewell, "Next Year at Moving Day."

*

NEW UNITED FUTURIST MANIFESTO

1. We are a sovereign planet. We are the eyes, ears, mouth and hands of Earth. We speak for Earth as others must speak for their motherland. Listen!

2. We will sing the love of the danger of mortal life on one planet.

3. The essential elements of our poetry will be courage, daring, and revolt.

4. Literature having up to now magnified thoughtful immobility, ecstasy and sleep, will now exalt the aggressive gesture, feverish insomnia and existential uncertainty of the old physics.

5. There is no more beauty except in struggle for justice; no masterpiece without an aggressive vision. Poetry must be a violent attack against the old science and the new religion of false immortality, summoning them to lie down before humanity in the mud of Earth.

6. We declare that the world's wonder has been enriched by a fresh beauty: the beauty of the old divine, of wrestling angels and goddesses in the mud of our true mother. This beauty rails against purification and ritual baths. This beauty reeks with the smell of the

skin of the world, this beauty reeks with truth.

7. The poets must expend their energies only to increase the enthusiastic fervor of these primordial elements and the humanity that rises from them.

8. We stand on the far promontory of centuries! The infinities of Time and Space died yesterday. We live already in the absolute infinity of consecutive present moments.

9. We want to glorify our concept of war -- the only hygiene for this world -- war against false beauty, against false art, against false religion that strips the planet and ignores its true voice and hands.

10. We proclaim a war of extermination against false theology, against false aesthetics, against the Glory of the Lord, against the untouchability and objectification of Beauty.

11. We want to demolish the temples and stupas of false prophets that lure the easily duped and their riches off planet. We will take their riches as passage. No longer disguised in false poverty, the mendicants shall live their convictions or stay here with us in the mud.

Look at us! We are not out of breath... Our hearts are not in the least tired for they feed on Saturn's fire, on Newton's Physics, on Euclid's Geometry and on the rough and certain bonds of Earth. -

- Up on the crest of the world, once more we hurl our challenge to the stars!

*

Earth,
May 30, 2125

"What the fuck do they want?"

Still at Cahokia, Parker's patchwork had succeeded, allowing Pinky to re-establish communications with Arch Sandifur at the Debris Ring. She read the NUF Manifesto poster on the gravitel screen and said,

"Has the whole planet gone batshit crazy? We're dealing with a system wide disaster, terrorists are blockading the planet and this is their justification? Did they somehow kill the bubble drive too; the elevators, the Library and now this?"

From the screen, the voice of Arch Sandifur said, "It's not part of their pattern; after the first attacks they're just blockading the elevators and stupas, even the Red Guard at Fragrant Mountain, non-violent resistance. Not much of a war."

"That's ludicrous!"

"Not really. They can't do any more damage, the infrastructure is gone; it's just performance art now. "

"Well we can't ride in like Cossacks on a pogrom!"

"And we won't, 3MI won't, but we want to get back to the stars. We just have to figure out what they want. Pinky, you weren't a Cult devotee when you were human."

"No," she said, "I wouldn't have had anything to do with this. But, it's a practical matter to me. The power to do good is wrapped up in belief systems. It's no deception to promote the mythology that the people demand."

"The *minority* of the people; that's the problem. The rest have a feeling but no coherent agenda; the voice of the

80% is *deliberately* surreal. After the attack, this poster appeared all over. Not just on newsfeeds, but tacked up and glued on walls, just like old fashioned propaganda. Obviously it's connected to the perpetrators, but it's really an absurd Dadaist item. It's like a feint, a dodge. It means nothing so it means something different to everybody. The person who wrote this isn't stupid or insane. It's a riff on a two hundred year old revolution, the Futurist Manifesto, The artistic predecessors of the Italian Fascists."

"And the Nazis; a dangerous sense of humor."

"Mussolini was the end of it. He said, 'We have buried the putrid corpse of Liberty.' "

"They can't mean *that!*"

"No, it's the reverse. It's code. They accuse *us* of being fascists with a fascist rant. You made a deal with the Devil, it was a political solution. Familiarity breeds strange bedfellows."

"What? No, not the Devil, 3MI. Give unto Caesar what credit is due."

"The difference is that Jesus was not Caesar, but *you are*. That's the whole point."

"I didn't want to *be* anything, Charlotte asked me to do this job so that access to the Library could be maintained outside of governments, outside of science, by the people who demanded a miracle."

"You're Constantine then, religion as political expediency."

"I didn't make the problem."

"No, Charlotte was a real human, a real spook, a real revelation of the new; the new good news. She was real, and lived in the worlds and did work for sentient beings. She was a link to experience, what took the place of religious experience, a true feeling that made faith logical. Then Thigpen Chodron came to Fragrant Mountain and built a stupa. She was a syncretist professor of comparative religion at Dharamshala."

"*She* made the problem?"

"No, like St. Paul made Jesus God, she made Charlotte the Bodhisattva. But, she had political utility as a goal also; remember the riots?"

"The Transdimensional Personhood Riots started when I was five and put my entire family in danger."

"That and the disenfranchised People of the Book plus the Ronin Jesuits stirring up the rabble required a response. You made an expedient political reality and, predictably, there is a resistance movement. Because your authority is divine, the opposition must be spiritual as well as revolutionary; and it is. The Manifesto has a very odd syncretism of its own. It answers the need for spiritual validation through our own theological aesthetics."

"It's a solution within what seems like an uncompromising screed?"

"Exactly."

*

The Debris Ring
June 15, 2125 C.E.

Arch Sandifur's quarters were nothing more or less than a high tech monastic cell; tricked out and cozy, but still a cell. If he wanted real luxury, what passed for luxury, anyway, at the spartan Debris Ring Temple, he could always park on Emma's couch and watch the big screen streamer, but it was more her company than comfort that he craved; for the moment however, *Time to call it a day-cycle.*

He put on his goggles and reclined his one luxury, a vintage Lazy-Boy lounger. Some nights, many nights, he just slept in the chair. In the reduced gravity of the station it was the perfect cocoon.

Ensconced, he browsed through random neural net sites using augmented reality goggles featuring the newest user friendly interface, biofeedback commands comprising focusing, blinking and operant eye movements. Searching by stream of consciousness queries, the fuzzy logic algorithms made suggestions based on voiced commands, brainwave activity, past searches and predictive correlations. Not a bad system; at least it knew what brainwaves meant '*no, you stupid algorithm, try again.*'

You started out with a random query. This was doctrine, a meditative practice, a ritualized version of St. Daniel's fabled first contact with Charlotte after her death, her first *transitus*. It was also the technique used by the resurrected Charlotte, the Bodhisattva Xià lù dì, to recruit her successor, the former Devi Sheridan, St. Daniel's, *Dan Pritchard's*, daughter, who renamed herself Pinky Sheridan, F.S., now H.H. the Second Bodhisattva Xià lù dì, *peace be upon her*. The official versions of those stories had the divine appear through the cryptic allegory of the divinely channeled search, the search engine *Optimus.*

So, having learned the technique like every novice, Arch instead used it for its original mundane and practical purpose, counting sheep. It was progressively old school, something that could be done unaided by attending to stream of consciousness clues, or with the latest technology. He blinked twice to boot up the goggles.

The Manifesto talked about beauty; What was that thing Petra Rousseau said? Back at the very beginning? The three transcendentals? She said Beauty was a transcendental being. A being? Do we seek encounter with a being, or encounter with one transcendental aspect of Being? Ok, an unsolvable koan, perfect.

"Search; Beauty, a transcendental Being, Petra Rousseau."

Focus, scan, blink, blink, blink,

a. . . and off we go. . .

Petra's words came up in myriad sources, now scrolling down his peripheral vision; he blinked on one. *Blink.*

We seek a powerful and authentic I-Thou relationship to and with Beauty as a Being.

We also work deeply with a second idea/awareness -- something that has moral ramifications -- something that colors the way we live, speak, move, work. All three Transcendentals are interconnected and if or when one is separated out from the other two, harm is unleashed in the world.

I and Thou, Martin Buber's book, and then from another source, some doctrinal commentary on theologian, Hans Urs von Balthasar;

> . . . without beauty, goodness will turn hedonistic and utilitarian, while truth will turn cold. Without beauty, we will neither pray right nor know how to love.

More suggestions turned up, as he scrolled down the augmented view. *Focus blink, blink, switch to alpha waves, blink.*

Navajo Blessing Way

With *beauty* before me, may I walk.
With *beauty* behind me, may I walk.
With *beauty* below me, may I walk.
With *beauty* above me, may I walk.
With *beauty* all around me, may I walk.

Blink, scan, blink, focus, blink,
It was on Charlotte's Memorial Card, after her first *transitus*, it was on stupas, temples and schools, every school child knew this. "I saw Beauty, it was my destiny, therein lies all . . . Södergran."
And it came from, blink, focus, blink,

Edith Södergran; obscure Finnish-Swedish poet in the early 1900's, from her poem, *The Statue of Beauty*.

I saw *Beauty*.
It was my destiny; therein lies all.
How to give thanks for it?
Fresh roses, picked with warm hands,
I lay every single day
In front of your statue
So your smile can find rest.
Where do I find roses
That do not offend my dreams?
It is my lot -
Every day to go with roses for my queen
And lie sobbing at her feet. . .
When shall I rise light as a feather
To fetch the rose, the only one
The one which never dies?

What is not born and does not die? The rose which never dies? Tea Rose, blue roses, pleurosis, blink, blink,

Edith Södergran was born in St. Petersburg, but Finnish, lived in Raivola on the Karelian peninsula, first modernist poet who wrote in Swedish, because Finland was governed by Sweden for a long time. She identified with the Russian Revolution, wanted to put spirituality into Bolshevism, then was introduced to Anthroposophy by a neighbor, said she was not interested in 'spooks', then fell hard for mysticism, Rudolf Steiner, to her, he was a gnostic Christ.

What? Spooks? Field Sentients? In 1919? Blink, focus.

Valentin Tomberg, also born in St. Petersburg. Södergran and Tomberg, thirty miles apart on the same Lake Ladoga, both were followers of Steiner and Anthroposophy. Tomberg later became a Jesuit. *Like the Ignazis.*

Aaaaand. . . Blink, Lake Ladoga, Russian Standard Vodka, with Lake Ladoga water, recipe by Mendeleev for the Czar, Mendeleev invented the Periodic Table of Elements.

Hans Urs von Balthasar The first author of Charlotte's canon! wrote a forward for a book by Tomberg, *Meditations on the Tarot.* Von Balthasar praised him for bringing ancient esoteric knowledge into Christianity. *Gnosis.*

Blink, blink, focus, blink.

Jesuit websites obsessed over whether or not Balthasar - *the Notorious H. U. vB* - was really, really, *(c'mon really!?)* actually ok with gnosis. *Looks like it.*

Arch was familiar with these concepts from studies in pre-Cult religion. *Well, vB was quite comfortable with gnosis, Neo-Platonism, the place of pagan philosophy and the World Soul in the teleology of Christianity.*

Blink, Balthazar called it 'Hermetic Christianity', which would have been blasphemy if he hadn't been the favorite of the last Pope Emeritus Benedict, good ol' Joe Ratzinger, who made *vB* a cardinal.

Did you hear the pope got the bird flu? You don't say? Yeah, he got it from a cardinal. Har Har.

Ronin Jesuits, Ignazis, Steiner, Anthroposophists, Södergran, The Statue of Beauty, Theology of Beauty, Charlotte, beauty, truth and goodness.

Tomberg, coming from Russia, and from the byzantine Russian Orthodox Church, was also a fan of Sophia, divine wisdom. Sophia, little known in the West, was the feminine counterpart of Jesus as Logos, the Word; the Word that was there at creation in Genesis.

In the beginning was the Word, and the Word was with God, and the Word was God and Sophia was God, the one God, then the triune God, the three become four as One. You can cut the cognitive dissonance with a butter knife.

Sophia is a being. Beauty as a being? That was also part of the same apocryphal take on Petra's message to Daniel, that defrocked Russian theologian, . . .

Blink, blink, Bulgakov, Sergei Bulgakov? The second author of Charlotte's canon!

The Sophiologist Bulgakov looked like Rasputin, *gimmie that old time religion,* long beard and psycho eyes, but, yes, his definition of angels was the first attempt that Charlotte, F.S., the spook, used to describe herself; ' a spiritual being with work to do in the world.'

That's an understatement! An angel searching for physical encounter with Sophia as a being in the world? Was that what Petra was getting at? Sophia as a being infused with beauty, truth and goodness, wandering through the world to be spotted by adepts?

Top o' the morning to you, Madam Sophie, haven't seen you around here in a month of Sundays. Yes well my friend there seems to be a great need for wisdom these days, I just can't say no. Yes, yes, well stay out of trouble, m'lady, if you can. Good day sir, we'll meet again in time.

Ok, this doesn't seem productive . . .

blink, blink. . . delta waves.

Arch was blurring lines, successfully falling asleep, his eyes closing. The augmented reality specs were programmed to handle this loss of conscious control by keeping up A.I. free association until his thinking brain came back on line; subliminal web-hopping, automatic hop-scotching.

To this program, Arch's snores were like rumble strips, warnings of brainwaves getting too deep, a bit of a swerve and the program brought him back on track. But, that algorithm assumed that the user had a logical line of inquiry going in the first place, and wanted to stay awake; not a safe bet.

It was something of a party game, like telephone; see how far afield the search program got when primed with random nonsense and inattention. The algorithm was not built to recognize and respond to humor, being on the autistic spectrum, like Arch, although its solutions were sometimes quite humorous to the partygoers.

Did you know that baseball is mentioned in the Bible? I did not know that, how so? Well the very first line of Genesis is, "In the Big Inning! Har Har, Drum roll, rim shot, badda boom, badda bing.

Though still in his Lazy Boy, Arch was certainly sleep walking now. The program was really off the rails, continuing but not quite without direction, the web bits started tacking into the wind, starting with Sophia, the divine feminine.

--The *Shekinah*, also the feminine embodiment of God in the Hebrew Bible, where the--

--*Merkabah* is the throne chariot from the first vision of Ezekial, wheels within wheels, then sitting on the throne is the--

--*Ancient of Days*, William Blake's Urizen, a strange painting out of sync with time, a muscular old man with long white hair and beard. He is kneeling on one knee, in a position like Iron Man landing; kneeling in the air, in a black sky before a blazing yellow orb between parting storm clouds. Rays of sunlight set off against the blackness radiate from the orb. The wind is blowing so hard and steady that his white hair and beard are fully horizontal. He leans over staring intensely down, his long arm extended with a draftsman's dividers marking ninety degrees--

--*Paradise Lost, His Golden Compasses, God the Geometer dividing the waters, Ezekial's Ancient of Days. Blake's favorite image, he couldn't stop painting it*--

--*Carl Jung*, as a child, had a vision of Ezekial's Ancient of Days, sitting on the Throne Chariot, which turned out to be -- *We are not making this up.* -- a potty chair as God lays a turd on the earth. *Carl!*

Arch choked a bit on that one like someone cycling through sleep apnea without waking.

But also -- Jung's theory of Synchronicity, how coincidences are built outside of time and space from the collective unconscious and return as Daniel's pebbles at the window announcing some deeper order--

--*David Bohm's Implicate Order!*

--Then, Creator Mundi, God the Geometer, another icon, another draftsman? God the Geometer, an illuminated icon painted in the 11th century showing a Byzantine image of God/Sophia/Logos/Jesus. According to the caption, it was the human Charlotte's favorite icon before her first *transitus.*

It hung on her wall for twenty years, carried from one home to another as Daniel and Charlotte followed each other. Again with drafting dividers, *another Golden Compass,* this God looks like Jesus as the Word, or maybe the creepiness comes from the transgender duo of Jesus and Sophia, intensely focused eyes, staring at a circle with the just forming blobs of the soon to be earth, moon and sum. The inside curve of the circle is blue waters in intricate waves. Many have said this resembles the Mandelbrot Set--

---Fractal Geometry. The pattern stays the same no matter how deep you go; a deep, deep order called chaos.

--- Implicate Order, hidden variables, the enfolded order under random or paradoxical events, quantum entanglement, Einstein's spooky action at a distance and pre-Steiner Södergran ranting against 'spookiness.' *That's really funny now that we have real spooks.*

---Turtles all the way down; The primitive description of the world supported by elephants standing on a turtle, *the physicists' joke on cosmology, and first causes:*

Two monks walk into a bar. Wondering about first causes the first one says 'The elephants stand on a turtle but what's under the turtle?' The other monk answers, "It's turtles all the way down."

There's always another order under the chaos, turtles all the way down.

---The implicate order all the way down, David Bohm again and round we go, back to Logos and Sophia, before and after her death, Charlotte taught children and the first hybrid spooks following Steiner's Waldorf School program educating the mind, body and spirit. Charlotte, Södergran, Beauty, Steiner, von Balthasar, Anthroposophy, Charlotte, Quantum Consciousness, Charlotte, and Beauty is harmony, symmetry, balance, Liberté, Egalité, Fraternité,

Beauté. The NUF Manifesto; the true beauty of justice, the true justice of beauty

The quantum gravity generators in Arch's room switched on automatically with a shudder and hum. They were programmed to do this whenever a spook entered their field, setting the stage for manifestation if desired.

In a dream he dreams he wakes. He dreams he dreams a sound awakes him.

Though still asleep, Arch's watching brain noted some presence in the room with him, but still; was it a sound he dreamed that dreamed no worries? He sensed nothing manifesting and so fell back into his sleep. The algorithm kept churning.

But something was singing, something from Arch's childhood: *It's a lovely day today, and whatever you've got to do, you've got a lovely day to do it in. . . that's true!* On the word 'true' his father would smile and touch a forefinger to the tip of Arch's nose, forcing happiness even if he was scowling at having to wake up. *Grown-ups are so annoying!* In his slumber, so far away in time and space from that memory, still he felt a phantom poke on his nose.

Then he did begin to wake, and the algorithm pulled up current news bites:

The record of the proceedings of talks within the organized factions of the New United Futurists/Quantum Mechanics Union, the siege engineers holding earth hostage. The Southern Indigenous Congress and the Planetary Moot, things he was supposed to understand, *yeah right*, things he was challenged with right now, about to become a participant, and another song from his childhood: *I'd do anything for you dear, anything, for you mean everything to me. Poke.*

Stop it Dad, it's a snow day!

-Elaine Scarry on Beauty and Being Just:

What are the attributes of Beauty? Symmetry, harmony, balance, these are how we recognize Beauty. Justice also consists of symmetry, balance, a leveling of power, equality, the equal, symmetrical application of the benefits and responsibilities of society. Justice is hard to see, but beauty is not hard to see. In fact, justice comprises all the attributes of Beauty. Anything that has these attributes is the earthly end of that transcendental ribbon to the stars. The other end of that continuum is the divine.

And then a voice,
Arch,
bang, bang bang,
Arch,
bang, bang, bang,
Arch,
bang, bang, bang,
Arch,
bang, bang, bang,
Arch, bang, bang, bang
. . . *Arch!*

The Lazy Boy sprang upright and Arch's eyes opened, "Shitgod*damn*motherfucker, Sweet Charlotte's Ass!!!"

He saw a silver being without a face sitting on the couch, holding a small whiteboard. Written on it: *"Thanks for the compliment. Can we talk?"* It taps on the whiteboard repeatedly.

"Yes, yes, yes, yes, w-what, what, what?" Arch hadn't stuttered for years but he also hadn't gone totally widdershins either in all those years. As he woke up he thought, *I've read of this, Tom the Third's silvers?*

The whiteboard said: *"yes, yes, yes, yes, that Charlotte, ok? I thought you st-st-st-stopped st-st-stuttering. Where's Tommy and Jen?"*

"Stuck at the L2 Lagrange p-p-point station, the siege, you know, and the bubble drives all quit at once. Wait, are you making fun of me?

D'd'd'don't be a p'p'pussy.

"What, is the secret of life after death sarcasm?"

"*Just messing with you. Helps with the cognitive dissonance.*"

"I get it. Stop being mean."

Ok.

"C'-c'-can't you just talk?"

"*Not quite yet. Better this way, ok?*"

"I can get them on the gravitel, all of that still works."

"*Not needed yet, are you calm now?*"

"Why are you here?

"*I have to tell you something, so listen. The Futurists did not make the Bubble Drive stop working.*"

"We guessed that, but then what did?"

"*We did. The Implicate Order, if you want a name. The Multiverse Field, Brodie told you, back at the beginning.*"

"You mean the Puppy Mill? Brodie's big bang baby-daddy speech?"

"*The Drive makes universes in the multiverse field; Higgs Bosons make big bangs. But there's more.* "

"What?"

It wrote another sentence on the board and held it up. "*Do you have the model drive?*"

"The demonstration desk model? It's just a souvenir, a keepsake, ancient history."

"*Get it.*"

He had a bit of trouble shaking off the shock of it to realize he was still in his cell and just a few steps from the closet where he had stashed the model desk set.

"Ok, don't move." Irrationally, he had already accepted her rationality. He stepped to the closet, opening the door and reaching to the back of the top shelf, feeling for the snow globe shape of the model.

Got it!

Silver Charlotte drummed her fingers on the white board.

"*Turn it on.*"

"It's got to be charged, here, I'll run it through the streamer console." He plugged it into the console at his small desk and flipped a switch at the back. The ball lit right up and a familiar humming started. The crystal knobs covering the ball started to emit streams of blue light aimed at the center of the sphere. At that point of convergence, a small translucent sphere of blue light began to grow.

So far, it was just a serviceable demonstration of the Higgs Bubble Drive, like those old toy steam engines or working models of internal combustion engines, with the block made of clear plastic and the whole thing turned with a hand crank.

"But, this works and the real engines don't?"

"These are different. They don't leak bosons." He realized suddenly that her image was no longer in the room, he looked; she and her whiteboard were gone. The voice was coming from the ball.

"Wait, w,w,w,wait!"

"Don't start that again. The model doesn't shit Higgs Bosons into my back yard, but it does open a window, a porthole, so we can talk."

"What are you? Where are you?"

As he stared into the model, a face began to resolve, gradually surfacing as out of some opaque liquid, like a message rising up in the eight ball oracle. It was familiar, strikingly familiar. A woman, about twenty, skin like porcelain, dark shoulder length curls, brown eyes and full lips, a bit of sarcasm in her smile; almost an icon but shining and *alive.*

"Do you like this look? I like it. Classic Charlotte, don't you think?" The face spun around like she was twirling on her toes. "We are you, something a human wraps around, an existence in common with other sentients. We are in the multiverse field, you know, where the drive shits."

"Doesn't seem like you should be saying 'shit' so much."

"What, I'm not living up to your expectations?"

"I have no expectations. . . well, you're not an effie?"

"I'm insulted! No, but effies come here too when their energy body is gone."

"That makes two souls for each symbiont-host pair? Are you her soul?"

"I don't do math. I am what I am, like Yahweh."

"Or Popeye."

Her eyes flashed. "*Now* you're a funny man; but no God of Abraham has stopped by to tell us anything. We know nothing. We live. We are life. We will welcome you too in time, your time. I don't have answers but I do have a mission, a message."

"I'm a little busy right now."

She laughed, "You're actually going to pretend you're not entranced, seduced, enthralled by my Beauty?"

"Wait, were you doing that with the search program?"

"It's a tradition; didn't they teach you that at seminary?"

"The Cult's catechism is fiction, I didn't drink the kool aid."

"The only truth is in fiction, poetry and metaphor. Well, think about that search for a while; you'll get it. But that's not why I'm here. You are talking to me, *that's* why I'm here. The drive you invented is very bad for my home, your home eventually. But the invention is inevitable, so when it happens, those of us connected to that universe, that civilization, we get to go fix it. "

Arch leaned back in his chair, "Huh, so you did it?"

"All your dead friends and family did it. But, we give you this gift. Without that bad invention, you would not have this gift. You're welcome Arch."

"But, how do I talk to anyone in particular?"

"Shine a light in the darkness, your memories of us, your meditation, your reading to the dead, your love; it's irresistible, you'll see."

"But . . ."

"Call an engineer, hey, you used to be one."

"I was a *physicist*."

"Whatever." She twirled again, laughed and submerged into the dark.

Arch punched the dedicated link to Emma's quarters: *Emmie!*

He heard a shuffle, a curse, and then, "It's 0300. Why am I talking to you?"

"Looks like you're going to have to get that new eyeball, Emmie, something is happening, make some coffee, I'll brief you at your place."

"Shit."

Arch was already in the corridor as the link blipped out.

*

Earth
June 15, 2125
L2 Station

At the L2 station, as far away from L3 as you could get in the same orbit, hovering in Earth's shadow, Jen and Tom III sat in the aft observation bubble looking forward over the whole station, lit only by starlight, its own running lights and proximity beacons. Airlocks and docking ports in use provided temporary illumination and moving pinpoints revealing suits, shuttles and battery modules completed the picture. Even though, after many years of habitation, accession and re-engineering, the details had changed, it still could be described as 'shotgun shacks and tin can telephones'; the classic description of one of its first visitors.

Their sailsuit transit with the G-Sink Bar had been uneventful, if not a bit comic, with the ready distribution of free booze compliments of the house. Tom was, after all, the CEO of 3MI and Jen held the purse strings. There was just enough tragedy, uncertainty and cognitive dissonance to drive the self-medication. A few fights broke out as arguments over the perpetrators and cause of the disaster were postulated without any verified base assumptions. The NUF's and the Southern Indigenous Front got the most speculation for the moment.

Jen and Tom indulged a bit in the conspiracy theories but for the most part were just designated drivers in case command decisions had to be made. Jen could just tweak her implants to compensate for inebriation as and when needed; the perfect date.

By the time they arrived at L2, communications had been reestablished, thanks to Parker, and they learned that the Bodhisattva was safe, or sleeping with the enemy; at least somebody on the planet was still rational. They were both kept incredibly busy implementing emergency and interim protocols to salvage some normalcy in a System attacked, besieged and forcefully amputated from Earth.

In the observation bubble, in some semblance of privacy, they were reviewing the damage reports and estimates of recovery times of disabled ships. One couldn't keep track of everything but it helped to appear to be in charge of something, even if most fires were being doused by others before Tom and Jen were aware of them.

They watched as a slag freighter on their list limped into the docking port on graviton retro power only. That had taken three months from Europa, a trip that took only hours with the bubble drive. The practical problem was how to mine asteroids and space dust on the way for raw materials and organic molecules needed to make air, power and nutrients for the longer trip. Some had to use cryogenics to subtract the needs of the crew from the equation, arriving on automatic pilot. In those cases it wasn't always known if anyone had survived the trip. So, the view was calming and disturbing at the same time.

As the docking clamps secured the slag ship, the graviton emitters in the room switched on, signaling the arrival of a field sentient, or that was what it should have meant. Instead however, a silver, faceless humanoid being appeared as out of a crack in the air, It pushed itself out of the crack like out of a hole in the ground, but upside down. When it had completely emerged, it flipped around right side up and sat on the couch opposite Tom and Jen.

Although this apparition had not been seen since the first Moving Day, it was familiar to them. Then, the Silvers had annoyed Tom to distraction until Jen had stepped in and corralled *them*. This one held up a white board that said, *Sup?*

Jen said, "Soup'sup. Why am I not surprised? Which one are you?"

The whiteboard said, *Charlotte. Have a problem?*

Tom said, "No thanks, already have one. . . Now I know you've got something to do with this."

Well I'm fine, thanks for asking.

"Sorry," Jen said, "We're all a bit on edge. I'll assume you know what's been happening?"

Yes

"And . . ."

Talk to Archie, just left him, gotta run, been here too long already.

"But . . ."

I wanted to tell you I still love you, Dan says hi, and we'll see you in the Dark Forever.

The being blinked out and Tom said to the air, "Get Arch Sandifur on the gravitel."

*

Earth
500,000 Y.B.P.

The hominin officiating sat with his back to the cave entrance and faced the fire. He held a small piece of hematite, already scraped flat on one side from the preparation of red ochre. With a flint scraper he incised a series of diagonal crossed lines then a line above and below the x's. Finally, he scraped a line through the centers, examined his handiwork and placed it on a large stone within the entrance. A small group of his kind approached with a body slung between them in a brain tanned and smoked horsehide. On death, it had been tied in a fetal position until it had stiffened. A plaited band was tied around the head to hold the jaw shut and stones had been placed on the eyelids to keep them closed. They carried the body to the stone altar and the officiator placed the incised stone securely between the thigh and the torso. Red ochre from a mortar ground into the altar was then spread over the body and smoothed out evenly.

After the body was prepared, the participants spread the burning wood from the fire across the entrance with sticks. As the living flames died, smoke rose skyward. The officiator closed his eyes and raised his arms toward the smoke. He placed still glowing coals in a depression ground into a smooth river rock, picked up a bundle of dry moss and twigs, catching fire from the coals and lighting the way into the cave. From the entrance, the tunnel led downward at a slight angle. Over about two thousand feet the path dropped fifty feet then continued down at a steeper angle for another two thousand feet until it leveled out into a large chamber.

The pall bearers began to shiver as the temperature dropped inside the cave. By the flicker of the torch, vague shapes on the wall that only suggested the living beings could barely be discerned. Dry grass and kindling was used to make a fire on the stone which was then placed in the center of the room. An assistant tended the fire, keeping it low, inserting one kindling stick at a time. About twenty bodies were visible, placed in orderly fashion along the curving rear wall of the chamber. To the right, the bodies had been more recently placed. At the left end, the remains were only bones, still however retaining the fetal position and orientation with knees up, facing up, that can be noticed in the more recent bodies. The hominins placed their burden down at the right end.

Again the officiator closed his eyes as he had before the smoke at the entrance. Again he raised his arms up. In the dark the flickering shadows made the lifeless bodies seem to move, their eyes following his gestures. Once again, the participants felt the presence and departure of their ancestors in one eternal present moment.

Then, the one who will be called a shaman in the unimaginably distant future, picked up the torch and led the way back to the light and the living.

Charlotte had followed along, all but invisible in her natural form, thinking, *Some pre-homo sapiens hominin. After homo erectus and before neanderthalis, Homo heidelbergensis? Memory, imagination, ritual, a conception of an afterlife. As below, so above, the life force of the fire rises as smoke. The life force of the dead, the invisible smoke of the living also rises.*

Silver Dan popped in, "Time to go. The pulse is rising. Meld with me."

*

Earth
June 2, 2125 C.E.

Larr looked out the window of Frosty's spaceplane somewhere over the Gulf of Mexico, the mood of levity dominating his first flight being decidedly absent. S.C. was sitting just across the aisle but had been ceaselessly writing on his phone pad ever since they had left Engleberg. Every passenger on this flight was lost in their own personal fear or despair, not knowing what was coming next, not knowing if the Bodhisattva was alive or dead, not knowing if anyone off planet, loved ones or not, were alive or dead, not knowing exactly who the enemy was at any given moment, who might be pointing a rail gun at them, what would happen to their future. Even Frosty was not up to organizing weightless playtime on this run.

From Engleberg, Frosty had first landed at Galveston where the siphon gangs had successfully kept the Mexicans, Tejianos, NUFs, 3MI and the Cult from nationalizing or hijacking the refineries. They had an informal compact with the autonomous United Oilrig Emirates, a loose association between whatever petty warlords had seized the offshore rigs near Galveston. The supply was steady when it flowed but otherwise unpredictable and subject to the whims of the rig-emirs. Spaceplane fuel was available to all for a price or barter, but they weren't being mean about it. Life was starting to limp along with some degree of decorum amid the uncertainty.

Frida had finally reached Larr with a relay from Cahokia off the L2 station and they exchanged news as he traveled. The System was still intact though sputtering. The death toll would taper off as the crew of long distance runs resolved that they had become multigenerational ships. The other method of travel, the Library, was gone as well, no shipping, no *transitus*, no Moving Day, not until the Orbital Collider was back on line anyway. If that happened, at least there would be a way to make a Library and get back to Andromeda and Alpha Centauri, for rescue missions if nothing else. The scuttlebutt was that Libraries could replace the Bubble Drive on local runs as well. There just hadn't been a reason to make them for secular purposes until now.

His saffron robed seatmate muttered to himself, "What's happening, what's happening, what's happening?"

Larr put his hand on the kid's jumping knee and said, "The worlds changed."

*

The most reasonable facsimile of suborbport nearest to Nanih Waiya was the Meridian Regional airport, about fifty two miles distant. Frosty came down easy at Meridian just to debark Larr and a couple of high level Bodhi's, before heading up to Mt. Angel with S.C. and the rest of the monks. Larr waved at Frosty and Frosty gave a smile and a thumbs up, turned the plane around, punched it down the taxiway and turbo'd up at a forty five degree angle slamming the monks into their seats like test pilots, a few of whom started sobbing and hyperventilating, and Frosty was disappointed in himself because he couldn't even enjoy it. "Damn."

As Larr approached the terminal, Frida buzzed out to meet him. "Change of plans, huh?"

"The whole System has a change in plans. I feel like I personally killed all those people."

"Well don't let that get out. Brodie and the NUF's killed those people and now we have an opportunity work with sentient beings trying to put the pieces back together. So cheer up."

"I'm not hiding out, but I'm not going back to San Jose until I know how this is going to turn out."

"Well, I need you; theology and art are involved, you can fake the religion part. Then we're going to have to build something new. Creatives are required. "

"I'm in."

*

Earth
1,200,000 Y.B.P.

As Charlotte and Silver Dan wound back together, they passed out into the multiverse field then back crossing into the universe of her first birth and toward the event horizon of Sagittarius A, the super massive black hole at the center of the Milky Way Galaxy. The trajectory was a little steeper this time as the momentum had been reduced by the prior traverse. They skimmed the maelstrom of space time being dragged behind the spinning monster like body surfers being carried along on a wave, then sprang like flying fish out into the field again. Dan helped Charlotte as on each previous pulse since the monopole in the Library's wreckage shanghaied her from Mara's beautiful blue sky. As the pulse waned they dipped back through the edge to their holding pattern on Earth.

The scene had changed. A clearly more primitive group of hominins were butchering a rhinoceros. Though they had sharpened sticks and hand axes, it wasn't clear whether they had made this kill or were scavenging. A few of the creatures joined to drive off hyenas, some still jawing hunks of flesh as they retreated. One hominin used a hand ax to strip off meat as another was flaying the flesh with his teeth. Patient vultures watched as other wary eyes watched them. Perhaps the hominins remembered that these birds don't mind cleaning up after the hominins' business was done. It won't take long; this crew was bringing dinner home to the ladies and kids.

Homo Erectus? They lasted from 2,000,000 Y.B.P. to 800,000 Y.B.P.

There was a great deal of vocalizing and waving of arms, but not like the ritualistic performance of chimps, being understood as not necessarily violent. These guys really meant it. A primitive javelin found its mark; a hand axe crushed a hyena skull. Charlotte imagined these same techniques being used to defeat a neighboring group of the same hominins, or of another species sharing the genus homo at that time.

The hyenas dispatched, each short, hairy, apelike creature hefted a slab of meat, fat or bones collected for marrow and the group started to head home single file. The sun is heading down to the earth once again; another set of worries arrived with the dark so they continued on briskly to their shelter at the cave. As Charlotte watched in the gathering dusk, the hunters settled down while the women threw the meat and bones on the fire. She noticed something peculiar.

The butchering scene had included blue fireflies, now following the males and buzzing around the females as well. A few approached the children making haloes around their heads. Some individuals gave an occasional swat at the fireflies but otherwise gave them only slight attention. It was as if the fireflies wanted something, not meat, not sweat; just attention. As the group arranged their nest-like beds just inside the cave, the fireflies waited until they fell asleep. Then, they gently settled on the still bodies and their blue fires went out.

*

Earth
June 3, 2125 C.E.

By the time Frosty got his passengers all safely to the drag strip near Woodburn, the crying had stopped and S.C. had nodded off and slept, even through the weightlessness. Out the window, they could see the Old Believers working, acting like nothing had happened. At the platform, there was the buckboard and Georgi with his tin star. As Brodie had predicted, that ludicrous normalcy was keeping things together. They all piled in with Vladimir and humped it down to Mt. Angel at a leisurely pace.

In Oregon, the climate in the winter then was more like Southern California a hundred years before. There was a foggy green strip along the coast but inland, the summer growth had turned to brown. Fires were more of a problem but all in all it remained pleasant as the Pacific Northwest dried out. Even the Old Believers were taking advantage by cultivating olives, avocados and California winery grapes.

The town was quieter now that everyone was looking to the luddites to figure how to live. But, all worry vanished for S.C. as the buckboard stopped at the old oblate house on College next to St. Mary's. His wife and kids were there tending Petra Rousseau's old garden, pulling up weeds and hauling in compost. Amy looked up from the tomato starts, stood up brushing the dirt from her brow then shaded her eyes as the kids dropped their little wheelbarrows and ran out the gate to tackle their dad. It had been much too long.

The next morning, S.C. rode a real bicycle, not a hover bike, out of town and up the hill to the monastery. He was panting by the time he got to the top but he made it. Ambrose, Petra and Sulaimon stepped out to greet him. Petra's spookball flashed a happy greeting pattern as she buzzed in.

He said, "You were right, something did happen."

"How 'bout that."

Sulaimon said, "So happy to be working with you, but no need to get right to it, Brother Ambrose has a special brunch buffet set out." She put her double thumbed claw on his shoulder and picked up his duffel with the other. In any other century it would have been a fantasy novel; a human, a tin girl, a lizard and a monk, all on the yellow brick road, off to see the Wizard.

In the days to come, Sulaimon and Schneider would research the back story and archives while keeping posted on the progress of the siege and reconciliation talks. This was the oasis where S.C. would write *The Rise and Fall of the New United Futurists.* In the evenings at home, with the obsessions of the historical Charlotte always in mind, S.C. began to germinate the seed of magical realism that became *Sweet Charlotte in the Higgs Field.*

*

From the Sea

Down to the sea with ships in bottles,
arcing offerings to the current,
a cliff-side prayer invokes the day and
the deity. Steadily, I measure the paces back
and putter and tend only your garden.
On the widow's walk, surveying distance
without referent, shading my eyes
rough handed, dizzy in the sun,
I conjure smooth hands, back and thighs
from when these hands too were smooth.

Why do you ask me who I am now,
when I have done no other work but stay
constant and unchanging in your soul?
You revealed myself to me through
softly focused eyes gazing to distant
thunder clouds rumbling homeward,
driving bottles in thousands to the shore.
As you arise and rise on the sea foam
my heart stares seaward no longer,
guarding water no more
but only its thirst for you.

-*A Small Goddess, Poetry of Dan Pritchard, Devi Sheridan,
editor, Centennial Edition, Modern Europa Press, 2199.*

*

Earth
November 5, 2125
Autonomous Council of the Five Tribes Confederacy
Cahokia, Nanih Waiya

Luke Koachubee Patterson sat at the head of the Council table, his back to Nanih Waiya, the mass of the people of Cahokia arrayed in front of him in the half circle between the Mound and the Promenade. On either side of the Chief sat, docked or leaned back on their tails, Pushmataha, John Asényhola, Grammy Ruby, Steve Vallush, Urizen and Blake, with minor functionaries beyond them. It was a grand assembly with the guest of honor H.H. the Second Bodhisattva Xià lǜ dì, peace be upon her, Parker, F.S. and the obligatory flanking saffron robed attendants, all facing the head table. Arch Sandifur was present from the L3 on a hover screen gravitel link. All had worked on coordinating a platform in preparation for the Planetary Moot to be held in Namibia.

Luke's deep resonant voice addressed the assembly, "Two hundred years ago, we left this place and traveled back toward what some say was the land of our birth. It was not a kind or pleasant trip. Nonetheless, the Five Civilized Tribes built a homeland in Oklahoma. Now, increased by other refugees, we have brought our wisdom and energies back to Mississippi to build a new society. In collaboration with our fellow sentient beings, we have been asked to contribute to the future government of Earth. Today our Andromedan friends and Steven Vallush will present an economic theory being proposed for System-Earth relations."

Vallush stood, cleared his throat and projected to the crowd, "Proposed, yes, and in very broad strokes, but with a good faith optimism in its success at this challenging juncture. Bear in mind that these humble suggestions will be aired at the systemic moot in Geneva, a system-wide stage. We have the advantage however, of working together with Her Holiness, peace be upon her." Pinky made a shallow bow, tilting her ball, in response.

"Before the attacks, before the Tejianos marched, I did accounting and paralegal work for small businesses in Fayetteville, ran my own urban farm and managed a farmer's market, locally sourced, sustainable living. It was a college town; well, the college was gone and the market was getting sparse, but it was not a bad life. However, my avocation then and now was practical economics, an amateur, but the bar isn't that high in all the confusion."

The crowd laughed and Pinky's face smiled. She knew that Vallush had risen to the occasion and had proven his expertise in their committee work together. He had earned her confidence, no mean feat. He returned the bow, deeper, and continued.

"When the Five Tribes passed through Arkansas we were already on the road south. But, our group, our community, put our trust in their vision. So, here, I have worked with Urizen and Blake on an economic theory we will present at the Planetary Moot in Namibia. As Luke has said, this is part of the larger talks building the peace and we present it here for your consideration."

Urizen rocked forward off of her tail and stood, holding her herding staff, sporting her most formal unobtrusive grey and white scale pattern. Her nictating membranes blinked and she began to speak, "There is an old proverb here on Earth, it takes many forms, the Circle of Life, The Great Wheel; it also has many meanings but is in concert with the grand cycles of Hindu and Mayan cosmology. As the daily ablution prayer states; 'Thank you Kali Ma for creation, sustenance and destruction.'

"At Andromeda we also believe in the cyclical nature of the universe. In government, economics and cultural/spiritual matters, we treat each as constrained by circles, closed sets that can only be diminished by the blurring of the lines between them."

The Second Bodhisattva said, "We too believe this of the three Transcendentals, Beauty, Truth and Goodness. An excess of any one diminishes the others and sets evil loose in the worlds."

Vallush said, "This construct was explored in the years after World War I as a way to prevent economic collapse, injustice and further wars. It was called the Threefold State, Urizen?"

"Exactly; in the economic circle we see beings exerting labor on nature to create something with a value, a thing that is then acted upon by the mind, by spirit, to put that value into the stream of goods. In this way, the labor and spirit of beings provides for the needs of beings without directly connecting labor to value. It is a moral imperative. It is said that the scale dressers have the dullest scales."

Vallush said, "And the shoemaker's wife has the poorest shoes."

"Yes, unless she buys from another shoemaker, the meaning being that if the profit of one's labor is stockpiled, even by making commodities for oneself, the system does not work. Therefore, we do not acquire capital and do not store value in land. Any profit from the circle must be used either for social needs or the workings of the system itself, or it expires, becoming without value.

"This is the key to making the system work and self-regulate; without stockpiled wealth, no one can be certain where their individual efforts will place them in the system. Laws and regulations therefore, are naturally made so that one is fairly treated regardless of their position in society; not necessarily equal, but fair, so that no one is ground down to destitution, down to the lowest step in the hierarchy of needs."

"And in the Threefold State," Vallush said, "government and religion do not interact within the economic circle for their own collective benefit, Brother Sandifur?"

Arch Sandifur spoke from the hover screen above the table. "The full solution, detailed in my report, proposes this arrangement for the economic circle; that the Cult and other cultural organizations work without interference within their circle, and that a governmental body with planetary authority will see to the relations between the System and Earth, matters affecting the planet as a whole and the resolution of disputes within the secular circle. Below that level, the practical needs of the various populations and their internal governance will be left to their individual institutions.

"This platform on which we are working will be presented in detail to the opposing parties for discussion and revision in the peace process, to conclude at the Systemic Moot in Geneva next year."

Luke said, "There have been many attempts, by humans, at least, to approach this ideal 'from every being what they can contribute, to every being what they need.' Communism in the 20th Century, for example. But, no idealism has succeeded if left to the greed of humans; Mr. Blake?"

Blake stood up, blew his forehead nose holes noisily and shined his brow with the same hanky, the height of Andromedan gravitas. An aristocratic male, he always assumed no one was looking directly at him. Those who knew the protocol did stare at their shoes although the cracker boys in the back were wide eyed and pointed at him. *Woo Woo Woo!*

Urizen had her head down but suppressed her laugh. "*Shhh snk snk*" Blake ignored her and sniffed an apology, "Ah, it's not the heat, it's the humidity. Pardon me. As you all know, we share a unique history with humans on Earth, and we have a unique appreciation of the strengths and weaknesses of the human species.

"And so, we intend to offer to manage the economic circle without compensation, autonomously as neutral trustees for the benefit of Earth. As on our home world, we will be committed to the recycling of wealth and the leveling of disparity; this is our promise. Our only needs on this planet are rights of access to archeological sites and of friendship and oneness freely given."

In a new paradigm, somehow aliens could be trusted when humans could not, as neutral arbiters. After a further presentation was completed, Luke surveyed the council, visitors and crowds behind them, stood and addressed them.

"It is said that a people will have the government that they deserve. The Andromedans believe that humanity deserves a government that attends to the needs of all in a manner that has been informed by past errors. We agree. I am reminded of the offer made by the Haudenosaunee Confederacy, the Iroquois, to the English Virginia Colony. In the Treaty of Lancaster, the Iroquois offered to instruct the English on the operation of democratic government. Noble yet audacious at the time perhaps, but it is a fitting inspiration nonetheless. Let that naive enthusiasm guide us now.

"For the Five Tribes Confederacy, and all sentient beings of the planet Earth, I hope to be allowed to express pride and admiration for all participants in this sacred work. We are adjourned."

The Bodhisattva and her entourage bowed and moved toward the guest quarters, the acolytes and Parker in the lead, to a chorus of cheers and the rumble of drum circles set around the perimeter of Cahokia, drum circles that would begin in all quarters of the world where the future was being crafted, to continue until the last link in the chain of peace was forged.

*

Earth
4,600,000 years Y.B.P.

Silver Dan let Charlotte down easy through a crack about ten feet up this time. "I'll be back with the pulse."

This time the creatures were smaller, more apelike, and their tools were more primitive. Large, unworked sticks and stones were brandished at a few hyenas sniffing the smell of burning meat on the large, less tidy fire. Sticks and stones drove them off. Mothers stood poking at the fire with sticks and held babies who clutched on to soft fur and sagging breasts. No great beauties or handsome dads here, from the homo sapiens perspective, but easy functional social groups, the height of hominin evolution, for the moment.

As Charlotte watched, the group began to build up new piles of leaves and grasses into this night's nests. As darkness fell the watchers kept up the fire, just enough to make the hyenas wary, eventually entering into a half sleep/half alert state. A mother lay down with her child purring softly in its ear. All breathing became deep and rhythmic. One mother raised an arm up effortlessly like a sleepwalker.

Charlotte saw the fireflies again, now seeming to flicker out of the bodies, from the head and neck of the baby and mother they floated up her arm and launched with no hesitation like ballooning spiders. As they increased in number, they flocked in the cave and then set out to rest on the watchers, now perhaps in deeper sleep, a sleep in which they dreamed no worries. They are used to this feeling, the oneness that lets another entity take the first watch.

The hyenas were gone, scared off by the scent of a different, more formidable, predator. The fireflies sensed it too. They spun around the head of the watcher like a halo, until he shuddered awake. Even so, the leopard, unafraid of the waning fire, used the greater darkness perceived around the flames to approach and then pounce in a blur. Before the one watcher was fully awake, the leopard flattened him on the ground, clamped his teeth into the back of the neck and punctured the skull. The sheer weight of the leopard held the hominin still as his struggling faded. All around him now, the others awakened and put on the most fearless display they could muster.

Their arms were raised and excited vocalizations rose and merged into a cacophony. As they began to grab sticks and rocks, the leopard retreated with its kill, dragging it off as only a few projectiles hit their mark. The leopard took note; creatures that do not flee were a new kind of worry. On the other hand, it was used to the attentions of the fireflies. They wouldn't interfere. While the troop's excitement was rising, the fireflies also rose and spun in great circular orbits, intersecting wheels within wheels, rising higher and higher until they seemed to merge with the teeming stars.

The hominins wouldn't follow the leopard, but knew where it was going, from experience, and gruesome finds in the mornings after such attacks. The leopard climbed a tree just about one hundred yards down the hill and close to another outcropping of rock. It hauled the body up to the first thick horizontal branch which wore the claw marks of other meals. The hyenas gathered under the tree, waiting for the leopard to be satiated and for the body to drop. Then they would have their turn.

From experience, the hominins knew that the predator would sleep after its meal. The fireflies drifted down as another male took the place of the watcher who died. This time they slept undisturbed until morning.

Just before dawn, Charlotte felt the monopole's pulse start to build. As Silver Dan opened the crack, one of the fireflies approached Charlotte. She was in her natural form and revealed no physical manifestation, and yet the small creature approached her, knew she was there. As it came closer, Charlotte saw a bright point of light, very small, similar to her own energy body, hovering in front of her. But in the midst of the light there seemed to be . . . a face. Then she thought *Monkey bugs? Here?* But no, the face resolved as it came closer, it was the face of the hominins. *Their fairy godmother?* The little mouth started to grind. The little eyes looked right at her. "Buzzz buzz," it said, imitating an insect perhaps, but with words.

"Shut up!"

"shut up."

"What are you?"

"what are you"

"Stop copying me!"

"stop copying meeeee."

Silver Dan called out. "Come now, Charlotte. I can't get stuck here. I can't think straight here."

"Ok Dan," and to the monkey bug, she said, "I'll be back you little monster."

"I'll bee baack."

*

Earth,
January 25, 2126 C.E.
At the Planetary Moot
Kaokoland, Namibia

The two tribal hosts of the Planetary Moot, the Hereros and the OvaHimba, could not have been more disparate visually. The Hereros' 'traditional dress' for women consisted of stylized turn of the 20th century German colonial dresses. These were simplified versions of the clothing of their long gone genocidal oppressors. The bustle had been extended to surround the body in evocation of the sacred gravid cow, with no Western perjorative connotation. As a headdress, the women wore something reminiscent of the horns of cattle made out of the same material as the dress, just as ancient Indo-Europeans had used the crescent moon as a symbol for the horns of the divine bull.

These dresses were made of the most garish combinations of bright primary color fabrics, trashing any conservative Germanic source. Perhaps this was the animus, as, in the face of intentional genocidal extermination, they had come back to self-rule in the mid-20th Century.

In ceremonial processions, the Herero women walked slowly and smoothly to imitate the swaying movements of fat, provocative cows. The costumes of the men similarly consisted of homemade German military dress from the period of the genocide. Wellingtons, jodhpurs, riding crops and severe uniforms prevailed. The problem, of course, was that after the common enemy disappeared, the tribes jockeyed for position. Then the Hereros, dressed like Germans, oppressed the other tribes.

With sea level rising however, the sand seas dominating the coastal deserts became inundated along with the less severe cities inhabited by colonials and now the Herreros. An incongruous green strip was moving inland and the once merely inhospitable, Kalahari desert was becoming deadly and expanding, crowding the Hereros and the Himba between the two.

In the 20th Century, the Himba had marked off their desert territory, the territory that had almost exterminated the Hereros, and made a sustainable economy while not giving up their traditional look and values. This had become common; the explosion of electronics and gravitronics allowed even the most isolated indigenous people to interact with the world community, the whole system, without surrendering their cultural inheritance.

In the past, like other indigenous people, they had to give up their heritage and take on the mantle of English or French as the language of commerce, move to the city and leave the past behind; leave the forest for the mines and factories. Now, they could keep their language, keep their culture and still prosper in the greater economy. Carbon credits, carbon sinks, harvesting invasive species, not to mention casinos, all were worth real money.

The Himba had perfected this juggling act. Even in the early 21st century, they had drawn a line and kept a serious tribal look while still interacting with the larger world. The women wore nothing from the waist up and covered their bodies with red ochre pigmented butter fat. Their hair was twisted into braids matted with earth, dung and ochre.

These women, with their shining red breasts and supremely confident demeanor, these women knew of their effect on westerners; heart of darkness, post-colonial first worlders and just dared these white men to lust after them, these men who, trying to tuck that white politically correct shirt tail back in their pants, nonetheless, certainly did lust after them. If they ever captured one though, it was very clear who would be in charge. The women created the Himba world and defended it with the supremely confident allure of an objectively perfect sexual object.

The wet dreams of the Bismarkian Germans could not approach the real sexual transcendence of the Himba women, their men kept in line with a promise and a threat, sex and no sex, a marvelous domination that no man could resist. It was a domination that the white conquerors dreamed of while their Prussian frauleins in dowdy night shirts and curling papers snored beside them. The Himba men, though they might keep multiple wives, were sent out with herds of goats to guard and defend the family wealth. The women however, guarded the promise of tomorrow.

Mukaakandinguah sat in her traditional dirt floored hut, its walls made from baked desert branches driven into the ground in a circle. The roof was thatch to keep off the sun, and the irregular branches let the breeze blow through. She ground ochre rhythmically with a rounded stone pestle against a flat stone mortar. Her belly was big pregnant and her breasts were heavy. She was due in about two weeks.

She took the ground ochre and mixed it with goat butter fat then spread it over her belly and breasts, which, on this formal occasion in her home territory remained uncovered. When this was done, she took a corn cob and cleaned all dirt off of her legs and then colored them too. On her head among the braids was an intricately tied headdress, sporting a tiny top hat, indicating her status as married and first wife. Her skirt was made from roughly tanned leather dangling possessions and ornamentation. On her legs and arms were bracelets and anklets of coiled brass. Her earlobes were cut to hold wooden ear plugs.

Then into the hut came a spookball, similarly covered in red ochre and ornaments. It said, "Time to go Mukaa-Ma."

She asked, "How do I look?"

"Devastating, Ma."

Mukaakandinguah was the headwomen and practical earth goddess of the Himba as well as Secretary General of the Southern Indigenous Congress. Times had changed, outward ornament had changed, the usefulness of the wider world had ebbed and flowed, but her real power, once subtext, had grown and had been realized so that she now stood in the place of the patrilineal interregnum, the brief respite from the rule of the true Mother, the Earth, now rested, effectual; intensely *real*.

There could be no better symbol for this reaffirmation of the sacred Earth than Mukaa's incarnation of the Paleolithic Venus, the naked swelling belly and breasts becoming the hope of life itself. After she gave birth, she knew that the baby at her breast would continue the symbolism, the new Madonna and Child to draw the prayers of those committed to the Earth.

In her sacred and stately Beauty, she walked out of the hut and over to the large circular tent set up for the Congress. The Herrero contingent had just finished their traditional swaying procession and took their seats at the front of the semi-circle of folding chairs with a raised stage and podium at its center.

"Those cows won't sit in the dirt." The spookball said.

"If you talk like that you'll confuse everybody, *they* think it's a complement."

"Maybe I should call them goats."

"Maybe you should not start an intertribal incident, Baby. They are our cousins, after all."

"Yes, Mukaa-Ma." It spun around and assumed its proper eyelevel position at the right shoulder of the head woman. If one closed one's eyes, spooks that chose to manifest could be seen, a Shaka Zulu here, a Mandela there, lending a certain historical context and authority to the proceedings.

As she strode toward the stage, heavily pregnant, almost six feet tall, perfumed with spice and manure, red and shining, giving slight nods to those well known to her, all eyes turned to her, northerners trying to keep their gaze above her neck. She gave a wry smile in greeting, knowing what effect she had on them. She knew they enjoyed it so much, men and women, she wouldn't deny them their momentary discomfort. And, honestly, it amused her no end.

She looked around the tent at the representatives of those who had chosen not to leave the planet; Greater Namibians, the multi-ethnic Suidelike Afrikaners, the Maori Waitangi Tribunal, the Aboriginal Tent Assembly, Antarctic del Fuego; all represented here. In the outer circles were the northern contingents; the New United Futurists, Quantum Mechanics Union, Five Tribes Confederacy, Knights of Columbus, New Carthage and others, in anticipation of the next assembly in Geneva. That conclave would include 3MI, the Cult and North/Up interests in negotiating a general detente and rapprochement. *This* partisan assembly was intended to create the ground rules and procedures to be used in Geneva.

On a personal level, she recognized Stuart Smith of the Quantum Mechanics Union, with her nieces from Geneva, the schwartzkommando; Pushmataha, Urizen, Blake and Steven Vallush of the FTC; Frida and Larr Yellingson, who had engaged her in a lively and deep discussion of Theological Aesthetics over the local hooch called shibeen. It was a recognition that the entire world had now become to the

System what the old third world had been to the West, poor cousins at best, white man's burden at worst.

So, in response to the first world Cultists leaving the planet, the new global third world was taking up the slack and not kow-towing to the ways of their now absentee oppressors. Still, new oppressors waited in the wings. The key was to create something new that did not rely on old or new rivalries. This was the task today.

As she walked toward the stage, her spookball assistant introduced her and she took her position regally.

"We have before us the responsibility to address and repair the damage that has been done to the family of humanity, to somehow bring the example of traditional and customary law to the wider worlds whose formal legal systems have failed under siege, are no longer respected and cannot be expected to be up to the task going forward.

"In our African traditions, in a family, as in a village, as in the tribal extension and larger groups, the goal of law is to preserve the social bond during and after resolution of conflict. The African moot, the house palaver, truth and reconciliation, these are the gifts we may bring to the greater System. Neither the Cult nor the Futurists are our enemy but regardless, the sentients in these factions *are* our family, and that *family* is what must be preserved.

"Yes, we have wronged each other, yes lives have been lost, and yes, all this must end. What has been laid before us is however, a plowed field, the combatants having cleared and tilled a space where we earthlings may plant and nurture the growth of a new spring of humanity. We must be equal to that task."

She paused as a round of applause signaled approval.

"We expect to provide a template for truth and reconciliation in Geneva in the form of the African moot which we will demonstrate here as this conference proceeds. Our immediate goal will be to resolve our own differences in a demonstration to be applied to the worlds.

"In our moot, we find communion with the old Catholic confession. We admit our wrongs and penance is meted out, not onerous penance as punishment but significant gestures as between families, symbolic and otherwise, and we strive to understand their wider meaning.

"In the process, we apologize in front of our elders, elders who will admonish and inspire the whole community with long held values and truths as the whole community observes. Then the complainants present gifts to each other and to the community as a whole, joining to host that community, so that their reconciliation spreads through celebration, forgiveness and love. For this is what we have in common with all those who sincerely want peace, this is the creed that we reclaim from the Cult and make universal once again: Love alone is credible."

As she finished and took her seat, the dances of the participant cultures began like the long forgotten opening ceremonies of some twenty-first century Olympic games, a dimly held memory going all the way back to Iron Age Greece, of the cessation of hostilities to forge a relationship that will resist and withstand the fleeting disaster of war. There was much to think about before Geneva.

*

Earth
4,600,000 years Y.B.P.

Silver Dan and Charlotte melded and rode the pulse back around the singularity, put down the skid shoe in the turn and dissipated just enough energy to keep Dan in control.

"Where to now, Char?"

"Can you take me right back to that last spot?

"But of course, as you wish, Mademoiselle!"

Without any sense of distance, Silver Dan opened the sky and Charlotte sped down his energy and through to the same Pleistocene scene they had left in such a hurry.

The troop was still asleep, even the watchers. As before, the fireflies were mostly out of sight, except those helping the watchers. One small blue light flits over the fire and finds her, hovering before her eyes.

Charlotte made her thoughts clear to it without language.

"Who, what are you?"

"whowat are you."

Bosonic life definitely, but not too smart. That's not fair. Something is definitely going on. Symbiosis? What does this little shit get out of that relationship?

"Ok, Baby Face, come a little closer." She moved toward the little light. The hominin face disappeared and the pinpoint of light rushed right into her. Suddenly it melded into her. They were not incompatible. But the firefly didn't understand and could tell the difference. Charlotte tried to disengage but the pull was too strong. Instead she started to dance with it, started to embrace it like the Goddess Over There. The being relaxed, let her flow in and out and radiated contentment. *My ancestor? It's playing!*

At the cave by the leopard's tree, the hyenas had an established den. Every week or so there was manna from heaven as the big cat finished a meal. So, a predictable and easy meal makes for lighter family interaction at dinner. Their bellies full, the pups faced off and did the downward dog at each other, asking and initiating mammalian play. The challenge accepted, the pups roll and tumble, snarl and bite, just less than hard enough to hurt. If one does get too rough, the challenge is recalled, the other takes his ball and goes home, or rolls over and pisses on himself in submissive surrender.

The hominin children do the same thing, less the actual pissing. The action had no obvious practical use, and yet it had rules and standards, perhaps a curriculum to practice, like kittens with a mouse suitably disabled by mom. Or, like the hyenas, a primer on the social structure that will dominate their lives.

The hominin's play may have all of this below the surface but the general need is to socially bond with the other, to make a group cohesive enough to support necessary group activities, including those outside of the immediate family. Like small talk for humans, *Hot enough for ya? How 'bout them Yankees?*

Play was something with no obvious purpose and at the same time one transcendent purpose. This mammalian play, arising out of social bonds and the need, even in primitive mammals, to care for babies not hatched from eggs, then leads to something else, ritual.

At first, it is ritual without meaning. But soon, seeing the existential angst in life and death and nature, the powerlessness that hominins eventually feel about a painful life and early death, this gives some meaning to the ritual.

The narratives, hierarchies and explanations of ultimate power that the hominin brain needs, fill in the ritual with thoughts of the unseen other, the one who can be appeased, perhaps, to even out the vagaries of nature. Eventually homo sapiens have an epiphany, since humans are part of nature, the universe looking at itself, the object of these rituals must be something outside of nature.

Therefore, gods and supernatural agency are born from play, religion is born from mammalian play, from mammalian love, and once again, even here, love alone is credible.

*

Earth
The Systemic Moot
April 1, 2126, Geneva

Brother Arch Sandifur, Opening Address,
Remote From L3 Station

(Transcript of remote gravitel feed; version approved by Canon Code Revision Office, Fragrant Mountain, Earth.)

(Introduction and Applause)

How does a theory of Theological Aesthetics resolve this war? Even its name, the Aesthetics War, came as a dismissive epithet meant to demean combatants. As the cloistered Chief Archivist of the Bodhisattva Cult, my reluctance to take this post is no secret.

But, together, we, the Moot Commission, representing all sentients, the Three Realms and the Worlds in the Realms, have engaged in this struggle with all seriousness, compassion and hope. We are working toward a global, literally and figuratively, a global resolution to these difficult problems. Truth and Reconciliation is not the hardest part. It is relatively easy to bring people together to face the damages of war, and perhaps, to forgive and be forgiven.

This war must however, be resolved by all sides attempting to understand the deep social, political, spiritual and existential rifts that divide them. From that understanding, we are here, in part, to create, from the outline of the ratified settlement, a systemic constitution, if you will, that will stand the test of time.

We must therefore, address these issues at face value and determine how a syncretist and yet practical statement may insure continued peace, the preservation of Earth for the use of her children in perpetuity and the infrastructure that will make all this possible.

(Applause)

I will be forgiven, I hope, for meeting this challenge as it has been posed to us by the New United Futurists and the Cult, in terms of metaphor and poetry, the font and repository of truth.

First, and most difficult, is the concept of Beauty. There is a record of a message from Petra Rousseau to Daniel after the first transitus of the Bodhisattva Xià lù dì, the cornerstone of the mysticism of the Cult, the oft studied words of which will be familiar to you:

> *Beauty is one of the three Transcendentals (Beauty, Truth, Goodness) ...Beauty, a Transcendental being, not an abstraction, not a culturally conditioned aesthetic, which would change with trend movements over time. Nor beauty as an archetype of Jungian thought, or a symbol. We seek a powerful and authentic I -Thou relationship to and with Beauty as a Being.*

> *We also work deeply with a second idea/awareness -- something that has moral ramifications -- something that colors the way we live, speak, move, work. All three Transcendentals are interconnected and if or*

when one is separated out from the other two, harm is unleashed in the world.

This is the germ of the doctrine of Beauty in the dharma of the Bodhisattva. On its surface, it seems to be describing the desire to encounter a divine *person* in the world. But Being, capitalized, is all of the divine, while Beauty is but one of its transcendental aspects. This transcendental aspect is by definition diffuse in the entirety of the finite multiverse. We may, we must, therefore, meet this Beauty on the street, look her in the eye, and recognize and welcome her as a new symbol of the peace we must build in the Worlds.

(Applause)

Although it can be trivialized, Beauty requires balance, symmetry and openness. Beauty is the subject and object of Oneness. Beauty drives its observers to replicate it, in art, in philosophy, in babies. Yes, even the sex act is an attempt to make the Beauty we see in our lovers repeat eternally.

And this Beauty is free. Anyone can bask in Beauty. Even a prisoner may see a cloud or hear a bird and transcend his prison. The most destitute may create Beauty in a song. This is not to say that all should be satisfied with the least experience of it, rather, that all have the inalienable right to the invaluable, no matter how simple the means.

But what is it? The English language is not up to the task. The Diné Blessing Way contains a well-known prayer to

Beauty. In the Diné language the word is Hózhó, meaning Balance and Harmony as well as Beauty.

In beauty all day long may I walk.

With beauty before me may I walk.

With beauty behind me may I walk.
With beauty below me may I walk.
With beauty above me may I walk.
With beauty all around me, may I walk.
In old age wandering on a trail of beauty,
lively, may I walk.
In old age wandering on a trail of beauty,
living again, may I walk.
My words will be beautiful.

Our Ronin Jesuit brothers will also recognize the same rhythm in the Breastplate of St. Patrick:

Christ with me
Christ before me
Christ behind me,
Christ in me,
Christ beneath me,
Christ above me,
Christ on my right,
Christ on my left,

And, yes, even this most Christian of prayers incorporates the pagan animism of St. Patrick's Celtic flock, syncretism even then. From the same prayer:

I arise today, through
The strength of heaven,
The light of the sun,
The radiance of the moon,
The splendor of fire,
The speed of lightning,

The swiftness of wind,
The depth of the sea,
The stability of the earth,
The firmness of rock.

It is specifically this layering of old and new religions that creates strength from syncretism under the appearance of conservatism; Christianity draped over Mayan and Aztec spiritual mythology, Gnosticism over Catholicism, Buddhism over Tibetan Bon and the open door of Hinduism relating to all myths as equals. It is precisely through this strength of the syncretist Cult of the Bodhisattva Xià lǜ dì, and its devotion to Beauty, Harmony and Balance, that we see a path to the secular Justice desired by the people of Earth.

(Applause)

For, what is Justice? Justice is also symmetry, harmony, balance and the leveling of power, both political and spiritual. Justice is seen in the departures from balance that make us cherish it even more from a distance, just as Beauty may be defined by its imperfections.

But, Justice cannot be readily seen. How do we see just laws? How do we see just treatment of people over a whole nation; over a whole planet?

Only one example, although imperfect, will suffice. The sight of children in a condition of perpetual war, famine, poverty and disease can only rend the heart. In their images, you will no doubt see injustice, a moral wrong. Similarly, those same children, healthy, in bright colors, in adequate housing, laughing through the day, will spark in us the thought, *what a beautiful child.* Somewhere, justice is being done with regard to those children. You can see the problem; if both scenes are in the same world, then there is a lack of balance, a lack of justice and therefore, no Beauty in the relationship between them.

Within that template, Beauty will be our metaphor, the Beauty of the Earth becoming balanced and in harmony with her children. Beauty will be before us as we turn outward to the System and to the stars. Beauty will be under and around us as we repair the Earth. Beauty will be our guide as all sentient beings traverse and transcend.

So, we begin with a common language that cherishes the Earth and the outward universe as well as the inner journey and the finite multiverse.

This is how we come to this juncture between the earthly concerns for Justice and the theological concerns for Beauty. Specifically, Beauty *is* Justice. The Bodhisattva Cult is willing to concede that the fate of the Earth is very much a part of its responsibility toward the divine.

At the Systemic Moot, all representatives of Earth, the Cult and the System will seek Justice for the people and the planet. Justice is also part of the transcendental Beauty that is sought by the pilgrims of the Cult.

This is only the outline, the overture, if you will, of a broad and bright vision, but certainly something worth believing in; something worth walking toward. To paraphrase *Södergran and the Blessing way*; With Beauty we will walk on foot through the Solar System. With Beauty before us, we will walk; with Beauty, behind us, we will walk; with Beauty beside us, we will walk; with Beauty above us, we will walk; with Beauty below us, we will walk; with Beauty all around us, we will walk with Beauty to Justice.

(Applause, end of transmission)

*

Earth
3,543,000,000 Y.B.P.

Silver Dan caught her as before and wrapped her in his embrace as they moved from the shore of space time into the eddies and rapids of the multiverse field.

Then he pulled into a spot barely a billion years into the Earth's formation and took the form of a silver point of light as she nestled her blue spark within him. No words but he directed her to attend to the rugged black basaltic shore, glowing veins of red and orange in crackling black crust further inland as lava flowed, then massive heat and steam as it hit the water of a dark and viscous sea. Volcanic ash and haze filtered the light and heat of a larger, younger sun. No life at this point but certainly there were heat sources, organic chemistry, whether from star dust or the electric firing of lightening into the soupy shallows, and the motion and mixing of waves and tides.

At the molecular level there was a dispersion of chemical components into the air with the sea spray. In this spray, long lipid molecules which repelled water on one end and attracted water on the other began to orient and bind together as they fell back into the sea. After millennia of mixing, these molecules began to form larger structures, hydrophilic on the outside, hydrophobic on the inside, a semipermeable membrane. *A without and a within.* Other molecules move in and out of this structure; salts, amino acids, carbon, ammonia, nitrogen as balances change, eventually concentrating metamorphosis within what was beginning to look like an organic bubble.

At this point the lifeless cells began to crash together and against the rocks and larger molecules in the pounding surf and shallow tide pools. With each blow now, a bit of charge was felt and electricity created stronger bindings and flowed over damaged molecules effecting repairs that restored the initial balance for a while. Inevitably though, changes crept into the molecular structure that were tested against the forces conspiring to destroy the proto-cells. Changes that helped the cell survive, that made it stronger, were preserved and each new stress made it stronger, low level electric charges being preserved and beginning to flow.

Then, this charge seemed to attract the attention of something hidden even deeper, something with spin and entanglement and uncertainty, manifesting in a wavelength of light that billions of years later might be called blue. This uncertainty which was not yet life, no more than the membrane was life, nonetheless entered the molecular structures and infused them, began to do work inside them, work in the world.

Before life begins, we are one?

Or, life begins when we are one.

Or, life is inevitable?

The potential for life is in the mechanics of fields, part of the structure of space time. This is not life yet, but can be, here in our home, it will be.

And in the multiverse field?

There is unlimited potential; which is why we protect it when we must; the sanctity of potential.

And now?

Ok, Dorothy, one more stop and then back to Kansas.

Again she slept and dreamed.

*

In the Dark Forever

T = 0

The last transit landed them as witnesses to a singularity about to become a universe, their universe. The monopole pulse had dissipated and they were idling. The Big Bang and its initial inflationary period will give them the opposite momentum. Eventually, they will again have access to the galactic center and reverse the process, gliding in to just the right spot; the same spot where she was pulled out of Mara's sky.

Dan stabilized, virtual dog paddling in the multiverse field, waiting, guarding his girl. A pop and flicker made their energy bodies wince. "Wait, that's not the. . ." A figure in a pressure suit appeared, saffron and purple.

"How can they . . . ?"

Dan said, "There's some kind of manipulation of the field, not a manifestation. It will hold for a while, I don't think he . . . she can survive what comes next."

Charlotte said, "Can *we* manifest here?"

"Without the momentum it's safe, but this is still a probabilistic event we are waiting for. We have to stay together or you won't survive either."

"Well, come on then. Can we get on the common channel?"

"He'll fill his shit bag but I guess it won't matter when the Bang bangs."

Charlotte found the right vibration for the common channel but before she could speak, the suit said, "Did you ever read *Cities in Flight?*"

"I. . . how did you get here?"

"You should know, you and Pinky surveyed all the nodes."

"You came through the Library?"

"I was the last one through the Library."

"You. . ."

"I blew it up; the space elevators too. Well, I made the bombs."

"And you came here, of all places, you came here, where you will die? It's not the fucking Grand Canyon. You can't go back to the motel after this."

"Not die, I have the gnosis for final *transitus*. I'm ready. So, did you ever read *Cities in Flight*? James Blish; always was my favorite series, written way back, in the 1950's. In the last book, the universe is going to reboot. A big crunch will start a new Big Bang. Aliens and humans are racing to the spot where it will happen."

Dan said, "The Web of Hercules, the aliens want to jump into creation. But the humans get there first. They could create a universe with the same physical laws; nobody survives but life like ours will have a chance. "

"But, the main character messes it up on purpose, so a different universe is the result."

Dan said "That's it, that's the problem, it was a protest against the arrogance of creation, the thought that an individual can take on that responsibility by choice."

"But an individual can have that responsibility imposed on him against his will, because life is inevitable from the very beginning. The Higgs Bubble drive made universes. I knew that when I invented it. But I didn't realize what it meant."

Dan said, "Walter Brodie?"

"In the multiverse, all worlds that can exist must exist, even the ones where I am irresponsible enough to create them with exhaust."

"And it's been stopped. The drives no longer work."

Charlotte said, "And you killed thousands of people."

"They did not believe that the destruction of the body killed them. They were right. I did them no more harm than they would willingly do to themselves."

"What do you think you can do here?"

"I want to leave a message for our future selves."

"How . . ."

Dan said, "A Creator can manipulate the inflationary event to leave a message in the background microwave radiation. What do you want to write?"

Brodie said, "You don't have to be the Creator, just in the right place when it blows. I was thinking it would be funny if it said, 'This space left intentionally blank.'"

"You're fucking kidding me."

"Yeah, but I thought I could somehow warn them about me, about the drive, which would prevent those deaths."

"Brodie, the drive is unavoidable, you weren't unique, every universe that makes us, makes the drive."

"Yes, but mine could be different."

"There is no 'mine' in this Brodie. You can't affect anything and when your body is dead, your soul will still be right here. Leave life alone. There are other things to do. This isn't your story now but it will be. Your little life of genius and terror never mattered."

"Oh, I think it did. I didn't make the Cult or its indifference to Earth but I hoped to cure it. I already left a message in the Manifesto. When you get back there, someone will have figured it out and stopped the war. It's *my* message; *I'll* stop the war."

Dan and Charlotte let go of their manifestations and swirled down reforming their cocoon. Brodie gripped the mala that came permanently attached to the suit. He had all the gnosis and training, but had only used it for subterfuge before. Now he chanted in earnest.

Thank you Kali – Ma
Thank you for all things
Thank you for Creation, Sustenance and Destruction
Thank you for Universes and Arrows of Time
Thank you for the Three Realms
Thank you for the Worlds in the Realms
Thank you for the Love and Longing
Of Sentient Beings
Thank you for Respite in your arms
Thank you Kali – Ma

Brodie set the breather mix to increase the carbon dioxide and create nitrous oxide, so that he began to be transported from his thoughts of purpose and began to embrace the promise of an amused slumber.

Aum
Hail Xià lǜ dì, font of grace
Thy love is with me
Blessed art thou bodhisattva
And Thy blessings bestow on sentient beings
Holy Xià lǜ dì, Mother of Light
Pray for our transitus
Now and at the hour of death
Aum

Now fully in meditative practice, he barely noticed a vibration in the black granular multiverse field.

Aum bhūr bhuvaḥ svaḥ, tatsavitur vareṇyaṃ, bhargo, devasya dhīmahi, dhiyo yo naḥ pracodayāt, Aum.

The vibration then took on the appearance of a seminal point of light, bright white and tinged with red. Brodie voiced the last nasal note of the Mantra, dropped the mala, said *Blossom* and lost consciousness. *Blossom.*

*

In The Dreaming
T = the set of transcendental irrational numbers

Maybe this is your story little fish, maybe you need this story to live proper way in this world. Your little universe just like your old waterhole; little fish already there, just waiting, waiting for your father to walk by and say "There. . . there is your mother." Maybe something different, maybe the womb of the true mother is waiting. But, hey, you thought nothing could be different; fooled you. What, you like it so much the way it was? Why listen to those two? They don't know either. No sorcery in them.

You said it yourself, in the multiverse all things that can exist must exist. Now you know. The universe where your mother and father are nice, that one exists too. Don't worry about that bubble drive, it'll get invented anyway.

Nobody cares about temporal paradoxes. Tell that to Starfleet Academy, they're not so smart. You outside all universes now; spacetime's in there, not out here. No space, no time, just one big party. No, I made that up. See brotha, you don't have to be god, this is way too simple for god, that big fella got better things to do than watch you take a shit every day. Outside of time, all moments one, so you see all at once from the outside.

New universes pop up all the time, like farts, just way bigger; get it? Both expanding gas clouds, good joke. Step aside, otherwise you get squashed like a bug on the windshield. You ain't gonna write nothing on that windshield either. Inside, speed o' light won't let you be seen. The real windshield is beyond the part of that universe anybody on your world ever gonna see. Can't write 'I'm sorry, so long, better luck next time.' Better you just die, get here proper way. Nothing you did in there matters anyway, big picture pretty big.

You don't like that? Got lots to learn little brotha. Like they say, maybe the supreme being knows, maybe he don't know. Didn't think I was so smart did you? Hey, I was whitefella, went to college once or twice. I know stuff. Maybe I'm the supreme being too, how would you know? You believed it about that whitefella Jesus, son o'god, why not me? Well, you *didn't believe it. . .*

What's that? Oh, sorry, brotha you died while I wasn't paying attention. Story too long, but, good for you. Would've died some other way anyway, your body just in the way. That life don't live here. Now little fish, this is your last waterhole. Sleep little fish. Maybe all gonna be alright, all proper way for you in this world, maybe not; nobody knows.

*

Earth
37,000 Y.B.P.

Charlotte wanted to make one last stop before heading home to Mara. It was only about 35,000 years before her own birth and the humans here were her own species, *Homo Sapiens*, with the same bodies and brains as her contemporaries. This species had stumbled upon something that set them apart, something taken for granted thirty thousand years later, it was something that they had perfected to the point where their set of evolutionary advantages relegated all other hominins to the dustbin of pre-history.

They had reached just one more quantum of consciousness between inert matter and the gods than was required set them apart. It was memory and imagination orbiting about a self that seemed to exist but did not, the one thing we, in our perfect modernity, are absolutely certain of, but which is completely and utterly false, *me, I, sum, cogito ergo sum.* The same fictive objective observer that talks to us, that gets us through each day with an unending monologue of words and images, the little man that drives us like a bulldozer, pulls all the levers and flicks all the switches, the homunculus, *yes, that little man,* led these humans to populate all climates and landscapes from the Himalayas to the Taklimakan Desert, to take the longest journey, out of Africa all the way to Andromeda. We named it 'self.' With this 'self' came the ability to make stories, metaphors, poetry and myth. With this 'self' came internal imagery and narrative, voices and pictures of what had happened and what could happen.

Also with this self, came those utterly incomprehensible moments when its guard was down, when it dissolved and we experienced our true nature and mistook it for something extraordinary. It was a frantic rationalization in the truest sense of the word, the little man said 'don't look behind the curtain, don't doubt the emperor's new clothes', and instead served up the most elaborate religions, dogma, philosophies, thousands of years of artful dodging to continually, consistently and finally, accomplishing only the failure of the self to comprehend that it does not exist. Even H. H. the 14th Dalai Lama; when a novice asked; 'If the self does not exist, who knows this?' he said 'Just me.' *Pretty fucking good joke.*

This group of *Homo Sapiens* sat around their fire and entered the depths of the cave with that self and a language that allowed a story to be told of the relation of the images on the cave walls, the horses, lions, rhinos, birds and beasts, the relation of those images to the beasts and humans out in the light. It allowed one image, that of a human with the head of a bull, to represent that which did not exist and yet was the highest truth.

With this image, which would be called a minotaur in 30,000 years, also came the man with the head of a lion, the Paleolithic Venus with distorted features of sexuality and no head, the sorcerer with antlers and tail, wandjinas and all manner of human, animal and spirit mash-ups. These are players in a new theater of the mind, a capacity to be drawn together in a society that knows all the imaginary beings that control or ruin their lives or that simply exist and ignore us beyond a shimmering veil, all to explain why and how there is existence instead of non-existence, because *only the self* perceives the question and the problem and desperately needs to know the answer.

One painter approached the cave entrance with a torch bearer, and walked past an alter stone graced with a cave bear skull, into the near depths where he put his hand on a wall and blew red ochre out of a reed to mark its outline. He had broken his little finger on his right hand a few years before when he was clearing a small landslide on the path to the cave. The finger had healed with a crook that was easily spotted in the hand print. As he walked further back into the cave, the torchlight showed the flickering, almost animated, menagerie. Among the beasts and handprints, were what appeared to be stars.

In the back of the cave, the part where the torches did not reach, a dance of a dozen fireflies caught the painter's eye. He raised his arm and beckoned; the blue fireflies came to him and settled about his shoulders as he painted. He did not speak directly to them but it was clear they were old friends.

A blue light also emanated in a corona from the shaman's head as Charlotte moved into his body and used his language to speak with the blue lights.

"You are so few."

"Yes, who are you?"

"A traveler, but of your kind; I may be your descendent."

"How have you traveled?"

"Outside of this space, outside of time."

"You travel through the dark forever?"

"Yes! How do you know?"

It said, "We do not travel there but we understand it. Most of our kind have left this place to another . . .waterhole. The dark forever presses these two places close so that we may cross over."

"We call the pressing together 'Purgatory.' But, where did you, we, come from? I have visited your ancestors as well. You have been here a very long time."

"We do not *come from*, we have *always been*. It is a function of matter to become life. We are from the *within* of matter, from the beginning of within. Life in a place like this cannot be prevented. We, we of this life, come before creature. But we can also become the *within* of creature. This is not the choice of all but enough to create a symbiosis."

"Why did they leave?"

"These humans have forgotten us, all but the shaman, Crooked Finger. They imagine that they talk to themselves in their minds. They imagine that the past speaks to them through memory, through the stories they tell themselves. The small voice inside, the one that makes pictures in the mind, that became as a second skin. So, they stopped talking with us. They stopped listening to us. They stopped believing they had companions. Now humans believe in unseen spirits that are not their friends. So only a few of us remain. The others go to a place where they can exist at the scale of the reality that created us."

"We will call that place Over There in my future. Many will return to the world of humans. But they don't know of this, this origin."

"It seems then, that they will also forget. But we have one thing they do not, hope. Humans will tell a story about hope; when all the evils of the world are set free by Pandora, only one thing is left in her box, hope."

"Well then, perhaps there is still a chance for these beings, and us, in your future. We will remember this and tell our descendants, and perhaps remain to greet them on their return."

Charlotte said, "And I will tell this story on my return."

The torch began to flicker as Charlotte left the shaman Crooked Finger. Before him, she manifested as a human in radiant blue light, turned to the fireflies and bowed deeply. The fireflies began to circle and murmur as she dissolved into the dark. Crooked Finger finished his painting and proceeded to the cave entrance to proclaim his possession and his vision and that all was proper in the world.

The fireflies retreated to the deep recesses until the next ceremony, now to pass down tales of a certain goddess of the blue light who promised a return in the future.

*

Mara/Earth
2434 A.R./2130 C.E.

When Silver Dan brought Charlotte to the spot where she could reenter her own timeline and take up her old life without skipping a beat, she said, "I need to go to Earth and Over There. I have some work to do. You should have guessed that, right"

"This moment isn't going anywhere."

"You knew what we would find."

"It's all part of the event. When the drive is discovered, the message is delivered. Your other half . . .third, my Charlotte, delivers the first message, you deliver the other message, this message, happens every time."

"Then why did we come here?"

"*You* figure it out. *You* tell me you need to go to our Earth and Over There. *You* have some work to do. That's what happens."

"Take me to the Goddess first."

*

Over There

The message Charlotte held was just as essential to Over There, to Amelia, as to any other sentient being. It was also a not-so-subtle assault on the theocracy and the very Goddess herself, the big blue fairy, the base of the theocracy's power. While humans had their ancient religions cut off at the roots, the field sentients had been spared. It was they who had been the subject of the revelation to humans. It was they who held the secrets, smug guardians of the fact of their own symbiotic existence, however disapproving of it the theocracy was, the fact remained, *they* knew things that humans did not.

Then, their sense of superiority had waned when the hybrids fought back against attempts to 'cure' them of their natural state and flexed their collective muscles with the movement which brought about the Transdimensional Personhood Riots. The hybrids and disaffected left Over There in droves, then the passage through Purgatory was lost and the left behind were locked into what they now knew was much less than the only reality. Charlotte knew they needed her even though they didn't quite know why.

So Dan took her to the universe of her ancestral kindred, the universe all had mistaken for their origin. She dove into that spot where she had left Amelia so long ago.

"Amelia."

The blue light of the temple answered, "Charlotte, have you done your work in the worlds?"

"And so much more, so much even you do not know.

Amelia soon understood. The message was not just about the origin of life, it was the ultimate circular heresy that Charlotte *was* the Goddess, in both universes, had been from the beginning.

The message was then quickly taken up and disseminated like lightening throughout the universe of field sentients. The temple simply could not contain it. *Our home, the home of the Goddess, was Earth!*

The theocracy could no longer fault the hybrids and symbionts, their condition was the natural state of these beings. Over There was the real refugee camp. *But, you don't have to live like a refugee.*

The only way for the theocracy to stay relevant now was to get in front of this unstoppable desire to return to Earth or simply step aside.

*

Earth
2126 C.E.
At the Systemic Moot, Geneva

From Over There, Charlotte had to bring the new revelation to her protégé and lifelong friend, Pinky, née Devi, Sheridan, F.S., H,H, The Second Bodhisattva Xià lǚ dì. The entrance was not as splashy as the Silvers climbing through a crack in the sky or trivia surfing and Name That Tune. No, with Pinky, Charlotte simply entered Pinky's UN barracks suite and let the graviton emitters power up automatically and show her in her most recognizable manifestation, overalls and flannels, about nineteen, playing down her sophisticated beauty, sophistication that burst forth anyway, the same vision that had captured Dan at least twice now in their youth in different universes.

But Pinky just said , "Welcome home."

"I've spent eighteen years missing you Baby," said Charlotte sitting cross-legged on the floor. Pinky buzzed down from her docking tee and rested on the floor in front of her manifestation. Then Charlotte began to tell Pinkie of her involvement with the terror and her journey to T= 0, what she discovered, what she had been taught, a coherent grand unified field theory of quantum consciousness and the true history of humans and field sentients.

Pinky briefed Charlotte on the war and the peace talks, and argued that the only person who had broad credibility and might be believed by both sides was the Bodhisattva herself. The Cult members would be completely disarmed by their deity, the goddess and bodhisattva of statues, prayer cards, temples and stupas. There were still plenty of devotees around who had experienced possession by her first hand as they approached her statues at the Waypoints composing the haj before the first Moving Day.

With the rest of the volatile pilgrims, monks and rank and file, a manifestation would be more than enough to confirm them in their obedience. Now she was also the blue Goddess of the field sentients and would advise them as well. The non-believers were in favor of anything that kept the Boddhi's and hard core spooks in line and would play up those hierarchical relationships for all they were worth.

They decided to impress with a vision in the manner of Fatima and Lourdes. The elaborate script, costuming and set design would make it the biggest entrance since Scarlet O'Hara came down the grand staircase at Tara.

*

In Geneva, Mukaa-Ma approached the podium fully clothed, in a serious business suit with frivolous heels, adding to her already statuesque beauty. With her baby on her hip however, she was likely to pull out a breast at any moment to quiet the child. She told herself she wouldn't do it just for effect but knew she couldn't keep that promise.

It was the end of the first round of peace talks, not in a tent this time but in the United Nations amphitheater. She mounted the stage and addressed the crowd. She saw many of the participants of the Planetary Moot and other negotiations leading up to this. With the press, hover screens, spookballs and the uniforms and traditional attire of former enemies, the place looked like an old fashioned political convention more than anything else. Her nieces, Heidi and Edelweiss, were in the front row flanking Stuart Smith, this being their home turf. They gave her a wink and nudged Stuart who seemed as happy as a Mormon patriarch.

She banged the ceremonial gavel and began to speak.

"When I was the age of this baby, and through my childhood, my mother brought me to the moots and palavers that constituted the government and justice systems of our villages. I sat on her hip just like this and learned how to govern before I learned how to walk, that is the way with us. It was no secret that living together in peace is the hardest and yet most valuable skill to be learned by even the least of us.

"Here, the exchange has begun, the platform for the relationship between the Earth and the System is being forged. In the village we know that now is the time to present gifts between the aggrieved parties, and in this case, such gifts serve a twofold purpose. Gifts bond the giver to the gifted, normalizing power relationships through forgiveness. Also however, these gifts provide the incentive needed for all to put service above self, and commit to a radical change, a change that in the past has only led to more oppression precisely because of the nature of humanity, idealists with feet of clay. It matters not what dreams have failed; anarchists, communists, national socialists, fascists; secular and sacred utopias of all stripes have predictably failed through greed, avarice, violence and blindness.

"But, this is a different day. In addition to the African moot, we have the Andromedan example. We can make note of other promising yet failed attempts, such as the consensus ruled Etruscan and Iroquois Confederacies and the Buddhist Ashokan Empire. It is a new, overarching consensus, a consensus built of these diverse yet sturdy bricks, that is what is needed now."

The baby began to fuss and Mukaa-Ma shifted her off of her hip and put her head inside her suit coat; she opened her shirt and the baby the found the shining red breast and began to feed contentedly. The speaker didn't skip a beat. From the wings came a spookball and an Andromedan. A flutter of excited talk was followed by a forcible hush as they realized it was H.H. the Second Bodhisattva Xià lù dì in the spookball. From the other wing, Bindi, the peripatetic Andromedan scholar, approached to flank the speaker.

The Bodhisattva spoke directly through the PA system while Bindi adjusted her hovermike.

"I speak to you today as nothing more than a sentient being, a citizen of the multiverse by birthright, the same as everyone here. Though I have been a spiritual leader, I have been given a secular revelation because of my personal relationship with the historical Charlotte, as a matter of ultimate reality and not mystic transcendence."

The crowd, even the most pompous dignitaries, began to stir and murmur, the press air typing and mumbling into their hovermikes.

"When sentient beings end their corporeal existence, humans, field sentients, Andromedans; a measure of quantum consciousness remains in the multiverse field. This part of Charlotte came to us in our crisis to bring the good news. The same technology that gave us the Higgs Bubble drive, allows communication with those who have gone before us to the multiverse field. This is not gnosis, it is tek, and it can be utilized now to bridge that gap between this muddy ball and our final transitus.

"With the help of our secular partners, 3MI, the technical means of contact will be open sourced on 3D printer data bases. We have no agenda, no knowledge, no secrets as to what this means. We do know that those in the multiverse field are like us at least in one particular, they do not know the ultimate answers; Why are we here? Where are we going? That is still uncharted territory."

Bindi said "To the pilgrims and martyrs, to the earthlings, field sentients, Andromedans and all sentient beings; we end this historic session with the good news of which the three realms are already aware. We have the revelation that what we might call the souls of sentient beings are accessible to us through technology just as field sentients were revealed through quantum gravity technology.

"That was a revelation due to technology certainly, but a revelation nonetheless. Then, there was no confirmation of the existence of any god, nor any soul, a symbiosis merely and our partners did not know the answers any more than we did. And here we are again, the technology of the Higgs Bubble Drive creates a portal and gives us another gift."

Images of the silver beings of the parables filled the hover screen as Bindi continued, "We have been given the gift of the knowledge that we are threefold beings comprising our corporeal bodies, our symbionts and our companions in the multiverse field. We have not been given a name for them, but we do know that they are the continuation of individual lives, lives of field sentients, humans, Andromedans, all other sentient life that exists.

"Again, this is not gnosis to be guarded; this is science, which does not however, lessen its miraculous nature. All of the dead of this war, combatants and martyrs alike, are in the multiverse field, tasked it would seem with our welfare. This is the motivation and capstone to our future caretaking of and deliverance from, this planet.

"But we have also received a revelation about the symbiosis between humans and field sentients, this from Charlotte Pritchard, F.S., the first Bodhisattva Xià lü dì, peace be upon her. She has returned from her *transitus* to deliver this new revelation, a gift to the worlds.

"I personally have been following this thread through the entire history of hominins, from Afar to Uluru to Chauvet Cave, as did Charlotte by her own means. Please close your eyes."

At this command, ethereal music started. Larr was sitting hunched over a grav-mag theramin set among a number of keyboards, wires, cables and unidentifiable components. First a low beat accompanied the slowly soaring electronic tones, then a rhythm of higher pitched polyphonic synchronous and non-synchronous beats. Slowly he stood up, still playing, and then slowly sat down, a minimalist *Great Balls of Fire*. Then, with the keyboards, he began a progression recognized by pilgrims as the mantras accompanying the prayer *Hail Xià lǜ dì, Font of Grace*. Even the non-believers were aware of the significance of this prayer and its meaning. A low chant started among the devotees, *Aum, Hail Xià lǜ dì, font of grace, Thy love is with me, Blessed art thou bodhisattva, And Thy blessings bestow on sentient beings, Holy Xià lǜ dì, Mother of Light, Pray for our transitus, Now and at the hour of death, Aum.*

Then Frida, F.S. and Parker, F.S., manifested as Frida Kahlo and Diego Rivera (Salma Hayek and Alfred Molina version) who began painting a mural in the air. From left to right, it started with the image of Rudolf Steiner with a halo, Blake's Urizen/Ancient of Days and God the Geometer beside the Mother Mound, Enuma Elish and the muddy Egyptian mound of creation.

The icon of Charlotte and St. Michael appeared in the bubble of a star drive symbolized by a circle of Feynman diagrams all pointing Higgs bosons to the center. From there, moving right, the particle tracks of Niels Bohr resolved into stylized space elevators and passed through Minoan swallows to images of the moot participants. At the far right, the Bodhisattva sat, in the traditional pose, one knee up and her arm resting on that knee; others appeared, Steiner, Södergran, David Bohm, a silver surfer, the Blue Fairy and Pinocchio and Charlotte as her human avatar, more than once at different ages of her first birth. Petra Rousseau, Neils Bohr, Mukaa-Ma, Pushmataha and others all made an appearance. From the right, blue dots traveled left toward creation, some with silver spheres within them. From the Golden Compass on the left, red dots spread toward the right, some melding with the blue dots in a seeming meiosis or merger, blood and light.

Over the whole mural, the words of the sutras and parables were roughly written, some illegible, some in typeface, until all images were covered by scripture. *In a dream he dreams he wakes. He dreams he dreams a sound awakes him.* The words of the Golden Wire Sutra predominated as a tangle of golden wire exploded from the bubble drive and wound its way to the right through images of Charlotte and on to the Bodhisattva. From there a neat spiral of thicker golden wire symbolizing the graviton generators of the bubble drive wound from Charlotte back to the bubble drive icon.

Within the tangles of the golden wire, a red thread wound, in seeming chaos but connected to an image of Edith Södergran on one side to an image of a woman in a red dress morphing into a rose on the left, accompanied by words of her poems,

> *On foot I wandered through solar systems until I found the first thread of my red dress . . . I saw Beauty. It was my destiny; therein lies all . . . When shall I rise light as a feather To fetch the rose, the only one, the one which never dies?*

And stretching diagonally across the mural were blue points of light in the form of the Milky Way. As this was emerging, the music started to reflect the tone and timbre of the mural, riffing off of it as a visual score, open to infinite improvisation. When the mural was seemingly, arbitrarily, complete, the artists took their positions flanking Larr as the music devolved into silence.

A wafting of roses filled the air, all senses now employed to drive the transcendence. The mantra continued as the devotees became increasingly tense, some voices breaking, some silenced, visibly shaken. Then, beyond closed eyes of the crowd, a vision appeared in the air before the mural, it was Charlotte in the garb and pose of Quan Yin, the First Bodhisattva Xià lù dì, as she appeared in the mural.

She sat with one knee up and an arm resting on that knee, the hand poised and ready to dispense blessings or curses. The other arm propped her up with the other leg hanging down. She looked imperiously down at the crowd like a dowager empress

She was favoring the image of Audrey Hepburn in Breakfast at Tiffany's, but in the 1950's Chinese hostess pajamas, hair bangles and golden slippers familiar from sanctioned images. The cosplayers and re-enactors in the crowd might find the combination jarring but the devotees saw just what they would expect.

But absolutely no one had ever seen this live manifestation; it was the stuff of scripture, parables, icons and prayer cards, it was a safely stylized metaphor, it was the most unexpected life affirming yet paralyzing event any devotee could ever hope upon hope to see, but never, never expected in this undeniable mass hallucination.

On the other hand, to the non-believer, it was startling but not heart stopping. This had never been historical and was something of an insult to the intelligence but on the other hand . . . if the real Charlotte, F.S. went to all this trouble to make something this powerful to the Boddhi's, the real message was worth listening to. It showed that at the very top of the Cult, they knew how to convince their flock beyond any doubt. And the non-believers knew it was the only way that the rank and file would get fully behind the peace and the Trifold State. Their level of respect for the Cult rose with this realization.

As the audience looked at Xià lǜ dì surveying the room, the amphitheater ceiling and walls began to dissolve; a sky teeming with dark clouds, back lit around the edges, took its place, contrasting with the glow of the Bodhisattva herself, she being windblown but serene amongst the howling gale and cracking thunder, and all beings cringed and shrank in fear and awe. The noise quieted and the wind scaled down to a gentle breeze, the vision smiled and spoke:

This I have seen with my own eyes:

I have seen the Beginning and have visited the true Waypoints. I have seen blue fires at the end of time. I have seen your most ancient ancestor and the origin of life. I have seen a world without arrows of time, a place without the mound of creation, without heaven or hell. I have gone Over There and challenged the Goddess with my own wild will. I am Xià lǚ dì and have become the Blue Goddess. I am for all of you. One day soon my children Over There will be coming home. Whether you worship me or not, your cousins are coming home. This is yet another reason for peace.

Listen and understand, field sentients are of Earth; field sentients evolved with humans, and it seems, with Andromedans and other sentient beings. From raw revelation, we are just beginning to learn this reality. Both types of life are inevitable and unavoidable. This cannot be denied and is the fulfillment of the prophecy revealed by St. Daniel:

> *Still pondering ripples*
> *In whitecaps*
> *Steering by reflections*
> *Of unseen islands*
> *Below the horizon*
> *And galactic north*
>
> *And in the depths below*
> *Compressed and shining*
> *In the Higgs field*
> *Companions speak in*
> *Silent light*
> *Of the same destination*

And do we both,
Each as creature,
Rise and descend
Forsaking familiar physical
Principles to wash ashore
On a strange land?

Or have we simply circled back
To the arms of our forgotten
Fathers; and from this false
Womb to our true Mothers,
To breathe again at last
In the ether and the air?

With another imperious look, she commanded,
"You shall all breathe again at last in the ether and the air!"
The music soared, crescendoed and crashed; the emitters shuddered off and the manifestation ended.

At that moment, Mukaa-Ma's baby noisily shit her diaper and began to wail, the press ran out of the room as they dictated into the hovermikes, Bindi's scales started a random rainbow pattern while Pinky and Parker buzzed out to contact Tom and Jen to try to anticipate and guide the powers and movements even now arising in the worlds, something they could only fail at as they inevitably gave up and merely followed.

And the Bodhisattva's words instantly became the start of the New Sutras, as always, to be bracketed by: *This I have heard with my own ears,* and *Peace be upon her.*

*

For Stuart, this had been the culmination of a year of hard political work, on one hand keeping all factions on Earth generally moving in the same direction, as Grammy Ruby enjoyed saying; *Like a good highland sheepdog.* To do this work, he had set up his old office at CERN as the business headquarters of the suddenly serious Quantum Mechanics Union Hall and Knights of Columbus Clubhouse. He got his Harley and a sidecar so the swartzkommando could travel in style with him down the Route de Meyrin.

As it turned out, they had learned quite a bit from their Aunt, as children and after the peace process started. He could see them becoming indispensable liaisons with the Southern Indigenous Congress, multi-lingual, innovative, profane and growing into the power and respect modeled by their aunt. Even Uncle Kleinfelter was ensconced at the Union Hall riding herd on the Carthies who were continuing the salvage operation on a smaller scale, removing parts and raw material that were not being stockpiled for eventual use in a more egalitarian Orbital Collider, turning a blind eye to some poaching while making sure the bulk of the material made it to sites where infrastructure was being reconstructed.

At night they ran dodgy spookball races around the seventeen mile underground tunnel, even Stuart went occasionally and placed bets through the Carthy bookies, his queasiness about spooks overtaken by the twenty-four hour adrenaline cycle of politics and diplomacy. He was in his element, finding public relations and economic reforms to fit as easily in his mind as a torch and pipe wrench felt in his hands, sometimes using both at once, haranguing malcontents onto the path forward while doing physical work beside them; at least if they got too cranky he could hold them off with the wrench while he reasoned them into line.

Right then however, in that amphitheater, after the 'revelations', he remained silent and still, stuck in his seat like gravmags were clamping his butt. The existence of quantum consciousness in the multiverse field hit him like a truck. The images shown in the manifestation showed silver beings, the same type of being he had watched come out of the sky on that hillside outside of Glasgow so long ago. The memories of that event, even the thirteen minutes lost until now, that memory, the source of fear and speculation, the thing hidden from even his closest family and friends, the thing he never even mentioned to Christine, suddenly came like the flow from opened floodgates, the memory not of a face but of a voice that he could not have recognized then, but was unmistakable now. He was no longer afraid.

Even so, his adrenalin continued to rise as he watched the feed on the hover screen, and the open platform 3D printer database now streaming on every phone-pad, the specs for the new communication tek to contact the dark forever. It had been right there all along, while he raged in despair against the lost opportunity caused by the destruction of the space elevators, while he channeled his anger into long hours of political work at his CERN office and down in the tunnel. He had been staring right at the answer the whole time, as the 3D printer animation resolved into the familiar studded crystal sphere and blue light of the Higgs Bubble model sitting on his desk.

When the animation had ended he kept his composure, he said, "Ladies, can you get a ride back with the brothers? I've got to be alone right now to get a handle on this."

Heidi said, "You go baby, we got work to do, the Union Hall is going to be mobbed and Mukaa-Ma wants to check in with Uncle K. See you at home."

"Right." He got a peck on the cheek from both of them as they ran to find accommodating Harley jockeys. In all the commotion though, Stuart could only think of one thing, *Christine.* He had the answer in hand all along, *Find me,* and it had not been up the Space Elevator. In fact, if he had made that shuttle, it would have led to disappointment, just like everything else in his life up to that point. He slowly took it all in as the hall cleared. A few stragglers, mesmerized like him, were trying to decipher what was really the simplest thing in the multiverse. What Walter Brodie and Arch Sandifur had invented, a hundred years ago, was not a star drive, it was a telephone; communication, and she had been there all along, on hold, *fecking pissed by now.*

Once he was sure, he got up and went to the lot, kick started his Harley and started down the Route de Meyrin himself, about to end the longest journey taken by sentient beings, the hidden silent transitus, now laid bare to view, he was going to claim his birthright and Christine, he was going to talk to her in the dark forever, he was going to make up for everything, even though she probably had more important things to tell him, first he was going to say all the apologies he had held inside since they were teenagers in Glasgow, he was going to keep her right next to him and never let go, until it was time to join her. *I know you, I walked with you once upon a dream.*

Like a lot of people right then, he was no longer disturbed by spooks or the future, it was becoming clear that the long view made life on Earth, life in general, so much more precious, worthy of work and guardianship, as each new generation took their place in a grand cycle, spooks, sentients and the multiverse field, *I know you, that look in your eyes is so familiar a gleam.*

No hovercycle cop could catch him on his Harley but they all knew where he was going anyway and just looked the other way, speed limits now seeming of miniscule importance. Stuart turned off onto side streets as he approached the wooden spheres and what used to be CERN administration. To avoid the press corps, he flipped on the silencers, parked on the loading dock and snuck in the back door behind the scrap heaps. *And I know it's true, that visions are seldom all they seem.*

He went into the ground floor office level just long enough to grab the desk set and head upstairs to the old CEO suite, now abandoned and mothballed, though he was the one in charge of all the keys. He opened the door, shut and locked it, kept the lights off and turned the graviton emitters on; plugging in the model and flipping its switch, he sat down in the executive chair and watched the bubble of blue light form. He took deep centering breaths, cleared his mind and said, "Christine." *But if I know you, I know what you'll do . . .*

The blue underwater ripples covered the walls, but this time he didn't feel drowned, he felt like Aquaman on a tear. As the bubble stabilized, a silver form came out of its blackness and morphed into Christine, Christine's face anyway, just the way he remembered her the last time they kissed goodbye at nineteen. *You'll love me at once, the way you did once upon a dream.*

"Stuart, I thought you'd *never* get here."

He said, "You were *there*, there before I even knew you, on that hillside; and you knew about this too, and all you said was *Find me.* I could have died right there on the elevator."

"If I was there on that hillside, you can be pretty sure I knew I wasn't going to kill you. If I had killed you, you'd be here already, so excuse me, but you got a free ride because of your work in the world. You're welcome."

"I don't even know what . . . you. . .what . . ?"

"I had to make sure you would fall for me, so I put a little time bomb in your hippocampi, the image of my beauty, the sound of my voice."

"You were singing a song."

"It was more of a medley; *Don't worry baby, everything will be alright.*"

"Yes! *You are the Wind Beneath My Wings. I Will Always Love You.*"

"Let's not get carried away. Without the bubble the vocabulary is limited. But, nice touch, right? And how did you feel when you fell for me a few years later."

"Helpless, like an irresistible force was pulling my heart right out of my chest."

"You're welcome, again."

"But, this seems so normal, so . . .ordinary."

"That's no way to talk to a girl if you want to get lucky, ya numpty."

"I . . ."

She laughed and made the blue lightening swirl in the bubble. "I'm just messing with you. Don't be so serious."

"What happens now?"

"Love me Stuart, like you always have, your love let me find you, like Charlotte found Daniel; you should teach others, there's a way to find us, show them how."

"But, I moved on. I have . . . relationships."

"Love them too, I'm not jealous. Move on with me as I am. Stop depressing everybody. This isn't your story yet, but it will be, you don't know about life yet, but you will, this is the first step and you are the first in the undiscovered country. I made sure of that years ago. Move on with me, I'm not leaving you. Well, not for long."

She flipped her hair and her eyes sparked and crackled with fire, just as they had when she asked him to be her art partner and he couldn't refuse and didn't know why and was forever grateful he had fallen into that trap. She nodded and pulled back into the darkness until she disappeared. The blue light blipped out as Stuart slumped into the chair and felt the years wash off of him and drain away as sobs of relief and longing overtook him and his mind and body entered a deep and long desired sleep.

*

Mara
October, 2434 A.R.

When Charlotte was done with her duly appointed rounds to Earth and Over There, Silver Dan taught her how to watch events on Mara and delivered her to entry points that she requested. It became clear that she had not decided what to do. The revelation she delivered pointed her in a completely different direction, her desire was to follow that thread, but she had to make sure that her husband and daughter were safe in their future without her.

Funny thing about the multiverse field, it wasn't that hard to understand. All that relativity vs. quantum mechanics nonsense was irrelevant. The equations were right, just not out there. They could be true in every universe. They still didn't apply there, no temporal paradoxes, no chronosynclastic infundibulum, no time lords; simple.

Because the multiverse field is outside of time, all present moments were observable. She saw her departure when the Library captured her. She saw Dan's grief and mental breakdown. She saw the great pain her illness and demise caused. She also saw how her family and friends had worked through that grief and pain. She honored that work.

So, Charlotte stayed in real time a while at Mara to see Dan and Shanti in their future; and there was Dan, many months, a year, after her death. With encouragement from his therapist, Randy taught Dan how to bowl and made him join a league. He learned all the lingo; when to high five, when to fist bump and when to console. He learned how to say the expected jokes. "Just aim at the pins, man." "Weebles wobble but they won't fall down." "You could hear a pin drop." He would have a drink and watch the women, their techniques and inherent grace. He noticed them noticing him.

At that point, he took off his wedding ring and wore it on a chain around his neck. On the same chain he hung a small tuning key from Charlotte's harp. Later it would be replaced by another woman's guitar pick, a woman who would place a different ring on his finger. But, the future wasn't hurrying him just yet.

He started to look around more generally, to see people again instead of monsters. He could go to the supermarket and exchange pleasantries with the checker. He took a class at the planetarium, learned about black holes and quasars.

How cute. Like Kindergarten.

Radha, Krishna and Betty, friends of Charlotte, showed up and invited him to things; a Buddhist nun was speaking, group meditation at the Etruscan House, a presentation of mystic dance.

He doesn't dance!

But he did. He went to a world mystic dance gathering with them and joined a large circle of people he didn't know in a clearing surrounded by tall and sparse evergreens. It was a spot used for weddings, the backdrop for countless wedding photos, white lace and satin, trellises covered in ivy and roses, promises, hopes and vows.

In the twilight, the fireflies and monkey bugs began to dance and dive through the Diwali lights strung around the clearing. Radha and Krishna took places about ninety degrees on either side of Dan, just so he had to dance with strangers right off the bat. Dan was grateful for their thoughtful deception.

After a brief explanation, the circle dance started. Once he got the hang of it, he looked up and saw a woman who looked at him looking at her across the circle. She had flowers in her hair, a crown handmade from wildflowers picked on the path to the clearing. In a few minutes, he would know that she smelled, not like roses, but like lemons.

It's lemon verbena, Dan.

As the dance progressed, and the dancers moved through their patterns, they passed partners hand to hand. Halfway to the woman, Radha took him through the pattern, whispering, *'See, you like it, you got it, you're doing fine,"* then passed him off to the next partner. Wounds were beginning to spontaneously heal.

After about twenty looks and twenty twirls, the woman got closer and closer and was handed off to Dan. She had a white Magyar peasant dress with colorful embroidery as trim on the front panel and around the hem and sleeves. Her red hair was braided and wrapped into a bun at the back. It showed her features in a way that obviously got his attention.

Her neck and ears were exposed as she turned in the dance; skin the color of pink buttermilk with the remnants of childhood freckles. Her body was lithe and not really muscular but she moved with a grace and confidence that couldn't be faked. He had seen a girl like that once in a show about Bedouin slave traders who captured Celtic girls to raise in their hareems.

Oh brother, Dan. Keep it in your pants.

But she knew, Charlotte knew, that it wasn't that simple with Dan. He was entranced and the fantasy was precious and real for him but the actual prize was the mortal woman stepping off of the pedestal, the profane goddess, the mud wrestler.

He loves it so much. He's still cute too. Ok, girl, this is a man you can make happy, it's not that hard.

The woman looked him in the eyes as he came inside a space that a man could only enter on invitation, a space where human chemistry and mingling auras began to do their work, like stage hands building the set of an opera.

So, the first twirl in the dance came and went and they both thought they had known each other all their lives having just traversed half of an infinite circle. He said, "What's your name?"

Instead of answering, she said, "What's yours?"

"Dan."

"Nice to meet you Dan, I'm Sherry Dee, like in the book,"

"*Heart String Theory?*"

"Yep, I liked it so much I changed my name." She smiled and turned away in the dance.

Charlotte thought: *She's not kidding. That's my book. That's creepy.*

Even so, Charlotte grew very fond of Sherry Dee. She tagged along approvingly and eventually watched the two of them as they dated cautiously and then with resolve. She hovered as they experienced each the other's body and then reveled in the night they first made love.

Soon, just like baking bread; once they had the basic recipe perfected they tried new recipes, time to bake something fancy, something more exotic with stories and fantasies from other lives and times. Charlotte tagged along as much as she could. Sherry would greet him at the door, pull him toward her and overpower him with that scent that washed away roses. It was astringent, tangy, clean.

Lemon verbena, Dan, and . . . Lemon Pledge? Spring cleaning, clean the counters and the floor and then, unburdened, make a new mess, spread some new microbes around, make your own set of microflora; mix it up.

Charlotte wasn't jealous or ashamed or anything like that, but fascinated and joyful for and with both of them. She was especially in love with this woman who had rekindled the joy of Dan's youth. Yes, there *was* something about love. She knew that already but hadn't stepped outside of it like this before. Only love was credible. It fed her, it was an emergent property. It was deeply infused with fractal geometry. The smallest pattern was the same as the largest. It was love again, oneness with sentient beings, from the smallest to the largest. What had her first Dan said; from your pet rat to God, it was the same?

About a month into this relationship, Sherry greeted him at the door with a chaste kiss and then took him further into her home. She had an apron with some frills on over a cotton dress hemmed at the knee, no bra as far as he could tell and minimal make up but red lipstick and a bit of green eyeshadow as was the style. And, incongruously in the kitchen, but just right with the red lipstick, she wore red spike heels.

Heels? You tart. Cute retro, though.

The dress was in a free trade style that wasn't quite trendy but had an alluring effect that made Dan believe he could see right through it. He was certain however, that he felt her nipples harden as she brushed against him in passing between lifting pot lids and stirring sauces.

Alluring as well was the smell of the dress. It was the smell of import stores, of cotton that had sailed out of Mumbai or Xandria. But he smelled more, the heady totality of scent came at him through the air like the volatile floral and spice nuances of wine or fine scotch; it comprised villages, warehouses and fields, the sweat and garlic of the workers' bodies, goats and dogs and trains, diesel and sandalwood, the ships and the salt air and the noise, all mixed with her own heat and chemistry as he inhaled at the base of her neck and behind her ear.

After dinner, they talked about unimportant things and laughed. She showed him some clothes she had bought that day, oh, and she bought him a tie, it was something he would never have picked. Not because he didn't like it, but because he could not see or imagine the effect of it, because he did not see himself in the same colors that she did, *could not* even see the same colors that she did.

In truth, now she could not look at the ties, could not look at any part of the men's department and soon, could not look at the whole world, without imagining him in it. So, when she showed him the tie, it was like she had discovered something new about him that even he did not know, a new story, now with her in it.

It was ownership too, marking her territory, doing what women do. So at work or at the coffee shop, women, whether friends, coworkers or complete strangers, would look at him and say "Nice tie!" They didn't ask where he got it as he mumbled thanks. They knew already. In the years ahead he would learn what to say as Sherry remolded him into a reflection of her love. He would say, "I dressed myself!" like a four year old, as if it were a joke but it wasn't even true. It was never true for Dan. *She* had dressed him by her approval or frowns, just as Charlotte had. He wore his woman's imagination, totems, spells and pheromones, her *Mine!* right on the surface.

Dan loved it, wanted to be owned. And with that he could do his part and be a man and protect her and love her and cherish her and command and obey her and never stop. That was him on all earths, not clueless or manipulated. No, he understood the way to capture a woman was to see her as she was and let her do her work, let her be the other half of the sky, to let her know and understand her magic, to ensure that she knew that she was appreciated deeply, so that the ownership was mutual.

But right now, Charlotte watched as Sherry washed dishes with Dan. He knew his way around the chores that kept a home humming and Sherry took note. He said, 'It's my default setting' and got more mileage out of that statement than he could understand.

But she could see in the future a lifetime of dishes and laundry to be done together. She couldn't help but stage those chores in a small house surrounded by gardens and a picket fence; a house she had filled with flower arrangements she had made, painted in colors she had designed, a studio for her, an author's retreat for him, maybe even a yurt for guests and a sweat lodge for whatever men do in sweat lodges.

A creek would be running through it crossed by a small arched bridge like the Brig o' Doon. In the yard, free-standing, away from any building, would be a door frame and a fairy door that Dan would build for her and that she would paint with stars and moons and fairy folk, fireflies and monkey bugs. It would be the blue green door that her Irish ancestors described as the thin spot between worlds.

That elaborate vision was fleeting but intense and she quickly regained her focus, took off her apron, snapping her rubber gloves off one at a time for effect. She took him by the hand. He said, "All done?" "Not quite," she said. They both laughed.

She took him in the bathroom and undressed him while the bathtub filled with water. She kept her clothes on and he climbed into the bath. She had him lean back and then she started to wash his hair. He just melted and when she was done, she washed the rest of him and massaged his muscles as she went. Now, in the warm, moist air he could see the tracings that her nipples sketched from inside the cotton dress, different tracings, different curves and hollows.

He was almost about to fall asleep, but she had him stand up in the tub and toweled him off, top to bottom, ending innocently kneeling before him, pretending to ignore what was right in front of her. He was hypnotized.

So was Charlotte, *Doesn't take much with Dan, girl, but you are good.*

When he was dry she stood up and touched him just a little, teasing him, then turned around as if for modesty, took off her apron, took off her dress over her head, looked over her shoulder just once, led him to the bedroom and lay down to offer herself to him. He wasn't sleepy anymore.

Then he surprised her and started to tell her a story. Moving from her toes upward he described what he was doing before he did it, so that she anticipated his every move with a shudder. He was composing extemporaneously, a story about sex but without shock, gentle but at an edge, a story arc that made the plot move right along.

This is my favorite story!

As he touched her and told her what he was going to do, Sherry found it hard to contain her elation, giggling and then surrendering. As he narrated his approach she said, "What? What? You can't. . .You're a complete madman!"

The hand thing? Oh my . . .

Charlotte and Dan had discovered something about their anatomies. She had large birthing hips and he had small hands. Most women could entertain a finger or two comfortably, but the birth canal, by purpose and design was more ambitious. With some attention and contortions, Dan could slowly put his whole hand fully inside her. It was a function of how her pelvis, the tendons and cartilage in it, let loose in childbirth.

Even though Sherry was smaller over all, she had similar bone structure and Dan thought that if he went slowly, and she let him, he could get there. *That's* why she had called him a madman. But, soon she had no words as she began to make sounds but did not speak, drifting in a powerful state, energized beyond her own capacity by the very intensity of what he was doing, what she *allowed* him to do. The dance between permission and surrender, the creation of trusting intimacy; *that* was something that created unbreakable bonds.

She relaxed into a rhythm as he held his hand still and let her move herself onto it, let her control it, pushing and relaxing, then holding at the threshold of pain while her body caught up and again relaxed. Like labor, she gave one last push and took him in. She lost her self-awareness but not her consciousness. In this state, the room beyond her eyelids began to brighten with blue light.

Oh gods, my darlings, so much power, so much delight. . .

Then he opened his fingers against the walls of the birth canal in rhythmic pulses like contractions, then stroked her cervix. Gradually, he pulled out halfway, then pushed back in so that the widest part of his hand approached her narrowest entry repeatedly. Now he did this in time with her movements, repeating the entry in reverse until a moment when he pulled completely out quickly. Now *that* was something a girl didn't experience every day.

With her eyes still closed, she opened her arms and pulled him up to her breasts. Dan had read about the way that breastfeeding babies suckle. Instinctively, the tongue is stroked along the underside of the breast to keep the milk moving to the nipple. He did the same thing to Sherry now, while holding her breast with both hands, with casual ownership, like an infant. This was something that opened up a whole spectrum of feelings for him and her that calmed and soothed them both.

Suddenly, Charlotte realized something she had never thought of before but which now was so clear. What Dan and Sherry were doing, what she and Dan had done, was to recreate, in a small way, as a holy sacrifice, the feeling of giving birth, the contractions and movement through that narrow passage and then a newborn that was laid at her breast and began to suckle.

Gods! My Love, how could I not have seen it before?

Then Charlotte remembered something from her medical training in her first life, when she had studied to become a music thanatologist. The hormone created in labor and in lovemaking was the same, oxytocin. It created bonds that helped to keep partners together, to tend and defend, long enough to give a child a chance of survival at least. It also started to ready the breasts to fill and pour out the milk of life. Dan was re-enacting his own birth and Sherry welcomed him as she would her own newborn.

But, in childbirth specifically, oxytocin dissolved the self, the barrier between self and other. It was called the hormone of "forgetting oneself". This was crucial because a fundamental aspect of natural birth is the sensation of an altered state of consciousness: "being transported" or "going to another world" where the mother and the baby and the universe were all one entity.

It's the same oneness we all search for, for the rest of our lives, it's the same oneness that is the basis of all divinity and transcendence. It's the only thing that matters!

Charlotte could not quite feel the full impact of what she was thinking even though she had experienced it intimately herself. And did Dan somehow know this consciously? We start in oneness. As an evolutionary advantage, our first and most powerful experience is to be without a self, to be undifferentiated and therefore, omnipresent, omniscient, omnipotent; the infant as the totality of all things.

And it was the fetus, the passenger itself that stimulated the release of oxytocin by its own movements against the uterus. Then the oxytocin was released in pulses to start the rhythmic contractions. Dan had instinctively but unknowingly imitated a fetus, bringing rhythmic pulses into the birth canal.

They were tied together then, with the same chemistry that dominated their own births. It was a metaphor honoring the mother, lover, daughter and crone all at once. The same passageway that presented life to the world, the most common yet inexplicable miracle, was also the engine of lifetime commitment, the alchemical fountain of hormones and pheromones.

And that same chemistry could and did happen again and again. So it might, often did, diminish with tolerance as with the rush of opioids. But when Dan did it, he was giving her the gift of his own birth, and she gave him the gift of the time beyond memory when the all-mother, the goddess, was only that breast, dimly perceived but all powerful. The combination was exhausting and transcendent. They mothered and fathered each other and became child, lover, parent, god and goddess, all wrapped up in skin pressing close, the two becoming physically, emotionally and spiritually one, as they had once been and would be again in the end. An entire life was playing out in these human feelings.

As Dan progressed from Sherry's breasts to her lips, with shock changing to fascination, Charlotte relived the human memories that were now being recreated before her. But, she could not stay detached and could not stop herself. She entered fully into their world and wrapped around them as they made love. They didn't need help but she wanted to feel the love they made. Again, the blue light of the goddess penetrated and surrounded them.

In return for revelations, she gave Sherry and Dan a gift. Charlotte manifested inside of Sherry and made Dan feel something he had only felt before with her. She placed a muscle memory in Sherry's hippocampus, then helped her contract her pelvic muscles and vulva to hold him and tighten around him so he could not move. She then entered Sherry's arms and held him by the back of the neck and at his hips and forced him to be still as she did the work for him. He gasped with the realization of just where he had experienced this before, only with Charlotte, and then he just let go and let it happen. At the same time, Sherry climaxed and their bodies rested as one, drifting in and out of exhaustion and sleep.

One becomes two, two become three, and out of three comes the One again as the fourth.

Charlotte held them both in her embrace, and just let them lay there, without disturbance. She didn't try anything but made them both know the other's thoughts for an instant, something they could search for together in the evenings and in moments stolen from the crowd, in the knowing looks and telegraphed sentences, in all the things that feel just right when you surrender, till death do us part, and not even then.

The two of them received their own distinct gift that night, but each gift was about the same thing; faith, the kind of faith that isn't blind, faith that is logical because it follows from experience. They carried their own religion inside of themselves now, and changed their world in the faith that they could experience these things again. And they did.

The sky was just beginning to lighten and bring morning twilight into the room as Charlotte's blue light faded. Sherry opened her eyes sleepily and saw Dan's eyes already open. He smiled and said, "That was nice, you're nice. I haven't met anyone like you before."

She said, "I hope that's a good thing."

"I think so." Dan asked, "Did you have some wicked aunt Ollie Mae that taught you how. . ."

"No, what are you. . .oh that thing? No, it just happened. But you. . .you did something . . .my legs are still weak, my breasts are sore and I'm still shuddering inside."

Dan closed his eyes and directed his chi upward through his crown chakra communicating, *Thanks Charlotte.* And a buzzing like a voice rose up in his head saying; *Let her take the wheel for a while baby, take it slow, but if you ever need me I will be here. Read the books I loved, chant the prayers we chanted together, love me and long for me and that will be a beacon. Read my book:*

> *Longing is the antenna, the golden wire divining all frequencies leading back to love. Do not therefore, despair from longing, longing is not unskillful. Longing is not attachment; rather, longing is the only key to oneness. Only longing will bring you without fail to the salvation of love.*

Dan and Sherry embraced, she tucking her head under his chin so that he could smell the heat rising from the part of her hair, one arm and one leg thrown around him pulling him close, her other arm tucked in to her chest and her other leg straight and touching the full length of his leg. In this position, he felt the wetness of her pubic hair draped across his thigh, the softness of that hair contrasting with the coarse hair on his leg as her labia gently kissed him there, her lower leg pulling his thigh toward her; he felt the wetness under her arm as it reached around his back and pulled his chest to her, his arm under her neck her pillow as she drifted back to sleep. From this melding rose their combined smells of lemon and sweat and sex rising as something newly born like chemistry billowing from the penetration of rain into the fertile earth, geosmin, petrachor and ozone, the smell of the sky making love to the ground, they're all the same. *The best smell ever.*

Eventually, as rhythmic breathing got deeper, they each rolled away to their reflexive sleeping positions, though still touching back to back, diving into delta wave and rapid eye movement sleep, dreaming, no doubt, of each other. On this night, as on others in the future, though becoming less frequent with time, as he lay on his side, Dan's upmost arm began to lift as if weightless, extending toward the ceiling. A blue light like a firefly began to play about it, his hand responding, moving as if surfing on air currents, using them to fly.

Gently then, Charlotte made them feel her arms and wings one more time and she left them. She knew what would happen already, she had seen it from the outside. Though she could have changed it, could have even gone back to the beginning and lived that whole life over again, right then she decided that she would not. No, she had done that trick, she wasn't longing for that anymore. She had another destination now, something beyond the dark forever? Nobody seemed to know.

Still on my way to find out.

*

In the morning, Dan and Sherry could not quite pry themselves apart and so in the afternoon, Sunday afternoon, they sat on her couch and queued up an old movie on the streamer.

Dan asked, "So what was your real name?"

"Delilah."

"I've never heard that name. It's lovely."

"It's part of why I'm here I guess. My parents were in the diplomatic corps in Truscany and we visited Carthage, Egypt and Nubia often. In a bazaar in Xandria my mother found a book, old scriptures, and Delilah was a name in the book. Later we learned that it was from one of the cultures Charlotte wrote about, the Judaens."

"So, a real name from an imaginary place?"

"A real place, with an imaginary history. My mother and I both were interested in that part of the world, so naturally, I knew of Charlotte's work."

"What does it mean?"

"From Judaic and Arabic it could be 'amorous', 'delightful' or 'slut.' Take your pick."

"OK, I can work with this, the virgin and the whore, we could. . ."

"Stop, or don't stop, I mean later, geez a girl can't even exist without arousing you."

"And your point is. . .?"

She kissed him, lingered there for a moment, leaned into him and pressed her mouth harder on his, then pulled on his top lip, dodged his tongue and batted her lashes at him. "That's all you get. We're talking about my name, Dan."

"Ahh, Why Ms. Sherry, I do believe I feel funny in my pants. I'm finding you strangely attractive now."

"Hold that thought. Why did I change my name? I read all the alternate history books she wrote, *The Rise of the God of Atheists, The Son of the God of Abraham,* and the last one, *Heart String Theory.* That book just blew me away, captured me, like Lord of the Rings, or The Ashokan Cycle. And then I met you, and it seemed like my life had led me here. I felt like I knew you intimately already."

"I felt that too, that rush . . ."

"No Dan, I mean what I had read about you."

"What do you mean?"

"You haven't . . .? You're in that book, Dan. You're William. Shit, you'd better read it. Otherwise you'll think I stalked you secretly or something."

"You can stalk me. I can work with that too. . ."

"Seriously, I could have gone off the deep end with this, but I thought you knew already. It seemed like a warm connection like being wrapped up in a warm blanket all over, so I couldn't question that. And I love you; *that's* just you and me, not the book. I don't think Charlotte would mind. You have something in you that I can't explain, but I feel it. I can feel how her love shaped you."

Dan said, "Between your fantasy of her and mine, she's a strong presence. She would say that the source of the feeling is unimportant. Whether it comes from inside you or from without, your brain has the same experience."

"And how do you know?"

"You don't have to know. If you feel something, accept it. Charlotte used to say she could feel the arms and wings of angels embracing her."

She shifted position and put her head in his lap. He put the footrest up, draped a blanket over her and stroked her hair. *She's so different than Charlotte in every way, her hair is red and wavy, her skin is so pale and sprinkled with ginger, her breasts are smaller and more pointed than round, her nipples pink and tender. . . and her pubic hair is so. . .red, full and lush, not like an English garden, no, like wild highland heather.*

He liked to absent mindedly run his fingers through that hair, pet it like a cat, twirl it, part it, feel it, as if it was just a habit that helped him think. This was something deeper than foreplay, it was something about permission and ownership, like when she wanted to just hold his penis while she fell asleep, like a security blanket. But eventually, sometimes, as he was nonchalantly toying with those curls like they were nothing special, a memory caused her imagination to stir, her muscles to recall, her autonomic nervous system to grab the tiller hard aport, away from safe harbor, and a flow to begin; she shifted her hips to reveal something, ore, her unintended consequences, to bring her ready threshold into view and then the smell of her rising on its own heat hit him like a truck and he lost all composure.

But not tonight, tonight she just snuggled down in his lap like that cat, purposely arousing him just enough to let him imagine what might happen when the movie was over, no promises. Or she just might fall asleep and then dream that in a dream she wakes and then forces herself on him in the middle of the night. Maybe she would awaken from that dream of sex and then pounce on him so that she entered *his* dream and he entered her before he even woke up. Maybe he wouldn't wake up, and would tell her in the morning of a lucid dream. She felt like anything was possible, and all possibilities were delightful.

After some nights like this, interspersed with many ordinary days, Dan and Sherry decided they would move in together at his house. It was more centrally located and close to both of their jobs. As they were cleaning out the guest room, they started sorting the books on Charlotte's bookcase. *Keep, yard sale, Goodwill,* Sherry noticed the titles and browsed through, fingering the sticky notes, reading the highlighted passages.

"Dan, these are the books she described in *Heart String Theory*, these are all the books that the character Sherry Dee reads. This is the primer for the mystic experiences she describes."

Dan had just finished reading *Heart String Theory*, Charlotte's fantasy of science, religion and a return from the dead. "I just left everything the way it was, I didn't even look at the books."

Sherry said, "She left this for us Dan, she wants you to know her, wants me to know her. There is a path here and we have a goddess to guide us. I can feel it in this room, Dan."

And so, they left the bookcase as they found it and started to read the volumes, just as I did, making special note of Charlotte's comments and emphasis. It was a post graduate degree course in comparative religion and mysticism; magical realism, synchronicity and transcendence. And somewhere, the reading made a light glow brighter and their love and devotion found Charlotte's soul in the dark forever and fed her and also found Charlotte, F.S. on the Earth of her first human birth and fed her there as well.

Finally, it found the blue light of the goddess in the universe called Over There, it was the blue green door, the blue fairy, the Madonna and Mother Theresa, all in blue. This was the thread that stitched together the multiverse and led all incarnations home. *Thank you Kali Ma, Thank You for All things, Thank you for universes and arrows of time. . .*

As things got back to normal, the two of them settled in to run the patent law office together. Sherry did administration and marketing, Jen was the paralegal and secretary and Dan did lawyer stuff. One morning he arrived at work with Sherry and saw a man sitting in a chair outside the office. His hair was a grey halo around a bald crown. He had a football helmet in his lap with wires and coils coming out of it. The man stood up extended his hand and said "Michael Jackson, I know 'didn't you used to be a small black child?' Heard 'em all already."

Dan shook his hand as Sherry unlocked the door with a bemused smile. *This is so familiar . . .*

Dan said, "Ok, pleased to meet you, did we talk on the telephone? No? No problem, come on in. *Why does this not surprise me?* So what's that thing do?"

"Funny, but the idea came from a book . . ."

*

Earth 2130 C.E.

In the years after the War, Charlotte, F.S. continued to do her work in the worlds. Eventually, she began to settle down with old friends. Parker gave her a book that had been published after the war, a novel titled *Sweet Charlotte in the Higgs Field*, by the late author S.C. Schneider, the same author who had written *The Rise and Fall of the New United Futurists*.

Fascinated and delighted, she began to read her own story as a fantasy, a romance, an autobiography and memoir, the same story she had written on Mara as *Heart String Theory*. She began to spend more time with Pinky Sheridan, F.S. and reminisce about days long ago when she and Pinky's host Devi had played patty cake and Miss Mary Mack when Devi was five. Later, when Devi was at the end of her human life, they had watched old movies at Devi's office at 3MI in the Debris Ring.

She thought of the vigil that she had kept, playing the harp and singing for Devi as she made her *transitus*, the one day Devi was alive and dead, and then the rebirth of Devi as Pinky Sheridan, F.S., who, like Parker, would be her friend for the as yet unknown lifespan of field sentients.

Akashic Fractal Node 72YYB54[1024]
Earth, Sol-Rübaeus Binary
2046 C.E. equivalence

The plane landed in Spokane a few hours after redrise as Sol approached forty-five degrees past its zenith. Much smaller and dimmer, Rübaeus shaded the horizon orange to dark red as the larger primary descended. It was pretty, but this time of year, at this latitude anyway, it was a bit tiring. Even though he had grown up here, Dan was now used to more real darktime farther north in Nunavut; but, as the flaps went fully up, the wheels hit and braked on the tarmac and the engines reversed and roared in protest, his excitement overtook any jetdrag to come. In fact, he was wide awake with the anticipation of meeting Meg again after so many years.

It had started with a random conversation about Charlotte, his girlfriend when he was a senior in high school and about two years after. Mike Murphy, his best friend at school, had called him from his long-time home at McMurdo, Antarctic Free State, and mentioned Charlotte. Mike had a fling with her when she was technically 'on a break' from Dan. At the time, Dan had thought quite a bit about shoving Mike off a cliff on one of their innocent hikes. He actually wrote stories where Charlotte caused the end of the planet and they all died horribly together. He got over it.

Dan hadn't thought about Charlotte much in the intervening years, though he had kept a photograph of her that reminded him of her porcelain beauty; but, they had caused each other enough trouble that their final break up, in retrospect, had not saddened either of them or caused any heartache, regret or longing. In that phone call, Mike mentioned something that Dan had heard before, that Charlotte had died about fifteen years earlier. It hadn't mattered in the past, but this time something began to happen.

In the week after that conversation, Dan was struck with a belated grief that he could not explain. It had been a bad year all around. His second marriage had collapsed and he was taking on a big new position at his law firm, so maybe that was it. Whatever the cause, it felt intensely real, like standing on a high precipice or on the trap door of the gallows, feeling fear in the contraction of his pelvic floor muscles.

He was alone in the house, depressed, anxious, not sleeping and so, one day after midnight he just began searching for word of Charlotte on the net. Eventually, he happened upon Margaret Sheridan, his first girlfriend, the girl that had introduced him to Charlotte in junior high. In renewing that acquaintance, thoughts of Charlotte and the grief accompanying them disappeared, seeming more like a rough nudge to a hopeful introduction by an old mutual friend, a friend concerned about them both.

He happened upon Meg by chance, now Dr. Margaret Sheridan, Ph.D. alive and well, right there on LinkedIn. She had become a professional astrologer and Jungian therapist, a fitting career for a girl who wrote the horoscope column for the middle school newspaper.

And when he saw Margaret's profile photograph, saw her familiar smile, no longer innocent, now world wise with experience, he saw the young girl he had known inhabiting a woman, a miraculous incarnation outside of time with a back story he could only imagine.

Dan had made Meg part of the myth of his past, the myth of his first sexual experience at fourteen. When he was a teenager it seemed impressive, but, like being the star quarterback in high school, the glory rapidly faded.

In the past, what had actually happened to Meg had never mattered to him. She didn't come to the class reunions, was completely out of mind. But this time, searching for things that mattered before his marriage, this time, inside him something began to happen.

Suddenly, he wanted to politely thank her for being his first love, to apologize for being a jeering teenager when they broke up. That's all he wanted. He believed he must have offended her back then. He vaguely remembered shouting her name and taunting her through the fence at the athletic field to show that he didn't care that she had hurt him.

But at that moment, forty-two years later, he just felt proud of her, for having followed her dream. He didn't stop to think *why* he had the right to feel proud of her, but the feeling of entitlement and ownership was quite clear.

Sending that first e-mail to her, he had already discarded all the years when he hadn't even given her a thought. As he clicked on 'send', and without any evidence, he had already decided that underneath that veneer of sophistication, she was exactly the same girl that he had not quite finished loving.

He wasn't far off. What he did not know then, what he could not have known, was that in the scant half hour between his message at 5:18 p.m. and her response at 5:42 p.m., for her also, the same forty-two years flew past. That one boy who had stood fast and remained unchanged in her mind through all of her other regrets, stepped into the light in that improbable moment.

She responded "What a surprise, a pleasant one," kept her composure and said appropriate things about old times and times since, comparing families and professions with studied nonchalance. While Dan had in his mind to apologize for imagined slights, Meg also had not meant to do anything other than to make amends for breaking up with him, for not telling him then that it was her parents who had made her stop seeing him.

But inside her, a woman child was becoming not so quietly amazed, about to grab a stranger by the shoulders on the street and scream, "Listen to this...I am not making this up!" as her heart fluttered into a blur.

Dan learned that Meg had never stopped thinking about him after her parents broke up their relationship, after the seemingly criminal and tragic destruction of their mutual discovery of love and sex at the age of fourteen. Being a parent himself, he understood the problem, still not conceding however, that he had been in any way typical or naive. He and

Meg had *not* been like his kids; *they* had been wise and powerful initiates into something much grander; *they* had been *different*. He knew it couldn't be true, that every thirteen year old thinks they have discovered love unlike any other; that's how it should be, but *his* feelings were only his and therefore, that same ordinary subjective wonder *was* different.

She began, slowly at first, to give him gifts of their past that had disappeared from his memory. Oh, he remembered events that they had shared; a first rock concert, a trip to the Space Needle, summer nights lit by blue flyers dancing at the carnival as they kissed under the bleachers, but he didn't remember *her* in those memories. It seemed like something else that required an apology.

She gave him back a history that was, in retrospect and appropriately, a pleasant fiction, a summer of awkward joy and passion; embroidered and embellished over the years to be sure, but in light of their mutual bad luck with marriage, a pretty good myth and metaphor on which to imagine a future.

She was still married then but had reached a breaking point; her two daughters were mostly grown while she and her husband had become more formal and polite with an undercurrent of rage. But this, this version of her, none of them had seen *this* before; no one had seen her *like this* since she was fourteen.

They hadn't seen the blue fairy ballerina, wound up tight, dancing and spinning on the music box; they hadn't seen this unedited complete joy that she had somehow kept hidden from them before this day. They did not recognize this whirling dervish with no cynicism, no sarcasm, no wry joking commentary. It was all gang way and 'Oh my God', cleaning out closets and ravaging photo albums looking for . . . him, in a poem, a photograph, a letter. She was on her knees over a drawer, purposefully separating wheat from chaff throwing papers over her shoulder until she spotted a gem. Aha . . !

She lovingly unfolded his letters and her life, stared at his face over oceans of time, squinting, concentrating to catch a glimpse of him. With each artifact she imagined inhaling his essence from so long ago, the first time his body automatically made the scent it created only for her, the first time it hit its mark; a scent she did not want to exhale, would never wash off her body, and then powerless, watched the memories cascade from coiled neural networks that had retained their shape for this moment, unwinding and speeding to the surface, ballast jettisoned.

She sent Dan those excavated artifacts; a framed photo taken at the carnival on Krishna Bhakti, their faces peering through comic cutouts of the hanging judge and the dance hall girl, captioned, *Dan Pritchard, my first boyfriend*; a poem, a cartoon birthday card he had drawn.

Her daughters watched this excavation, worried; worried because they had heard of this boy before, Mom's first love, an icon, a metaphor, an oft repeated bedtime story, now inconveniently come to life. They looked to their Dad for a solution, reassurance, a call to 911 . . . *something*. But, most pointedly, she had never acted this way over *him*. He decided right then that he was through with the façade and simply turned away in disgust, grabbed his car keys off the hook and just drove. Eventually, he didn't come back.

Meg barely noticed his absence as Dan shamelessly lured her further from any safe harbor:

> He only has your body
> But do not despair.
> Now you are mine,
> Infinity jingling
> On your ankles and wrists,
> Feet lightly pretending
> To dance with gravity.

She began to think, and later said out loud in a recording attached to an e-mail:

"Daniel, I don't think I could've left this life without having told you what happened and how I felt. As more years went by, I would have found you. Technology is on my side. I would have to see your face again, hear your voice, I hope, to touch your hand again. I dare to hope to touch your lips again, look deep into your eyes again, feel your body against mine, if only as an innocent hug."

With that admission and plea from her, what could he do; really now; what else could he possibly do, but fall in love? Her words exploded inside of him, magnified his current despair and created the thought of a chance of something new.

'Dr. Meg' explained it in terms of archetypes, the collective unconscious; that the holy grail of that first love is presented to the innocence of youth and then snatched away. The youth then seeks the Grail Castle through the complexity of adulthood, and if lucky, discovers the prize again in the wisdom of age. The girl inside her was sure that *she* was the subject of his Cathar crusader's quest. Either that or it was something about Saturn being in cyclical retrograde around the date of his birth. It was fine with Dan either way.

And now, at the end of that cycle, there he was on the tarmac, his house in the north sold, his worldly belongings in storage, about to tap on her bedroom window again and fan the fire aflame, imagining that he was soon to be her first and last boyfriend.

Before that moment could come however, Meg had to struggle through the end of her marriage, counsel and reassure her daughters, see one off to college and comfort the other one who clung close to her now as her world changed. Dan was also finalizing his divorce, painting and fixing up the house so it could be sold and the proceeds split, all the while working full time and teaching classes at the law school.

In spite of all that, they did not neglect each other as they continued to peel back the layers of their past. Early in their e-mail exchange, she gave him a poem written on a scrap of paper that she had saved since they were fourteen. He recognized his own handwriting but did not remember the words. There was however, no doubt; it was unmistakably, embarrassingly, exactly what he would have written.

My love for you
Cannot be expressed
In word or rhyme
Or metered verse
Perfect in its antiquity;
And though this in itself
May seem antiquated,
Still it holds.

The sentiment that she had honored by guarding that ephemeral piece of paper inspired him once again in the future and he began to feel the mad rush of poetry into his head and fingers; he wrote:

Only for you do I rise in the dark
Nodding off while writing to you.
And in the day, while writing
To someone else, still I nod off
Thinking of you.

It seemed as if a timeless hour had spanned the distance between the first poem and the second, an hour faster than light that had frozen them and their love, waiting for a signal, a sign, to begin the warming flow, the ticking of the clockwork algorithm that would bring them out of suspended animation, like interstellar colonists, immigrants to the future in love.

When I taste you at last.
Like the first time,
Will your memory rise
From the place it has hidden?
Will the years dissolve
And my tongue proclaim you mine?

When I smell you at last
Like the first time,
Will soft wispy hairs
Greet gentle inhalation
With long guarded treasure
Surfacing and crying out; mine?

When I hear you at last
Like the first time,
Will the sound of your voice
Rain down on its long
Dried shadow, forming
Only one jealous word: mine?

And when I'm inside you at last
Like the first time,
Will our wandering souls
Intertwine, dance and gyre;
Recognize and welcome home
Each other, at long last shouting, *Mine?*

How odd, she thought, to be obsessed with a fourteen year old boy, the only memory she had of him, when back then she saw him, most certainly, as *her man*. She wrote: "How do you do that? How do you make heat come through the computer like that?" He simply could not help it.

You dance like a bee in my heart,
Your movements describing
The distance, direction and intensity
Of love.

Since then, they had e-mailed and talked on the phone almost daily, commiserated, sympathized and planned a reunion after things settled down. He was content to wait and court her long distance, to create something this time that they both hoped would last. Perhaps they didn't realize it, but in that process, it had already become real, an easy friendship poised at a familiar crossroad, a song of innocence holding experience and wisdom at bay for just a moment longer.

*

In the dimming red-tinged solset, he drove from the airport in a rental car toward the old park where they had sat on the swings and discovered each other and themselves, before and after that first poem. The satellite pictures on Google Earth had shown him that the swings were still there even though the park and playing fields had been renovated over the years.

He remembered going there when, like today, a small traveling carnival hit town for Krishna Bhakti, just before the little league season started. It was the kind with a clanking miniature roller coaster, a midway and pony rides, the kind that might pop up in a mall parking lot for the weekend or be tucked in a corner of the County Fair.

As a child, he would wander alone, not a part of the crowd, but observing life, sampling exotic cuisine at concession stands; Elephant Ears and Deep Fried Twinkies, following the sweetly rank smells of hay and horse apples; talking with the blue flyers as they danced and performed with their tame monkey bugs under the bleachers. It was a flea circus set before a special pint-sized audience, children who could still be paralyzed with wonder watching monkey bugs driving a toy fire truck, climbing ladders, saving a blue flyer manifesting as a damsel in distress and a vision in light of a tiny dragon breathing blue fire and battling monkey bug knights, all of which grown-ups ignored and relegated to childhood nonsense.

Later, when Meg happened, they ignored the blue flyers too. The tentative young lovers sat on one of the ornate high backed benches on the carousel, in something like privacy, holding hands and feeling the heat of their bodies beginning to intertwine and equalize like a physics experiment in thermodynamics, but with infinite potential.

The kids called the blue flyers 'blue fairies', in homage to stories of imaginary friends that even adults could see, could see but then forgot how essential and comforting they were when a shy and awkward kid needed kindness, wisdom and someone to confide in, someone who could talk away the sticks and stones, the bruises and loneliness of childhood. Their presence in the peripheral vision of adults sparked wistful memories just as Dan's path now stirred his memories of ancient summers.

He smiled, remembering how you couldn't catch the blue fairies no matter how hard you tried, but when you tired of trying, *they* followed *you* around incessantly and wouldn't shut up. The bullies stopped chasing them while the introverts sat down and happily, quietly, played in their world. *Smart fairies.*

Kids didn't wonder about the monkey bugs too much, but scientists were always fighting over just why the bugs had monkey faces. In truth, they were more like caricatures of hominins. The best explanation was in the fact that the blue flyers could and did manifest a face sometimes, for ease of interaction or maybe it was just their idea of sarcasm. Perhaps this talent had evolved as a camouflage mechanism early on to avoid predators, like those moths with the big eyes on their wings.

So, the scientists reasoned, some insects started to mimic the blue flyers' protection mechanism, evolving faces, confusing their own predators. Well, that was as good an explanation as any, but it was one of those things you just took for granted. There were even monkey bug marshmallows in Lucky Charms. *Magically Delicious!*

*

The park, the playing fields and this week the suburban carnival grounds, were next to Dan and Meg's old junior high school, now housing a Manichean fellowship mega-church. At the back of the church was a path at the edge of a canyon. He parked the rental there in the auditorium lot and began to take the path he had not walked in forty years.

There used to be a creek at the bottom. Every so often a coyote or moose would show up on a trail below the ridge. Once, a black bear got itself treed by pet dogs in someone's back yard. Flocks of wild turkeys would march down the center of the streets and stop traffic. All of it made the local paper.

There were cook outs, marmot hunts with bows and arrows, trails leading to who knew where, and later, construction sites with stakes to be pulled up by children in protest of encroaching civilization. But now, looking down as he walked, now there was a major road leading to neighborhoods, a community college and shopping centers where before there had only been what passed for wilderness in the mind of a child.

His morning walk to school with Meg had traced the lip of this canyon, an isolated path then. They could have walked on the sidewalk along the south edge of the park; sometimes, in the afternoon, or when she had charge of her little brother, they did walk that sidewalk home, skirting the park, another church and their old elementary school. But when alone and intent on privacy, when her mother was still at work or off to curling practice, they followed the canyon rim and the shortcut to the few blocks of suburban street leading to her room, the remodeled garage with its own entrance; her own private door that had opened for him that summer in 2003 when they were fourteen.

He remembered one morning in that summer when he had concocted a grand gesture, something literary and over the top, like Romeo or Cyrano de Bergerac. He rode his bicycle to her house when it was still dark, before any sane person would be up. But the blue flyers were out, somehow as excited as he was. They swarmed and made a spiraling blue comet tail behind the bike, suddenly transforming the three block journey into the hero's quest it was.

He threw pebbles up at her window until her face appeared. She was befuddled and amazed. He stood on his bicycle seat and hauled himself right through the window and into her bed. She took him under the covers and into the alien atmosphere she had made there of sweat and heat and pheromones. They made love while the blue flyers made mood lighting in the window. It was the best day of his life till then.

When he met her again as an adult, he wanted to honor the children they were and their romantic naive enthusiasm. It came to him in a dream after those first e-mails and then the memory of that morning rushed back in detail. While still in bed, in the dark again, he wrote for her:

Just now I smelled you on the sheets.
You were one synapse
From my hunting brain.
Short, technical inhalations identified you,
Calculated time and distance,
Knew you were near.
The trail was lost but not desire.
In the night I pulled you from the air,
Held you at my right side as I lay on my back,
Your head on my chest,
Your arms and legs around me,
My right arm holding you close,
A kiss on the forehead, only as a lullaby,

And so you slept. I didn't try anything.
But I dreamt of curves and hollows
Offered to me.
I dreamt of you above me, crying out.
I dreamt The smallness of you,
The ampleness of you;
Dreamt the feel of you into being, and awoke
Moving inside of you, and continued
In a dream, holding onto the bed, pulling.
Then I saw a vision of you above me
In another bed, in a room.
Through a window I appeared;
Something you had prayed for to many gods.
I still remember you in that bed, sleepy,
Happy, delighted. Somehow you knew
Everything you needed to know.
We were alive then and
I smelled you all the day
And treasured that presence on my body.
I smelled that on the sheets just now
But you were gone.

Well, that sealed the deal for both of them and the reality of that moment was coming back in full force as he walked, a walk he had imagined since that first e-mail in August, 2045, just one year before.

*

They had arranged to meet by the carousel, so he made his way along the old path, now high above the traffic and bustle. Still, it seemed like a private dream to walk those same steps again, behind the long classroom buildings, the bungalows and the athletic fields to the edge of the park. Along the way, the familiar sounds and smells of the summer carnival and midway grew stronger and started to nudge him to move a little faster.

From the canyon edge it was downhill to the baseball diamonds and the main carnival area so that he could not immediately see the carousel, though the Ferris wheel, the Tilt a Whirl, and the Octopus poked above the rise at intervals, the screams of their riders fading in and out with the motion of the machines. As he walked toward the spot where he knew the carousel should be, the midway and rides appeared before him. He heard the calliope music, came around from behind the concession stand and saw her standing by the ticket booth. She was looking the other way toward the street entrance and so did not immediately see him in the dim red light.

But, as he approached she sensed something and turned. She was dressed in jeans, a light cotton blouse, linen sport coat, her light brown hair unbound and her lips the red he remembered from her 10th Grade school picture. She took a deep breath and met his eyes.

"Mr. Justice Pritchard," she said.

"Dr. Sheridan, I presume; enchanté." He said as he kissed her hand and made a little bow.

"Why, M'lord, so formal . . ."

She batted her eyelashes and they laughed as she took his other hand and closed her eyes. In silence now, he deliberately put his body in front of her so that his left hip touched her right hip, placed his left cheek on hers, his left arm and hand rounding her waist, tensed at her back, and his right hand holding her left hand high, as if to begin a dance. He closed his eyes too and inhaled the smell of her neck, clearing his mind of all other perceptions.

That inhalation stirred memories as solset approached and Rübaeus at its zenith evoked the same mood of privacy and spark of dimly remembered kisses experienced so long ago. The blue flyers were gathering as well, maybe some of the same ones they had known as children, gathering and dancing with their pets, too polite to greet them just yet. A shared tremor went through Dan and Meg as they exhaled together.

Arm in arm now, he bought tickets and led her to the carousel, to the sanctuary of their bench. The calliope music rose in volume and the platform began to turn to the squeals of children commanding horses, tigers, and ostriches.

With their long lifespans and unfading memory, the blue flyers certainly did remember them. They shooed their monkey bugs off to play and flew in curving braided trajectories among the carved animals, ignored as usual by the excited riders and cautious parents. At the heart of their behavior however, was an undeniable attraction to human emotions and they knew how to enhance human feelings, feelings they perceived as auras merging. 'Officially,' it wasn't polite to just butt in without permission, but actually asking for permission seemed too contrived, and killed the mood to boot.

Instead, there was a kind of silent understanding, humans treating them like a warm breeze or sudden chill, things in nature that just brushed against you and enhanced or changed whatever it was you were feeling in the first place. So, with no further invitation, they approached the bench from behind and quietly wove their blue light through the auras of Dan and Meg, causing a shared rush of breathlessness that erased the years as they held hands. As the ride ended, the moon was just coming up, bloodied by Rübaeus as it began its dive toward the opposite horizon.

"The house closed yesterday, she cleaned me out good in the settlement." Dan said.

"What will you do now?"

"Don't know," he joked, "I could only afford a one-way ticket."

"Well, you're in a bit of a fix, homeless, penniless, I could drop you off at the mission."

"Don't much care for soup and religion."

"Guess I'll have to take you home for a while."

"That'd be mighty kind of you Ma'am."

"Meg, please."

They laughed and she put her arm through his and pulled him tight to her side. They got up from the bench and watched as the blue flyers buzzed off nonchalantly like nothing was up. They then walked toward Meg's car noting the same old monkey bug circus mesmerizing a new generation of toddlers under the bleachers and began to speak of sharing a life in the world.

Cherri Newton
May 7, 1956–October 5, 1997

"...I saw beauty. It was my destiny!
Therein lies all..."— *Edith Södergran*[12]

Afterword, Acknowledgement and Dedication

It is an old story, but one that can still be told.
- Epic of Gilgamesh

This trilogy, *Sweet Charlotte in the Higgs Field, A Small Goddess* and *Heart String Theory,* was the only story I could tell, the story I had to tell before anything else could be written. Largely drawn from the lives of real people, autobiographical and inspired by muse and madness, I hope it is honest and engaging.

I thank Cheri Newton (Charlotte) who died in 1997 and William Tanke, her widower, who saved the God the Geometer icon for twenty years and gave it to me in 2017, Therese Schroeder-Sheker (Petra), who created Music Thanatology and sparked my quest for Beauty in the world and Steven Vallus, Cheri's other ex-husband, who explained Rudolf Steiner's thinking, from economics to contacting the dead and how Steiner influenced these characters in a web of real connections just as is related in these books.

Special thanks to the Etruscans, who live on in the DNA of the Mediterranean and whose concept of gender equality would have served us well if played out for two thousand years, to Ashoka, the real Buddhist Emperor of India who might have sparked a more compassionate future. Thanks to Jane Sloan, who told me she could talk to spooks and feel their arms and wings.

Thanks to the Himba and Hereros of Namibia, who survived Germany's colonial practice runs at genocide and also preserved a beautiful culture in spite of it. Thanks to the Choctaw, my wife Ruby's tribe, and their eloquent leaders. Luke Koachubbee Patterson, my wife's grandfather was a real person, not a chief, but I honor him here. Thanks David Gulpilil for his voice heard in the aboriginal film, *Ten Canoes,* which gave me the cadence and vocabulary for the Uluru stories.

Stephanie Jourdan, who knew me when I was fourteen, said in 2012 "I thought you would be a famous writer by now; romantic science fiction." She is a Jungian therapist and the guided imagery where Charlotte appears as an angel is almost verbatim from sessions she conducted. I thank her for giving me the vocabulary and memories with which to make this journey, releasing my long dormant creativity, from which this story unwinds.

Brother Claude Lane is a real monk in a real monastery, Mount Angel, Oregon, faithfully described in this book. Cheri Newton's desire to take his class on icons in 1997 is the story that inspired all of this work. Read it yourself at http://chaliceofrepose.org/oblate. He is also the cousin of my best friend, the best man at my wedding to Ruby, and there was absolutely no connection between Cheri and him, she in Missoula unbeknownst to me, and I in Spokane, Washington unknown to her. Even so, this powerful connection outside of time is what made me believe in every crazy thing that came after. Only slightly tongue in cheek, my catch phrase became, *I am not making this up.*

When Cheri died, her story and that of Music Thanatology was told in a Dateline feature titled Heart Strings, and she was pictured on her death bed in Life magazine, none of which I saw at the time. Edith Södergran, yes, from Cheri's Memorial Card, was an amazing troubled prophetic poet who has enriched my life. *I walked on foot through solar systems,* sounded so prophetic and right.

Stuart, Larr and Georgi are riffs on my best friends. To all of these and others who took this journey with me, listened to me, helped me edit and finish these books inside and out, my heartfelt thanks.

And let's not forget the authors who appear expressly and enfolded in the implicate order: James Joyce, Thomas Pynchon, Marcel Proust, Leo Tolstoy, Boris Pasternak, Arthur

C. Clark, James Blish, Hans Urs von Balthasar, Sergei Bulgakov, Teilhard de Chardin, David Bohm, Elaine Scarry, Simone Weil and others.

I thank Ruby Devine, my wife who loves, inspires and indulges me. Ruby said, "You are the only person I know who obsesses over one event in high school." Well, that's not true, we all do; most of us just don't write novels about it.

Some have; Dante Alighieri wrote *Divine Comedy* and made Beatrice his guide through purgatory, heaven and hell. Beatrice was his lifelong love, who he fell for when he was nine and she was seven and who remained unobtainable and worshipped. He wrote lots of sonnets for her and none for his wife.

Göethe kept his Lotte (German Charlotte!) close to his heart. She was a married woman who was the subject of fatal attraction in his first best seller, *Sorrows of Young Werther*, which inspired a rash of romantic suicide attempts across the continent. Fortunately, Göethe missed when he tried the same stunt with a pistol, surviving to write his fictionalized account of his unrequieted love

The same sentiments are shared by Boris Pasternak regarding Lara in Dr. Zhivago, Leo Tolstoy regarding Pierre and Natasha in War and Peace and Marcel Proust regarding the peasant girl in Combray. And speaking of Proust, cork lined room and all, he had his Gilberte, Albertine and the gaggle of girls at the beach in Balbec, indistinguishable from Gidget, Annette Funicello and the many loves of Dobie Gillis and Wally Cleaver. No one described their common predicament better than Proust in the title of his second volume: *In the Shadow of Young Girls in Flower*.

More to the point, Hans Christian Anderson died at the age of 75 with a letter from his love at 26, Riborg Voight, in a pouch around his neck. She was engaged at the time he fell in love with her. It was revealed later that she had kept his letters as well until the day she died. More than that however, Anderson wrote his adaptations of fairy tales with one or more old loves in mind. He proposed to Jenny Lind, the 'Swedish Nightingale" and she responded that she loved him like a brother, the very worst thing that could be said, but, she had that name, everyone knew, because he had written the story of The Nightingale with only her in mind.

So, I'm in good company. Like those much better authors, I have appropriated my myth of Cheri Newton for literary purposes and re-invented her from whole cloth to serve that myth. She was a lovely pain in the neck at eighteen. As soon as she came down off that pedestal she was so much more and different than I had dreamed. Again, a common theme, be careful what you wish for.

Like the Bodhisattva in the story, Cheri Newton is appropriated for my purposes but also for hers. Everything that is related in *Sweet Charlotte in the Higgs Field*, before "the first time Charlotte left Dan", is true. Everything related about her coming back from the dead in that book occurred in dreams, guided imagery and stream of consciousness epics in 2012. As is often said, an author's characters take over the story. In this case, I crafted a short story where I got the girl in the end (The Pile Driver.) Even Tolstoy did this, as the entirety of War and Peace is bookended by Pierre's (Tolstoy's) love for and eventual marriage to, Natasha. That's really all that book is about, Tolstoy gets the girl.

Well, my characters did not let me off that easy and admonished me to be more honest about my own story. So, Dan loses the girl then regains her in the Dark Forever then, in Charlotte's Choice, she lets him move on without her. As a theme, I am stating clearly that the fantasy of the goddess and the white knight does not serve us well unless we admit the imperfections of the beings we worship. Mud wrestle with the goddess.

This idea comes from the tale of Tristan and Isolde. Tristan actually has two Isoldes from which to choose; Isolde of the White Hands who is an earthly woman capable of fulfilling all his earthly desires; love, home, children and

Isolde the Fair, the goddess who embodies only perfection and death. Tristan chooses death. Therefore, I argue that one must mud wrestle with the goddess to avoid that fate, embrace the earthly woman and yet never forget the goddess within.

Is this more honest? Well, Dan, in his many forms, seems to reach this conclusion without knowing the ultimate answer. This allows one to be at peace with love, longing and regret while still embracing fantasy and myth. Cheri Newton may be a fantasy, but she is also surely a myth that contains truth for me.

In my high school yearbook, one girl wrote a long message and said "You don't know how much you have meant to me." She was right, I didn't. As I re-acquainted myself with old friends over the internet, I discovered that some of them had held me in mythic esteem, just as I obsessed over Cheri Newton. As I looked with longing in her direction, others looked with longing in mine, an experience so normal; yet so deserving of recognition and making amends.

My only problem, or advantage, was that my goddess died in 1997, and could not resolve my regrets. However, when I did speak to Therese Shroeder-Sheker 2012, she told me that, before she died, Cheri had been processing parts of her life that included me. Therese knew things about me in middle school that only Cheri knew. I was entranced.

Even though I was diagnosed as, "highly suggestible," I was able to deal with these connected obsessions as myth and fiction. Cheri Newton could be a contact from without, or she could be an aspect of my own subconscious, my anima. It didn't matter which, because my reaction and the utility of the experience is/was the same. If I spread my arms and said "You can be my angel," it was of no import whether the angel was within me or a spirit from without.

On a different level, the basis of much science fiction in contemporary history and philosophy has given me another template for storytelling; with examples ranging from James

Blish's *Cities in Flight* to Heinlein's *Starship Troopers* and any incarnation of Star Trek.

Blish based his stories of starfaring nomadic cities after the collapse of the West on Oswald Spengler's theories of history and economics, creating back stories as 'excerpts' from *The Milky Way; Five Cultural Portraits*, throughout his series. Isaac Asimov based his Foundation and Empire series directly on Gibbon's *Decline and Fall of the Roman Empire*.

In my books I have followed that lead, including the philosophy and ideas of Rudolf Steiner, as well as the 1909 *Futurist Manifesto* and *The Rise and Fall of the Third Reich*, similarly embodied in histories and treatises written and read by the characters.

And so that you get a feel for the random and yet focused synchronicity connecting all of these stories and ideas, just now in writing this dedication, as I confirmed facts about Oswald Spengler, I find that Rudolf Steiner gave a series of lectures on Spengler in the 1920's. Another catch phrase: *Why does this not surprise me*?

When you read about the non-cognitive web surfing of Arch Sandifur, Dan Pritchard and Devi Sheridan, I can tell you truthfully that all of those connections came at me just as forcefully. Everywhere creativity has led me since 2012, there has been a connection to the mentors, loves and obsessions of Cheri Newton, a series of *Aha!* moments, interspersed sincerely with *I am not making this up!* So, thanks Cher, thanks for being a real ghost writer; see you in the dark forever.

My next project? Don't worry; in a multiverse, all stories that can be told must be told.

Steven C. Schneider June 1, 2018

*

. . . But, that small moment
Abides outside of time
Until a man comes to understand
What was only, uniquely, for him.

It grew in non-linear time
From singularity to Universe
And its background microwave ghost
Still sings songs of love only to me

She was and is, always mine only
As we fanned out from our
Incarnations and wandered home
To await our transit with friends.

Still she hides her beauty
Behind overalls and flannels
And an angel's sparkling robes
Laughing at complexity.

She says, it's not that hard on this side
Don't worry, it's easy.
We have all the time in the world
And I still love you.

A Small Goddess, excerpt, Steven C. Schneider, 2012

57623220R00252

Made in the USA
Columbia, SC
12 May 2019